MW01153729

The Search for Melchizedek

Jeffrey Tiel

Copyright © 2012 Jeffrey Tiel

All rights reserved.

ISBN: 1477520465
ISBN-13: 978-1477520468

FOR TRUE FRIENDS

ACKNOWLEDGEMENTS

For review of earlier drafts of this book, I offer my thanks to Greg Behrens, Jennifer Dean, Joel Dean, Alyssa Guthrie, Patricia McClellan, Rebecca Smith, Sean Templeton, Dorie Tiel, Julia Tiel, and Richard Tiel. I am grateful for Sarah Black's photographic help. I especially appreciate the many hours of work of my special editorial assistant, Tyler Millhouse. While each of these people deserves my gratitude for the role that they played in helping this novel reach fruition, none of them is responsible for any errors or omissions in the text, nor should they be taken to hold any of the views advanced by or condone any of the actions taken by the characters. Finally, I would like to acknowledge the inspiration of the oceans of the world, without whose steady waves many a coarse stone would remain unpolished.

FOREWORD

I have taken some licenses with the texts from which I've drawn much of the interpretation necessary for the background of the story.

For my use of part of the prayer of Ptesosiris, I am indebted to the translation of Miriam Lichtheim in *Ancient Egyptian Literature: Volume III: The Late Period (Ancient Egyptian Literature)*, ISBN: 0520248449, University of California Press, 2006, 44. For the riddle in chapter 66, I am indebted to en.wikibooks.org/wiki/Puzzles/Riddles.

The storyline depends in part on a modest identification of the god, *Yah*, with the eventually developed Jewish God, *YHWH*, or *Yahweh*. As this name is traditionally so holy that it is impious to pronounce it, I've adopted the standard usage of substituting *Adonai* for *YHWH* whenever the latter should appear in speech. This may be confusing for some readers, trying to figure out how *Yah* connects with *Adonai*. I therefore have Agent Quarston mistakenly speak the holy name *YHWH* in order to clarify the connection to *Yah*. This is not meant as an offense to my readers, and Quarston is himself corrected during the dialogue where this occurs.

Except for real literary or historical characters whose fictional use by me should be viewed as fiction, the names used in the story are not meant to reflect real people. In particular, no reference to the real Rothschild family line is intended. Nor should references to agencies or people involved with Egyptian archeology be viewed as genuine or descriptive, since to my knowledge reputable archeologists should and do follow all prescriptions regarding their work by the Egyptian Antiquities Authority. No references to political or military programs, especially those suggested for the fictional characters in the Israeli and American governments, should be taken as representative of authentic policies of the governments of either the State of Israel or the United States. Finally, the theological views of various fictional characters within the novel should not be taken as official teaching of any religious organization or person.

"For this Melchizedek, king of Salem, priest of the Most High God . . .

was first of all, by the translation of his name, king of righteousness, and

then also king of Salem, which is king of peace. Without father, without

mother, without genealogy, having neither beginning of days nor end of

life, but made like the Son of God, he remains a priest perpetually."

—Epistle to the Hebrews (Author Unknown)

PROLOGUE

79 A.D. Herculaneum, The Eruption of Mount Vesuvius

Marius slammed open the door and gasped for breath. All too quickly a savage cough pierced the clean air of his patron's villa. He hacked, grasping at his chest, and spat a black slurry on the dusty floor of the apartment. The gloom filtered through the narrow windows of the villa, and Marius could just make out the ornately carved stone staircase at the far corner of the room. Marius wiped his sweaty palms on his tunic and then pressed them against his throbbing temples, struggling to calm his racing heart. But he could not wait. His legs lurched forward, duty and desperation driving, carrying him up the uneven stairs. The room was bathed in the same pallid gloom, but here a haze of fine ash saturated the air. Marius lunged for the manuscripts, desperately collecting his patron's belongings in the eerie quiet born of the thick layer of ash outside which insulated the villa and deadened the air. He drained the contents of a wine skin into his parched mouth and tucked the skin under his elbow. Arms full, he scurried down the stairs with precise footfalls to avoid a headlong dive onto the floor below. He crossed the room and passed through the doorway, leaping from the high curb into the uneven street.

The silence was broken. He was jostled and prodded, kicked and elbowed. Marius winced through the stinging ash and struggled to keep his footing as he raced beside frantic faces. The ashes clung thick to their dripping brows. Smoke and ash filled the sky, and though it was midday, torches could scarce penetrate the darkness. A slave or a thief, he knew not which, rushed past, clenching a fist of flashing jewelry. It did not matter. The democracy of chaos had descended with the ashes. Soldiers, noblemen, gladiators, actors, merchants, bakers, artisans, and slaves all trampled one another, as they streamed down the streets and alleyways toward the city's gates and the refuge of the sea.

A chariot plowed its way through and over the crowds, knocking him off his feet and scattering some of his patron's books. Desperate to recover them, he scrambled off the sidewalk and into the street. His hands had just seized one manuscript when a violent shake of the earth knocked him back onto the sidewalk. Spitting blood, he sourly recalled his confidence that he could make one last run into the city. Marius tried to stand, but the dizzying ache in his head spun him back into the street clogged with the coughing and wheezing citizenry. Abandoning the rest of the books to the press of the crowd, he ran under the ash shrouded gates and made for the great villa that doubled as a school of philosophy. Stumbling along the uneven and shaken earth, he at least breathed easier as he pulled the empty wineskin from his sack and inhaled from its precious air reserve. He had paid careful attention to his patron's instruction to inflate the animal skin with fresh air to use as a spare lung. Now it was saving his life, as he rushed into the villa and up to the library. The students frantically packed their costly manuscripts into large urns and carried them into the cellar, through the harbor tunnel, and down to the sea and the waiting ships. Grimacing as he pushed aside his favorite plays of Euripides, he snatched up his patron's manuscripts from among the thousands of scrolls. With a final breath from the wine skin, Marius raced down the steps, narrowly missing a young pupil panting on the stairs. He reached the ground floor and tossed the books through the open cellar hatch, giving chase as he scaled down the ladder to the dirt floor below.

A violent explosion shook the mountain to its core. All eyes turned upwards, as an eruption of explosive volcanic gasses blew the top of the mountain into a roiling cloud that flooded the sky and then rushed earthward, surging toward the city. Minutes later, the searing hot blast wave incinerated everything in its path. Frescoes, statues, columns, and even the images of the gods were engulfed by the insatiable heat. Few buildings could endure that inferno, that indifferent and unyielding surge. In moments the city of Herculaneum died, buried under a river of mud and ash.

Thrown to the cellar floor by the explosion, Marius heard the door slam behind him and rubble pin it tight. He snatched up his patron's manuscripts in his trembling hands. The screams of the dying, faded and ghostlike, seeped through the ceiling above. Steeling himself to their agony, he hurried toward the tunnel's exit. Out into the eerie orange light he ran, his feet slipping on the ash-coated dock. Marius screamed for them to wait, but his parched throat was silent. The oarsmen strained with all their might, as the ship drew away from the dock's edge. Marius leapt for the boat and slammed into its side. Clawing for a handhold, he felt himself falling toward the raging water below. Suddenly, a powerful hand grabbed at his tunic. He felt the man's strength as he was easily lifted onto the deck. Panting with exhaustion, Marius squinted through the haze into the eyes of his patron.

"Marius, did you get them?"

* * * *

Present Day

The impeccably dressed gentleman walked down the long hallway past his palatial bedroom and into the library. The room was filled from floor to ceiling with rare and first edition leather clad books. Renaissance cartography graced the walls, and embedded in the floor lay a stunning, red Egyptian marble rendering of the *fleur-de-lis*, the symbol of Florence. Yet not here was the true value of the room. Crossing the great seal, he approached the ornately carved wooden paneling. Pressing gently on one panel indistinguishable from the others, he heard a faint click. The panel unlocked and slid back to reveal a security console. It required his fingerprint, retinal impression, and a code. The panel then lit up, satisfied as to the identity of the gentleman. The richly adorned shelves to his right swung free from the wall to reveal a staircase that descended to a vault far beneath the villa's Renaissance foundations. No other living man had ever seen what the vault contained.

Vividly painted Theban warriors guarded the entrance to the first room which contained treasures that had long since faded out of the memory of men. He gazed into the vacant marble eyes of Augustus Caesar, the life-sized sculpture so perfectly crafted it would have left the art world drooling. Yet it was not for them that these treasures were kept. He stepped up to a great sarcophagus, the product of the most exquisite Hellenic artistry. Inscribed in pure gold he read in Greek letters, "Alexander." Stepping past a lost dialogue of Plato, he passed out of the Gallery of the Ancients and into the Renaissance Room.

A remarkable number of priceless works had "disappeared" into France in the centuries following the Renaissance. They had in fact been quietly collected. Forgotten sculptures by Michelangelo, paintings by

Leonardo and Raphael, even ancient jewelry some owned by Cleopatra herself and ornately set by Verrocchio, all of this lay before him. Shelves overflowed with books, most the only copies in existence. Three complete codices of Leonardo's, totally unknown to the world, sat on the shelves untouchable by anyone but him. And then there were the best of the holy relics, a nail from the true cross of Christ, some of his hair that the Romans had ripped from his beard, even a wooden cup reputed to be the grail itself. He was skeptical of all these religious artifacts, of course. His ancestors had collected these prizes in the hopes of gaining eternal life through the church. But catering to the church was not his idea of eternal life.

The gentleman approached the final room of this vault of wonders, but unlike the others it held but a single pedestal standing at its center. Three faint columns of blue light emanated from the domed ceiling, illuminating the floor around the pedestal. He approached the single stair upon which the pedestal was raised and stepped up to gaze at the sealed titanium sphere that secured this, what to him was the real "holy grail," since it offered the best clue to the true source of immortality. He looked down at the console that jutted out from the front of the pedestal and observed the two familiar buttons: one gold, the other red. Pressing the gold button, he watched as the titanium sphere opened up and then rolled back into the pedestal, the triangle of blue lights fading into darkness. Suddenly, a faint cone of white light illuminated him and the dais upon which he stood. Set in the center of the open sphere he saw the familiar crystal case, so perfectly transparent that he thought he could reach out and grasp what it contained. Amidst a perfectly inert gas to guarantee preservation, lay a series of yellowed and gnarled parchment pages.

The man gazed at them with a desire approaching lust, for he knew the promise that they kept. They were written over a span of three hundred years by the same man. Someone out there had lived for at least three hundred years. And he wanted to know how. This was not religion, nor was it science fiction; it was fact.

CHAPTER ONE

Washington D. C.

Roger Quarston glanced up at the clock superimposed over the news program on the high definition television monitor that hung at his gate. Only twenty more minutes to boarding, and then a quick one hour shot back home to Boston. He sighed thankfully. He ran over to the snack shop, passing over the many candy bars, and grabbed a Nutri-Grain bar and a bottle of spring water. After paying the clerk for his purchases, he found a seat at his gate. It wasn't difficult, as his was the last plane leaving for the evening.

He settled back into his seat and reflected on the hours before. It'd been a long day, closing out his latest case with his superiors in D.C. It disturbed him to think over the details, even though they'd gripped his every thought for the past few months. He longed for a shower, to wash the grime of the whole sickly affair out of his mind, and hopefully out of his dreams.

The thought of grime stirred his memory. He pulled the ever-present slip of paper from his shirt pocket and jotted down the name of his favorite stainless steel cleaner to pick up tomorrow. He chuckled loudly, annoying the well-dressed woman sitting across from him. He didn't know anyone else who had a favorite cleaner. Imagining the other FBI agents around the water cooler arguing about whether Comet was superior to Soft Scrub only made him laugh aloud again. This time the woman glared at him for a moment before returning to her romance novel.

Quarston tried not to care, but her displeasure still bothered him. He hadn't been able to make a fulfilling connection to a woman, and now in his mid-thirties—okay, he smirked again, late thirties—he felt that he was running out of time. Perhaps it wasn't really time that was the problem, he admitted to himself. He possessed the self-awareness to realize that a thirty-something agent who was enough of a neat freak to make Jerry Seinfeld look like Oscar from the "Odd Couple" had a serious burr up his ass. He felt the familiar emptiness creeping into his consciousness, the darkness that haunted his dreams, and he knew, shattered his few attempts at relationships. Just four months before, he had again awoken screaming from a particularly disturbing dream. But he hadn't been able to tell Jessica. He had felt he had to protect her from the crap that was his job. Someone had to stay clean, pure from the cesspool that he inhabited. She had left him the next morning. He had known it wasn't her fault. But he couldn't tell her anymore than he'd been able to open up to Theresa or Maura before Jessica; he couldn't stain the very people whose good-natured lives he counted on.

But he couldn't cope with it himself either. He had gone to the shrink, even been honest. But honesty didn't fix anything. And he wouldn't start a relationship with anyone on the job. He wanted to go home to get away from human filth. Some place that was clean. Some place where everything had its place. And that made him somewhat crazy, he knew, "obsessive compulsive" was the term the shrink used.

Quarston peered over the last bite of his granola bar at the glum, well-dressed woman across the way, quickly shooting his eyes back to a raisin to avoid her glare. He glanced up at the terminal television screen and noticed a Dateline NBC story about women who married convicts serving life-sentences. He laughed aloud so hard that the face of the woman across from him contorted, and then to his surprise she seized her leather bags and stormed away to another seat.

Perhaps a prison bride would do it, he thought. Yeah, that'd be perfect. He couldn't marry a normal person, because they'd never understand what he confronted every day. He couldn't marry another agent who would just duplicate his issues. So maybe the answer was to form a relationship with a convict.

He sobered suddenly, feeling that the solution was to leave the Bureau. No more stress, no more chasing people who slaughtered each other over inanities. But it wasn't the right answer either, he knew, as he got up from his seat when the ticket agent called his flight number. He was a detective, plain and simple, just like his father before him. Okay, he was a Fed, he corrected himself. But he'd refused promotion several times to work the streets, to do what he did best. In spite of his ex-partner's death six months before, his superiors still hadn't required him to partner up with another agent. And he knew that that spoke volumes of their respect for his success at the Bureau.

Quarston finished the last bite of his bar and tossed the wrapper into a trash can, before answering the call to board. He handed the ticket agent his boarding pass and complimented her kindly, as he had learned from his father. "Small kindnesses mollify the meat-grinder of life," he'd say. Yet all Quarston felt was the grind. He walked down the jet way and up to the stewardess at the aircraft door and was directed to his seat. After jamming his long legs underneath the seat in front of him, he closed his eyes to calm his mind. He was rewarded with the suggestion that he clean underneath his refrigerator. He smiled before drifting off to sleep.

*　*　*　*

A few rows ahead of the worn FBI agent, a large well-built man slipped into his seat on the aisle. He had boarded the aircraft at the last call just as he always did. In his line of work information meant survival, so he constantly surveyed those boarding ahead of him. He easily identified air marshals but kept his watch for anyone whose eyes suggested professional surveillance training. He made no effort to disguise his own appearance, knowing that his anonymity was his best defense. He had never been arrested, never even been issued a traffic ticket in any of the some thirty countries in which he had operated. Moreover, there was no possibility of evading the facial recognition systems that now protected the European and North American countries. He traveled under the same passport, always. Changing passports with the same face would red flag anyone. He was himself, he mused, plain and simple.

As he buckled into his cramped seat for the flight to Boston, he reflected on the assignment he had accepted. The stewardess began to explain emergency evacuation procedures, including the use of an oxygen mask in the case of sudden loss of pressurization during flight. His mind flashed suddenly to the old chemist he had killed only three weeks before, the feel of the plastic of the man's oxygen mask still cool against his skin. The carbon dioxide gas he had injected into the oxygen line had done its work quickly. He never killed the same way twice. He also made sure never to accept an assignment on a high profile target. His aim was survival and a bank account of two million euro. He was patient and he was thorough.

The stewardess completed her final check of the cabin and then buckled herself into a jump seat while the plane taxied toward the departure runway. As the plane rumbled along, the assassin wondered about his target for the next evening. He wouldn't ordinarily accept a contract of this kind. But the provider, whoever he was, had offered three times the usual rate. So, he had agreed to meet the contract, relieve him of some rare manuscripts, and then finish things. Initially, he'd feared losing the element of surprise, but the target was a man in his later years without any kind of professional protection. So, he nestled into his seat, intent on relaxing his nerves and again going over every detail of the mission.

* * * *

Mr. Hentersheim, an unassuming old book dealer, teeter-tottered down the cobble-stoned avenue in Boston's warehouse district to approach a large, well-built figure that emerged from the shadowed doorway. Fear paralyzed him where he stood, so he nervously fidgeted with the *tefillin* in his pocket.

"Do you have it?" the assassin insisted.

He watched Hentersheim bite his lip and swallow hard, trying to answer. Instead, the worn man just nodded and pulled open his haversack to remove a rag-covered object. Before handing it to the assassin, he stammered, "And my grandson? What about my grandson? You tell me where he is!"

The hooded assassin nodded and moved closer to Hentersheim, placing a gentle hand on the old man's shoulder and whispering something in his ear. Hentersheim looked relieved and relaxed his grip on the parchment. His eyes opened more in astonishment than horror as a knife drove through his ribcage and into his heart. The hooded assassin stared deeply into the old Jew's clouding eyes, watching the life recede as his heart struggled to beat around the cold steel invader. He withdrew the blade, wiped it on the old man's tweed jacket, and then dragged the body toward the open doorway. Pouring kerosene all over the body, he withdrew from the building, but not before tossing a match into the pooling fuel. Ten minutes later he glanced into his rearview mirror at the orange glow that filled the sky.

* * * *

An arson-murder case would not normally be assigned to an FBI agent, but when the burned building belonged to a front company for one of the biggest crime families in Boston, the FBI ensured that its people were on the scene the next morning. Everyone assumed that the body had some connection to organized crime, so a yawning Agent Quarston was surprised to see the charred *tefillin* hanging from the badly burned corpse.

A religious man, Quarston mused, and Jewish too. Not your usual mob hit. Bending his six foot one frame down close to the corpse to examine the Hebrew characters written on one of the little scrolls that survived the inferno, Quarston felt the wear in his knees and hips. He had a hefty build and was certainly not overweight, but he suspected that his thirty-eight years of age were finally demanding some respect.

It wasn't just his age, Quarston admitted to himself as he returned to his car several hours later and looked at himself in the rearview mirror: it was his eyes. They were worn, but not by physical exertion or age. He grimaced and said aloud, "Maybe I need a vacation."

*   *   *   *

The autopsy that followed offered a further surprise: the victim was a male of some seventy to eighty-five years. And when the dental records revealed his identity as one Myron Hentersheim, a rare books dealer from New York City, Quarston abandoned the mob connection theory and wondered what he had stumbled into.

Quarston arrived in New York late in the day and drove directly to the old Jewish section of the Lower East Side, whistling in amazement at the collision of cultures. A Chinese restaurant and a hip-hop delicatessen pressed in against the venerable Eldridge Street Synagogue. He wasn't sure which was more out of place, the spicy aromas wafting in from the restaurants or the Gothic and Moorish vaults of the old synagogue. Approaching the turn of the century tenements, Quarston located Hentersheim's tiny rare books store hidden in a side street and parked his car. The splintered door hung crooked on its frame, and a nudge from Quarston's shoulder allowed him to squeeze through. Shelf after shelf had been overturned on top of carefully stacked piles of books. Quarston noted the musty odor of old leather, aging paper, and decades of dust hanging in the air. Apparently, someone had removed each book and examined it, but in finding nothing, had turned to the shelves and sparse furnishings as well as the wood floors and fading burgundy walls. Quarston gazed at the shattered sheet rock and gouges in the flooring boards, revealing pipes and wiring unseen in eighty years. Reaching down to a thick volume, he picked up a work by Montesquieu. Its pages had been ripped from their binding. He found more books subjected to the same treatment. Rage, Quarston mused. Whoever had killed Hentersheim had been looking for something, and when he hadn't found it, he'd gone on a rampage.

In the rear of the shop, Quarston found a tight staircase that led him to Hentersheim's small apartment nestled comfortably above his rare books shop. It too had been torn apart. Hentersheim's deceased wife's jewelry lay scattered among the debris.

"What were you looking for?" Quarston asked aloud.

Stepping over the splintered coffee table and around the overturned sofa, Quarston examined what remained of Hentersheim's computer station, just the monitor and peripherals with their sliced wires. But the computer couldn't have been the primary target, Quarston thought, since it was in plain view. No, these criminals had been searching for something else, and when they couldn't find it, they'd settled for grabbing the computer, probably hoping it would contain information leading them to what they'd really been looking for.

Glancing out the window, he noted the butcher shop across the street with its proudly labeled sign, Goldman's Kosher Meats. What grabbed his attention was the condensation circle on the window and the two little eyes staring at him over its top. Quarston finished looking through the book shop before casually leaving the premises and walking down the street. Using his peripheral vision, he noticed a head popping out of the butcher shop and glancing his way, so he crossed the street and the head disappeared again. Moving rapidly back up the street to the butcher shop's doorway, he waited just a few seconds when a little old head peered around the corner and stared right into his eyes. The man started and leaped backward, crashing into the doorway's far frame. With a yelp of pain, he tried to scramble back inside the shop, but Quarston was already in the doorway, offering him a hand. The tired old man looked up in surprise but accepted the hand. Quarston offered him a seat on a small stool and sized up the little man who in turn scrutinized the government agent.

"Police?" queried the wizened old fellow, trying to regain his dignity.

"FBI," answered Quarston, suppressing laughter.

"Ah."

Regaining his professional bearing, Quarston began, "Do you know Mr. Hentersheim?"

"We are very close friends," replied the butcher in a faded German accent. "We met on the ship bringing us to America in 1937. We had little else but the shirts on our backs."

The FBI agent frowned. The old butcher would soon have to hear of his friend's death, but perhaps that information could be used advantageously. So, he answered, "I'm after the people who tore up his shop."

"Tore up his shop? What happened? Is Myron all right?"

"I'm afraid not, sir," replied the agent with affected sadness, pulling his stoic face into a tight frown. "I'm sorry to have to tell you this, but your friend was murdered in Boston two days ago."

Quarston paused as the Butcher pulled his face into that same tight frown Quarston had perfected. He continued, clearing his throat, "I came to the city to investigate. . ." Quarston trailed off, bothered by the butcher's stolid face, as if it came as no great surprise to him that the old man had been killed.

Quarston cleared his throat. "Did you see anyone hanging around the book shop?"

"No," answered the butcher quietly. "I didn't see anything."

Quarston noticed that the elderly man had softened a bit and his chin began to shake. Inured to the grief of others by years in the Bureau, Quarston pressed the man for what information he was now convinced he possessed.

"Did Mr. Hentersheim relate to you that he was having some problems?"

"No, he wouldn't tell me anything," replied the butcher half-desperately.

"But you were aware he was in some kind of trouble?" Quarston continued.

"Yes, yes," he answered. "But he changed so quickly!"

"Changed how?" queried Quarston, trying to conceal his growing confusion.

"Well, he seemed so cheery about a week ago, like he'd hit the lottery, but not about money, you understand," the butcher proceeded quickly. "It was more like he was in on some great secret, or at least it felt that way to me, since he wouldn't tell me the details."

"Okay," answered Quarston, "so some event occurred a week or so ago which made Hentersheim seem very positive and optimistic. But then it all changed, is that it?"

"Right," continued the butcher. "Just a few days ago he came to me very early in the morning, around 5:00 AM! He never does that. I couldn't understand who would be banging on my shop door at that hour, maybe the police, or . . . anyway, you get the idea."

"Definitely," echoed Quarston. "So, what did he tell you?"

"Well, it wasn't what he told me, but what he gave me, you see," answered the butcher excitedly. "Like it was all some big mystery—only he seemed so sad, and maybe a little frightened too."

"But what did he give you?" pressed Quarston.

"Oh, right," the Butcher hesitated before shrugging his shoulders and adding, "a key."

"A key?" wondered the FBI agent. "Why did he give you a key? Were you supposed to just keep it for him, or use it for something?"

"No, not use it, only to keep it for him in case anything went wrong."

"Went wrong? With what?" asked Quarston.

"With whatever it was he was doing," mused the butcher. "But he wouldn't tell me that, said it wasn't safe, the less I knew the better. How does that make any sense? If something happened to him, and I didn't know anything—which I don't—then how could I help him? I feel less safe now, because I don't know what he was up to. I mean we were the best of friends!"

The old Jewish man choked back tears, as Quarston paused to review what he had learned. Something had changed, all right, something that had turned Hentersheim around completely and led him to that dark alley in Boston. The old man suspected the danger, and he gave his trusted friend the key.

"But to what?" Quarston wondered aloud.

"Hmm . . . what's that?" asked the butcher, his solemnity disrupted.

"The key," emphasized Quarston.

"Oh, right, I don't know what it's for, but maybe you can figure it out. If I can find it, that is," offered the butcher.

Quarston watched in amazement as the man reached down into his meat freezer and pulled out several legs of lamb. He opened the first and felt underneath its skin, and then proceeded to the second. From this second lamb leg he pulled a small key. He squeezed some sanitizer from a large tube and washed first his hands and then the key, before turning it over to the FBI man.

Quarston left the butcher shop soon after and mused over the meaning of the changes in Hentersheim's emotions over the past weeks. What had so animated him in the first place? And what had changed to arouse such fear and caution? Quarston guessed that the old man had come upon some object or information of sufficient value first to raise his hopes but then to make him a target of someone else's interest. He drove towards his hotel as the last rays of the sun slipped into the West, flipping the key over in his free hand. The key suggested that whatever Hentersheim had gone to Boston for, he had kept something back, maybe as a bargaining chip. Quarston now knew that he was one step ahead of the murderer, because whoever killed Hentersheim hadn't yet discovered what the key would open.

* * * *

Quarston pulled his car over next to the Chinese restaurant he'd noticed earlier, rolled down his window and took in the aromas wafting from the kitchen. He glanced at his watch, twisting the outer dial indecisively. At any rate, he couldn't press the case much further that evening, so he headed into the restaurant and placed his order at the front counter. Choosing a table next to a large faux-stone dragon painted in brilliant reds and yellows, Quarston plunked down to await his meal, the sound of sizzling food crackling in his ears. His hungry eyes darted around the room and stopped on a perfect view into the bustling kitchen. Quarston stared dumbly as the chef coolly handled his large wok, flipping snow peas, broccoli, and carrots into the air and back down onto the searing surface. The chef picked up a squeeze bottle and fired a jet of transparent liquid into the wok. Steam engulfed the vegetables, and the fragrance of ginger wafted over to Quarston's table.

While he watched the cook, Quarston pulled the mysterious key from his pocket and stared at it. He couldn't figure it out, but he knew someone who could. As the waiter arrived with his steaming platter and a bowl of fried rice, he lifted his phone and called to his favorite FBI lab technician, Harry.

"Hi Harry, how are things?" asked Quarston as innocently as he could sound.

"Just great, Boss," humored the techie. "What do you have for me at this hour?"

"Just a key," answered Quarston, realizing that Harry was probably already back home. "I need to know what it opens right away."

"You have the new Bureau issued phone, right?" asked Harry.

"Of course," Quarston replied, lifting the first bites of rice to his lips.

"You know how to use the camera on it?" Harry continued.

"Oh, I see," answered Quarston smartly. "Just give me a second, and I'll attach a couple of photos of the key to a text message to you."

"Got it, boss," laughed Harry. "I'll call you once I get it."

Quarston pressed the END button to conclude the phone call and then set up the phone's little camera. Placing his chopsticks on the side of his plate, Quarston positioned the key on a clear spot on his table and took several photographs. He heard a man at a table not far from him ask, "EBay?"

Quarston laughed as he sent the photos to Harry, "Yeah, right, I'm selling old keys on EBay."

"Actually, you'd be surprised how much really old or rare keys sell for," replied the man as he sipped his soup.

"Is that right?" asked the FBI agent, as he poked his chopsticks into his own meal. "How do you know so much about it?"

"Oh, I buy and sell all kinds of little knick-knacks on the Web," he answered. The man coughed and adjusted his tie. "You know, I pretty much work from home."

"Uh-huh," mused the agent, choosing not to look too closely under this particular rock. "And what do you know about keys?"

Perusing the key, the man replied, "Well, my best guess would be that it opens something small, like a jewelry box, but as for age, it looks very new to me."

"How do you figure that?" asked Quarston.

"There's no grime on it," the man answered.

"Couldn't it just have been cleaned recently?" pressed Quarston.

"When was the last time you cleaned your keys?" retorted the man.

"But if someone wanted it to appear new . . ." continued Quarston.

"Oh sure, but now you're talking fakes," replied the man with a laugh. "But I don't see anything special about this key that would make it worth faking."

Quarston nodded, "True, and the teeth don't look worn at all either."

"Right," answered the man. "So, it ain't a new key masquerading as an old key, since it looks just like a new key!"

Quarston laughed, "Yeah, you're right. I'm a cop, so . . ."

"Of course!" chuckled the man in turn. "That explains it. Nothing is ever at it seems, eh?"

"Not in my business," laughed Quarston.

The man shrugged and returned to his newspaper, while Quarston munched his egg roll waiting for Harry to call him back. Quarston's ex-partner had introduced him to Harry, the "whiz-kid," he'd called him. They'd hit it off immediately, Quarston always respecting talent, and the whiz-kid flattered by the attention the agents paid him.

Quarston's phone buzzed and he answered Harry's call.

"So, what did you find out?" he asked.

"Looks like a safety deposit key," replied Harry. "But I'll have to run it through the computer in the lab to identify the bank."

"Sounds great, Harry," answered Quarston gratefully. "Call me tomorrow morning once you know the bank, and I'll check it out here in the city."

Harry promised that he'd be on it first thing in the morning, so Quarston returned to his plate finishing the last bites of his Szechuan chicken. He turned to examine his bill and noticed the fortune cookie sitting in the little tray. He laughed and removed the cookie from the plastic, wondering what his fortune would be this time. But the crack of the cookie didn't bring the expected amusement. "Love is sure to make its appearance," he read soberly, staring into the empty chair between him and the EBay-tycoon. Right, he thought.

Gathering his empty dishes, he rose from the table to leave, but hesitated as he noticed the three grains of rice that had fallen from his plate. He paused, considering that it'd probably be good therapy to leave them there. "Aw, hell," he guffawed, and swept them onto the tray.

CHAPTER TWO

New York City

The assassin winced as he slowly drew a third shard of glass from his shattered fist. The pain from each draw with the tweezers focused his attention. Never before had he so completely screwed up a mission. As the anger rose in his chest again, he plunged the tweezers back into his knuckle. The pain felt like the ice of upper Siberia, quickly dissipating the self-loathing that had only complicated his problems. He sat on the floor of his hotel room, surveying the results of his tirade. Art work lay shattered among the splinters from the cracked and twisted furniture. The electronics and casing of the television were enough to give away its former use, but beyond that . . . he grimaced again as a fourth piece of the mirror emerged from his hand. He knew he had to regain self-control. His survival depended entirely on passing unnoticed, being completely ordinary. A call to the local police for hotel damages would place him on their radar.

But that wasn't the worst of his troubles. What was he going to do about the missing manuscripts? That was the question that haunted him. He'd searched everywhere the old Jew might have hidden them, torn apart the old man's shop and apartment, but found nothing. He couldn't keep his mind from going over the confrontation with the bastard yet again. Why hadn't he checked the package first? Obviously, the mark would have wanted some security against his grandson's life!

But the truth was, he'd never accepted a contract like this before. He was a killer, pure and simple. Exchanges in the dead of night were another matter entirely, required a distinct set of skills—he now understood that clearly enough. Bottom line? He'd failed to complete the contract. He had only one of the articles that he'd already been paid to retrieve. Walk away . . . could he just walk away? Dump everything, pay off the hotel, and slip away into early retirement? The network he worked for employed a double-blind contracting system, so neither employer nor operator was aware of one another's identity. But no system was beyond penetration. If they wanted to find him, they would. He shook his head again, furious with himself for his stupidity.

Crunching over the shards of the crushed dresser drawers, he entered the bathroom and rinsed the blood from his hand before expertly treating the wound. At least none of the damage would be permanent, he sighed. On the other hand, he continued his previous train of thought, he had terminated the mark and retrieved the one document. He'd looked it over and noticed the stain on the one side, just as the contractor had indicated. Would it be enough? He'd only been paid half the money, so maybe if he just delivered what he had and called it even, the contractor would be mollified?

It was his only option, because disappearing was just too dangerous at this point. If the employer blew a gasket, then yes, then he'd have to disappear, or at least try to. He kept his multiple outs ready and updated monthly. If he had to get out, he'd at least have a decent head start.

Walking over to his bag, he pulled out a worn copy of Melville's *Moby Dick* and turned to the page with the word he'd chosen to file the phone number under. He had spent years mastering the medieval memory system of associating information with locations in rooms in his mind. But he used physical indicators, widely available indicators like passages in books, to concretely preserve the associations, an admission that the electronic age had sufficiently worn down human memory that he could never hope to match the old scholastic theologians for sheer volume of information.

He'd make the call, he decided, but first he'd disclose to the hotel manager that his wife had just called to say she was filing for divorce and taking the kids, the car, and the house. That would create enough sympathy that the ten thousand dollars he'd offer to pay to cover the damages to his room should do the trick. He smiled wearily and pressed the '0' key.

* * * *

Maurice St. Claire sat at the mid-Western Starbucks sipping what the Americans thought should pass for cappuccino. But the well-practiced boredom that men in his profession used to deflect attention masked his displeasure. The whining of his phone disrupted his demeanor. He hoped that the distinctive whine meant that the mission had proven successful.

He listened silently for a few minutes as the assassin related to him the last few days' events, relieved to know at least that the Jew was dead and that the one artifact had been retrieved. He wasn't sure how his own employer would respond to the loss of the others, but he was a professional, and rarely did an operation of this complexity run perfectly. He smirked at the suggestion that he keep the remaining payment, assuring the worried contractor that he'd be paid in full. St. Claire would have the man in his debt, a debt that might one day make the difference between life and death. It was a lesson he'd learned from his employer's family: complete liberty of action existed where everyone owed you something modest. If they owed you too much, well, then you suddenly became an attractive target yourself. He suppressed the self-congratulatory smile that almost emerged on his well groomed face. He'd been at this so long, he nearly thought like his master. In some matters at least. He finished his coffee, disposed of the cup, and headed to Hopkins International Airport. He would retrieve the package in Paris before heading home.

* * * *

The assassin pulled a glove over his pained hand, shielding the bandaging from prying eyes. Surveying the hotel room one final time, he left nearly five hundred dollars on the table to tip the service staff, and headed down to his taxi, his bag wheeled behind him. Just one more professional leaving the city, he thought, as he reviewed his appearance in the mirrored elevator. A simple nod to the desk manager garnered the pained sympathy that convinced the assassin that all would be well, most well indeed.

After the cabbie tossed his bag into the trunk, the assassin rode with his briefcase bulging on his lap. He asked the man to stop at a FedEx Kinkos, where he held the cab. Everything appeared normal to his trained eye, but he hesitated before entering the shop. He'd been watching for local police cars or any other sign of surveillance, since he left the hotel. But he'd not been followed on foot or by vehicle so far as he could tell. Caution, not arrogance, was the central habit of his life, so he knew the differences between what he could tell and what might lie hidden just around the corner.

He entered the FedEx Kinkos and ordered packaging materials. He withdrew the document carrier from his bag and stared again through the glass at the meaningless and faded markings that constituted a justification

18

for murder. It didn't bother him, but he often wondered what motives underlay his contracts. He shrugged, pleased to be nearly free of his burden. After carefully securing the document in the package, he addressed it to the location he'd been given in France and approached the clerk. Tightening his grip on his briefcase, he handed her the package and paid the bill in cash. Relieved, he turned away from the friendly clerk. Not two steps away, he noticed a less than friendly glance from one of the patrons, a man not carrying any packages. Tension replaced the ease that usually accompanied a finished mission, and he wondered if he'd been followed after all. He quickly scanned the remaining people in the shop but noticed nothing out of the ordinary. They all just stood in line not talking to one another, perfect New Yorkers. But then the clerk had seemed rather friendly, he thought worriedly. As he approached the suspicious customer, he shot a glance over his shoulder at the young lady greeting the next customer. Nothing odd there, he thought. He stumbled into the man without a package, and apologized gruffly, while expertly feeling him for weapons. Finding none, he realized that the patron might be in line for something else. Perhaps, he thought with concern. One could never be sure. But one thing was clear. He needed to get out of the United States immediately. He headed toward the exit and inhaled deeply, easing his strained nerves. Then he left the store and leaped into his taxi, relieved to be heading directly to the airport.

CHAPTER THREE

Mossad Headquarters, Israel

Tucked away several hundred meters beneath one of Tel Aviv's supermarkets, the center of Israeli intelligence hummed with its usual activity. But what Yaakov Katz had just learned pushed this day outside the usual. Raising a hand to halt the report, he stood to his feet and brushed past the two surprised case officers who had been briefing him. Passing through the array of frenetic activity that characterized a nation that was perpetually on a war-footing, he approached the heavy titanium door that separated the two levels of the facility. In spite of knowing exactly who it was that approached him, the soldier guarding the door followed every detail of his security check. But Katz was too deep in thought to give it any notice.

As the heavy door jerked open, Katz walked in silent consternation down the tubular hall, sterile under the florescent lights above. Not even his footfalls made a sound on the floor, constructed with enough elasticity to absorb a nuclear impact on the city above. Katz jerked to a stop in front of his office and ducked inside. The place still reeked of cigarette smoke, in spite of his attempts to overcome that temptation. He crossed the Persian carpet he'd added to offset the building's stifling sterility, and pulled open a file drawer. Katz's hands worked quickly, sifting through the file cabinet and withdrawing a red folder. He opened the folder deftly and silently perused the pages within.

It made little sense that the book peddler should suddenly turn his attention away from his own and toward *goyim*. When Myron Hentersheim had first approached Israeli intelligence, everyone thought he was another of the apocalyptic crackpots, but when he offered proof of his claims, Yaakov had immediately classified the operation under the strictest secrecy and reported the case solely to the Prime Minister himself. When Hentersheim turned down an initial offer of money, and then in a bar rejected the sexual overtures—he was a bit old after all—it became clear that he had approached Israel either out of love of the country or out of hatred for someone else. A careful background check on Hentersheim had revealed no enemies. And his religious and community service hinted at religious or patriotic motives, the distinction between the two being important but often overemphasized in a country with such a profound religious history. So, Mossad had concluded that Hentersheim was the real thing. Katz snapped the folder shut and reached for his blue sports coat.

Their relationship with him had been developing solidly for two months. Its abrupt cessation could be explained by what? A change of heart? That didn't seem likely in a man of Hentersheim's years. A counteroffer? But Hentersheim wasn't in this for profit. So, that left coercion of some kind. And Hentersheim's sudden disappearance suggested just that. Someone else had entered the market, someone that he would track down.

*   *   *   *

Cleveland, Ohio

The fog was almost as thick as the smell of lake water in the air and it glowed incandescently with the light of the full moon shining silently down on Lake Erie. No other boats were in sight as the small yacht swayed under a slight wind, the cold water lapping against its side. Shrouded in the half-dark of the fog, the securely weighted body of Zechariah Hentersheim, the formerly healthy twenty-one year old grandson of the murdered book dealer slipped over the side of the yacht into the murky depths. The fish would eliminate any evidence of Zechariah's identity before anyone ever found the young man. The yachtsman then raised his sail and caught the breeze fully, the prow of his boat slicing through the icy water. With one last sweep of the horizon, he ensured that no one had seen him. He then spun the wheel hard over to the starboard, directing his boat away from the watery grave. Popping the lid off a bottle of beer, he relaxed and gingerly continued his journey toward the state of New York. His mission was complete, and his money would be well-spent.

*   *   *   *

Yaakov Katz finally arrived at Metsada, the special operations division of Mossad, and impatiently headed towards the encrypted signals department. Forty years of work in intelligence had slowed the tired, heavy set Israeli patriot. His slight cough and mottled skin did little to disguise the fact that he'd only recently given up smoking. But his expressionless eyes masked an extremely fine mind, adept at ferreting out threats to the security of his country.

Arriving at the signals room in the super-secret facility buried in the side of a desert mountain, he ordered that a directive be forwarded to his most prized asset, an Israeli agent deep within the US Federal Bureau of Investigation. He wished to know just what the United States knew about Hentersheim. And so he made two requests: what did the FBI have on the Hentersheim murder? And what did the FBI have on the name, 'Melchizedek'?

* * * *

Lake Erie

The yachtsman looked with concern at the clouds developing on the horizon, as the winds churned the waters into increasingly larger swells. The moon's full sphere now illuminated the night, as the cold front descended on the lake shattering the fog that had concealed him. Had he not been involved with body-disposal, he would never have ventured this far out of sight of the land in the first place. The lake was well-known for its unpredictable, dangerous storms, and this night as the bow of his boat angled sharply into an oncoming wave, the yachtsman began to worry. He thought of calling for help, but that would officially place him at the scene of the disposal should the body ever turn up. His worries were interrupted by metallic sounds coming from below. Glancing into the cabin, he noticed several galley cups sloshing on the floor. Hurriedly, he descended the ladder and entered the cabin. Sure enough, he had left the porthole windows open to clear out any stench from the body, and now as the boat swayed with the crashing waves, water poured into the yacht. After securing the portholes, he headed into the hold to start the pumps. Reaching behind the pump to hit the switch, he felt some unfamiliar wires. Concerned that the storm might have thrown the pump against the bulkhead and damaged it, he grabbed a flashlight and strained his neck to peer over the pump at the switch mechanism. A knot instantly formed in his stomach and his tongue stuck to the roof of his mouth as he saw the unmistakable form of a bomb. Apparently, he thought darkly, his employers had decided to dispose of two problems on this trip.

CHAPTER FOUR

Langley, Virginia

F red Billings left the director's office for what had by now become a weekly report on his counterintelligence investigation. His best efforts could not bury the smile that erupted in his features each time he left that office, especially as the Attorney General and the Director of the FBI followed him out and joined their entourages back to their own offices in the Capitol. The case was unprecedented and in an extraordinary act of interagency cooperation, the FBI director had actually requested that the CIA handle the investigation. Billings knew that the FBI director just couldn't be sure how far Israeli tentacles reached into his agency, and rather than compromise the case with an investigation of his own, he had handed it over to an outside agency. It had required a special appeal to the President and then the Attorney General to permit a domestic investigation of this kind by the Central Intelligence Agency.

Billings waited for the elevators to return. He would happily wait for twenty elevators if it enabled him to continue his leading role in ferreting out the full duplicity of the Israeli spy. Spotting the coffee machine down the corridor, Billings ran over and deposited a few coins. But just then the elevator offered its familiar ding, drawing him back with hot coffee sloshing over the sides of his cup and onto his hand. The stinging irritation called to mind the fury that had consumed him when he was first assigned to plug the leak at the FBI. How any American could compromise the security of his own country was beyond Billings' understanding. It was bad enough, he thought, when the newspapers revealed classified operations under the people's alleged "right to know." It wasn't that Billings was naive; he knew the power that US intelligence wielded, and he knew there had to be accountability. But accountability wasn't the same thing as some "right to know."

But the difference with David Goldblum—Billings almost spat the name out, the man so disgusted him—was that Goldblum served not a distorted sense of loyalty to the principles of his own country, but instead served a foreign power. And a friendly power at that! Billings reached his own floor and headed down the hall to his, now larger, office. He looked at the painting hanging behind his desk, depicting the British burning the White House to the ground during the War of 1812. He kept it there to remind himself of one fundamental principle: other nations weren't ever your friends. They all served themselves first.

And so, here he was, spying on a spy working for an ally nation, one of America's closest. Yet once Billings' teams had tracked Goldblum's pattern and identified his drop point, he had been ordered not to make an arrest. At first rankled, he eventually agreed with that assessment. Why waste an opportunity to counter-spy on a spy and thus turn Israel's spy into a source of information on Israel itself? The hen had become the fox.

It was a master stroke, suggested by the CIA director himself, to the ready agreement of the Executive Branch. Naturally, the FBI had taken some convincing. For the past year US intelligence had been retrieving and copying Goldblum's packages before the Israelis picked them up. From what Goldblum was sending to Israel, the US learned what Mossad wanted to know. That in turn enabled them to read Israeli intentions. Working together, the two agencies had also given Goldblum access to fabricated programs so as to misinform and misdirect Mossad. The US had turned Mossad's highest placed US agent without either the agent or his handlers being privy to the scheme!

Billings' reflective euphoria gave way to a sudden jolt in his right knee, as he slammed it against the inside of his desk. The damn thing was just too small, he thought angrily. He picked up the phone to see about getting something larger, while nursing the old football injury that occasionally evidenced a slight limp. The lithe mid-Western ex-receiver pushed the memory of that awful day to the recesses of his mind, pleased that his redirected career had proven so successful.

After being assured that another desk would be found somewhere, he returned the phone to its cradle, just in time for his secretary to approach him with another pile of decrypted Goldblum intercepts. Glancing at the clock, Billings sighed. He thanked his secretary, noting that she was wearing her overcoat. His would stay on its hanger for many more hours.

Billings headed down to the bathroom to refresh himself before devouring the latest communication between Goldblum and his handlers. In the mirror he saw the sandy hair that sat atop a round mid-western face ordinary in all respects except for his piercing blue eyes. Dousing himself with cold water, Billings appreciated the invigorating chill. He headed back toward his office musing on the oddities of the intelligence business. The grand schemes to discover or conceal—without which no nation could really be safe—made it almost feel like a great political game. Everyone lied to everyone else and did so with a twinkle in their eyes. Might as well be kissing babies, Billings laughed, as he entered his office again.

Returning to his desk, he deftly jammed his muscular body into the measured space before sipping from the coffee that had scalded him earlier. As it warmed his body, it also sharpened his sensibilities, making the pain from his leg injury more pronounced. How ironic that the coffee that warmed him nevertheless increased his discomfort. Just like espionage, he thought grimly. The information that his government craved came at an awful price. Real people were caught in the services of their rival countries. It wasn't a game. No doubt, Goldblum believed himself a patriot, just as Billings did. But Billings rejected the appearance of moral parity, confident that when Goldblum was finally arrested, he'd not lose any sleep over his life-imprisonment. Looking at the large file in front of him, Billings yawned in anticipation of another long night.

CHAPTER FIVE

Giza Plateau, Egypt

Franklen Bartleby gently hammered on the rear of his chisel in the stifling heat of the Giza plateau. Desert winds swirled outside, occasionally blasting against his chafed skin. The shade provided by the tomb's entry room offered little relief, as his body struggled even to produce sweat. Forty-five years failed to slow the sun-bronzed archeologist whose silver rimmed eye glasses offered a metallic counterpart to his bleach blond eyebrows and fair hair. He wore the expected khaki colors of a desert explorer, while a canteen hung from his belt and a notebook bulged in his shirt pocket. His sturdy boots, worn and dusty, steadied him as he crouched before the plastered doorway. Taking another swig of water from his canteen, he returned to his task. With a final tap, the chisel broke through the ancient plaster to reveal a dark hole, unseen by human eyes for nearly three thousand years.

Like so many other ancient Egyptian tombs, this one had yielded whatever treasures it once possessed to the ever-efficient grave robbers. But though the treasures were not replaced, the ancient authorities had repaired the entry ways to the various vaults within the tomb by covering them with plaster.

Bartleby had finally obtained the permission of the Egyptian authorities to crack open the plaster wall, and now with a single shaft of light penetrating the darkness, he slipped a small camera followed by an illumination lamp into the hole. Flicking the power switch to the equipment, he gazed down at his visual display, as his aide manned the camera's remote controls.

Both men sighed slightly as the camera revealed what they had told themselves was very likely the case, that the mummy had been ransacked by the original robberies. What remained of it had been respectfully laid back into the cracked and broken wooden sarcophagus by priests in antiquity. When the camera light turned to illuminate the far wall of the burial chamber, however, the series of beautifully painted reliefs brought delighted gasps from both of them. Bartleby and his assistant spent the next few hours photographing every detail of the reliefs through the small entry opening. Once finished, Bartleby stuffed a rag into the hole, intent on preserving the interior walls from the ravages of the desert sands.

* * * *

Lake Erie

Staring at the bomb attached to his boat, the yachtsman feared that he had only moments before it exploded. Frantically searching for the bomb's detonator, he realized that it was not wired to the pump mechanism or any other part of the ship. Dismayed, he tried to think clearly. Why hadn't it gone off already? It certainly didn't have a motion detonator, since the ship had been rocking in the storm. So, what did that leave? A timer, most likely. But how much time did he have left? There was no way he could tell. He knew that unlike what they show in the movies, real timed bombs do not include LCD displays with a countdown; why would one bother giving a potential bomb disposal unit any information?

So, what was he to do? Throw it overboard, his mind screamed. He reached over the bomb to see how it was attached to his boat. Disgusted, he saw that it had been welded into place. There was no hope of removing it quickly. Frantically, he grabbed for his emergency supply kit, as well as his compass, weapons bag, emergency radio, and portable GPS. Racing topside, he yanked the tarp off his small dinghy and hurled his supplies into its bottom. Expertly working the small cranes that held the boat in place, he dropped the dinghy's stern into the dark water. But the bow line tangled in the mechanism. Sweat poured down his face as he struggled to free it, occasionally glancing back at the dark hold of the yacht as though he might get some sudden warning that the bomb would detonate. Finally, the line came loose freeing the little craft from the yacht. The yachtsman dove into the boat and reached for the oars. He had rowed just forty feet away through huge swells, when the sky lit up with a massive explosion, showering his body with splinters. He lay dazed in the bottom of the dinghy grateful to be alive.

* * * *

The explosion off the port bow of his patrol craft surprised Coast Guard Lieutenant Rick Sanders. Part of the Ninth Coast Guard District Fleet, the self-described "Guardians of the Great Lakes," his boat usually worked to interdict cigarette smugglers from Canada, but in rough seas he augmented the larger ships in sea rescue. The gale was sufficiently strong that he hadn't even seen the yacht prior to its disappearance in the fireball, but he hurried his fast boat toward the debris field. His first mate called from the lookout position that a small dinghy was adrift and possibly occupied, so Sanders turned his boat toward it.

The yachtsman was still too dazed to notice the approaching patrol boat, so when he heard a voice calling to him from the dark night, he spun around in complete shock. Seeing the patrol vessel hovering above his tiny boat, he acted precipitously and reached into his bag for a pistol. But a powerful searchlight suddenly illuminated him and just before a voice echoed over a loudspeaker ordering his surrender, he heard the distinctive clicks of several weapons being cocked. Desperate to escape, the yachtsman considered going over the side of his boat, but even if he escaped the Coast Guard in the black water, he'd very likely freeze to death before he ever made it back to land. Hearing a forceful repetition of the order to drop his weapon, the yachtsman let it fall from his hands and raised his arms above his head.

Lieutenant Sanders was amazed at the exhausted and blood soaked man led aboard his ship in handcuffs. It was clear to him that their sudden appearance had surprised the yachtsman into revealing his criminal intentions. Capitalizing on this knowledge, he approached the man with a cup of hot coffee and a blanket, as his crew retrieved a first aid kit to treat the many cuts that continued to spew blood.

"That was a bomb on your boat, you know," offered Sanders simply.

He received no verbal reply, but the menace in the eyes of the yachtsman told him what he wished to know.

"They tried to kill you," the Coast Guard officer stated.

"Yeah, I know," answered the yachtsman. "Some deal, huh?"

"Some deal," echoed Sanders, handing him the coffee.

After the man's wounds had been treated and the coffee had warmed him, Sanders continued, "Perhaps you'd like to talk about it?"

Sanders could see that the yachtsman reflected on what he asked him. Criminals were loyal only if they thought that that loyalty would be rewarded. Here he had a chance to uncover whatever larger plot was really at work, so he added, "You'll do better with us than with them."

Sanders watched the exhaustion and fear that had been omnipresent in the features of his prisoner suddenly give way to a decision.

"I'll tell you what," offered the yachtsman craftily. "How about we make a trade? I'll bet that bombs at sea are rather unusual for you, right?"

As Sanders nodded, the yachtsman continued, "Then you get me dockside and set me up with the Feds. They'll want to know what I can give 'em. But I need complete protection and a new identity. Otherwise I don't talk."

Thoughtfully, Sanders replied, "If you don't talk, I doubt you'll survive for long in the system—not after what I just saw."

But the yachtsman refused to be bullied and just repeated, "Protection, or you get nothing."

CHAPTER SIX

Lake Erie

The yachtsman sat handcuffed in the swaying coast guard vessel, as Lieutenant Sanders turned the boat towards shore. By mid-morning of the following day, they had entered Cleveland's harbor. Sanders turned his catch over to the senior officer at the base who listened in amazement to the yachtsman's story. The officer then called the Cleveland police and asked for a detective from homicide. He had little doubt that this would eventually involve the federal authorities, but protocol was protocol.

* * * *

New York City

The local police enjoy cooperative relationships with banks, and so it did not take Quarston's lab tech, Harry, all that long to work with the NYPD to identify the safety deposit key's source. He arrived at Citibank and introduced himself to the branch manager who, upon receiving a fax of Hentersheim's death certificate and reviewing Quarston's identification, took him into the vault to the waiting safety deposit boxes. The manager's key matched the one Quarston had obtained from the butcher, and with the turn of both keys the door opened. The manager carried the box to a table and left Quarston to his privacy. Quarston took a deep breath and lifted the lid on the large box.

The yachtsman's real name turned out to be James Beecham, a long-time resident of Cleveland with no connection to any criminal ventures whatsoever. Detective Larry Burke found this fact puzzling after hearing Beecham's tale. The deceased and probably irrecoverable Benjamin Hentersheim proved to be connected to a Myron Hentersheim who had himself only recently been murdered. And Beecham's story definitely connected the two events. After confirming what he could of Beecham's account, he would contact the detective working on the other case and set up a joint investigation. Because the crime apparently involved an interstate kidnapping, he knew he would also have to call the federal authorities. He dialed the number for the FBI.

* * * *

Quarston stared in wonder at three glass frames containing what looked to him like ancient manuscript fragments. He could not identify the script but knew it was neither Greek nor Latin, since he'd studied the classical languages as an undergraduate at Boston College . . . okay, so it wasn't a dialect of either language that he knew, he admitted to himself. Attic Greek, the Greek of Pericles, Socrates, and Sophocles was itself developed from an older variant that employed Phoenician script. But his knowledge of ancient languages did not include Phoenician or Egyptian or Akkadian or any of the other important literary or political languages, not even Aramaic. He suddenly wondered about that, but the symbols didn't appear to match the shapes of contemporary Hebrew characters that he had seen. He recalled that ossuary box that had turned up a few years back, a box that some said held the bones of James, the brother of Jesus. And the letters of that script did not appear like the Hebrew lettering he was familiar with either, even though it was Aramaic, a close relation to Hebrew. People write the same letters in different ways; that's what it came down to. So, he'd have to find a paleographer to examine and translate these texts. And he'd have to find out how old they were, their country of origin, and . . . what was that? One of the three pages had a dark stain along its right side. Mud? Ink? Blood? He wondered. Ancient substances did not have the same coloring as their contemporary cousins. He would need a sample of that substance for testing as well. He really hoped that these documents weren't of archeological value, because if word got out that he had them, and that he was cutting them up for testing . . . no, word would not get out, he suddenly decided. He would conceal their existence for now, because he was determined to solve this crime.

Quarston dusted the frames for prints, but discovered only one set, which he compared with the coroner's report and confirmed were the book-dealer's. The butcher had never held them. Quarston felt relieved that his impression of the butcher's truthfulness was on target. Quarston supposed that Hentersheim had been nervous about the safety of the documents and had entrusted the key to his life-long friend, but for some reason hadn't taken him fully into his confidence. Why? That was the question. Embarrassment? About what? Quarston couldn't be sure yet. He needed more information.

Quarston next carefully opened the glass frames of the manuscripts and excised a small piece of each for analysis. He made sure that he retrieved some of the stained portion as well as some of the smudged ink, taking great care not to disturb the writing itself. After taking numerous photographs of the scripts, he restored the manuscript fragments to their original location in the box and watched as the manager replaced the box and locked the door. The bank was the safest place for the documents for now, he had decided. Quarston returned to Boston that afternoon and dropped off the samples for analysis and the film for development. The next day he would head back to his *alma mater* to talk to one of his old professors who might offer him guidance and possibly even translations of the texts.

* * * *

Paris

Maurice St. Claire edged along the arched gateway of the train station in Paris, observing a young man with a newspaper under one arm munching away at his baguette. Oblivious to his surveillance, the man waited in the package receiving line and then handed the clerk his confirmation number. The clerk checked the number and soon returned with the package from America. Placing his newspaper on top of the package, he finished the last bite of his baguette and tossed the wrapper into the trash. He then entered the main terminal of the station.

Close behind him, Maurice St. Claire tailed the young man. St. Claire spent most of his time observing the people around his package carrier, watching to see if anyone looked too closely at him or appeared to be following him. As the man boarded a train, St. Claire hopped aboard himself and grabbed a seat in the rear of the crowded car. At the appointed stop, the man exited the train and left the terminal. He gingerly headed to the small cafe where he was soon to earn himself one hundred euro. It had taken him quite some time to find the place the first time, because it was

32

so out of the way. He had initially wondered if there was something criminal going on, but the dazzling eyes of the art student who had hired him squelched that line of thinking quickly. He saw her waving to him from inside the café, so he quickened his pace.

St. Claire observed the man order a coffee and sit down with the girl. She flirted with him for a while, chatting animatedly, and then handed him the money they had agreed upon. The young man accepted it thankfully and asked if she was interested in meeting up with him later that evening. She agreed to meet him at a favorite club, and he got up to leave. St. Claire glanced at the street, and then back into the near empty café. As the young man brushed past him, St. Claire walked past the café and further down the narrow street. Within moments, the young lady walked up to him with the package.

"Here you are, Maurice," she reached out to him.

"Thank you so very much, Bridgette," he nodded to her. "You won't see him again, right?"

"Just making him feel comfortable," she answered airily.

St. Claire nodded, satisfied. He handed her one thousand euro, and she immediately headed away and toward the train station. St. Claire walked slowly down the street in the opposite direction of Bridgette. His eyes continued to look for any changes from what he'd seen on his surveillance runs the last few days until he felt satisfied that no one had tracked the exchange.

* * * *

Boston

After a refreshing night's sleep in his own bed, Quarston retrieved his developed photographs and headed toward the college. On the drive to Boston College's campus, Quarston recalled the wonder of his college education. He had gone to school with naïveté and ambition; he knew he wanted a career in law enforcement, and he knew he wanted a serious education. But he was wholly unprepared for what hit him in his first day at school. He had enrolled in a philosophy course with a witty and logically skillful professor. Quarston had always assumed that justice was what the police enforced and lawyers and politicians played with, but after a semester with Professor Williams, he realized that justice of the criminal or political kinds was just that, a *kind*. What is justice itself? This was the stunning question that drove him into Plato's *Republic* with a passion. Socrates's cross-examination and unstoppable fervor for the truth matched his own passion to uncover the truth in criminal ventures, but Quarston had realized what Socrates would have asked him: what's it all for? Why bother with fighting crime? What ends are achieved by this activity? And are those ends good? To figure that out, he had to know what goodness for human beings really was. And that was the central subject of Plato's book. He had never read a book like it before or since. In fact, he had kept his pledge made fourteen years before to reread Plato's *Republic* every year, and every time he read it, he was amazed to find the book of even deeper interest and satisfaction than the last time. That Greek knew human nature, and Quarston continually found it beneficial both to his career, in figuring out deformed criminal nature, and in his own life, as he sought to lead the best life he could. But in spite of his moral zeal and professional success, he hadn't found happiness. The philosophical optimism of his youth hadn't translated into the kind of justice he really sought. With these mixed feelings, he parked his car at the security office, glad for his agency sticker, and ventured back into his academic past.

* * * *

Paris

Maurice St. Claire greeted the elderly woman who ran the small inn with a bouquet of flowers and then carried his package and a new bottle of Bordeaux up to his room. He pulled the cork from the bottle and sniffed it expertly, before pouring himself a glass and resting it on the mantel of the small fire place in his room. While it took in the air, he opened his suitcase and retrieved a small scalpel.

St. Claire looked at the package that rested on the table in front of him. He had spent so much time in the past few weeks arranging all the details that made its presence before him possible. He was pleased with his success and relieved finally to be outside the United States. His travels in Ohio had been necessary. Loose ends had to be tied up. But it was all for what lay in that package, he thought eagerly.

As he cut open the top of the container, he thought about what had led him down this odd path, quite out of the ordinary of his usual security work. His employer had made this project a top priority for him, expending significant sums. He reached through the bubble wrap and pulled out the glass container and looked at the faded and aged paged within. Sure enough, it was stained significantly on one side, just as his employer had indicated. Apparently, that stain was the main interest, not the text or the document itself. He didn't know why, he didn't really need to. He had spent years in the service of his employer, confident that whatever plan was in motion would ultimately yield its weight in gold.

With extreme care he opened the glass frame and slid the document partially outside, sufficiently far to enable him to slice off a section of the stain. His employer had been precise about this. He dropped the excised piece into a pre-addressed, biohazard bag and sealed it. Placing it on the table for mailing the next day, he returned his attention to the document and gently prodded it back into the safety of the glass frame. Confident that he had carried out his instructions exactly, he returned the glass case to the bubble wrap and closed the package.

Satisfied that he had done what he'd been instructed to do, he returned the glass case to the bubble wrap and closed the package. He then turned to his glass of Bordeaux and sipped thoughtfully.

* * * *

Cleveland

Roger Quarston's office phone rang several times without an answer, so Detective Burke left a message for Quarston to contact him on the Hentersheim case and then left his office for a weekend on the lake. He was planning on taking his boat to Cedar Point. He had learned over the years that women had a soft spot for roller coasters and fun, even from afar. And so, his standard dating tactic was to grab a case of beer and take his gal over to the Point to where the world's highest roller coasters would stencil the setting sun. He threw his gun, badge, and cell phone on to his dresser; this was one date he didn't want ruined by police business. He had met Cindy only two weeks before at a NASCAR race in Mansfield. They had stumbled into one another at a refreshment stand, spilling beer all over themselves and landing in a clump on the ground. She had looked at him in a shock that quickly turned to contagious laughter. She then poured the remainder of her beer over his head, and he admitted that he deserved it. That won him the sympathy date, where they discovered that they shared not only a love of beer but engines. A woman who knew the value of cars and beer? Burke decided that maybe his luck was finally changing.

CHAPTER SEVEN

Boston College

Professor Beaufort's office door was open as Quarston approached. Beaufort was sixty-one years of age, with thick salt-pepper hair atop a long, narrow face with thick rimmed glasses. His tall form evoked an awkward physical presence with long lanky legs and ill-fitted clothes, almost like a human daddy long-legs, Quarston smirked. But Quarston had also taken Beaufort's course in ancient cultures and knew that the man was a genius with languages.

Beaufort was seated behind his desk with stacks and stacks of papers that needed grading. Good professors spend far more time grading papers and talking with their students outside of class than teaching within the classroom, and they always love the opportunity (or excuse?) to do the latter in place of the former. And so Beaufort's face erupted into a huge smile when he saw Roger Quarston's face peer around the office door. Quarston looked sheepish, as he always had when he caught Beaufort's gaze, but Beaufort was thrilled to see his former students, and immediately rose from his chair and warmly shook his hand. Quarston swallowed the gulp that had formed in his throat. He suddenly felt again like the junior college student he had been when he had first met Beaufort, but his old professor offered him a chair and coffee (always the coffee, he remembered), and sagely asked about his life and career. This enabled Quarston to become for his professor what he had become for everyone else, a highly successful field agent of the FBI. He explained some of the drama of his recent cases and mentioned that his partner of many years had lately died leaving him alone on his current case. And that naturally led to his serious business.

"Professor," Quarston began, "I'm here in an official capacity, because I need your help on a rather sensitive matter."

Beaufort smiled at Quarston. 'Sensitive' meant 'secret,' he well knew, and so he offered his help, "Roger, you can trust my discretion. How can I assist you?"

Quarston opened his briefcase and withdrew the photographs he had picked up at the office that morning, handing them to the Professor. Beaufort examined them carefully for several moments, yanked open a desk drawer to reach for a magnifying glass, and stared again at the photos. Suddenly, he stood up, grasping multiple books off one of his shelves. He opened them one after the other in his usual jerky movements that had entertained Quarston's classmates. Whenever Beaufort became excited about something, he would move about with jerks and twists, talk two or three times more rapidly than anyone could record, and literally smash chalk on the chalkboard as he tried to write. So, Quarston became increasingly intrigued by his professor's spirited examination of the documents.

Finally, Beaufort stopped everything, fell into his chair, and exclaimed, "My God!"

"What is it?" Quarston pressed him.

Beaufort waved him toward silence and tossed his glasses onto the desk, as he sank deeper into his chair with his eyes fixed on the ceiling. In fact, he had ascended to another dimension of history, language, and culture, all buzzing about in his brilliant mind. Finally, he turned back to Quarston and asked, "Okay, where did you get these?"

Quarston was taken aback, and replied, "I'd prefer not to say at this time, Professor. I was hoping you could translate them for me."

The professor stared at him hard, and then a suspicious grin formed on his face. "Roger, you wouldn't be pulling a prank, would you? Driving an old professor over the edge into complete madness? I mean, I know I'm partly mad already but . . ."

"No, Sir," Quarston exclaimed, "this is entirely on the level; these are photographs of . . ."

Quarston trailed off. He was about to say, "genuinely ancient manuscripts," when he suddenly realized that he didn't know that at all. Maybe they were complete forgeries. But if so, why would anyone kill over them, assuming someone had. He decided that he needed the results of the sample analysis, but in the meantime he would still get the translation he needed. So he answered the Professor.

"Sir, these are photographs of what might be ancient manuscript fragments, or so it appears. I'm having them analyzed," Quarston paused at the look of consternation that spread over Beaufort's face and then hurriedly continued, "No, no, I've been quite careful not to damage them or obscure the writing or mishandle them in any way."

"But you handed them over to a bunch of lab technicians?" the professor exclaimed in shock.

"No, I just excised some small samples and kept the original fragments safe," he replied.

"You just cut them up, you mean, but you didn't 'damage' them?" the professor inquired quizzically. Quarston began to feel like he was in class again.

"Look sir, someone has been killed over these documents, and I'll be damned if paleographic care is going to impede my investigation. I only cut the edge of the documents; I was extremely careful."

Beaufort stared at him again, and Quarston stared back. There must have been a full minute of silence between them. Quarston had seen this before; the professor was wholly comfortable with silence, and when he would ask an unanswered question of his classes, he would often just wait and wait and wait, and finally the class would realize he really meant to be answered. But Quarston now played the same game back, and after another three minutes, the professor was forced to speak first. Quarston would remember this moment as a lifetime achievement.

"Very well, I suppose you have your job to think of, but these texts, Roger! Do you have any idea what they are?"

"No, Sir, that's the problem. What are they?"

"They are written in Sumerian cuneiform script but in ink on vellum, not on clay tablets as are almost all Sumerian inscriptions of which I'm aware."

"But why would someone use ink rather than a stylus on clay? Wouldn't the characters be hard to write with a quill if they were usually made with a small chisel?"

The professor chuckled, "Roger, what do you think letters are? They are nothing but scratches on a page. We add interpretation to the scratches with our minds. Whether they are inscribed into clay or written with ink, knowing what strokes to make is the point."

"Right, I see what you mean," acknowledge Quarston, a little embarrassed. "But it's still strange to find someone writing on vellum a language from a place where everyone uses clay inscriptions. Is that it?"

"Exactly," answered the professor.

"So, it'd be like someone from our century used to paper found himself in ancient times in Babylonia. He might just as well prefer to write in ink, after he learned the ancient language," mused Quarston.

"Yes," the professor reflected. "Suppose he was an Egyptian, for instance."

"Then he'd be used to writing with ink and quill on papyrus, but if he somehow got stuck in Babylon . . ." Quarston trailed off.

"Then he might still write in his old way," finished the professor.

Beaufort continued, "The language is Akkadian used by the great ancient Mesopotamian cultures including both Assyria and Babylonia. In one of the texts the form of the Akkadian language is neo-Assyrian, while in these later ones it is late Babylonian."

"Okay," replied Quarston, "so they are written in two different forms of the Akkadian language, from two different eras, though back to back eras, correct?"

"Right," replied the professor, "and so they could be from the same time period, but not necessarily. You'll need carbon-14 dating for that. The vellum . . ."

". . . is animal hide and so was alive at one time," broke in Quarston. "Carbon-14 dating will offer a fairly precise date."

"Exactly," said the professor.

"But what are they about, Sir?" Quarston asked.

"That's what's so intriguing," replied Beaufort who then continued. "Let me begin with the Assyrian scripted fragment. It refers to a great battle by Sennacharib in Phoenicia, and then mentions his turning away from Salem!"

"And what's the big deal of that?" asked Quarston.

"Salem is Jerusalem, Roger. This text refers to an event in the Hebrew Bible in which Sennacharib's army is decimated by an angel forcing him to retreat from a possible conquest of the kingdom of Judah."

"Oh, you mean the Hezekiah story?"

"Just so, son, just so. Amazing, isn't it? I mean, we have no other references to the cause of that retreat save the Biblical sources."

"Okay, and the other ones?"

"One of them merely refers to some raiders or an army, but it seems more like bandits formed into something like an army, so I use the term 'raiders.' Apparently, these raiders attacked the town of the writer, and he was injured in the raid. He mentions being just able to ferret away his books, making it appear that he was more than a scribe."

"Why?"

"Because he owned books."

"But wouldn't a scribe likely own books?"

"No, a scribe would write books, but they would belong to his master."

"So, he owned books . . ." Quarston hesitated, waiting for the professor to continue.

"Yes, he owned books, but he also wrote books."

Quarston suddenly caught the point, "He was a literate man who owned books!"

"Right," replied the professor, "and that means more than a scribe, more likely a wealthy educated person. Common today, not so common in the ancient world, though in Egypt and Babylon we find that combination more often than in many other cultures."

A thought struck Quarston, "Which manuscript number is the 'raider' one?"

"You have it numbered as the third," replied the professor.

"The one with the stain."

"What's that?" asked Beaufort.

"One of the manuscript fragments had a stain along one edge, number three."

"I see," replied the professor, "and you wondered if it is blood, and if so, how old?"

"Right."

"A good question. I guess your lab techs will prove invaluable after all," the professor admitted with a wry grin.

"Apparently," Quarston smiled back and then continued, "and the last fragment?"

"That's the strangest one of all!" exclaimed the professor, increasing the speed of his speech by fully three times.

Quarston choked back a smile and managed to ask, "That's the other Babylonian one?"

"Right! The other Babylonian one." The professor just stared at Quarston apparently stunned again into silence.

Quarston probed, "So? What did it say?"

"It refers to Belteshazzar, chief of the magicians and sorcerers of Babylon in the time of Nebuchadnezzar."

"Well, if it's from the time of Nebuchadnezzar, that proves that it must have been written at another time than the Sennacharib piece and by someone else," concluded Quarston.

The professor's profound amazement was broken by this erroneous inference. "No, no it doesn't, for they all could have been written at the same time, even about events occurring 150 years earlier."

"In different languages?"

"Why not? Who knows? No conclusions yet. The carbon-14 dating will assist you there."

Quarston still thought his hunch would be vindicated, but went on, "And what is the significance of Belteshazzar? I mean, everyone knows who Nebuchadnezzar was."

"Oh dooooooooooooo they?" the Professor droned and gave him a sharp look. "*You* know who Nebuchadnezzar was, but ask my freshmen who he was! What they don't know any more. What do they teach them in the schools these days?"

"Okay, so Nebuchadnezzar was the greatest king of Babylon and is the guy who sacked Jerusalem and carried away the Jews into their exile. And Belteshazzar is who?" queried Quarston.

"The Hebrew prophet, Daniel."

Beaufort and Quarston stared at each other again but this time there was no question on the table. They were both completely and utterly stunned into incredulity.

Beaufort finally broke the silence with a matter of fact conclusion, "And that, my boy, is why someone is pulling a magnificent hoax on you!"

"Right," replied Quarston. "Hitherto unknown texts written in Sumerian script—which one rarely if ever discovers in ink—referring to Biblical events. Has to be a scam of some sort."

"Just so," retorted the professor. "The question is why you are interested in them. Some big wig worried he got ripped off?"

"No, and that's the problem, Professor," answered Quarston. "Someone was murdered over these documents, or at least that's my hunch."

CHAPTER EIGHT

Boston

Quarston asked Harry again whether he had done the test correctly, and the lab technician assured him that he had. Quarston just could not believe what he was being told, namely that the three documents were some 2,500 years old.

"Actually, carbon-14 is a rather accurate dating system, and we can place one of the documents at about 2,800 years, another at 2,600, and the third around 2,500 years."

"I see," murmured Quarston, looking again at the aged vellum under the microscope.

"What's more," added the technician, "I subjected the ink to carbon-14 dating as well, and . . ."

"Same dates?" interjected Quarston.

"Right," replied the technician. "And the coloring of the ink and its fading rates confirm the carbon-14 results."

"Okay," summarized Quarston, "so, we've either got authentic documents here or someone went to an enormous amount of trouble and tracked down 2,500 year old paper and ink to forge them."

"Well, yes, I thought of that too, so I checked on the ink, and it cannot be stored that long. It is itself a biological product, derived from a snail in the Mediterranean sea. My research on it showed that it was commonly traded throughout the Bronze Age. But get this: it degrades over time if not used."

"How do you know that?" queried Quarston.

"Well, for one thing, the ink compound is chemically unstable, but for another, vials of the ink were found on a Mediterranean wreck some fifteen years ago."

"How on earth did you discover that?" wondered Quarston.

"I saw a Discovery Channel special on this dive on an ancient Phoenician merchant wreck in the Med that contained multiple bottles of ancient wine. I always wondered if you could drink the stuff—I've since learned that the answer is no. But anyway, that got me to thinking. If wine can be found on old wrecks, why not ink? So, I did some searching and found out about the wreck with the ink vials. And sure enough, the ink vials were degraded just as indicated."

"So, you are telling me that these documents were actually written in what . . . 500 B.C. or so?"

"More or less. Remember that the documents differ by some 300 years from one another."

Quarston found himself feeling unsettled at this conclusion when the technician continued.

"Sir, I also subjected the samples to handwriting analysis, after noticing an odd similarity in the shape of some of these symbols. See how this line tends to bisect this one here, and then over here too?"

Quarston peered into the microscope and noticed the bisected lines.

The lab technician continued, "That is not a regular feature of the lettering, from the expert I consulted."

"You discovered that they were written in Sumerian script too?" asked Quarston.

"Yes, though I don't have a complete translation . . . you were working on that, correct?"

"Right, but tell me what the handwriting analysis showed."

"They are written by the same hand," he exclaimed.

"Oh, come on," rebutted Quarston, "that just cannot be right, or else you are telling me that we've got a guy who's at least 300 years old."

"Look, Sir, I double checked the dating, the handwriting analysis, and I put the language through a stylometric analysis program that confirmed that even stylistically they are from the same person."

"Well, this is just too much to believe for one week," Quarston replied and then added, "Look, you must have some idea of the implications of this, right?"

"Yes, Sir, I do. We've got a guy who was alive for some 300 years between 800 and 500 B.C. That's very, very odd."

"Yes, 'odd' is one word for it. 'Insane' is another. You really expect me to believe this?"

The technician just stared at him with that serious "you ever want me to expedite a case for you again?" look.

"Okay, okay, so we've got a guy living a very long time."

"Oh, and another thing, you were right about the blood."

"Blood?" inquired Quarston.

"Yes, the stain is . . ."

"Blood!" interjected Quarston and asked, "But whose blood? The author's?"

"Unknown Sir, but we could run a DNA analysis to learn more about whoever's blood it is."

"Very well," replied Quarston cautiously, reluctant to widen the scope of those aware of the documents' existence. "I'll consider that."

"Sir, what did they say?" asked the technician curiously.

"Hmm . . .?" murmured Quarston, still musing over this colossal discovery.

"You got the full translation, right?" he pressed.

"Oh, that . . . right, I did. Grocery lists, ancient grocery lists," Quarston answered.

The lab tech peered dubiously over his glasses at Quarston, who then added, "For now, just grocery lists. I'll fill you in once we know more. And remember, Harry, this is completely between you and me, or no Christmas gift this year."

"Right, Sir, I understand."

* * * *

Back in his own cramped office, Quarston sat deep in thought. He was convinced now that something strange beyond his comprehension was going on, but the facts were irrefutable. He had checked and cross checked both the data and his reasoning. The paper and inks were roughly 2,500 years old. The languages in which they were written were in use at that time. While the parchment could have been employed in a forgery, the ink could not. That ruled out modern forgers. An ancient forger was certainly possible, but how could he account for the handwriting analysis? Adding the data together, he had a guy living over a span of at least 300 years who wrote about Biblical events. Such a discovery could easily account for a murder. That much was sure. But how could anyone live that long? And was Daniel a real person? Weren't those stories about the lion's den and the fiery furnace just children's fables? None of it made any sense to him, so he decided that his best move was to return to Boston College and have another conversation with his old prof. Maybe he could shed some light on the implications of this discovery.

He noticed the message light flashing on his phone but ignored it, deciding that he couldn't risk any delays pursuing this case.

* * * *

Boston College

"They are *how* old?" asked Professor Beaufort.

"They were written between 800 and 500 B.C.," answered Quarston.

"Right around the time of the events recorded in the texts," the professor said to himself. "I never would have believed it . . . you obviously did something wrong here."

"Why?" asked Quarston.

"Because everyone knows that there is no archeological evidence supporting the existence of Belteshazzar."

"But wouldn't this text confirm it?"

"If it were genuine, which it can't be."

"But why?" insisted Quarston. "Look, I'm a practical guy, I don't go for all this ancient Biblical stuff; I deal with real people and real crimes. But the data is the data."

"If the texts were real," answered the professor, "then by now someone would have discovered them."

"But what of the Qumran texts?" queried Quarston. "Those texts sat undisturbed for 2,000 years."

"No, no, no, Qumran is completely different."

"How?"

"The Dead Sea Scrolls have a definitive history and context. Your texts appear out of the blue, right? You have no idea as to their origin?"

"None," admitted Quarston, and then added, "Yet."

"Well, then they are forgeries," insisted the professor.

"But how can they be forgeries if the science proves that they are authentic?" demanded Quarston.

"I don't know, Roger, but they've just got to be. It's the mark of the best forgery, isn't it?"

"There's something more, Professor."

The professor shook his head wearily. "More?" he asked weakly.

"Yes, more. The documents are separated by 300 years, and yet are written in the same hand."

The professor just stared at his old student for a few minutes open-mouthed. Then he rose from his chair and paced about a bit, muttering, "The same hand? It can't be; it just can't. There is no way. It's impossible."

"What is it, Sir? What's impossible?" queried Quarston.

The professor motioned him to silence, while he went on pacing. Finally, he returned to his seat, opened his desk drawer and withdrew a bottle of Irish whiskey. He was so absorbed in his thought that he poured only a single shot for himself and drained it before pouring another.

The professor then whipped open his Rolodex, examined several cards, and grabbed his phone. But Quarston pressed down on the switch hook and prevented his acquiring a dial tone, much to the professor's surprise.

"You want to get to the bottom of this, right?" Beaufort asked him.

"Secrecy, Professor, we must have absolute secrecy."

"But Roger, unless we consult with my old buddy in Biblical Studies, we'll never resolve this question. I've got a hunch, you see. Bob Jacobson and I go way back, and back at Cambridge he got a little bit drunk now and then . . ."

"Just him?" interjected Quarston, staring at the half-empty whiskey bottle that he had never seen as a student.

"Okay, maybe not just him, but that's not the point. The point is that he talked a good deal after he'd had a few pints, and one night he advanced a really odd theory."

"Which was?" asked Quarston.

"Which was that Melchizedek might still be alive," answered the professor. "Mind you, I think he is nuts, but then . . ."

"What? Who is Melchizedek?" Quarston asked.

"That's my point. You really need to talk to Bob, so let go of my phone."

"Very well, but you must swear him to secrecy as well."

"Done," replied the professor.

46

CHAPTER NINE

As Quarston and Beaufort walked toward their meeting with Bob Jacobson at the faculty lounge, Beaufort filled Quarston in on some of his colleague's theoretical eccentricities. By the time they met Jacobson, Quarston was puzzled about the value of their meeting. But when the sixty-three year old Jacobson lifted his hefty body from a leather armchair and turned to meet Quarston, his balding round face, hearty deep laugh and twinkling eyes brought Quarston up short. Jacobson was a jovial man with a relaxed carriage in spite of his girth and mild jowls. And the immense smile and deep personal warmth of the man gave Quarston a feeling of such ease, that in moments they had found a private corner in the dark cherry-paneled room and were discussing what to drink. They ordered vintage port, a 77 Fonseca Quarston noted with surprise and delight. Faculty salaries must have really gone up, he thought, as Beaufort said, "We can just charge this to your FBI tab, right?" It was really more of a statement than a question, Quarston realized with a gulp, but nodded submissively. His port just wasn't going to taste quite as good as he'd hoped, he decided.

After cheese, nuts, and three fine cigars were brought to them, Beaufort started the serious part of the conversation.

"So, Bob, like I was telling you, Roger here is an old student of mine who has since joined the FBI. And he's on a very strange case involving ancient manuscripts."

Jacobson's eyes widened in increasing surprise, as Quarston related to him the story of the murder, the recovered fragments, their ancient dates, the content of their scripts, and the stunning fact that they were written by the same person. Beaufort interrupted here and there to offer his skeptical rejoinders to the whole story.

After Quarston finished, Jacobson managed to mutter, "Okay, so the world just turned upside down, but what does this have to do with me? Why are you here? Presumably not because you wish to publish this, though God knows you ought to."

"No," interrupted Beaufort hesitatingly. "It's because of Melchizedek."

Jacobson just stared at him.

"Melchizedek," he murmured, taking a handful of cashews and settling back into the comfort of his luxurious leather chair.

He had not thought much about that name since his graduate school days when he had spent a full year and a half researching the man for his master's thesis. He had examined every ancient reference to him in both the Biblical and extra-Biblical literature, and he had arrived at a bizarre theory that he had not presented in the published monograph. So he thought for a few minutes as his last swallow of port lingered on his pallet.

"We're going to need Scotch for this," he asserted confidently, and Quarston's face fell. How would he ever get his supervisor to sign off on this? It had always amazed him how they could pay drug-addicted informants hundreds of dollars for tips, but couldn't buy a couple of professors excellent wine without all kinds of red tape.

The Scotch they ordered was old, naturally, and had been sitting in port pipes for several of its 21 years of age. The port offered a mellowing to the natural bite of the whiskey, making it exquisitely smooth with hints of plum and honeysuckle. It was the best Scotch he'd ever tasted, and he owed the Balvenie people a letter of gratitude, unless of course he ended up having to pay for it personally. He suddenly wondered how professors afforded a taste for such drinks, and decided wryly that on another occasion he'd have to launch an investigation of the matter.

Once they were all settled well into their Scotch, Jacobson shifted in his chair and began.

"Melchizedek was a king, the king of Salim or Salem, what eventually might have become Jeru-salem. Remember that there were Canaanite civilizations in the Holy Land well before Abraham arrived from Mesopotamia. According to Genesis, Melchizedek was a priest of God, *El Elyon*, 'God Most High,' to be precise, but he was a priest before the time of Moses and the giving of the law."

"Wait a minute," interjected Quarston, "You are saying that he was a Canaanite priest who nevertheless believed in the Jewish God?"

THE SEARCH FOR MELCHIZEDEK

"That's what Genesis indicates," answered Jacobson. "Though you might have the order backwards there."

Jacobson and Beaufort both laughed at Quarston's puzzlement, before Jacobson continued, "It is more likely that the 'Jewish' God was already the Canaanite deity who called to Abram of Ur to come to the land of Palestine. Remember that Ur was thoroughly Sumerian with its deities, and we find no mention of *Adonai* there (recall that we use '*Adonai*' to avoid voicing the true name of God, *YHWH*). By contrast, we find definite mention of *YAH* in Palestinian pottery from the time of Abraham and Melchizedek. And remember that if Melchizedek was a priest of this God, then it might be better to portray Abraham as coming into the sphere of this God, than to suggest that Abraham brought this God to Palestine."

"So, there was worship of the Jewish God prior to Abraham," pressed Quarston.

"No, there weren't any Jews yet," answered Beaufort. "So there wasn't any 'Jewish' God."

"Right," emphasized Jacobson. "And remember that even Abraham's family remained loyal to Sumerian deities, as we see from that Genesis text where they have their household idols with them! Moreover, there are other examples in the Hebrew Bible of non-Jews worshipping the same God as the Jews, as well as a few famous examples of monotheism from the pagan world."

"Right, like that nutty Pharaoh worshiping the sun disk," replied Quarston thoughtfully.

"Precisely," continued Jacobson, "but in replacing the worship of Amun and the other Egyptian deities with the sole worship of the Aten, the Sun disk, Akhenaten was not explicitly worshiping the same god that the Jews would come to worship. But Melchizedek seems to have—at least given Abraham's recognition."

"And the others?" queried Quarston.

"The others include Balaam, an apparently pagan prophet in the book of Numbers who is hired by a local king to curse the Israelites. So far, he seems completely pagan. But when he goes to curse the Israelites, blessings come out of his mouth instead. The king who hired him is incensed and tells him to go back and do it again. Balaam tries, but again blessings and prophecies come forth! You see Balaam apparently *was* a real prophet, or at least was a fake who was overcome in these instances by the Jewish God. The king threatens Balaam, so he heads out to try a third time to curse these Israelites, and on his way his donkey runs into a field and refuses to follow the road."

JEFFREY TIEL

"Oh, that's the story of the talking donkey!" exclaimed Quarston, while Beaufort rolled his eyes.

"Right," answered Jacobson excitedly. "The donkey asks him why he is hitting him, and Balaam answers about how proper donkeys ought to stay on the road. He's apparently so angry at the beast that he forgets to be shocked that his animal is talking to him! And at that point God opens Balaam's eyes to see an angel standing in the road with a fiery sword ready to kill Balaam had he gone any further toward cursing the Israelites."

"Wow," replied Quarston, noting Beaufort shaking his head.

"Yeah," said Jacobson, "it's pretty scary when you think about it. But the point is that Balaam's cursing Israel might have had real effects, so this angel was sent to prevent it. And that suggests that Balaam all along was a non-Jew with genuine spiritual capabilities, possibly on some level worshiping *El*—the generic name for God—or even *Adonai*, although that's not clear from the Numbers text."

"And the others?" asked Quarston.

"Another example is the Syrian captain, Namaan," answered Jacobson. "Namaan gets sick and his captured Israeli slave-girl informs him that a prophet, Elisha, exists in Israel who can make him well. So, he heads down to Elisha, and after some interesting events, does become well. In thanking Elisha, he makes a very odd request of him. He asks if it would be pious for him to take a bit of Israelite soil in a small box with him when he went home, so that he could take it into the temple of the Syrian pagan deities and when pretending to pray to them, he'd really be praying to *El*, or God!"

"You're kidding!" exclaimed a shocked Quarston. "Elisha didn't go for that, did he? I mean, what kind of faith is that?"

"On the contrary," answered Jacobson, "he did accept this faith, however small. You have to remember: how could a non-Jewish believer in the Jewish God survive? Namaan was not going to convert to Judaism! And the Jewish texts themselves make very clear that eventually all the blessings of God were to be poured out onto the entire world through the Jewish people. So, the idea that some of those people should have come to know the God of the Jews earlier should not come as a great surprise."

"Well, that's not the kind of faith I heard about as a boy. Nothing like the faith of the martyrs!" replied a sullen Quarston.

Jacobson answered him, "Look, Roger, you've got to remember that the number of martyrs compared to the number of ordinary Jewish and then Christian men and women is extremely small. Not everyone can be a

50

Moses or St. Peter, or even should be. Most people should live out their lives in relative peace and charity."

"I guess I can see that," said Quarston. "Are there any others who worship *El Elyon*, but nevertheless are not Jews?"

"Well, the other interesting case comes from the book of Daniel in which King Nebuchadnezzar himself appears to be writing an entire chapter about the incident in which his pride was crushed by the Most High God. In the end he asserts the supremacy and glory of the God of Daniel, but he certainly never becomes a Jew."

"Nor is there any cuneiform evidence of such a statement by Nebuchadnezzar, is there?" interrupted Beaufort, "Do tell the boy the whole story."

"No, there isn't," admitted Jacobson, "but until now we never had any non-biblical evidence of Daniel either, did we?"

"Okay," answered Quarston, "so you two have competing theories about the veracity of these stories. But the larger point is that the Biblical texts have multiple instances of people outside the main Jewish tradition who nevertheless come to believe in *El Elyon*, God Most High, who the Jews discover through Moses to be *YHWH*, right?"

"Remember to substitute *Adonai* for *YHWH* whenever you speak the self-given name of God, Roger, for his very name is holy. But on the whole, yes, I think you've got it," replied Jacobson.

"I'll remember to do that," Quarston paused awkwardly before continuing. "And Melchizedek, the guy we are apparently interested in, believed in *El Elyon*, God Most High, long before Moses?"

"Indeed he did," asserted Jacobson. "This Melchizedek is both a king and a priest . . ."

"Wealthy and educated," interjected Quarston to Beaufort, who nodded before refilling their scotch glasses.

" . . . a king and a priest," Jacobson repeated. "Note that, since it becomes very important later on. Anyway, Abraham has just defeated a group of raiders . . ."

"Raiders!" exclaimed Quarston. "But one of our fragments talks about raiders!"

"Yes," replied Jacobson gently, "but those raiders were from a time much later in the Assyrian Empire. Raiders, land pirates in effect, were a problem throughout much of the ancient and even medieval world with the Viking assaults on coastal cities. I mean, why work, when you can just steal from the working man?"

"Sounds like politics," chimed in Beaufort with a grin.

51

"Indeed," laughed Jacobson, "indeed it does. Well . . . where was I?"

"Raiders?" offered Quarston.

"Oh yes, Abraham had defeated a large group of raiders, and recovered the loot that they had stolen. Melchizedek approaches Abraham and blesses him, and in return Abraham gives Melchizedek a tenth of the spoils from the battle."

"That's where the concept of the tithe comes from, not from work, but from battle spoils?" queried Quarston incredulously.

"Well, yes. Interesting, isn't it?" answered Jacobson. "Then there is a reference in the Psalms to Melchizedek, what is clearly a Messianic Psalm, Psalm 110. And in that Psalm Messiah is compared to Melchizedek as being a priest in his 'order,' a priest who lives forever."

"Forever?" repeated Quarston, feeling as though something was falling into place.

"Forever," replied Jacobson.

"Hence the divine nature of the Messiah that links up with what the Christians maintain about Jesus," Beaufort interjected.

"Exactly," answered Jacobson. "And that brings us directly to the Christian Biblical text of Hebrews, the one book in the entire New Testament that no one has a clue who wrote!"

"No one but you, you mean," poked a grinning Beaufort.

"Well, I suppose," answered Jacobson.

"You're losing me," replied Quarston.

"Here, look for yourself in the seventh chapter of Hebrews," said Jacobson.

Quarston took the Bible and opened to the seventh chapter of Hebrews and read from the end of chapter six into chapter eight. A detective always examines context when he looks at evidence. The two professors found this pause an excellent excuse to order some more scotch, some cashews, and a cheese and fruit tray filled with fresh strawberries, luscious grapes, pineapple, and asiago and pecorino cheeses. When Quarston finally looked up, his face was mixed with confusion and confidence. Something had become clear, but that clarity drew him into a darkness for which he was wholly unprepared.

"You see?" asked Jacobson.

"Yes, I see," answered Quarston who then helped himself to several strawberries.

CHAPTER TEN

Cairo

Franklen Bartleby tossed the photos from the Giza tomb onto his desk. He stomped his boots and a cloud of fine dust puffed into the air. Looking around the office for his professional attire, he located his badge. "Director of Egypt Exploration Society" he read aloud. From the time he was a young boy, Bartleby had been fascinated by the tales of ancient Egypt. Pharaohs and mummies, then hieroglyphs and temples, and now ancient tombs had occupied his attention so much that he hadn't had time for even a romantic romp let alone a serious relationship. Occasionally that bothered him, but the bureaucratic requirements of running the Society occupied any spare time that he had. He chuckled to himself, as he pulled his tired boots from his aching feet. Of course he'd describe his leadership of the Society as his "spare" job. The digs were the real work. Others didn't see it that way, of course, and now he had to make a series of calls to placate the various benefactors that made most of the archeology of Egypt possible.

Bartleby dialed the number for Laurence Rothschild who provided nearly two-thirds of the operating budget for the Society itself, as well as underwrote almost every dig in any way related to ancient libraries. Bartleby thought that Rothschild's motivations were eccentric, for he suspected that his benefactor hoped to find the "lost" Library of Alexandria. Of course, all serious scholars knew that the Library had been damaged repeatedly in the ancient world and finally destroyed completely. But donors supported archeology for all kinds of reasons and occasionally eccentricities paid off enormously. Bartleby was happy to report to

Rothschild that the tomb he was excavating connected Thoth, the Egyptian god of scribes, wisdom, and magic, with a repository of scrolls.

"But Sir, you need to understand that the reliefs of Thoth in this tomb date from at least 1700 B.C."

"I understand," answered Rothschild, "so they have nothing to do with the Alexandrian library per se, but they still link Thoth to an ancient repository of texts. Those texts might have eventually comprised part of the Alexandrian library."

"Yes . . . that's possible," Bartleby assured him, wondering at the penchant for amateurs to turn mere speculative possibilities into investment probabilities.

"Then do send me the complete report," added Rothschild, "with photos. You do have digital photos of the reliefs?"

"Yes, of course, Sir," added Bartleby, recalling the stifling heat of the tomb. "I'll send them within the hour."

"What about the location of the Thoth library? Any hints or indications as to its original location?" queried Rothschild.

"It's too early to tell," reported Bartleby. "At this point we've conducted only a preliminary analysis of the reliefs. You are welcome to take a stab at it yourself, of course."

Bartleby was patronizing Rothschild, but his benefactor took it all in stride, "Perhaps I will, Franklen. Thank you very much for the report. And rest assured that you will enjoy my continued interest."

Bartleby returned the phone to its cradle, pleased by Rothschild's use of the term "interest" which, if translated into Egyptian hieroglyphs, meant one thing: money.

*   *   *   *

Boston College

"So, Melchizedek is alive, is that it?" asked Quarston, having reviewed the Biblical passage that Jacobson had given him.

"That's my theory," said Jacobson. "How else can the Christ follow his order of living forever if Melchizedek died?"

"But some Christian scholars interpret the appearance of Melchizedek in the past as an appearance of the pre-incarnate Son of God," interjected Beaufort. "We need to acknowledge that."

"Yes," answered Jacobson, "except that that makes no sense whatsoever, because how could the Son of God be a priest after himself? Melchizedek in Genesis is portrayed as an historical figure who rules an entire city and chats with Abraham. Jesus is said to be a priest after his order, not after himself."

"But no one else thinks your theory is correct?" asked Quarston.

Both professors laughed. "He'd have to be insane to actually try to publish this!" proclaimed Beaufort.

"Which is why I've kept it to just a few friends," admitted Jacobson. "But with what you are saying, about a three hundred year old guy recording historical events . . . it looks like you have credible evidence that I'm right."

"How's that? I mean, how can you identify your Melchizedek character with our manuscript author?" queried Quarston.

Jacobson thought for a few moments, and then answered, "I have a theory on that which I'll explain. But with your photographs of these fragments of Melchizedek's Record, I have little doubt now that my theory is correct."

"Melchizedek's Record?" queried Quarston with anticipation.

"I think that Melchizedek's job is to record all of human history and to stand as a living human witness to the failure of any human regime ever to rule justly."

"Why?" asked Quarston.

"Well, let's begin with the book of Daniel, shall we? There are multiple prophecies there about divine interaction with human kingdoms, and extensive hints about the role of the angelic powers in their affairs. But you get the impression that God is going to allow kingdom after kingdom to rise and fall until finally Messiah arrives like a great heavenly rock that shatters them all with one blow."

"So, we're not doing so well, eh?" asked Quarston.

"No, we're not," replied Jacobson soberly.

"But the world has become so much more democratic," retorted Beaufort disconcertedly.

"Perhaps," nodded Jacobson, "but recall your Plato. Democracy isn't good in itself. In fact, it can bring about tremendous harm. Even the mixed regimes that we now advocate, republics, aren't good unless the people in them are good. And that has always been the divine objective."

"Which is part of the reason Jesus, like Socrates, wasn't a politician," answered Quarston, happy the conversation turned toward Plato.

"Probably *part* of the reason," laughed Beaufort.

"The Biblical texts also speak of a judgment of nations as such, not just persons, so there must be a record of their deeds," Jacobson continued.

"But why does it have to be a human record?" asked Quarston.

"It doesn't," acknowledged Jacobson. "But if there's one thing you get from a life-long study of the Scriptures, it's that God has a flair for the ironic! And wouldn't it be just dazzling for him to produce one of our own to present the record of our own failure as a species?"

"But that's hardly proof!" retorted Quarston.

"No, I confess that you are correct, so let's move on, shall we? Further evidence is found in our literary traditions. Over and again we find references to a stranger, a witness, a wanderer who walks the earth generation after generation and watches and observes. It's as though the poets are prophets on some level."

Quarston's right eyebrow rose at this suggestion. "You're kidding, right?"

Jacobson replied, somewhat ruffled, "Look, Quarston, truth can arrive through the poets too, Plato be damned!"

"Okay, fine. Sorry, Sir. You may be right. But we need something solid here," answered Quarston.

"All right . . . how about this? And remember that my point is to draw all of these pieces together into a large puzzle . . . the Nag Hammadi library!"

"The Gnostic texts?" queried Quarston.

"Yes, in one of these texts Melchizedek is mentioned, even further, apparently is quoted for a short section. Part of his description includes the following line: 'that I might tell all of the aeons, and, in each one of the aeons, that I might tell the nature of the aeon.' That sounds like a record of historical periods, doesn't it?"

"Yes, it does," answered Quarston. "But did Melchizedek write that?"

"It's not clear in the text whether Melchizedek or Jesus is supposedly saying that. But there is a section directly attributed to Melchizedek in which he again refers to the 'aeons' being revealed to him, possibly by an angel."

"But if he were there, why would he need an angel?" asked Quarston.

Beaufort finally erupted in laughter. "Exactly! Just what I've been telling him for years, Roger!" he exclaimed in delight.

Jacobson's tight lipped face turned into a grin, as he acknowledged the long, unresolved dispute. "Yes, I know, it's slim on evidence, but can you offer a better motive for God putting him into the world, Beaufort?"

Beaufort laughed again and admitted, "No, I can't, but this is *your* theory, not mine."

"That's a cop-out, and you know it," quipped Jacobson and then continued. "Here's my hunch: every people group in the world is given its chance for political dominion. Notice that no people have ever re-ascended to mastery. New nations rise and then fall. They are given their chance, and when they fail, Melchizedek records it for the final judgment of all things."

"That's a fascinating theory, but we don't even know whether those Gnostic texts referring to his recording the aeons are actually quoting Melchizedek accurately, do we?" asked Quarston.

"No, no, we sure don't," answered Jacobson. "But like I said, it's just a theory."

"But a theory with consequences, for if you are right, then somewhere on this earth there is a large depository of ancient books recording all of human history, and periodically there is some old guy who drops off new ones or recopies the old ones, correct?" asked Quarston.

Jacobson and Beaufort both stared at him in astonishment. They worked in the past, not the present, and these implications had never really occurred to either of them.

"Well, I suppose that's possible," answered Beaufort precisely. "But why do you think he's 'old'?"

Quarston looked at him in surprise, "Because he's thousands of years old. Hence, 'old.'"

Beaufort nodded, "Okay, fine, old in actual age, but if he really has been deteriorating for thousands of years, he'd be a rather withered old fellow, now wouldn't he?"

Jacobson added, "Right, the paradox of the goddess Eos. Remember it? She asked Zeus for immortality for her mortal lover, Tithonus, but neglected to ask for eternal youth as well. Big mistake."

"Right," answered Quarston slowly. "So, he could be young-looking."

"Exactly," answered Beaufort. "And as for an ancient library, that's possible, but consider an alternative: what if he has updated all of the books on some kind of digital medium?"

"How on earth would he know how to use a computer?" Quarston started and then stopped short, as both professors laughed again.

"It's not like he traveled here in a time machine, son!" Jacobson exclaimed. "I mean, the guy's knowledge must be incredible. Surely he would know how to drive a car, run a computer, etc., just like anyone else, depending on where in the world he lives. And remember that we don't know whether he's still in the East or not."

"It's like looking for a needle in a haystack," replied Quarston.

"But are we looking for him?" asked Beaufort.

"Someone is," answered Quarston. "It's now a question of who finds him first."

CHAPTER ELEVEN

Florence, Italy

Laurence Rothschild sat at his desk in the opulent 14th century frescoed study on the top floor of the old Medici country villa that overlooked the famous renaissance city. Though he was over sixty years of age, he appeared at least ten years younger, displaying constant vigilance toward his health. Rothschild carefully examined the photos of the tomb wall reliefs that Bartleby sent him via the internet. There was the god, Thoth, represented as a man with the head of an Ibis. Lunar symbols surrounded him, and scribes sat at his feet. Thoth was indeed blessing or directing what appeared to be the building of a temple that contained scrolls. Rothschild wondered if the builder might be the owner of the tomb that Bartleby was excavating. Perhaps there would be clues as to the temple's location. Two large obelisks stood before the temple in the tomb wall etching that Rothschild perused. Instead of the usual pyramids capping them, he noted the full and half crescent moons, indicating that this temple was devoted to Thoth.

Rothschild smiled as he noticed the walls of the unfinished temple complex covered with two large baboons. If not represented as a man/Ibis composite, Thoth was usually represented as a baboon. And sure enough, the full and half crescent moons crowned the baboon god on the temple walls. The temple was definitely devoted to Thoth, and it was distinct from the main temple complex uncovered in Khmun, the City of Thoth. For all that remained of that complex were two enormous free standing baboons erected by Amenhotep III, Rothschild remembered. This temple on the other hand had its two baboons forming part of the temple pylon's supporting wall. So, it may yet survive. But where? Rothschild wondered if it could be found in Giza near Bartleby's current excavation, an as yet undiscovered part of Khmun, or some other location entirely.

Rothschild could also see that priests were carrying chests filled with sacred scrolls into the temple's hypostyle hall. He looked carefully to see how they treated the texts. The priests were grouped in alternating sets of four and eight, the magical numbers of divine completeness for the Egyptians. Priests burned incense at each stage of the scrolls' journey. That meant that the scrolls they carried were sacred, holy to the god Thoth.

He wondered aloud, "Could it be?"

He had spent years pursuing the elusive Book of Thoth, the ancient book of magic and wisdom that allegedly contained the secrets of the power of immortality. Perhaps it was finally within his reach.

Rothschild hastily sent Bartleby's complete report to his man at Columbia University. While Rothschild's own knowledge of ancient languages including Egyptian hieroglyphs exceeded that of many professionals in the field, he needed a true specialist to ensure that his own preliminary findings were correct. Moreover, the symbology of the reliefs might yield the clues that he desperately sought.

* * * *

Boston College

Beaufort summarized Jacobson's argument and began to link it to Quarston's manuscripts, as they all refilled their glasses of Scotch. Quarston strained to focus his mind through the warm feeling that descended on his senses from the alcohol he had already consumed over the last couple hours.

"So, let me summarize, all right? Bob has a theory about a guy who doesn't die writing history over the aeons, while Roger here has apparently authentic manuscript evidence to support an ancient author recording history for approximately three hundred years. And besides our being asked to believe that all this is true, we're also being asked to believe that Bob's Melchizedek is Roger's author. And if that identification is to be believed, then we've got a guy who is some six thousand years old still walking around. Does that capture where you all are?"

"Well, do you have a better theory? Something that fits all the data? How do you explain the handwriting analysis, or the carbon-14 dating, or any of it, Professor Beaufort?" queried Quarston.

"I can't, and that's what troubles me," offered a frustrated Beaufort, sniffing his glass for some relief.

"That's why I like him—his honesty," smiled Jacobson warmly.

"I don't believe in people living six thousand years either," insisted Quarston. "But I've already got evidence of someone living for three hundred, and before this week, I'd never have believed that!"

"Well, I've long suspected it," offered Jacobson. "But I've always kept it to myself, since if this guy really is out there somewhere, the last thing I would wish to do is to draw attention to him. Can you imagine all the reasons people would have for trying to capture him?"

Quarston's detective skills now flew into full gear. "Right! Motives!" he exclaimed.

"He'd be of incredible value to the Jews, that's for sure," offered Beaufort.

"Perhaps, but then again, perhaps not," answered Jacobson.

"Look here," rebutted Beaufort. "He could confirm the Jewish claim on Palestine. He could confirm that God really spoke to Abraham and gave it forever to the Jews."

"Wait a minute," interjected Quarston. "Nobody grants land claims on the basis of divine right! That would lead to perpetual wars."

"Well, that's partly true," admitted Jacobson. "But even the philosophical foundations for our own republic make allowance for this."

"They do?" Beaufort and Quarston said in unison.

"Yes, they do. In his *Treatise* Locke argues that given the equality of all men under the natural law, no man has natural ascendancy over any other, and therefore all just government depends upon the consent of the governed, right?" he asked.

"Right," Beaufort offered, "and that is why there is no room remaining for divine claims to ascendancy. The whole point of that book is to deny the divine right of kings."

"No, that's not the whole point of the book," rebutted Jacobson, "though we will shortly need the skills of a real Locke expert. Locke states explicitly that those rules of self-government can be abrogated only by the person who created human beings in the first place. So, if God should by clear signs—and that's important—raise one person in ascendancy over his fellows and make him king, God can do that."

"Okay, I guess that does make sense," admitted Quarston. "But kingship and land are quite different."

"No, they are not, not in the ancient world at least. The 'king-dom' is the dominion or realm of the king, so they are much more closely linked. Moreover, if God can authorize a king, why can't he also authorize property rights?" added Beaufort, supporting Jacobson's point.

"But that would lead to perpetual strife, since every nation will claim divine right over something!" interjected Quarston.

"Just so," agreed Beaufort. "In fact, my sister just returned from Kenya where she has been working for thirty years as a nurse in a clinic, and she told me about the Maasai tribe. They value cows as their chief sign of wealth. Well, they believe that the gods gave all cows in the world to the Maasai, so that any cows not possessed by them (like the cows in Texas) were stolen from the Maasai. And would you believe that a neighboring tribe has the same belief, that the gods gave *them* all the cows in the world? So, in real politics, these sorts of views lead to perpetual blood-letting."

"You are correct in any case with competing claims to divine revelation, but the Jews and the Muslims have the same father, Abraham!" countered Jacobson. "And Melchizedek knew and blessed Abraham, so he could literally decide the matter. And don't forget too, that Melchizedek was a Canaanite king and might well support the Palestinian's identification with those ancient peoples' claims to the land."

"But what difference would it make?" asked Beaufort. "Whatever Melchizedek said, the other side would murder him and suppress the story."

"That sounds about right," admitted Jacobson. "But it wouldn't stop either side from trying to get him, would it?"

"Okay, so that's a motive," acknowledged Quarston, "a clear political motive for acquiring Melchizedek. But it also assumes that either the Israelis or the Palestinians are aware of his existence, and we have no evidence as yet to suggest that."

"Correct," answered Beaufort. "But this inquiry is to identify who would have a motive to capture him if they *were* aware of his existence."

"And there's a correlative interest on the part of the Christians who believe Melchizedek is a type of Christ. That's the argument of the Hebrews passage," added Jacobson.

"A 'type'?" asked Quarston.

"Think of a 'type' as a figure or image of something else. Like the shepherd is an image of Christ caring for his church, his lambs. Melchizedek is the type, the priest-king, who is the image of Messiah."

"But the Jews agree with that, given the Psalms passage," responded Quarston.

"Yes, they do, but not with the identification of Jesus as the Christ. And that's the main argument of Hebrews, the identity of the Christ. Imagine if the church unveiled Melchizedek himself!"

Quarston interjected, "But might not Melchizedek side with the Jews against Christianity? I mean, after all, he blessed Abraham, right?"

"Well, consider this," retorted Jacobson. "There's one Gnostic text in which Melchizedek is quoted as saying that he was baptized. So, he lived into the Christian era for certain, and then became a Christian."

Beaufort and Quarston both shifted in their seats, before Beaufort exclaimed, "Well, I don't know about that! That's a real stretch, Bob."

Jacobson was about to reply, when Quarston broke in, "Right, we certainly don't know about the authenticity of those Gnostic texts, do we? But regardless of their veracity, we've still got a Christian motive, don't we? It looks like we've now got a triangle of possible religious/political interest in Melchizedek: Christians, Jews, and Palestinians would all have motives for finding him."

"Okay, so we've considered religious and political motives, but for what other reasons might someone be after Melchizedek?" Beaufort asked.

"Well, I'd definitely think of a fountain of youth possibility," said Jacobson.

"So would I. The biotech companies would give their right arms to dissect him. Imagine it: eternal youth!" offered Beaufort.

"But if he was divinely granted life, why would examining his DNA help anyone?" asked Quarston.

"God might well have given him life naturally," answered Beaufort. "We die because of a failure of cellular regeneration. Perhaps God offered him DNA that regenerates cells indefinitely. That would be priceless in its value medicinally."

"So, we'll have to look at firms engaged in biotechnological research focused specially on the ageing process," commented Quarston.

"Right," said Beaufort, and then added, "But don't forget governments, even our own, that may have classified agendas in this regard."

"Or the crackpots out there, if they found out about this," added Jacobson. "That's another reason I've kept most of this stuff to myself rather than publishing it. Any discussion of Melchizedek lands one immediately in the realm of UFO's, pyramid forces, and the like. Just do a Google search some time on 'Melchizedek' and see what turns up!"

"I've got more suspects than ever I could have imagined," answered Quarston glumly.

CHAPTER TWELVE

Katelyn stood right on the edge overlooking the sparkling lights of the city beneath her. She was high enough that the sounds of the cars below her could not interfere with her sublimity. She gazed at the stars on this crystal-clear night and knew peace for the first time in her short but agonized life. She donned her earphones and flipped to the next to last piece on Evanescence's album *Fallen* that had alone touched her soul. Oh, she'd thought she'd been 'touched' before, touched by God she thought. She had raised her hand to receive Jesus at age five, again at age eight by a camp fire (camp fires have a way of bringing this out in people), and again at age fourteen at a church conference on virginity. But it never amounted to much in her inner life, a life haunted by loneliness and sadness, so different from those around her. They were all happy, or so their stamped smiles told her. She tried to expose her pain, but she could never talk to anyone that understood, and so she found that she could cut the pain into her body, a cutting that relieved the sorrow on the inside by matching it on the outside.

As she edged closer to the last step of her life, she lit a cigarette and remembered the boy who 'loved' her. She had never been in love until she met Travis. Travis was a fraternity brother, an amazing catch, she'd been told. He showed her a cool kindness and flattered her until the night he raped her and then gave her to his friends. He did drive her home the next morning, but that somehow convinced the police that she'd fabricated the whole story. When her church counselor explained that God was trying to teach her to forgive, she knew that she was utterly worthless. She'd cut that night till she bled, something she'd never done before. But the pain in her soul could no longer be matched by any pain in her body. She knew that only death could save her now. As the haunting notes of Amy Lee's voice faded into the night, Katelyn flicked an ember off the glowing end of her cigarette and watched it float toward the ground far beneath her. When she could no longer see it, she took one last pull on the cigarette and then carefully rested it still burning on the ledge beside her. Looking one last time at the scars on her arms, she stepped off the edge of the building.

* * * *

Mrs. Crawford was just returning from a retirement party after finishing her last day as an elementary school teacher, when the windows of the parked car she was approaching exploded. She did not notice the feminine form falling onto its roof. She instinctively turned away from the impact site straight into the path of a truck whose right wheels rolled up onto her vehicle, crushing her instantly. The truck driver could not control his rig either, as the entire vehicle flipped over onto its left side and threatened to flatten a small Civic.

David Goldblum was thinking about the requests he'd received from Mossad headquarters that afternoon. An operation or person named 'Melchizedek'? And what did that have to do with Hentersheim? He resolved to search the database the following day to resolve these problems, as the truck on his right started rolling on to the top of his Civic. He was so surprised by this event, that he did nothing but watch through his sunroof as he and his car were crushed. In that moment he died, leaving a major gap in Israeli intelligence. For Goldblum had served two masters, and the Mossad just lost their highest placed asset within the FBI.

* * * *

John Horn was the chief resident on duty in the emergency room on what the press dubbed "The Night of the Jumper." Multiple cars crashed into the ones containing the initial fatalities. And those fourteen occupants suffered burns, serious lacerations, impact injuries, and broken bones. Three pedestrians were injured by the glass flying from the car, one critically. Another woman was hurt when the hubcap of the car the suicide landed on flew directly into her face.

All that would have been manageable were it not for the fact that the truck knocked over a telephone pole into an internet café. A huge power spike surged through the computers in the café blowing up the monitors right into the users' faces. As the victims started arriving at the hospital,

Horn's well-oiled team had already prepared a triage area. He moved his twenty-nine year old, medium built frame forward with steady deliberation, though it protested with the fatigue from too many sleepless nights. He shook his head in frustration as he noticed his appearance reflecting off a brightly polished stainless steel instrument tray: haggard looking and ghoulish, he thought to himself, before laughing aloud at the bright blue fully engaged eyes. He found the irony between their unremitting fiery intelligence and the bags and wrinkles that surrounded them a bit too amusing, knowing that the vacation he planned with his sister was long overdue. Reaching the triage area, he took a deep breath, knowing that this would prove another long night, and then dove into his work.

* * * *

Boston College

Quarston felt that he had pretty much exhausted the subject of Melchizedek by the time that he and the professors had finished their third glasses of scotch. As he rose to leave, the scotch and a question from Beaufort landed him heavily back in his chair.

"What will you do with him if you find him?" queried Beaufort.

"What do you mean?" asked Quarston. "I'll bring him in for his own protection."

"Who is going to protect him who would not have an interest in exploiting him?" asked Jacobson.

Beaufort furthered this line of questioning, "Look, Roger, who in the FBI knows about this?"

"Well, no one, actually, as I've not reported my results as yet . . . okay, there is one technician who knows about the photographs and the handwriting analysis, but he's sworn to secrecy," added Quarston.

"You cannot tell your superiors about Melchizedek," warned Jacobson.

"He's right," added Beaufort. "I mean, I still can't quite believe any of this, but if Bob is correct . . ."

"Then what am I supposed to do about these murders?" asked Quarston.

"Find the murderers and arrest them, but leave Melchizedek out of it," replied Jacobson.

"That might prove easier said than done," answered Quarston.

"Well, Melchizedek has survived this long, so presumably he must be well-equipped at hiding his identity," offered Beaufort.

"But no one knew to look for him then. Now they do," Quarston concluded.

CHAPTER THIRTEEN

Florence

Laurence Rothschild stared up at his chief of operations and head of security. He thought his subordinate almost looked like an angel with his head framed by the ceiling frescoes of clouds, trumpets, and scrolls, except for his intelligent and watchful eyes, small mouth and tight lips. This was a man who inspired fear, thought Rothschild. Fortunately, he was very well paid. Rothschild rose from his ornate chair, a gift from the Pope to a Medici prince many years before. He walked to the great open window that overlooked the city of his ancestors, where Maurice St. Claire joined him.

"Well?" asked Rothschild.

"Almost everything is going as planned, Sir," answered his loyal subordinate, "but we didn't get all the documents."

St. Claire offered a full report of the assassin's activities from the clandestine meeting in Boston, to the stolen packet and murder, and finally to the futile search of Hentersheim's residence and book shop. One document was all that had been found.

"And you are sure that the professional you hired to carry out the assignment isn't holding out on us?" Rothschild queried.

"Well . . ." St. Claire paused, "if he is, he hasn't made any demands. He's a consummate professional, so I really doubt it. He conducted a thorough search of Hentersheim's shop and home, but found nothing. I think that it's Hentersheim who was holding out on us."

"But now he's dead," answered Rothschild flatly, pausing. "I suppose there's a kind of ironic justice in it, though, since we killed him."

"Yes, sir," acknowledged St. Claire, knowing there was nothing more to be said.

St. Claire opened his briefcase and handed Rothschild the package containing the manuscript fragment.

"You mentioned that you still wanted this, even though I already sent the sample to the lab."

Rothschild nodded, his keen eyes narrowing on the glass frame as he removed it from the package. He held the frame up against the sunlight and stared through the glass at the faint lettering.

"I will want to study this too," he mused more to himself than to St. Claire.

Rothschild admired the restraint of the man who had over the years almost become a friend. Obviously, he yearned to understand the full meaning behind his mission to the United States, but he maintained a perfect professional detachment. Rothschild took St. Claire over to a finely carved coat of arms, consisting of six orbs against a shield.

"You know what this is, Maurice?" asked Rothschild.

St. Claire nodded, wondering where this was going, "It's the Medici crest, Sir, your family heritage."

"But my name is Rothschild," his employer answered. "Do you know why?"

St. Claire answered cautiously, "I'm not sure, Sir. My understanding is that the Medici heirs all died out . . ."

Rothschild nodded, "Yes, they did, the main line at least. But there were others, there always were in those days. It was no longer safe for anyone to bear the name Medici. Do you know why?"

St. Claire admitted, "Not really, Sir. Ancient history is not my professional specialty."

"Not 'ancient,' my friend—Renaissance history," Rothschild explained quietly. "The Medici were fools in truth."

St. Claire started at that remark, but allowed his silence to indicate his interest.

"In the end the Medici thought they were gods," Rothschild explained.

"You are referring to the Holy Family portraits, Sir?" St. Claire inquired at Rothschild's silence.

"Oh, that surely indicates their caprice. To paint yourself not adoring the Virgin and child, but instead as the Virgin and child . . . takes a very special kind of . . . well, lunacy, I suppose," he admitted thoughtfully.

"You know," Rothschild continued, pulling St. Claire back to the window overlooking the city, "it all started so grandly. Cosimo the Elder, the building of the Duomo right over there, and the greatest of them all, Lorenzo d'Medici. The heights of glory."

"Then why did it all collapse?" asked St. Claire, not used to his employer's ruminations.

Rothschild nodded slowly, "Yes, that is the question, isn't it."

Moving toward one of the walls in the villa he pointed to one of two portraits of men clothed in the white papal vestments. "Leo the Tenth."

St. Claire gazed at the pomp and authority in the face of the Renaissance pope.

"The man spent the entire sum of the papal treasury in just a single year," Rothschild explained. "Nightly dinners of over sixty courses each. They yearned for the ancient glory, Roman glory, just as we all do."

"Their excesses helped bring about the reformation . . ." began St. Claire recalling his schooling.

". . . and the collapse of the family power, yes," continued Rothschild.

"A great pity, Sir," St. Claire consoled his boss but was surprised at the reply he received.

"No," answered Rothschild sharply. "They never achieved real glory, only fame. Do you see the difference?"

"I'm afraid not, Sir," St. Claire admitted uncomfortably.

"We seek power, yes?" Rothschild exclaimed. "Financial, social, political power. Always more, built not on noble titles and golden crowns, but on a myriad of relationships formed behind the scenes."

"Right," offered St. Claire admiringly.

"But why?" asked Rothschild. "What differentiates Caesar, Moses, Alexander and even Lorenzo my ancestor from so many others throughout history who also had power, perhaps even greater power?"

"Control of history, managing the perceptions of future generations," answered St. Claire.

Rothschild nodded, "Yes, that was Machiavelli's analysis. Glory lasts. Fame is fleeting. The next pharaoh replaces your name with his own."

"That makes sense to me," agreed St. Claire.

"But not to me," retorted Rothschild sharply. "What good is Caesar's glory to him now?"

St. Claire nodded slowly, as his employer continued, "If glory were the aim, one might as well become a historian and relish the accomplishments of the past, fancying oneself both as doer and inheritor of nobility. *That* was the real Machiavelli. Utter stupidity."

St. Claire's confusion grew, as he wondered where Rothschild was going with all of this.

"Come with me. I want to show you something," instructed Rothschild, his slim figure turning briskly and marching halfway down the hallway before St. Claire hurriedly followed him through the richly decorated rooms. The sounds of their footfalls echoed throughout the grand chambers. Rothschild finally came to the old family chapel, where apostles and prophets carved from pure white Carrara marble stood serenely. Storming into the room and past the holy altar without the customary nod to the martyr's bone it contained, he headed to the reliquary at the chapel's rear.

"Look!" he exclaimed to St. Claire.

"Yes, bones and hairs of the saints, I see them," replied St. Claire without understanding.

"This is what they really sought," emphasized Rothschild. "It's what we all seek."

"What are you talking about, Sir?" St. Claire exclaimed, dropping his usually controlled exterior.

Turning to his trusted aide, Rothschild adopted a more paternal approach, "Tell me, Maurice, what do you think would exceed even political and military glory?"

St. Claire thought for a few moments before answering, trying to merge his own thoughts with the meaning behind these reliquaries. Finally, he offered, "I suppose not dying at all."

St. Claire looked at the expression on his employer's face, and suddenly realized that he was coldly serious. And as everything fell into place, he blurted out, "You mean, you are after real eternal life? That's what the saints all sought."

"Exactly," explained Rothschild.

"But that's all Sunday school nonsense!" retorted St. Claire.

"Yes, that's all it's ever supposed to have been," offered Rothschild mysteriously.

"So we're not on some kind of religious quest, are we, Sir?" St. Claire spoke flatly. "That's why we've been investing so heavily in all those biotechnology companies."

As Rothschild smiled at him, St. Claire's admiration for his boss grew all the more, "You mean, Sir, that you've actually done it? You've figured out how to prolong human life indefinitely?"

"Not exactly," answered Rothschild, his smile intact. "But tomorrow morning we're going to get an important clue."

"The manuscript fragment?" asked a bewildered St. Claire.

"Indeed," replied Rothschild smoothly before leaving him alone with the bones of the saints.

*   *   *   *

Rothschild slept fretfully all that night and finally awoke well before dawn the next morning. Following his usual impeccable grooming routine, he slipped into another of his fine Italian suits. His roiling stomach would not tolerate breakfast, so he walked silently through the halls of the magnificent summer palace that he now called home.

Entering his office he gazed out onto the sleeping city of Florence nestled in the valley beneath the villa. No city captured his awe like Florence. His ancestors had given it its glory, but they had been shoved aside and replaced by the modern world. Rothschild wished for real glory too, but he wanted to enjoy it. He wanted to live. It was for this reason that he had invested so heavily in cutting edge biotechnology with all its promise of prolonged life. And he had a special reason to believe not only that long life, but actual immortality was possible. For deep beneath the villa he had constructed a special vault in which lay the evidence of immortality, a series of manuscript fragments written by a man who had lived for centuries. Just hours from now a key piece to the puzzle would lie in his hands. Soon, he would possess the DNA map to eternal life.

Sliding his fingers through his graying hair, Rothschild reflected on how his family had come across the scroll fragments four centuries earlier in their quest for "secret" knowledge. The Medici had pursued ancient wisdom as had everyone else at the time, though it turned out that ancient mathematics proved the real key to classical glory. Brunelleschi's genius enabled him to discover the mathematics underlying the dome over the Roman Pantheon, and then use that knowledge to erect his own dome high above the Florentine Duomo. Rothschild smiled at the verve of Cosimo the Elder, family patriarch of the Medici, supporting Brunelleschi's quest amidst the conservative skepticism of the Florentines. Lasting success always required decisive action, he thought. Rothschild looked up at the portrait of his ancestor. He liked him.

But the Medici also pursued what in the end turned out to be alchemy and religious nonsense too, for at the time, no one knew what would pan out. Technology and magic are really forms of the same thing, Rothschild mused, both attempts to manipulate the world. The myriad of reliquaries held by the Medici did little for their souls, he was sure, but the sciences discovered by Galileo and Leonardo among so many others ushered in an age that surpassed the Greeks.

Rothschild gazed at another portrait of a German Cardinal, clothed in the scarlet of his office. He had offered the scroll fragments to the family, eager to make his escape from Germany following its Lutheran conquest. The Medici had paid the Cardinal an enormous sum for them, because of what they were reputed to be, namely, part of an ancient chronicle written by Melchizedek. The fragments simply sat in the family vault for years, until he, Laurence Rothschild, had subjected them to scientific analysis and discovered their secret. He had then gone through the ancient records trying to determine how the cardinal had come to possess them, but nothing could be learned. So, he then looked to the future and had for three decades wondered how their author, Melchizedek or whoever he really might be, had lived for so long. Rothschild suspected that he might yet be alive.

These musings always made Rothschild anxious, more so now that he was closer than ever before to the truth. He found physical exercise a useful distraction, and headed toward the gym. While he prepared for a long ride on the exercise bike, he reflected on the events that led up to this moment.

Rothschild had years before put out feelers throughout the worlds of rare book dealers and antiquities smugglers seeking additional scroll fragments with the kind of Sumerian script used in his fragments. Nothing had turned up until very recently when a book-dealer from Bonn repaid a loan to one of the family's many banks. The dealer had repaid a two million Euro loan on the spot, something the branch manager noted with interest, and when asked about the source of the funds, the dealer mentioned that he had sold several scroll fragments to a dealer in New York City. Given the secret directive concerning book dealers and ancient Sumerian manuscripts that he had received, the branch manager immediately arranged a complimentary suite for the dealer at one of the family's many hotels in the city, and then invited him to a champagne and caviar brunch the following morning. The attention lavished on the dealer produced the desired effect. After several glasses of champagne, he had explained that the manuscript fragments were apparently written in Sumerian script, a great rarity, since surviving Sumerian documents were typically clay tablets imprinted with a stylus or cylinder seal. The Bonn dealer had acquired them through the will of his uncle who had himself acquired them sometime during World War II. And that meant that they had been seized from someone else under circumstances for which there would very likely be no record. Of course, Rothschild had checked. He smiled at the memory—he checked everything meticulously. But no record of the origin of the manuscript fragments had been found prior to their Second World War appearance. The Bonn dealer further explained that he had made inquiries on the antiquities e-network and been offered a fortune from the New York dealer but received not even an inquiry from anyone else. So, he'd made the deal.

The branch manager had provided his superiors with the identity of the New York dealer, and the entire case was presented to Rothschild himself within a day. Rothschild had arranged a significant reward for the branch manager as well as a promotion within the city, and then set himself to purchasing the texts. He had been concerned as to why the New York dealer would pay so much to acquire them. Could he be aware of their true significance? So, he had sent representatives to offer the dealer, a Mr. Hentersheim, a considerable sum for their sale. But Hentersheim had insisted that he had no interest in selling, and he refused to discuss his own reason for purchasing them. Rothschild had wondered if there was some connection to family losses during World War II, but Hentersheim's ancestry proved for the most part Spanish, not German, though his grandmother had lived in Germany before the War in comparable wealth. Perhaps she had lost them during the War and Hentersheim had been trying to reacquire what he could of the family's lost fortune. But Rothschild knew that this motive amounted to nothing more than speculation.

Rothschild wiped the sweat from his face, enjoying the soft comfort of the Egyptian cotton towel. Dismounting the exercise bike, he poured himself a glass of nutritional supplements mixed with orange juice. As the juice rejuvenated him, he recalled how when Hentersheim had refused to sell the manuscripts, he had called his special bureau, a very discreet organization within his financial empire that carried out clandestine activities, usually in the areas of industrial or political espionage. He had explained to its director, his confidant Maurice St. Claire, his need to acquire those texts from Hentersheim. He had already given Hentersheim his chance, so he authorized St. Claire to take whatever action was necessary.

Heading into the ornately decorated bath room, Rothschild prepared to slip into the cool pool for a swim. Just then his phone buzzed and he listened intently to what he was being told. A slight smile formed on his face, as he returned the phone to a side table and then dove into the pool. His muscles hardly strained as they pulled him through the water for the first of several twenty-five meter lengths. Rothschild stuck to his routine, knowing that St. Claire would soon arrive that afternoon with the results he was waiting for.

CHAPTER FOURTEEN

Florence

In the sterile conditions of his state of the art private laboratory, Rothschild spent the early afternoon hours evaluating the ancient document retrieved from Boston. He had spent an enormous sum to convert this wing of the Medici villa into a secure lab, appearing from the outside like any other of the many halls that snaked through the labyrinthine palace. Rothschild turned off the magnetic imaging backlighting behind the newly encased Melchizedek manuscript, and the faded ancient text replaced the glowing cartouche. "Just like the other ones," he muttered to himself, as a smile formed on his thin lips. A special signal light glowed on the wall near the lab's entry, calling him back to his study.

Maurice St. Claire knocked on the ornately carved wooden door and heard the familiar call of welcome from his employer. Even though Rothschild was nearly ten years older than he was, his employer's sixty-three years were masked by a vigilant devotion to health. St. Claire stared into his master's tapered face, his thin lips tightly pursed and his eyes narrowly focused. He couldn't help but admire Rothschild's distinguished look, his sharp features crested by a slightly receding hairline. Rothschild carried himself with an air of finesse and sophistication bred from his high culture and extensive education.

"Well?" his employer looked up at him eagerly. St. Claire's six feet exceeded his boss's height by some three inches. His usually cold, watchful eyes placed narrowly on his tight lipped, squared face gave way to a huge grin.

74

"She'd done it, Sir, the mapping is complete," answered St. Claire, referring to their biotech expert Michelle Andover who had talked with him earlier by phone. "You should talk with her yourself, because I don't fully understand what she's discovered."

"Very well, superb, I'll do it," answered his boss hastily.

St. Claire soon had Dr. Michelle Andover on the phone from her bio-engineering lab in northern New Jersey. Rothschild took the phone and introduced himself to her. Dr. Andover had never before talked with the person who had only three years earlier bought out the company she worked for and elevated her to the head of research. Rothschild had always used intermediaries, and she was flattered by his sudden attention. She began by thanking him for his trust, but he quickly turned the course of the conversation to her analysis.

"Yes, Sir. Mr. St. Claire sent me the stained manuscript sample, and sure enough, it was blood, just as he, I mean you, suspected," she began. "I followed the classified instructions that you sent and began with the manuscript material itself."

Rothschild nodded and listened eagerly as she continued.

"It's very old, Sir," she offered eagerly. "Carbon-14 dating places it around 800-500 B.C., just as you speculated."

"Excellent," replied Rothschild. "And what did you discover about the blood?"

"Well, it's very strange. The first thing I noticed is its capacity to mask its appearance."

"Mask its appearance?" echoed Rothschild.

"Yes, Sir," she continued. "When I examined it under the microscope, I kept seeing changes in color, shape, and even texture. It was akin to some sort of dramatic chameleon effect."

"But the blood is dead, isn't it?" asked Rothschild.

"Yes," she answered, "and that is extremely puzzling. It suggested some microbiological or physical property."

"Were you able to isolate it?" he asked.

"Yes!" she answered triumphantly. "It's genetic, from what we can tell. But I've never seen anything like it, and given the security on this research, I've not talked to anyone else about it either. But my researchers found nothing in any medical literature on such a genetic anomaly."

"I see," Rothschild mused. "And it is responsible for this chameleon effect?"

"From what we can tell, yes," she answered, "but there is more— much, much more."

"Go on," he ordered.

"The blood indicated extremely complicated immune responses, as though he has natural immunities to all kinds of illness or he's been around a very long time to develop that immunity."

"So, he could have lived as long as I've thought. And he could still be alive?" he asked.

"Given all that we know so far, I don't see any reason to suppose that he couldn't still be alive," she answered confidently.

"Could you determine the origin of his perpetual regeneration?" Rothschild asked hopefully.

"No," she answered glumly. "The source of his cellular regeneration is still a mystery. It may be organic, but we won't know until we can actually examine him."

"But we still have no idea where he may be, or who he may be," Rothschild murmured.

"Not yet, we don't," she answered, a bit too jubilantly.

"Tell me," he retorted. "What have you got?"

"We might be able to track him!" she answered.

* * * *

Langley, Virginia

Fred Billings was furious when he learned that his prize had been dead for fourteen hours before anyone had notified him. Ignoring the ever-present pain in his leg, he raced down the hall to organize a CIA retrieval team to examine everything that the traitor Goldblum possessed at his home, in his car, in his office, anywhere. It would all be kept ultra-secret, he well knew, and Goldblum would probably receive an honorable funeral to prevent Mossad from knowing that the CIA had been reading their requests and Goldblum's answers for months. Billing's face fell, as he wondered when, if ever, they would acquire an asset as important as Goldblum had been. Before leaving his office, he put in a call to the encryption lab, telling them to hurry the decryption of Goldblum's last orders.

* * * *

Doctor Horn crashed onto his cot, exhausted after over twenty-five hours work in the ER. Both emergency shifts had been called to duty to deal with the victims of the Night of the Jumper. He glanced up at the clock and wondered in his weariness whether the two o'clock was morning or afternoon. He reached for a water bottle, sat up, drank half, and then poured the remainder over his head. After grabbing a towel to dry off, he tossed it into the chair but inadvertently knocked over the picture of his younger sister. He quickly replaced it on the little stand next to the cot and whispered a prayer for her safety and well-being. He drifted into sleep wondering once again if he should have continued his research in hematology instead of clinical work in the ER. At least his well-earned vacation to see his sister was just around the corner.

* * * *

Billings opened the decryption file and read Goldblum's last orders from Mossad. He had been tasked with acquiring any information that the FBI had on a Hentersheim and a Melchizedek. He called his supervisor to request access to the classified database, and upon receiving approval, left for the elevator. He despised the gravity shifts in elevators, as the inevitable "bump" when they started or stopped always shot bolts of pain through his right leg. But it beat the stairs, he thought to himself.

Two floors down he walked into a highly secure area within the CIA, and once his identification was confirmed and approved, entered the computer room. There he pulled up the active case database and entered the name "Hentersheim." He discovered an ongoing Federal investigation, only days old, that involved a murdered book-dealer. An FBI agent from Boston named Quarston was heading the investigation, and it appeared mob-linked. He noted Quarston's contact information and planned to place a call to him later that afternoon. He then entered the name "Melchizedek" but nothing turned up. He switched databases to the code names database, and again came up empty. Then who or what was a "Melchizedek," he wondered. On a hunch he decided to try the insecure but often useful web once he returned to his office. One could not access the web from this location, as any ability that the CIA might have to access the outside offered a hacker possible access to the CIA's classified databases. As such, this room was completely cut off from all external electronic connection. The room was so secure that it literally had its own electricity generator to ensure that it was completely isolated from the outside world.

* * * *

Back in his immaculate office in Boston, Quarston mulled over what he had learned from his conversation with the professors. The idea that a Biblical character was walking around the twenty-first century world— apparently without a big beard and a shepherd's crook, he smiled to himself—turned his notions of order on their head. Mythical characters were supposed to stay in the past, in an era that believed in all that stuff. He struggled to cope with what it might mean.

The flashing message indicator on his phone was really beginning to annoy him, so Quarston decided finally to attend to it. A detective in Cleveland had found Hentersheim's dead grandson. But Detective Burke offered a bonus: he had the killer in custody. And he was talking.

Quarston immediately called Detective Burke, but Burke's phone only switched to his voicemail. He then called Burke's Cleveland Precinct, but they too were mystified as to the detective's whereabouts. He was due a few days off, but apparently, he hadn't taken his phone with him. Frustrated, Quarston asked about an opportunity to interview the subject. But the Precinct Captain explained that Burke would have to be there for any interviews, and he was due back on Monday. Quarston arranged for a flight to Cleveland that afternoon.

* * * *

Returning from the secure database room, Billings opened the door to his office, sat down in front of his computer, stretched out his sore right leg, and then pulled up his web browser. Activating Google's search engine, he entered the term "Melchizedek." He discovered that "Melchizedek" was the name of a car shampoo, a priesthood in the Mormon church, a text in the Nag Hammadi Gnostic library, as well as a figure in the Bible. He frowned and decided to call Special Agent Roger Quarston.

* * * *

Florence

Michelle Andover walked out of the airport and looked for the car that Rothschild promised would be awaiting her. Andover's short stature was offset by her fine figure, prominent bright eyes, and round almost innocent face. In spite of being in her mid-thirties, her soft features and pony-tailed hair gave her a youthful appearance. But she wore no makeup and never bothered looking for a relationship, because she was, as she liked to describe herself, all-scientist. She believed that science would eventually provide a world beyond the threat of death, and so even though her employer's methods sometimes alarmed her, she knew that the end result was so important that slight sacrifices had to be made.

She made her way past the taxi cabs down to the curb of the main road, still surprised by her employer's sudden interest in having her come immediately to Italy. He had spoken of the next phase of the project, and that he would need her here at once. She peered down the long line of small cars and scooters, more than she'd ever seen in the States. She hoped that her ride would arrive soon, as she knew almost no Italian.

A sleek black sedan smoothly pulled up to the curb next to her, and the driver took her things and opened the rear door for her. Andover was surprised to find Rothschild himself sitting inside the car waiting for her.

"Sir, I'm sorry, but I'm not really . . ." she stammered, hastily flattening out her wrinkled clothing.

"I know it's been a long trip, Miss. Andover," he answered soothingly, "but I need to know what you've come up with since our last conversation."

Andover sighed and settled into her seat before replying, "Well, remember my telling you about that chameleon gene in Melchizedek's blood?"

"Yes," Rothschild answered, as the sedan pulled away from the curb. "I'm still curious what that would mean for his body."

"Me too, but it's hard to tell. Perhaps he has chameleon properties," she offered. "But we really don't know yet."

"Okay, that makes sense, but what about tracking him?" he queried.

"Do you remember that atomic isotope we were working with last year?"

"Sure, what of it?" he asked.

"The chameleon gene is proto-radioactive."

"Meaning what?"

"Meaning that with just the right energy, namely the kind arising from that atomic isotope, the gene will irradiate him," Michelle exclaimed.

"And we can track the emissions?" Rothschild asked her.

"No, I'm afraid that would be extremely difficult. Our most sensitive equipment might not pick it up even if we were right on top of him."

"Then how does this help us?" Rothschild pressed her.

"Because he'll get sick! Radiation sickness!" she exclaimed again.

"I see," Rothschild answered. "But what about his immunity?"

"Well, immunity works against disease, but radiation sickness is not really a disease. It's a disruptive effect on the cells."

"But you thought that his cells probably possessed remarkable regenerative powers?" he asked.

"Yes, they do," she admitted. "But the question is how long the regeneration takes and whether or not if all of his cells become subject to the radiation, those regenerative properties will function properly or even at all. If a specific organ causes them, perhaps that organ itself will be affected."

"Will this kill him?" Rothschild asked.

"Not before we find him," she answered confidently. "The World Health Organization requires that hospitals report all cases of radiation sickness in order to track down any nuclear accidents as soon as they occur. So, once he seeks treatment at a hospital, we'll find out about it, and find him."

"Very well," Rothschild responded optimistically. "But will we be able to treat him?"

Michelle explained, "Yes, we'll isolate him from any further contact with the isotope and cleanse his blood of the vector. And then either his regenerative capacities and/or a blood transfusion combined with standard radiation sickness therapy should bring him around fairly quickly."

"How are we to expose him to the isotope though?"

"Well, that's where the genius that you are paying for comes through," Michelle answered jubilantly.

* * * *

Cleveland

Quarston emerged from Cleveland International Airport and grabbed a taxi to take him to see Detective Burke. As he settled into the "comfortable" back seat, his phone rang. He didn't recognize the number, but then in his business he rarely did.

"Quarston," he announced into the phone.

"Hello, Agent Quarston?" asked Billings.

"Yes, who is this?"

"My name is Fred Billings. I'm with counterintelligence in the CIA. I understand that you are working on a murder case involving a Myron Hentersheim. Is that correct?" Billings queried.

"Yes, it is," answered Quarston, filling Billings in on the essential details of the murder together with the fact that he was now on his way to meet the murderer's accomplice who was in the custody of a Detective Larry Burke in Cleveland. Quarston omitted any reference to the documents or to Melchizedek.

"So, you have a double murder of the elderly man and his grandson," Billings mused.

His own curiosity aroused, Quarston asked, "Why the interest of the CIA? Was Hentersheim involved in espionage?"

"At this point we don't know," admitted Billings before continuing deceptively. "The truth is, his name came up through an NSA intercept, and we'd never run into him before. I was assigned to prepare a preliminary case file on him, when I discovered that he'd just been murdered. That seemed an odd coincidence."

"I see," said Quarston thoughtfully. He figured that Billing's story made enough sense to be believable, but with the CIA one just never really knew.

"Perhaps I can join you in your interview in Cleveland? I can be there in about three hours," offered Billings.

"Sure, why not? I'll meet you in Detective Burke's office."

"Good. Till then . . . oh, one more thing," added Billings, "does the name 'Melchizedek' mean anything to you?"

CHAPTER FIFTEEN

Mossad Headquarters, Israel

A knock on his office door brought Yaakov Katz back to the present. A soldier handed him another red-folder intelligence report, indicating its high classification. Signing for the document, Katz showed the officer out, and then opened the folder. He frowned as he viewed the report. Goldblum was dead, and his death was allegedly the product of a traffic accident.

But Goldblum was a critical asset. Had he been identified by the Americans? Had they killed him? It wasn't their usual practice, at least not a practice that they publicly acknowledged. Katz knew that sources died routinely of the same ailments that plagued the rest of the population. But when a top source suddenly died, and when that death was violent, it was his job to remain incredulous. Katz longed for a cigarette, but his doctors had finally frightened him into halting that habit. He turned instead to a piece of nicotine gum, but the chomping sound was magnified by the silence provided by the ultra-secret, sound-proof facility. Frustrated, he spit out the gum.

Turning through the pages of the report, Katz evaluated the kind of accident that had killed his source. No, it wasn't an isolated accident in some remote location. Multiple vehicles were involved. Would the Americans sacrifice several of their own citizens? Perhaps . . . Katz leaned back in his chair, feeling the familiar clunk where the old springs had long since given up their supporting role. He gazed at the photograph of Langley he kept on his office wall. Americans were very hard to predict. Their actions wavered between pure sentimentality and ruthless pragmatism.

They could annihilate one hundred thousand Iraqi conscripts in the deserts of Iraq, and then they could wring their hands over the rights of the vicious brutes in Saddam's regime who ordered those conscripts to their deaths. He shook his head. It never made any sense. And so, events in America as well as the actions of the Americans were a continual source of both amusement and consternation to Israeli intelligence. Israel depended upon the Americans for military, political, and economic support, and so she spied on the Americans almost as much as any other nation. Determining and influencing American policy was the full-time job of a significant portion of the Israeli foreign services. Katz stood up and stretched his aching muscles, forcing himself to re-focus on the issue at hand.

What caused the accident? That was the crucial question. It didn't take much to cause an accident, and in congested traffic, highway hits could lead to major pileups. But these kinds of assassinations were very hard to engineer and that, together with the attention they drew, made them undesirable. Still . . . that very undesirability could provide the cover to make the death appear accidental. That was the endless mind-game of the intelligence world. So, a truck drove over Goldblum's vehicle. Another vehicle had turned into the truck, because the driver was distracted, distracted by a parked vehicle's sudden explosion. He noted that with alarm until he read the next lines of the report. The weapon detonating the car was not a bomb, as he feared, but a suicide, a woman jumping to her death from the top of the building next to the parked car.

Katz sat back down and thought carefully. Could the Americans have thrown someone from the building onto the car? That would require extraordinary aim. If the person was already dead, it'd be easier. But how would a body's hitting a car prove sufficient to cause a multi-car accident? It couldn't be guaranteed. And professional kills were designed to offer a near-guarantee of their success. There would be many other ways to kill Goldblum. So, perhaps it was accidental after all. Still, he'd have his people run a thorough review of Goldblum's work in the last three years. You just never knew what might turn up.

* * * *

As their black sedan approached the old Medici Villa on the outskirts of Florence, Michelle Andover completed her explanation of how they could track Melchizedek.

"We will use a genetically modified virus to inject Melchizedek with the isotopes," she asserted.

"But how will we ensure that the virus actually gets to him?" Rothschild asked her. "He could be anywhere."

"Then we'll spread it everywhere," she answered.

Rothschild started at that suggestion and then paused, considering. "Only Melchizedek will become ill, because only he has the reactive gene."

"Right, Sir, that's it, exactly," Michelle urged. "I've modified the original virulent and dangerous strain to render it benign. We won't have to worry about long term mutation."

"There will be no threat of an Andromeda strain?" he asked.

The Andromeda strain was an extraterrestrial virus in an American novel that killed all human life until it mutated itself away from its lethal propensities. But if a virus could become benign through mutation, it could likewise become lethal through mutation. So, safeguards had to be in place to prevent the kind of multiple regenerations that might lead to dangerous mutation. Michelle smiled at her employer's foresight.

"No, but we cannot limit the number of viral replications," she answered," because we need the virus to multiply and spread across the world. So, I've chosen a virus for which there is nearly worldwide immunity. It will be recognized by the immune systems of all those infected which will limit its duration, but not before it can be spread to others. And since I've already rendered it benign, anyone not already immunized won't be harmed anyway. Thanks to the world wide effort at immunization, I estimate the maximum life of the virus to only a couple weeks, greatly inhibiting the risk from mutation. But because of its extreme virulence, the virus should multiply over the entire globe in just a few days; another week, and it'll be gone."

Rothschild asked her, "But the radioactive isotope is a physical, not a biological product, so how can you make enough of it for the virus to carry? And from where will the newly replicated virus acquire the isotope?"

"That's where the real genius comes in," she asserted proudly. "We're going to employ nanotechnology as part of the viral code, so that when the virus interacts with the target's DNA, it will begin to produce the extremely small nano-machines necessary to produce the isotope. When new virus is replicated in host cells, the nanites will also be produced and with them, the isotope!"

"So, we prepare rapid reaction forces stationed across the globe ready for action the instant our people within the WHO hear of a single case of radiation sickness," Rothschild concluded.

"And then we grab him and begin the dissection," Michelle answered.

"How long will it take you to manufacture the virus?" Rothschild asked.

"Not long, as our genetic modification systems are already fully operational. We'll just need to move the resources out of the United States to avoid legal repercussions there."

"Because the isotope will be identifiable?" Rothschild asked.

"Oh yes," she answered. "Our company alone has the patent on the isotope isolation and production techniques."

"Then it will have to be stolen, won't it?" Rothschild asked.

"Yes, I suppose it will," she answered slowly, "and the theft might just motivate us to move our operation here."

"So it will. The destruction caused by the clumsy thieves will be extensive. Alert me once you have moved the essential equipment to the departure site," Rothschild ordered.

* * * *

Cleveland

Quarston nervously adjusted his grip on his phone.

"Melchizedek?" Quarston repeated after a second's pause, hoping Billings didn't notice.

But Billings noted the hesitation instantly. Law enforcement personal were trained to ferret out liars, not imitate them. Quarston was no exception, and Billings instantly grew suspicious of the other agent. So, he continued.

"Yeah, does that name mean anything to you?" he pressed.

"No, it just sounds weird, like, oh, I think I heard that name in church," Quarston explained. "Why do you ask?"

Billings considered that for a moment. Perhaps Quarston paused because of a passing familiarity with the name? He wasn't sure. He'd wait to see how things developed once they met in Cleveland. So, he answered, "The name came up in my investigation. We think it might be a code name for some operation. But you are right that it is in the Bible among other strange places. Who knows where it will lead? I'll see you in Cleveland later this afternoon then. Thanks for your help."

* * * *

Larry Burke, Fred Billings, and Roger Quarston finally met in the interview room of the Cleveland Homicide Unit. In spite of the lack of outside light and the stark furnishings in the room, Burke greeted them both warmly. He was pleased that both an FBI agent and a CIA counterintelligence official needed his man. Burke was confident that the information that Beecham would provide would open quite the can of worms.

Burke began the conversation. "I'm glad you both could make it for this initial interagency interview."

"So, how are we going to approach Beecham?" asked Quarston.

"Well, he's been fairly cooperative with me, though the Coast Guard couldn't move him," laughed Burke.

"Right," acknowledged Quarston, "not exactly professional interrogators, are they?"

"Hardly," Burke agreed, "but working the Lake Erie like I do, you realize how much we need 'em."

"Beecham has no criminal record, then?" queried Quarston.

"None, not ever been arrested either," added Burke. "That's good for us."

"Why is that good for us?" questioned the CIA agent.

Quarston nodded to Burke who explained, "He has no experience with the police, so we can work him."

"I wouldn't have thought of that," admitted Billings.

"Different jobs, same team," smiled Quarston.

"All right then," declared Burke. "I'll have Beecham brought in."

* * * *

Beecham's resolve in front of the Coast Guard officer had begun to wane of late. He was tired. He wasn't eating well. He was scared of his cellmates. He hated jail and couldn't imagine a life in prison. He missed the lake. He missed freedom. And here he was sitting in chains attached to a serious sergeant who held the keys to his life.

The sergeant received a call and yanked Beecham up. Beecham could barely walk, shackled as he was hand and foot. He followed the sergeant into another windowless room where three men stood around a single chair waiting for him. He recognized one of them as Detective Burke with whom he'd chatted before, but the other two were new to him. Beecham gulped and sank wearily into the seat.

Detective Burke smiled warmly to him, "Sergeant, I think we can remove his restraints."

The sergeant grunted and slowly opened the shackled and hand cuffs, letting Beecham rub his swollen wrists. He noted the intense gaze he received from the other two men. One of them looked at him with an air of finesse but with a powder keg in his right eye, striking Beecham with real fear. That one also had a bum leg. The other one seemed distant and thoughtful, like he carried the weight of the world on his shoulders. But his eyes were infinitely dark like he had no soul. Beecham felt like everybody hated him here, and he just wanted to go home.

"How are you doing, James?" asked Detective Burke kindly.

"All right, I guess," he sputtered.

"James, you don't look that well to me. You aren't sleeping, are you?"

Beecham didn't want to answer the Detective, but he couldn't help respond to human feeling. He felt tears welling up in his eyes, but he stifled them with a snort.

"I'd like you to talk with these two men here, okay? Tell them everything you told me, and we'll see what we can do about making things better for you."

"Hello, Mr. Beecham, I am Special Agent Roger Quarston with the Federal Bureau of Investigation," indicated the one whose eyes suggested he'd seen too much of this life. "Perhaps you can tell us exactly how you were involved in this murder?"

Beecham began, "Well, to begin with, you should know that I was contracted to kill the Hentersheim kid and dispose of the body. It was nothing personal."

"Who hired you?" broke in the other man directly.

"I don't know that exactly," replied Beecham. "I was contacted over the Network."

"The Network?" asked Quarston.

"Yes, that's what I wanted to talk about," he answered, feeling like he might be getting the upper hand in the conversation. "And Detective Burke here tells me that you will be mighty interested in my information."

"That depends on its value, now doesn't it?" countered Quarston coldly. "Let's hear what you've got to say."

"What is this 'Network' you spoke of?" pressed the one with the bum leg.

"But I want some kind of guarantee . . ." he started forcefully.

"We've got you red-handed for murder one. That's the needle, Beecham!" shouted Burke. "You answer the man right now, if you want any consideration whatsoever!"

"All right, all right. But you gotta understand. I'm guaranteed to be a dead man unless I get witness protection if I tell you this," he whined.

"If it's that good, you'll get it," promised Quarston quietly. "Now let's hear it."

"All right," he replied, anxious to make the detectives happy. "The Network is an organization of assassins."

"How many?" interrupted the bum-legged man.

"I'm not sure of the number," he answered.

"Then how did you get involved with it?" asked Quarston.

"I was invited in. I worked for the US military doing various kinds of wet work, and I planned to get out of that line, when I was approached with this huge offer . . ." he started.

"How much exactly?" asked the unidentified man.

"Oh, maybe two hundred fifty thousand," he paused, allowing that figure to set in.

"And the target?" asked Burke, interested in these new details.

"You remember Johnny Blazeman, that real estate tycoon?" he asked proudly.

"Yeah," answered Burke. "That murder was never solved. Very professionally done. That was you?"

"Yeah, that was me. That was my first hit. After that, I was given a special internet address and identity through which potential clients could contact me. That's the Network."

* * * *

Quarston felt his phone vibrate indicating he had a message. Irritated at being bothered during the interview, his curiosity nevertheless got the better of him, and he glanced down to see Harry's name on the phone. Excusing himself from the interview room, he headed to the top of the building where he could ensure privacy, and then walked out onto the roof.

"Hello, Harry? This is Quarston, what do you have for me?" he asked his lab technician.

"Hi, Sir. I thought something was odd about the manuscript fragment you gave me. The edge appeared thickly layered. So, I peeled back the layers and discovered a small bit of gold lying between them."

"What do you mean, gold?" asked Quarston confused.

"Well, vellum is often prepared in layers of dried animal skin. But something is lying between these layers, Sir."

"What is it?" Quarston asked.

"It's gold, whatever it is, so that suggests something important," Harry replied. "But I'm going to have to see the whole manuscript fragments in order to conduct an MRI scan to discover what's really in there."

"So, you need the pages, is that it?" asked Quarston reluctantly.

"That's where my investigation is, Sir," Harry answered. "Of course, it's your call."

"Okay Harry, I want you to go to my house. If you move the statue of the lion that's out front, you'll find a key to the house. Head downstairs into my workshop, and look underneath my bench. You'll find a little hide-a-key there. Remove the key, okay?" explained Quarston.

"Okay, and what do I do with it?" asked Harry.

"Take the key to Citibank, and it will open up safety deposit box number twenty-nine. You'll find the manuscripts there. Take them and conduct your analysis, but Harry?" Quarston almost whispered into the telephone.

"Yeah?"

"Tell no one about this, and when you are through, return the fragments to the box, and the keys to their places, okay?" asked Quarston.

"You bet, Sir. I'll take good care of them."

"I'm sure you will," concluded Quarston before hanging up his phone and heading back downstairs to the interview room.

* * * *

"Okay, who runs this Network?" asked Billings, as Quarston returned.

"I don't know," answered Beecham.

"Look, James, let me be straight with you. You'd better tell us the whole story. This Network has to take a cut of the proceeds. So, you must have some further connection with them," insisted Billings.

"Yeah, I suppose that's true," admitted Beecham. "But what is offered to me is a set figure."

"So, the Network must filter the clientele first," suggested Quarston to the others.

"Sounds like it," said Burke. "Which means it's likely centralized enough to take down in one fell swoop."

"Right," answered Quarston. "We've got to put an entire FBI office on this information. We could track down hundreds of killers all over the world, people totally unknown to us, since I imagine none of the Network assassins have any criminal records?"

Beecham nodded, "That's right. It's a condition of membership. And if you get caught, you get killed. That was my understanding."

"Yet you were succeeding with your Hentersheim contract, and somebody tried to kill you anyhow," murmured Burke.

"Yeah, tell me about it. There's the rub, isn't it? What would have been the point of that?" asked Beecham.

"Somebody puts a hit on the hitter—somebody very determined to maintain his secrecy?" asked Billings.

"It sounds like it," explained Quarston. "Tell me this, Beecham, do you have any idea who hired you or who might have planted the bomb on your boat?"

"No, none. I kinda hoped that if you cracked the Network, you'd find that out too," explained Beecham.

"All right, then, let's get into the details of the Hentersheim killing itself. You were hired to kill him or hold him for ransom or what?" asked Quarston.

"Kill him. There was no talk of any ransom. Besides, ransoms are the easiest way to get picked off by the Feds. No professional does jobs like that anymore," Beecham assured him.

"But you didn't kill him right away?" asked Quarston.

"No, I was supposed to wait for an authorization call, to actually kill him," explained Beecham.

"And when did that call come in?" pressed Quarston.

"The night I headed into the lake. No sense leaving a body to be found," exclaimed Beecham.

"We're going to need his phone," said Quarston to Burke. "Did you retrieve a phone in his apartment or wreckage?"

"No . . ." started Burke, when he was interrupted by Beecham.

"That phone went down with the boat."

"What do you mean 'that phone'?" asked Burke.

"I mean, that I got that phone in the locker, with the down payment," said Beecham.

"Locker?" asked Burke. "What locker? You never said anything to me about a locker."

"I guess I just forgot about it. The issue is the Network, not some locker," explained Beecham.

"The issue is whatever we say it is," asserted Quarston. "Now where is this locker?"

"At the train station," answered Beecham. "Number B224. I had the key, but it's lost now too. It went down with my boat."

Quarston looked to Burke who immediately left the room and ordered that the locker be printed and searched. Who knew what they might find in it? After Burke had left, Quarston continued the interrogation.

"What was the down payment?" he asked.

"Half the money," answered Beecham.

"And where is that money now?" asked Quarston.

Beecham hesitated, but before he could think very far ahead, Billings thundered, "Beecham, you listen to me, you little weasel. You are never going to touch a dime of that blood money. You hear me? Now you answer the man and you do it now, or so help me God, we'll hang your carcass out in the public eye so far that you'll be dead by sunset."

Beecham looked genuinely terrified. In fact, Quarston found himself intimidated by Billings' tone. But it worked.

Beecham replied, "Okay, I deposited the money, and I'll tell you where. I'll give you access to the account, but you've got to promise to protect me."

"If you are straight with us, if you tell us *everything*, then you'll get your protection," Quarston promised.

"So, how was the target identified, and how was payment made to you?" asked Billings.

"We'll be right back," Quarston interrupted and then walked with Billings out of the room. When they were alone, he continued.

"Fred, we've got somebody in Cleveland who put that money and phone into the locker."

"Right," Billings answered. "Not to mention whoever, maybe the same person, planted the bomb on the boat."

"Yeah, that's right. What's more, there is the concurrent killing of the elderly Hentersheim and the search of his book shop and rooms. We've got a fairly sophisticated international operation here. Isn't that kinda down your alley?" asked Quarston. "You gonna tell me what interest the CIA really has in this case?"

Billings looked Quarston over and reflected for a few minutes before answering, "All I can tell you now is that we've been involved with a major counterintelligence operation that suddenly went bust. Hentersheim's name came up."

"Came up from outside the United States?" pressed Quarston.

"Yes, obviously, otherwise we'd be in violation of the law," asserted Billings.

Quarston paused momentarily. He knew that the law did forbid the CIA to run operations involving purely domestic persons, but he also knew that in important cases, those laws could be by-passed. So, he went further, "Was the FBI involved in this counterintelligence operation?"

"All I can tell you is this: since our operation involved surveillance of persons within the United States, we had an FBI liaison and a Federal judge's authority behind every move we made. So, it's all legal."

Quarston immediately drew the erroneous conclusion that Billings was running this operation against someone within the CIA itself. Otherwise, the FBI would have been assigned to run the case. Counterintelligence, thought Quarston. Somebody inside the CIA had been exposed as a spy, and Billings had probably been assigned to thwart or use him. And that person worked for some foreign intelligence agency, an agency that wanted to know about Hentersheim and Melchizedek. How was that possible? Quarston didn't know, but he realized that this case was rapidly growing beyond him. He wondered about taking Billings into his confidence, but thought that perhaps he'd best wait a little longer.

When Quarston and Billings returned to the interrogation room, they found Burke conversing further with Beecham. Burke explained to them, "James here thinks he remembers the number that his employers called from."

"Well, why didn't you say that before?" asked Billings menacingly.

"I wasn't sure about it," murmured Beecham. "And you scare me. But if you really will protect me, then I'll give you that number."

"So, you thought of it as your insurance, did you?" asked Quarston.

"Yeah, it is my insurance, because you've got nothing else," tried Beecham unconvincingly.

"On the contrary," bluffed Quarston, "the FBI has already seized your computer, and we've cracked the Network. We'll have the entire organization soon." Quarston was pretty sure that the FBI would be able to crack into the Network's organization, but he knew that it would take more time than he really had.

Burke added, "And the Cleveland PD just took apart that locker of yours at the bus stop. We'll have your accomplice's name from his prints by night fall." Burke's teamwork with Quarston yielded the desired effect.

"Give me a pen," demanded a frustrated Beecham. And he wrote down the number.

CHAPTER SIXTEEN

While the Cleveland Police traced the phone number and examined the locker at the train station, Beecham explained the details of the contract on the young Hentersheim.

"I was supposed to go to the train station and pick up a telephone."

"That was the phone that went down with the boat?" clarified Quarston.

"Yes," answered Beecham and then continued. "I was to call a prearranged number twice, once when I'd obtained the target and again when I'd disposed of the body. Then the money—three quarters of a million—would arrive in the train locker. And I'd dispose of the phone. Very simple, really."

"But there won't be any money in the train locker," Billings mocked him.

"No, it'll be empty," acknowledged Beecham, realizing finally that his employer's plan to murder him guaranteed there'd be no payoff.

Quarston evaluated what they'd all heard. "Clearly, whoever hired Beecham had someone leave the phone in the train locker, someone who had to have been in Cleveland."

"Right," answered Burke, "And someone—maybe the same guy?—was receiving the calls Beecham made."

At that moment another detective knocked on the observation window calling for Burke's attention. Burke opened the door to receive a note with an address for the business linked to the phone number, a biotech firm in New Jersey. When Burke revealed this information to the others, Billings replied, "Well, that means that there are at least two different people working on the contracting end, someone who delivered the phone and set the bomb on Beecham's boat, and someone who received the phone calls in New Jersey."

"So, what is this company in New Jersey?" asked Quarston, satisfied that they finally had some solid leads.

"Oh, it's a biotech firm that just burned to the ground, if you can believe that. I doubt you'll find anything left there, but you could still check it out," Burke answered him.

Quarston called the New Jersey Bureau's office and learned as much as he could about the fire at the company. Sure enough, a fire had consumed much of the central offices and destroyed the lab. It appeared to be arson, so an investigation had begun. The FBI agent reporting to Quarston explained that they had recovered the badly burned computer server but discovered that prior to its fire damage, someone had used a fairly sophisticated virus to destroy all data on the drives.

"So, we're talking about industrial espionage here, with a fire to cover what was stolen?" asked Quarston.

"Yeah, that's what we're thinking," explained the agent. "Either that, or someone burned down his own company to protect crucial data. But something doesn't add up there."

"Oh, what's that?" queried Quarston.

"Well, we found the central office in the lab and there we found the fire-proof safe. And you'd think that anyone destroying his own lab would remove everything from the safe. Thing is, we found personal financial information from the company's lead researcher, a woman named Dr. Michelle Andover. And get this, she's gone completely missing. That makes it seem like she was involved in causing the fire, except that she'd be foolish to leave these personal records, because they are foreign bank account records."

"Oh? And what have you learned about the accounts?" asked Quarston.

"So far, we've determined that there is something like twenty-three million dollars in one of them. The banks holding the other two accounts have proven uncooperative. So, if this woman burned down her own lab, why would she leave a trail to her money? And what motive would she have for burning down her own lab?"

"Good questions, and if someone else burned it down, they'd not have searched the safe? Only you found nothing in the safe except for those records, right?" pressed Quarston.

"Exactly," answered the agent, "almost as if someone deliberately left them to be found!"

"And that would direct our attention to the missing doctor," surmised Quarston.

"To mislead us from the real motive which would be what?" asked the agent.

"I don't know," confessed Quarston pausing. "Tell me this. What kind of research was this lab involved with?"

"Hang on a minute, and I'll check," answered the agent.

While the agent was locating this information, Quarston revealed all that he had learned to the other two detectives.

Burke remarked, "Well, this is certainly turning into a tangled web, isn't it? I wonder what happened to the doctor."

"Probably dead and buried," answered Billings. "That's what I'd do if I wanted an investigation to die with someone."

"Right," whispered Quarston with his hand over the phone before adding, "Give us a nice clean package and we dig no deeper."

The New Jersey agent suddenly spoke up again on the other end of the telephone line. "Okay, I've got that information. The company was researching advanced regenerative technologies."

"What does that mean, exactly?" asked Quarston.

"Says here that they were looking to prolong the human life-span, possibly even to overcome death!" laughed the agent. "Fat chance. Sounds like a sure loser of an investment, if you ask me."

Quarston laughed too, when he suddenly felt a tingly sensation in his spine. Life prolonging technologies? Melchizedek! He almost spoke the name aloud but managed to contain himself.

Billings noted the change on Quarston's face and asked him, "Well? What did the agent say? What are they involved with? Biological weapons?"

Rapidly composing himself, Quarston answered a little too matter-of-factly that the company researched extending human life. He then added the joke that the New Jersey agent had made about its being a poor investment. Burke and Billings both laughed, but Billings' suspicions of Quarston were growing. He was confident now that the G-man knew much more than he was letting on.

The voice in the phone again caught Quarston's attention. "You won't believe this, either, but it seems that something like two-thirds of the lab equipment was recently shipped off to Italy."

"Where in Italy?" asked Quarston.

JEFFREY TIEL

"Um . . . let me see. Ah, here it is . . . Napoli?" offered the agent.

"Naples—right. That'd be the port of entry. And from there?" pressed Quarston.

"Nothing here indicates what happened to the equipment then," admitted the agent.

"Okay, tell me this: who owned the New Jersey firm?" queried Quarston.

"Good question," answered the agent with frustration. "We've been trying to piece that one together for an entire day, and you would not believe the complicated net of corporations all over the world that seem somehow connected but not in charge of this company! I'll let you know once we finally pin it down though, okay?"

"Thanks very much," answered Quarston hanging up the phone.

"So, we're off to Italy?" asked Billings to Quarston with amusement.

"If only," laughed Quarston. "I have a friend at the American consulate in Milan, and I'll ask him for help in tracing the shipment past Naples."

"Well, Gentlemen, neither my interest nor my budget permit me to go gallivanting all over the world, so I'll wrap things up here with Beecham and look forward to hearing from you on your end?" concluded Burke.

"You bet," answered Quarston. "And thanks so much for your help."

*   *   *   *

Rothschild smiled as he heard Michelle Andover explain that she had reestablished her lab at the site in Fiesole, an old Roman town overlooking the city of Florence. Purchasing the old convent at the crest of the hill in Fiesole had proven rather simple, as new novitiates to the order were increasingly rare. Hiding the path to eternal life within a convent brought a certain ironic satisfaction to Rothschild. But Michelle added something that drew him from his musings back to the matter at hand.

"Since this equipment is extremely sensitive, it has to be safeguarded against earthquake. I checked the seismic data for the area and noticed that the fault line that runs beneath Italy is showing more activity lately."

"Yes, that is true," answered Rothschild with a smile. "People say that Vesuvius is due to erupt again soon."

"Sure it is," Michelle chuckled. "But we cannot take any chances with this material. So, I'm going to requisition some special balancing equipment that will keep the primary machinery steady in case of a minor earthquake."

"I understand. Don't worry about the costs. How much of a delay will this cause in the viral production?" he wondered.

96

"Not long, maybe just a few days," she answered. "A German company produces exactly what I require."

A subtle frustration, alloyed with some emotion Andover could not capture, clouded Rothschild's features. "Do it."

* * * *

After returning to Boston, Quarston visited the FBI lab to see where Harry was with the analysis on the manuscript fragments.

"Just completed, Sir; take a look at this!" exclaimed the lab technician. "I found all or part of it in all three document fragments."

"What is it?" asked Quarston staring at the image from the MRI scan.

"It's a cartouche, Sir, made of solid gold," explained Harry.

"What's a cartouche?" Quarston asked.

"It's kinda like a name, but mixed with titles, for important ancient Egyptians. They write the hieroglyphs in a vertical line like this," said Harry, pulling out a pad of paper and hastily drawing some symbols. "Then they circle them with a rope that merges in a knot at the bottom of the name, like this," he continued, adding the figure to his drawing. "Kinda like this, see?" he asked Quarston.

"Okay, I do see, but what do the symbols mean? Whose name is it?" asked Quarston.

"Got me, Sir. I never learned ancient Egyptian. But I do have a theory about why the cartouche is found in all these texts."

"Oh, really, wonder boy," remarked Quarston, "and what is that?"

Harry laughed, "Well, you know how we use watermarks on our paper these days?"

"You think it's like an ancient watermark?" interrupted Quarston.

"Yeah, because it's in the same basic place underneath the writing in each fragment. I think that whoever constructed these parchments measured out the pages in advance, and placed the cartouches under them. They marked them as his, and vouched for their authenticity to anyone who ever found them."

"Pretty expensive watermark," muttered Quarston.

"All parchment would have been expensive at the time these were constructed, Sir. And if our guy could read and write, he worked for someone with lots of money," Harry concluded.

Quarston smiled at his up and coming apprentice, "Okay, Sherlock, well done. In the meantime, I know who to call to help with the translation of the hieroglyphic symbols in that cartouche. Can you return the manuscripts to the safety deposit box and re-inventory the key?"

"You bet. Uh . . . one other thing?" asked Harry.

"Sure," said Quarston.

"When am I going to find out what this is all about? My curiosity is really piqued!" explained the technician.

Quarston looked Harry straight in the eye. "I know, Harry, I really do. But people have been killed over these documents. So, for right now, the best thing is that you don't talk about this and forget you've seen them. Okay?"

"Then I guess I'll take a bottle of Jack Daniels," said Harry reluctantly.

"For Christmas?" laughed Quarston.

"Yeah, don't forget!" said Harry laughing.

CHAPTER SEVENTEEN

Maurice St. Claire approached the richly decorated doors to Rothschild's palatial office. The familiar Medici crest with its six balls dominated the wall above the doorway. St. Claire knew that he was only one of a handful of people in the world that were aware of the connection between the Rothschild and Medici names, so successful had the Rothschild family been in obscuring any connection to the infamous family.

Buzzed in by his employer, St. Claire entered the room to report on the status of their operation in the United States. But before he could begin, Rothschild jumped up from his desk and greeted his special operations director warmly. St. Claire was surprised at the show of affection, until he realized that his boss must have made some progress on the manuscript fragment research. He listened intently as Rothschild described Andover's discoveries and operational plan. Rothschild explained the scale of the operation necessary to distribute the virus, and the unique makeup of medical and urban commando personnel necessary for the special action teams. St. Claire had a wide network of persons to choose from, and since money was plentiful, he offered his confidence that he could prepare the teams with instructions for capturing Melchizedek and flying him to Florence. Additionally, Maurice assured him that the American operation was complete. The assassin in Cleveland had killed the younger Hentersheim before succumbing to an unfortunate boating accident, while his own men in Cleveland and New Jersey had gotten out of the country safely.

"And the New Jersey situation?" asked Rothschild.

"Secure," answered St. Claire. "We erased all the research data, as well as all communications between you and Dr. Andover."

"And the banking records?"

"We added those to her safe. Pity she'll never know how rich she really is," laughed St. Claire.

"Indeed," answered Rothschild. "An awful lot of money to send the American authorities on a wild goose chase."

"But well worth it," offered St. Claire. "The Americans hate loose ends. They'll be looking for Dr. Andover now, though. But she's safely isolated here, and depending on what you want done with her, we can revisit the question of her appearance and identity or eliminate her."

"Good. For now we need her. She's critical to the next phase of the project."

"Yes, I understand that. I'll make the arrangements you've asked for. But please be aware, Sir, that an operation of the magnitude you envision is unlikely to go unnoticed by the Western intelligence agencies."

"I do understand that," answered Rothschild. "And that's why Michelle Andover is actually part of something much larger than she or anyone but myself knows. When the time comes, our rivals in Turkey will have a great deal to explain."

St. Claire laughed. He was always astonished at the brilliance and irony he found in Rothschild. He had worked in military intelligence for years before going free-lance and eventually being hired by Rothschild. He'd initially marveled at working for someone who actually understood the intricacies of espionage and covert action, but after ten years with Rothschild and with close to two hundred million dollars in his own network of secret accounts, he was confident in his employer's conjuring.

* * * *

Munich, Germany

Otto Rosenberg received a phone call with a special code indicating that he was to assemble for a meeting with his commando cell leader. After serving with Israeli special forces but being discharged for a 'misunderstanding,' he had worked in nearly every theatre of military operations across the world as a mercenary.

Walking into the pub in Munich indicated by the coded phone call, he noted one of the others near the staircase in the rear. As Rosenberg headed toward him, his colleague nodded up the stairs, where Rosenberg found most of the other members of the team assembled in a quiet room overlooking the bar. His cell leader, Reinhardt Drexler, announced that they had a special assignment with rewards equal to four times their usual requirements. They all squirmed at this, figuring this increased the likelihood of their deaths as well. Drexler only smiled at their discomfort, explaining that they were merely on call to pick up a single sick individual from a hospital . . . if he showed up at all. When Rosenberg asked whether they were supposed to kill the sick man, his commander answered no, they were supposed to turn him over to a special medical team that would be joining them.

Rosenberg raised an eyebrow and asked, "What kind of 'sickness' does this guy have? We're not getting involved in a biological weapons operation, are we? Just how expendable are we on this mission?"

"I've checked into that carefully," Drexler replied wryly. "Apparently, our employer wants this one man, because he thinks that he is a unique match for donation for an organ transplant for his son."

Rosenberg laughed dubiously, and the rest of the team joined him. Drexler continued, "Yeah, that's a good story. But nothing in the orders indicated any special handling by us or the medical team picking him up. It sounds like they just want to apprehend this guy."

* * * *

A satisfied Rothschild finished his tour of the Fiesole facility on the outskirts of Florence. Michelle Andover proved herself over and again not only as an eminent scientist but also as an effective manager. She had converted the chapel of the old nunnery into the centerpiece of their new production facility and was already half-way through the viral production itself. An old icon of the immortal Christ lay tossed aside on a pile of rubble, as the ultra-modern machinery hummed. Rothschild just began an ironic smile, as Andover interrupted his reverie.

"Sir, we need to think about two things at this point."

"Right," he acknowledged. "How we distribute the virus and how we render it untraceable to us."

"Precisely," she smiled.

"I assume you have worked out the former, and you expect me to accomplish the latter."

"That's what I hoped," she added. "We'll need to distribute the virus on multiple continents at the same time in order to maximize coverage. You have your retrieval teams ready?"

"Yes, they are ready at key urban centers within eight hours flight time of any location in the world."

"My distribution teams are currently training on handling and dispersing the virus. We need to deploy it at the major international airports. Each viral deployment requires only one agent and a driver. So, I'm prepping sixty-seven agents for the actual dispersal. They will carry a simple hair spray bottle in a shoulder bag, and they will use it in a ticketing line, so as to avoid security entirely. Then they will simply exit the airports and drive off. Since they have all been independently contracted, none of them are traceable to us."

"Excellent," replied Rothschild. "Since we have a retrieval team here in Italy, you will be assigned to it . . ."

"As if Melchizedek will turn up here in Italy!" she exclaimed, interrupting him.

"Yes, well . . .," he began. "I realize that's a long shot. In fact, I hope it's a long shot, because it would be unnerving to find he's been living across the street all along, wouldn't it?"

"Indeed it would," she acknowledged with a glance out the window. "But then I guess he could be anywhere, couldn't he?"

"Or anyone," he added, before continuing. "In any case, you will return here to your lab to conduct your research once Melchizedek is found. In the meantime, you can deploy with the Italian retrieval team."

"Good," she answered, "and we'll be prepared for him when he arrives. We have a superb secure medical facility in addition to our lab. My only real concern is what the major Western countries will do when they discover that an engineered virus is working its way around the globe."

"And they will discover it?" Rothschild asked.

"I wouldn't be surprised," answered Andover. "Ever since 9/11 the United States has invested heavily in biological detection technologies. And I would assume that the NATO countries are working together to prevent biological terror attacks."

"But this won't be an attack at all," objected Rothschild.

"Correct, which means they won't be alerted by dozens of sick people arriving at hospitals all over their countries. But they might well detect a new virus working its way across the globe, and if they test it, they'll discover it was bioengineered. That's the question: will they bother to test it at all?"

"We don't know. But we must expect that they will. The 'robbery' and destruction of your facility in New Jersey went perfectly, so they will have multiple possible suspects. Your people still in New Jersey are working with the authorities to help identify what was stolen and who might have taken it. The police have so many theories and possible culprits, they will be spinning their wheels for weeks. I see no evidence that they suspect we planned the fire," Rothschild added deceptively.

"Good," she answered, "then we are relatively safe. If they identify the virus together with the isotope, it will appear as though it was an action done to exploit our work by someone else with nefarious purposes."

* * * *

Munich

Otto Rosenberg sipped his beer, staring at all the happy German couples making love with their eyes. He would never fit into this country, he mused, in spite of his Germanic heritage.

Pushing his half-eaten sausage aside, Rosenberg wondered about his latest assignment. If teams were being assembled all over the world, combining paramilitary and medical elements, and if those teams were being funded at his team's level, then the cost of this operation had to be huge. And that meant national involvement. The United States? Britain? He couldn't be sure.

Finishing his fourth beer, he wondered if his old employers might not find his latest activities interesting. Maybe it was time to go home. And just maybe, if his information proved big enough, they would forget the past.

* * * *

Israel

Rosenberg's information found its way to Mossad headquarters and the attention of Yaakov Katz. Still trying to get used to his nicotine gum, Katz chomped away as he reviewed Rosenberg's file. A broad smile erupted on Katz's face, as he remembered the "little misunderstanding" with the foreign minister's daughter that had ended Rosenberg's career. Rosenberg had been a fool, to be sure, but he'd also been away from the nest far too long. And Katz agreed with him; it did appear that a major operation was underway with the kind of resources usually available only to nation-states.

Katz closed Rosenberg's personnel file and focused on the details of the report. The operational target appeared to be an individual person, someone known to be ill. Rosenberg had provided minimal details on the composition of the medical team attached to his unit. In fact, it was what he didn't provide that drew Katz's scrutiny. He initially suspected that the target was someone deliberately injected with a biological agent transforming him into a living bomb. But the expertise necessary to treat a person carrying a biological weapon was not included in Rosenberg's team. The team members seemed to include experts in hematology. While specialists on human blood would be important for a hopeful transfusion, Katz agreed with Rosenberg that the transplant account had to be a cover story. A donor who was ill was a risky donor. So, whose blood was worth a one hundred million dollar investment?

Or maybe it wasn't the blood. Maybe the blood was being used to identify a particular person whose value might exceed a hundred million dollars? But why try to identify someone through his blood? And how particular could blood be? Any given gene combination might well yield tens of thousands of people. But with DNA it could be exact, he mused. So, perhaps the operational sponsor had in his possession the DNA of a particular person who was worth a great deal.

Yet the target was known to be sick. How would that be known? If the sponsor already knew that the person was ill, then he'd likely know the identity of the person in the first place, in which case an operation of this kind would be ludicrous. Either he had intelligence that his particular target was sick, or else . . . or else the sponsor had made him sick! That was possible, he considered. Rumors had surfaced approximately fifteen years before that both the Russians and the Americans were working on means to reengineer viruses to target and either kill or incapacitate specific individuals based on a DNA match. His own people cringed at this possibility, because of the likelihood that the next Hitler would turn this into the perfect eugenics weapon, targeting Jews.

Katz looked over Rosenberg's report again. Sure enough, the operation was apparently world-wide. So, a virus would have to be created and employed on a global scale. If it could be collected and analyzed, its engineering would reveal a great deal not only about the technology necessary to engineer it, but also about the intentions of its creator. Katz decided that this information required the attention of the Prime Minister, who could then order a coordination between Mossad and the biological weapons detection apparatus within Israel. If a new, engineered virus was circling the globe, Katz's suspicions would be confirmed. In the mean time, he would continue to glean information from Rosenberg about the operation.

Katz lifted his phone and dialed the number for personnel. Rosenberg was about to be reactivated.

CHAPTER EIGHTEEN

Quarston returned to Boston College for yet another interview with his professorial consultants. He checked his wallet before meeting them in the faculty lounge. "More scotch, no doubt," he muttered under his breath as he entered the lounge.

"Roger!" exclaimed Beaufort, walking up to him. "How good to see you again."

"Hello, Roger," smiled Jacobson warmly. "How is your investigation going?"

Looking around him carefully, Jacobson then added in a whisper, "Did you find him?"

"No, not yet Professor," laughed Quarston.

"Too bad," began Jacobson but then added, "Well, maybe not."

"I've found something else, something inside the manuscript fragments that I thought you might be interested in," explained Quarston.

"You thought we'd be interested in it, or you needed our help to understand it?" asked Beaufort.

"A little of both," answered Quarston sheepishly.

"Uh-huh," nodded Beaufort, "just as I thought. Well, what do you have for us? Out with it!"

Quarston sat down in their now-familiar corner of the lounge and began to reach into his bag, when Jacobson interrupted, "Aren't we forgetting something, gentlemen? How can serious men have a discussion of this magnitude without the appropriate beverage?"

Quarston shook his head, as Beaufort exclaimed, "Yes, by God. I think you are right! Roger here must have thought we'd forget about that requirement for our service, don't you think?"

Feigning hurt and surprise, Quarston pulled not the manuscript photographs but his wallet out of his bag, "And I was just about to order us drinks!"

They all laughed, as a waiter came over to receive an order for yet another bottle of fine scotch, an assortment of nuts, a fruit tray, and three Macanudo cigars.

After they had all received their drinks and cut and lit their cigars to their satisfaction, Jacobson suggested, "Well now, my good boy, what do you say that you show us what you've got for us today?"

"Indeed," added Beaufort, leaning forward and selecting a berry.

Quarston reached into his bag again and this time withdrew a folder containing photographs of the cartouches. Only one manuscript fragment contained the entire cartouche, so he began with the pictures of the cartouche fragments and revealed the picture of the complete cartouche last.

"You mean that you found these inside the layers of the parchment?" asked Beaufort incredulously.

"And these images are from an MRI, right?" asked Jacobson right on top of his colleague.

"Yes, and yes, again," replied Quarston to them both.

Ignoring Quarston, both professors carefully studied the photograph of the complete cartouche. Jacobson turned to inquire whether Quarston had brought along a magnifying glass, when Quarston, already prepared, handed him one.

"Can you read what it says?" asked Quarston.

"Of course we can," replied Beaufort. "It's what it means that has us puzzled."

"Right," murmured Jacobson. "I mean we've got a royal cartouche all right, but instead of the usual sun disk following the *Sa* symbol, we've got an ibis. These are mixed images."

Beaufort put down his cigar, "But look at the name, Bob, the name! That would be the Egyptian form, wouldn't it?"

"It sure looks like it to me," replied Jacobson. "If I were an Egyptian, I'd probably represent the name pretty closely to that."

"I'm not sure I'm following any of this," interrupted a confused Quarston.

"Okay, here's what we've got," related Beaufort excitedly. Reaching into his bag, he pulled out his ever-present yellow pad and his trusty red pen. He motioned for Quarston to move his chair closer to his and began to draw a circle with a knot on its bottom.

"This is an Egyptian cartouche, or *shenu* in their language. It conveys continuous life or eternal life, and you'll often find it held in the claws of the vulture god Nekhbet. Okay so far?" he asked Quarston.

"Sure," Quarston answered, intrigued.

"Now, the royal families of Egypt wrote their names inside of cartouches . . ." began Beaufort again.

"Oh, I see," interrupted Quarston. "It would symbolize long life for the King, sort of like when we hear the phrase 'Long Live the King!'"

"Very similar to that, indeed, Roger," answered Beaufort, "though we should add that it symbolized the continued life of the king after death too."

"Okay, that makes sense, given the Egyptian emphasis on preparing for death with pyramids and mummies," Quarston nodded.

"Exactly. In order to fit an Egyptian name into a *shen* sign, however, you have to elongate it into a vertical oval, like this," Beaufort continued, drawing an oval on the yellow pad with the familiar knot tied beneath it.

When Quarston nodded, Beaufort added hieroglyphic symbols within the cartouche and then asked, "Guess whose name that is?"

"I wouldn't know . . .," began Quarston, "King Tut?"

"Good guess!" answered Beaufort, and then pointing to the symbols in turn, he pronounced, "Tut-ankh-amun."

Drawing an additional oval cartouche next to the first, he inscribed it with a further series of hieroglyphs and added, "And this is Ramses, one of the most famous royal names in Egyptian history."

"Since for the most part only royal family members inscribed their names in cartouches, the Egyptians had to find a way to distinguish the King's royal name from his family members," explained Beaufort.

"All right," answered Quarston. "How did they do that?"

"Well," continued Beaufort, "kings had five names, what we now call a five-fold titulary, because the names were also titles belonging solely to the king. Usually we find two of those names together on monuments built under a particular king's reign. The first of these we call the throne name, which during dynastic reigns tended to identify a whole series of kings."

"Like Ramses, you mean?" asked Quarston, making sure that he understood.

"Yes," acknowledged Beaufort. "We have a whole series of Ramses that we now distinguish by adding roman numerals, just like we do for European monarchs or popes of the same name."

"Right, like King George III," laughed Quarston.

"Correct," nodded Beaufort. "The other name we might liken to our first names, a way of distinguishing the various kings of the same dynasty from one another. We call these 'birth names' to distinguish them from the throne names. Would an example help?"

"Sure," laughed Quarston again. "It never hurts to see it, does it?"

"Seeing sure helps believing," replied Beaufort, altering the usual form of that cliché. Drawing another cartouche next to King Tutankhamun's cartouche, he next inscribed it with an additional series of symbols and then read them aloud, "Nebkheperure."

"That is King Tut's first . . ." Quarston hesitated recalling the technical term, "or birth name?"

"Yes," answered Beaufort, "and when he ascended to the throne of his father, he received the addition of the royal throne name."

"Okay, I see that," acknowledged Quarston. "Then tell me how you could tell that Nebkheperure was a king rather than just a prince."

"Right, the main point, indeed," nodded Beaufort.

Drawing a tiny bird and then a small sun disk together above the cartouche, Beaufort turned to Quarston and said, "We translate these symbols as *Sa Ra*, or 'son of Ra', and this indicates the birth name of an Egyptian king."

"And only an Egyptian king would have such a symbol?" pressed Quarston.

"Absolutely," answered Beaufort, "for only he could lay claim to being the son of the sun god."

"Hmm . . ." Quarston mused, glancing over at the photograph of the cartouche taken from the recovered manuscripts.

"You see some similarities?" asked Jacobson.

"Yes, I do," replied Quarston, as he reached for the photograph.

Pointing to the cartouche in the picture, he continued, "This cartouche would mean that whoever's name lies within is a member of a royal family, right?"

"Correct," said Beaufort.

"And atop the cartouche is the little bird that you translated as *Sa* or 'son of', but it's not followed by the circle, the sun disk, so it doesn't mean 'son of Ra'?"

"Perfect, my boy, just perfect!" exclaimed Beaufort delightedly.

Breaking in, Jacobson added, "Instead of a sun disk, in your manuscript cartouche we find another little bird known as the ibis."

"So, this guy was not a pharaoh, a king of Egypt?"

"Definitely not," Jacobson answered Quarston, "but he was of royal blood . . ."

"Because his name is inscribed within a cartouche," Quarston nodded confidently.

"Right," continued Jacobson. "The ibis bird is one of the three ways of indicating the god *Djehuty* which is sufficiently difficult to pronounce that we tend to use the popular Greek rendition, Thoth."

"What are the other ways of indicating Thoth, Professor?" inquired Quarston.

"Well, he is often portrayed as man with an ibis bird head, or as a baboon, or as either of these with the lunar symbols of a full and crescent moon as his crown. If you've ever noticed the way baboons sit on their hind legs like a dog but with their paws raised up toward the warming sun, you'll understand why the Egyptians adopted that position as the position of worshipers before the gods—you'll see this position in Egyptian painting. Thus, the baboon became a creature of divine significance for them."

"And who is Thoth exactly?" asked Quarston.

"Thoth was the god of wisdom, writing, and magic. The Greeks equated him with Hermes, the messenger god," explained Beaufort.

"Just so, just so," agreed Jacobson.

"So, this guy was the son of Thoth, not the son of Ra, meaning he was not a pharaoh; but he was an Egyptian royal, a royal who somehow worked for Thoth as a priest or something similar?" asked Quarston.

"Yes, except for one detail," answered Jacobson mysteriously.

"What's that?" inquired Quarston.

"We don't think he was an Egyptian royal," stated Beaufort.

"Why?" asked Quarston, confused.

"Because an Egyptian royal person might well take on priestly offices, but those offices would represent major monarchial gods or their queenly consorts—gods like Amun or Horus, or consorts like Isis or Hathor," answered Jacobson.

"What was Thoth's status, then?" asked Quarston.

"Thoth was more of a lesser deity, a service or courtier god, recording the biddings of the ruling gods or judging the deeds of men."

"So, a royal identifying himself as a priest of Thoth would be like a Kennedy working bar?" asked Quarston, trying to grasp the significance of the professor's point.

"Something like that," laughed Beaufort.

"Well, if our guy is not an Egyptian royal, then I guess he'd have to be a foreign royal person, right? Is that possible? Could a foreign king be represented in a cartouche?" asked Quarston puzzled.

"Superb reasoning, Roger," answered Jacobson. "It's just what we were thinking."

"Right," agreed Beaufort. "In the great treaty between Ramses II and the king of the Hittites inscribed on the wall of the temple of Karnak, we find that the Hittite king's name is indeed inscribed in a cartouche."

"But without the *Sa Ra* indicator, right?" asked Quarston. "Because that would identify him as the Egyptian pharaoh."

"Precisely," answered Beaufort.

"Okay, so we've got a foreign king somehow associated with the god Thoth, is that it?" summarized Quarston watching the others nod. "Then I guess we'd better turn to his name. What do these hieroglyphs in the cartouche in this photo mean?"

"Why don't you guess whose name they spell out," offered Jacobson with a wicked grin.

"Melchizedek!" exclaimed Quarston.

CHAPTER NINETEEN

Florence

Back in his home in the palatial Medici villa, Rothschild stared again at the portrait of Cosimo de Medici, reflecting on his ancestor's calculated flirtations with danger. Rothschild knew that exposure in an operation of the kind he envisaged would lead to catastrophe, and so he had taken extensive steps to avoid vulnerability. Once the virus was released, global scrutiny would fall upon Michelle Andover. The robbery and destruction of the research facility in New Jersey would ultimately direct the attention of the Americans to her. Her presence in Florence was a secret. He had ordered her to fly first to Paris where her passport was replaced. Ostensibly, she was vacationing in the French countryside. That might buy her a few weeks. But once she went permanently missing, all attention would be directed toward her apprehension.

Rothschild considered that sacrificing her was only a modest loss. He rarely invested personally in people, because people were always willing to betray him. Greatness brought out the betrayal instinct in lesser men. Still, he liked Andover. Her intellect came close to matching his. Her knowledge of the Melchizedek mission had been a necessity. Moreover, eliminating her might not completely reduce his exposure, since one of his companies held a majority of the stock in her company. Granted, an investment connection wouldn't provide the grounds for a criminal indictment, but it would attract a hard look. Rothschild wasn't naïve. Princes of states acted as they always had, eliminating threats to their power without the niceties of criminal proceedings unless some advantage could be found in the propaganda effect of a trial. Why else did all of the Western nations employ highly trained covert operations units? What did the British Special Air Service or the American SEALs or Russian Spetsnaz do if not bring instant death upon persons declared without trial to be enemies of their respective countries? Rothschild did not relish the possibility of becoming a target of such an operation. His survival was based upon a carefully constructed false front.

Still, only Andover's direct testimony could assure the Americans that he was responsible for the virus. And the Americans killed based on solid information. Moreover, they liked 'lone gunman' theories; he could sacrifice Andover as a crazed scientist if necessary. But he needed her now, and keeping her anonymity in Italy would prove important. After the operation to capture Melchizedek was complete, he would keep her hidden indoors, away from the likely facial recognition capable satellites orbiting the globe, until he could alter her appearance or eliminate her. Preparing for the worst imaginable from one's enemies had proven to be a superb survival strategy for him, and so he had prepared his Turkish initiative to ensure that the Americans would find hands other than his behind the controls of Michelle Andover.

* * * *

Quarston poured the professors another round from the bottle of scotch, as they all puffed on their cigars and reflected on the significance of the cartouches found within the manuscripts.

"So, your technician friend thinks that they functioned like an ancient version of a watermark, eh?" asked Beaufort.

"Yeah, makes sense to me, but then we're not scholars," admitted Quarston.

"Well, we are, but we don't have any better hypothesis, because we've never seen anything like this before. The fact that the cartouches are found in all the manuscripts fragments does make your friend's hypothesis likely. It's just remarkable to think that he ordered entire scrolls constructed with these small cartouches buried inside them. Even though the gold content is minimal, it's still quite a lot of work," explained Beaufort.

"But it would dramatically indicate that the parchment belonged to the Melchizedek Record, wouldn't it?" asked Jacobson.

"Sure, it would," added Quarston.

"All right, that makes sense, but here's something that doesn't," began Beaufort. When they both turned to him, Beaufort continued, "Why would Melchizedek, a priest of the God Most High be working for Thoth?"

"Yeah, I've been kinda wondering about that too," explained Quarston.

"Good question," began Jacobson who thought for a moment before continuing, "I think I have a possible answer."

"Shoot," replied Beaufort before exhaling a perfectly formed smoke ring.

"You know that the worship of *Adonai* by the Jews was only monotheistic in a sense, right?" Jacobson asked Quarston.

"I'm not following," admitted Quarston.

"Well, what is monotheism?" Jacobson began dialectically.

"The view that there is only one God," answered Quarston.

"Is that 'god' with a capital 'G'?" asked Jacobson.

"Er . . . I think so," began Quarston puzzled, "Why?"

"Because when we use the upper case 'G,' what kind of being do we denote?" asked Jacobson.

"The supreme being," replied Quarston.

"Correct. And how many supreme beings can there be?" he pressed on.

"Only one, on pain of contradiction. I remember metaphysics. Supremacy is superlative, so there cannot be more than one. If there were two omnipotent beings, then they'd cancel each other's power out, and neither would be omnipotent. So, there can be only one supreme being," concluded Quarston.

"Well argued," replied Jacobson. "Now, what does the term *elohim* in Hebrew denote?"

"God," replied Quarston.

"Lower or upper case 'g'?" asked Jacobson mischievously.

"I want to say upper, but your face suggests lower?" wondered Quarston aloud.

"Correct, lower. So, there are multiple gods, *elohim*, throughout the Hebrew Bible. But there is only one *Adonai*," explained Jacobson.

"All right, one supreme being among lots of lesser beings, and the lesser beings are 'gods' in a lower-case sense?" asked Quarston for clarification.

"Right, to be a 'god' is simply to be an immaterial being," explained Beaufort.

"You mean, like an angel?" asked Quarston.

"Just so, in fact in the Psalms God speaks to the angels and calls them the 'gods'!" exclaimed Beaufort.

"Really?" asked Quarston. "You mean the Hebrew Bible recognizes that there are multiple gods, a pantheon of sorts, but that *Adonai* is the supreme one?"

"Almost," clarified Jacobson. "Not supreme among the group, but supreme intrinsically, in other words, the supreme being himself. So, *Adonai* isn't just the king of the gods like Ra, for *Adonai* is different in kind from the other gods. *Adonai* is *the* supreme being, the infinite being. This is why the prophet Isaiah spends so much time clarifying that there is no other god like *Adonai*; there is only one supreme being, and *Adonai*, the Lord, is he."

"Okay, I think I understand that, so . . .?" Quarston inquired.

"So, just to give you one example and then I'll make my larger point, do you remember the story of Moses fighting the sorcerers in Egypt?" asked Jacobson.

"Sure, he threw down his rod and they threw down theirs, and they all turned into snakes but Moses' snake ate the other ones," answered Quarston.

"Right, and then the ten plagues come upon Egypt, right?" asked Jacobson.

"Sure, ten awful plagues as judgment on the Egyptians for enslaving the Israelites and not releasing them," added Quarston.

"Not exactly," began Jacobson.

"What do you mean?" interrupted Quarston in surprise.

"I mean that several times the text of Exodus depicts *Adonai* as saying that he is judging not only the Egyptians but the Egyptian deities. Each of the plagues is directed against an Egyptian deity. *Adonai* says that he will obtain glory from these other gods."

"So, the other gods are real beings, in competition with *Adonai*, and *Adonai* is going to defeat them through the plagues, because the Egyptian gods will be unable to protect the Egyptian people in the very areas that the deities are supposed to lend their protection, is that it?" asked Quarston.

"Right," asserted Jacobson.

"So, how does Melchizedek fit into this?" asked Quarston.

"Is Thoth targeted by *Adonai*?" asked Jacobson.

"Oh, I see what you are getting at," interrupted Beaufort. "You mean that Thoth might not have been a demonic being at all, and that Melchizedek in serving him might have been serving a true servant of God, an angelic type of servant?"

114

"You mean that some of the pagan deities might actually have been good guys, angels, who people mistakenly worshipped?" asked a surprised Quarston.

"Possibly," acknowledged Jacobson.

"Well, if I were an angel, I'd be kind of chagrined to have people worship me!" objected Quarston.

"Absolutely!" affirmed Jacobson. "And they were! How many times do the angels of the Biblical texts have to tell people, even the heroic saintly ones, 'Don't worship me!'?"

Quarston stared at him, a little bit puzzled, before he finally ventured, "They don't, do they?"

Jacobson stared at him with that professorial look of disapproval.

"Okay, I guess they do," Quarston changed his answer. "But seriously, I really don't get that, because if I met an angel, I think I'd be scared out of my skin! Who would have time to worship such a being if he were running for his life?"

"You're right," Jacobson continued. "That's the other reaction the angels usually get, so they're always saying, 'Fear not' and 'Peace'!"

All three laughed at that remark and then took a moment to refill their glasses.

"So, Thoth, one of the gods of wisdom may be a noble angelic being. Remember that the Proverbs of Solomon represent wisdom as a goddess, and then St. John's Gospel as well as the Epistle to the Hebrews identify wisdom with the Word, the logos of God," explained Jacobson.

"Well, that may be a stretch, for the angelic 'god' of wisdom may just be an angel, not the Son of God himself," qualified Beaufort.

"And isn't it also a stretch to say that just because Thoth is not targeted in the Exodus story—and I figure you know that because there are no baboon plagues—that somehow he is legitimate, while the other Egyptian gods are demons pretending to deserve worship?" objected Quarston.

"If that were all I had by way of reasons, yes, but now we know that Melchizedek served as a magician or priest under Thoth, so why would he devote himself to the service of a demonic being?" asked Jacobson.

"Especially if as you argued earlier, he is supposed to represent the kingship and priesthood of Christ?" added Beaufort.

"Right, and notice too how his cartouche carries both kingly and priestly symbols. Isn't that fascinating, given Melchizedek's status?" asked Jacobson.

"It's astonishing, frankly," admitted Beaufort, while Quarston examined the cartouche again. "I mean what we seem to be saying is that

Melchizedek made his way to Egypt and somehow was recognized as a foreign king by the Egyptians and was given a priesthood under the god Thoth. Given something to do, I guess, a kind of royal appointment."

"And that some of the ancient gods were actually real beings, finite spirits who were either good or bad, angelic or demonic, and that Thoth must have been a noble one, more like an angel," surmised Quarston.

"And Melchizedek served, but didn't worship Thoth," added Beaufort.

"That's what I'm thinking," concluded Jacobson with feigned smugness, until he burned his fingers on his cigar wrapper when he tried to pull one last draft through the nearly consumed stogie.

"So, now I've got another connection for Melchizedek, in Egypt!" exclaimed Quarston after laughing at Jacobson's predicament.

"At least you have an ancient connection," noted Beaufort.

"Very well, gentlemen, I trust that you will continue to keep this little secret just between ourselves?" Quarston asked.

"Someday you'll tell us the whole story of your investigation?" asked Beaufort.

"I promise I will tell you all I can," replied Quarston.

"Very well then, the secret remains between us," asserted Jacobson, and Beaufort raised his glass in honor of the commitment.

CHAPTER TWENTY

Michelle Andover listened intently to the receiver of her secure telephone in the office of her new Fiesole lab. Smiling, she finished the call and then dialed the number for Rothschild's secure line. As she waited for him, she couldn't help but be drawn yet again to the beautiful crucifixion scene frescoed into the wall of her office, what had been the quarters of the superior nun who had originally run this former convent. It was the feeling of pity for the man that drew her to the figure painted at the crossroads of the medieval and renaissance eras. Sounds on the other side of her call drew her away from her reverie.

"Sir?" she addressed Rothschild formally, as always.

"Yes Miss Andover," he replied, ignoring her multiple doctorates. She had become used to his formalism, recognizing that in his view he lived far above his employees, and frankly, as she thought about his assets, manner, and capabilities, she accepted it. Americans liked to live in the illusion that everyone is equal, but the who's who of invitations to important events in the States told another story.

"We're ready," she emphasized happily.

"Already?" he asked in surprise. "You continue to impress me, Miss Andover."

"Thank you, Sir," she replied, somewhat frazzled that she found herself blushing and straightening her lab coat. "We are operationally ready: the virus is complete and has been transferred to the deployment agents who will commence their actions at the world's international airports in just under twenty-two hours."

117

"And you have kept Mr. St. Claire aware of your progress?" he asked her.

"Yes, indeed," she answered confidently. "Mr. St. Claire assures me that both the medical and paramilitary components of the retrieval teams are prepared."

"Excellent," Rothschild answered, his own excitement stoked. "And once the virus has been released . . ."

". . . it will spread across the globe in about a week," she answered his unfinished question. "And then we'll have him, sir!"

* * * *

A day after talking with the professors again, Quarston received a call from Billings in Washington.

"I spoke with your Jersey agent," Billings explained without any preliminaries, "and then put my classified research branch onto the case. Seems that the ultimate owner of that burned lab is a Frenchman named Laurence Rothschild."

"Oh, a Frenchman? Not Italian?" asked Quarston disappointedly, thinking of the Italian destination of the cargo sent from the burned out lab in New Jersey.

"No, he's French all right," answered Billings, pausing and then adding for effect, "At least now."

"What do you mean?" asked Quarston noting the way that Billings was toying with him.

"Two things," offered Billings. "First, he lives in Italy now, in Florence."

"Okay, that is interesting, isn't it?" mused Quarston.

"Yeah, and second, this guy's family history extends way, way back. I mean, this guy is politically and socially connected to *everybody*, even the famous Medici banking family."

"The Rothschilds go that far back?" pressed Quarston.

"Definitely, this branch does, very far back and always very powerful and wealthy, and their activities are cloaked in secrecy. These aren't the wine-making Rothschilds, you understand. It was damned difficult just to trace the family lineage, something you'd think they'd be proud of."

"Well, maybe not," offered Quarston. "What do you know of the Medici?"

"Actually, very little—just that they are famous," confessed Billings. "Who are they?"

"It's who they were," Quarston emphasized the last word for effect.

"You mean that they are gone now?" asked Billings.

"Yep, died out in the mid-18th century or so, but before that they owned nearly everything and everyone in Europe, because they held everyone's loans. And I mean everyone, kings, popes, dukes, you name it," explained Quarston.

"Well, how do you know so much about them?" asked Billings with admiration and growing curiosity about Quarston.

"Oh, they figured importantly in my college studies of the Renaissance," answered Quarston.

"Speaking of the Renaissance and Italy," continued Billings, "what did your man in Naples figure out?"

"He's in Milan," corrected Quarston. "But he's supposed to call me some time today with the results of the Neapolitan police investigation of that cargo sent from the New Jersey lab."

"Okay, give me a call once he does," answered Billings.

"You bet," Quarston answered and then hung up the phone.

Quarston leaned back in his chair wondering just who this Rothschild was and how they'd ever manage to pursue a case against someone whose political connections were better than those of the President of the United States.

*   *   *   *

Florence

After flying to Italy with the rest of their team from Munich, Rosenberg and Drexler met with the head of their medical attachment, a doctor who introduced herself as Janet Langley. She explained that they were looking for a person exhibiting a special pathology, and that they expected him to turn up in a hospital. Since they did not know where their target was located, combined medical/paramilitary retrieval teams were being deployed all over the globe to extract him once he was found. Using Florence as their headquarters, Langley explained that their team would be responsible for Italy as well as Southern France, Switzerland, and Sicily. Langley added that if their target were located in a hospital within their search area, then Drexler's military team should be prepared to support his extraction from the hospital covertly. They would support the medical team's entry into the hospital ostensibly to transport the subject to a facility with increased capability. Drexler then added that his team had already adapted the requisite medical equipment to conceal their weapons. Rosenberg decided this was the moment to acquire more information, so he asked Langley, "What kind of resistance are we expecting from the target?"

Michelle Andover had adopted the identity of Janet Langley in accordance with Rothschild's instructions. She answered, "Very little. We expect him to be rather ill."

"Then why the need for such a heavily equipped military team?" he asked.

"Because we must be prepared for the unexpected," she answered.

"Unexpected? You mean he has friends? Or others are pursuing him?" Rosenberg persisted.

"We have no intelligence to indicate that. But one cannot ever be sure," she explained.

"Well, what kind of sickness does he have? Is it contagious? Do we require special protections?" Rosenberg queried.

"No, we will all be safe. He is not contagious," Langley answered and then left the meeting.

Rosenberg didn't really expect her to identify the illness of their target, but he was pleased to know that Langley's own team wasn't taking special precautions. That meant two things. First, the target was likely not contagious. And second, it narrowed down the possible illnesses he might have. Mossad would find that information invaluable.

* * * *

Quarston hung up the phone and frowned. His connection in Milan proved less than helpful. The cargo from the burned out NJ lab had landed in Naples, all right, but as with so many things in Naples (so his contact had explained to him), the paperwork filed with the port authority claimed the equipment headed south for ancient Rhegium, now called Reggio di Calabria, on the straits of Messina. But the equipment's destination turned out to be a burned out warehouse and it naturally never arrived there. Moreover, Reggio di Calabria was hardly a cutting edge scientific community, so the equipment must have been destined for some other location. But Quarston's contact had no clue where that might be. A dead end, he thought, frustration growing. He called Billings to inform him of the results.

* * * *

New York City

A woman stood in the international ticketing line for American Airlines at JFK. A sleek brown purse hung over her shoulder, and she towed a Briggs & Reilly roller suitcase. She kept fussing with her hair, irritating the family behind her in line as well as the elderly couple in front of her. The line dragged back for seventy-five feet before one even approached the roped off zone. Finally, the woman reached into her purse returning her brush and extracting a bottle of hair spray. Twirling her hair this way and that, she sprayed copious quantities of the spray all about her head. The man behind her swatted at the air before realizing that what was falling upon him was not a spider web, but the fine mist of her spray. He was about to say something to the woman, when she abruptly looked up in alarm, and cried out that she'd forgotten her passport. She rushed past the irritated man, who thought with satisfaction that it served her right.

The virus found its way quickly into the lungs of about fifteen people. It infected the cells of the lungs and rapidly manufactured more of its benign cargo, before the defense mechanisms of its hosts recognized it as belonging to a family of invaders that it had seen before. The immune response was fairly rapid, the re-engineered polio virus instantly coming under the guns of the fully prepared body. Before completely overwhelming the virus, however, the irritation to the lungs caused a few coughs, spreading the virus onto still more unsuspecting victims. The same scene was repeated at international airports all over the globe. Within a few hours, the virus had made its way to virtually every corner of the industrial world.

* * * *

Washington, D. C.

Doctor John Horn was relieved as the airplane finally left the runway for the long trip across the Atlantic. He settled into his seat, weary from weeks of intensive work in the hospital. The thought that he'd be standing with his dear sister in front of the Florentine Duomo in about twenty-four hours was just enough of a stimulation to prevent his dropping off to sleep until they reached a cruising altitude of thirty-eight thousand feet.

* * * *

Israel

The first indication that his theory was correct was the sudden increased chatter in the intelligence community first in the United States and then in Britain, Germany, France, Italy, and Spain in rapid succession, and finally Russia about twenty minutes after that. Within thirty-five minutes of the quadrupling of the volume of encrypted radio traffic, Yaakov Katz received an emergency communiqué from the Israel Defense Force's own biological warfare detection unit. Katz had already issued orders for the study of the vector, even to the point of identifying in advance the most likely alterable and useable viruses. So, when he received news that it was an engineered strain of benign polio, his elation at his own predictive success was tempered only by his worry as to the full nature of this emerging threat.

Deciding to play his political cards when he had them, and figuring that the United States would identify the biological agent within another hour in any case, Yaakov called his counterpart in the Central Intelligence Agency and reported what his biological warfare detection team had discovered, namely that someone had spread a bio-engineered benign version of polio across the world. The Director of the CIA had already heard about the virus, but not its identity, and he thanked Katz for his help in identifying the virus. Katz smiled bemusedly, detecting a hint of aggravation in his counterpart. Now the CIA owed him a future favor. Given that the virus was benign, the Director explained that the United States would not be releasing information to the press. Katz sighed before answering; he never did understand how the United States Constitution had been interpreted so as to give their newspapers the status of a fourth branch of their government without any of the checks and balances placed upon the other powers. Dealing with the American government nearly always required political analysis on potential press response, something that frustrated serious professionals like himself. But Katz forced the unwelcome reflections out of his mind, so that he could concentrate on his objective. Physically smiling into the telephone to increase the congenial sound of his voice, he offered to send a liaison from the IDF bioweapons unit to coordinate with the other NATO powers in a joint investigation as to the perpetrator of this serious if not lethal incident. The CIA Director worried that this might be the precursor to a real attack, a feint intended to gauge Western response capability and timing. Katz confided that he agreed with that assessment and had placed IDF and intelligence forces on full alert to just that possibility.

Of course, Katz knew much more about the real purpose of the "attack" than did the Americans, but he would happily permit them to squander precious time drawing the conclusions he already knew. Part of the reason for the call into the Americans was to determine the degree to which the Director displayed panic. Katz suspected that a nation-state was involved in the attack, but the responses by all the powers he thought might have planned it suggested their surprise and genuine concern. Their mobilizations of costly assets showed that either they had planned for this level of deception, or else they really were taken by surprise. In which case, Katz wondered who was behind the attack, and what target was worth this much cost and risk of exposure. He would await the analysis by his bioweapons experts and any new information that Rosenberg might offer, before proceeding further.

* * * *

Quarston read the telex from Italy concerning his request to interview Laurence Rothschild. The man was currently unavailable, but his company's statement indicated their confidence that the police within the United States would soon discover the arsonist behind the fire in the New Jersey lab. Quarston was not surprised that the Italians would protect Rothschild. The United States would not likely detain one of its own citizens, especially someone of Bill Gates's financial status, merely on the request of an allied nation. Quarston would have liked to gauge Rothschild's response to his questions, but Rothschild, whether involved or not, was not going to make that very easy for him.

Quarston read over the additional research that the Bureau had conducted on Laurence Rothschild since his name had come up in the investigation. The man appeared to have fingers in pies all over the world, and most of them were innocuous if not noble. He supported medical research of all kinds, archeological digs throughout the world but especially in Egypt, and his business interests were eclectic. Quarston thought about what held all of these interests in common, and given his discovery of the cartouche contained within the manuscripts, he wondered if Rothschild's support of Egyptian archeology together with his interest in life-prolonging technologies might not indicate a possible connection to Melchizedek. He thought about the discussion he'd had with the professors regarding reasons people might have for trying to acquire Melchizedek. What's more, Quarston thought, Rothschild had the financial resources to run the sizeable operation that was behind the string of criminal actions in the United States that Quarston was convinced were all linked. So, means, motive, and opportunity? The wealthy always have opportunity, chuckled Quarston, because they can always pay for an alibi or simply contract someone else to do their dirty work. More and more Quarston suspected Mr. Rothschild. He looked over the file again, and saw that on the face of it Rothschild was a saint, decorated and honored with dozens of awards for his significant philanthropic efforts.

Quarston shook his head when his beeper activated. It was the Assistant Director's number, his immediate supervisor he saw, so he quickly called in to his superior's office, and was alarmed to discover that the nation's Biowatch early detection system had been activated. He was to report to the Assistant Director's office to await instructions, as all other investigations would be put on hold.

CHAPTER TWENTY-ONE

Rome

John Horn disembarked from his plane in Rome's airport, retrieved his baggage, and then purchased a ticket for a Eurostar train to Florence. He was extremely pleased to be back on the ground. The all-night flight had given him more sleep than he'd had in months, and he felt sprightly and eager to see his sister. He boarded the train and sat back into his seat for a nap for the trip to Florence. He heard a few people coughing a bit in the background, but nothing in their coughs alerted his medical sensibilities to any particular danger.

* * * *

Florence

An elderly gentleman, dressed not in the youthful chic of the wealthy Florentines but in the attire of a humble shopkeeper, emerged from a worn doorway onto the cobblestone streets of the city. He moved silently and unnoticed among the many tourists hauling their suitcases with their eyes fixed on the grand sights overhead. He skirted this way and that to avoid being run over by them, but eventually a pack of excited British school girls knocked him off his feet and onto the ground. Their embarrassed shrieks soon found him raised to his feet and hastily brushed off with rounds of apologies and urgent hopes that he was unharmed. The two carabiniari officers walking by cast an additional eye his way, but moved on steadily. One of the girls offered him a flower but coughed slightly when he reached out to accept it.

* * * *

Rothschild stood nearby, as Michelle Andover's team monitored the World Health Organization's medical alert network like hawks. Always a patient man, the excitement of the last few weeks put even his staid bearing to the test. His pager sounded, calling him away to the secure phone in his study. There he called back the number of his friend at Columbia who was reviewing the photographs he'd sent of the Thoth temple reliefs that he had received from Bartleby in Egypt.

"Hello, Laurence. You have made an impressive discovery here," offered Nikolai Borechnekov in his booming Russian accent.

"What have you learned, Nikolai?" asked Rothschild.

"It is clearly a dedication of the site of a new temple to the god Thoth. Thoth himself is dedicating the temple to himself. That is strange. Perhaps the Thoth figure is a priest of Thoth. I can't be sure of that, but the god figure is wearing priestly garments mixed with monarchial markings. That is what is so confusing. He has the marks of the baboon and the marks of Horus, the falcon god who guards the king. It's as though this figure is a mixture of god, priest, and king. It's really odd. I've never seen anything quite like it in my experience."

"Priest, king, and god?" asked Rothschild, his eyes narrowing.

"Yes. But that's not all. I agree with your archeologist's assessment that the tomb of which this wall relief is a part probably belongs to the architect or builder of the temple. This temple was his most significant achievement. I'd be willing to bet that the mummy bears the markings of Thoth in addition to the usual gods of the dead. He was probably a priest of Thoth himself."

"Okay, so you agree that the relief points to a genuine temple . . ." started Rothschild.

". . . in the process of being built at the time of this man's death, yes," interrupted Borechnekov. "Otherwise, the temple would not be deliberately left incomplete in the relief."

"So, was it ever completed?"

"I don't know," answered Borechnekov. "I've certainly not seen it at any site known to me. But how much of Egypt have we uncovered? We just cannot tell."

"Where would one look?" asked Rothschild.

"You mean where would one look to find the Book of Thoth?" retorted Borechnekov.

Rothschild smiled. Borechnekov wasn't stupid. The Book of Thoth had been a source of wonder and speculation for centuries. According to the legend it contained esoteric knowledge of the gods of Egypt delivered by the messenger god, Thoth. Those who read the book were imbued with magical powers, but no one ever made use of them according to the ancient myths, because the book's readers always collapsed into catastrophe and insanity. The moral of the story was that some knowledge was too wonderful for human consumption. Divine mystery was reserved for the gods. Some fragments alleged to belong to the book had turned up here and there, entire chapters of the book if you asked the occult groups that sought esoteric enlightenment. But nothing in these writings had ever seemed particularly magical or dangerous to Rothschild. He had read them all, of course, fascinated with the legend and its possible connection to Melchizedek. So far as he knew, he was the only person alive that realized that Melchizedek was in some way connected to Thoth. He had come upon the evidence quite by accident, when he had subjected the Melchizedek document in his possession to a number of different forms of backlit illumination. But he had never spoken of the remarkable discovery of the Melchizedek cartouche contained within the manuscript to Borechnekov. Nevertheless, Borechnekov was well aware of the allure of the genuine Book of Thoth, though Borechnekov's academic realism left him pessimistic that any part of it would ever be found.

"Yes," answered Rothschild after a pause. "Aren't we all interested in that book?"

Borechnekov laughed, "Laurence, Laurence, when will you ever grow up? Still pursuing your childhood mysteries?"

Rothschild bristled slightly at Nikolai's jibes, but calmly pressed the central issue. "Nikolai, what did you discover about the location of the temple?"

"You have the reliefs in front of you of course . . ." he began.

Rothschild rapidly pulled up the images on his computer. "Yes, of course."

". . . then do you see the river with the reeds in the background of the temple?"

"Yes, you think it's the Nile?" asked Rothschild.

"It may be. It would make sense. Khmun itself lies alongside the Nile. So, perhaps the temple is within eyesight of the river."

"That's not much to go on, Nikolai," said a somewhat dejected Rothschild.

"No, but I'll keep looking at the reliefs. I'll tell you this, though. That temple was definitely started, and those books the priests are carrying are the books of Thoth."

"Books?" Rothschild asked.

"Yes, definitely. Books!" answered Borechnekov. "There are chests and chests of scrolls, yet the names on the chest are all the same, and the sacred treatment of the scrolls is likewise the same. I think that it is a collection of books."

"A repository of ancient books, you mean?" asked Rothschild.

"Something like that, yes, perhaps an ancient library," replied Borechnekov.

"But in some way linked to Thoth?" questioned Rothschild.

"Yes. Perhaps the entire library is under his protection. Perhaps the books are all part of a massive sacred text. That is unclear to me. But do you see on each chest's corner a hieroglyphic figure?"

"No . . . oh, yes, I do," answered Rothschild. "They are . . . numbers!"

"Just so," answered Borechnekov. "That's why I suspect they are parts of one large collection of books or multiple chapters in one large book. Something on that order."

"Then if it is the Book of Thoth . . ." started Rothschild.

". . . it would have to be huge," finished Borechnekov.

CHAPTER TWENTY-TWO

Florence

The old man walked through the Piazza della Signoria approaching the Palazzo Vecchio slowly, passing the spot where Savonarola's body had burned at the stake. He paused there, as if remembering, and then moved on past the Loggia and towards the Uffizi. Suddenly he straightened up and then lurched forward vomiting profusely before starting to shake uncontrollably. Passersby called for help in a number of languages until members of the local police whose headquarters was housed in the basement of the nearby Palazzo rushed to his assistance. They found him collapsing into shock and called for an ambulance.

* * * *

John Horn walked through Florence, ever closer toward the massive dome that peeked through the streets of the ancient city. His sister was due to meet him later that day in the Piazza della Republica, so he decided to sneak ahead and view some of the city's legendary sights. The Duomo of Florence had been built by Brunelleschi displaying an ancient genius gathered, it was said, from his reverse engineering the design of the Roman Pantheon. Brunelleschi was the first in a series of brilliant Renaissance engineers produced by the city. The finishing touch, the great ball atop the dome, had been built by Verrocchio's school including his young apprentice, Leonardo da Vinci.

An ambulance rushed by him, its sirens blazing. Horn relaxed himself in the knowledge that he was on vacation. He decided to begin his tour with the Baptistery dedicated to St. John the Baptizer. During his college years he'd wondered about Byzantine influences on early Florentine art, and there was no better place to begin than with the Baptistery. Checking his watch, he confirmed that he had two hours to explore before meeting his sister.

* * * *

The Italian doctors quickly recognized the signs of radiation sickness in their patient. The treatment was straightforward and before long he was medicated and stabilized. They were keenly interested in how he had been exposed to a radioactive dosage sufficient to make him sick. But since he carried no papers, they would have to wait until he regained consciousness. In the meantime a nurse contacted the Italian Ministry of Health, alerting them to the potential radioactive hazard. The Ministry in turn contacted the World Health Organization.

* * * *

A whirlwind had taken Quarston's life by force over the last day, as the Biowatch protocol had been enacted in the United States. Quarston's boss as well as several other senior agents had taken him straight to Washington for a senior level meeting at FBI headquarters. Quarston now sat with other senior FBI agents as the Deputy Director introduced the Director of the FBI himself. The Director explained what they knew so far, that a virus had been identified spreading across the globe, and preliminary examination showed that it was the polio virus. Murmurs of surprise arose all around the room, as the Director hushed them, so he could continue.

"It's benign, people," he began.

"Benign?" asked one of the agents.

"Yes," the Director explained, "we received word from one of our allies, who detected the virus earlier, that it was bioengineered to render it harmless."

"Then what was the point of releasing it at all?" asked the agent.

"That's part of what we need to find out," answered the director. "We'll have our medical teams coordinate with the CDC to determine the nature of this bioengineering, exactly what it was for, and who might have done it, as well as where the original Polio sample came from."

"And our job will be to discover motive?" asked the agent.

"Yes," explained the director. "I want you to split into several teams to pursue every possible motive. Frankly, we are worried that someone released this merely as a test case to determine the effectiveness and vulnerabilities of our new Biowatch defense system. But that's just a hunch.

You are to consider every conceivable motive. The Deputy Director will work to coordinate the investigation and keep me informed."

The Deputy Director took over the meeting as the Director left, and the agents brainstormed to derive every conceivable motive given what they knew already. They agreed that they would be able to narrow down the options once the analysis of the virus was itself complete.

Quarston sighed as he was forced to redirect his attention to this new national threat. To his surprise, however, the Deputy Director called him over after the meeting and explained that he had been following Quarston's progress on the Hentersheim case and wanted Quarston to follow up the leads he was developing and their connections to the current crisis. He also wanted him to keep the CIA channel to Billings alive, so he was going to arrange a joint investigation headed by Quarston and Billings with all the support and additional agents that they would require. As the executive left the meeting room, Quarston whistled softly, amazed at the turn of events in his case.

* * * *

Israel

Yaakov Katz reviewed the report in front of him. The virus had been engineered to render it benign, but its extreme sophistication initially suggested work done in the United States or Russia. The biological weapons team evaluating the virus had then concluded that it had been developed in the United States, New Jersey to be exact. Amazed, Katz read of their identification of a unique radioactive isotope programmed for production within the virus. Katz called his secretary and asked for everything that he had on the New Jersey biotech firm.

* * * *

Florence

The technician monitoring the World Health Organization was surprised to see the report on the radiation sickness incident appear on his screen. He had been told to expect it anywhere in the world. That the incident occurred in Florence itself unnerved him. Was he in danger? Might his own family be in danger of getting sick? He had to dial the number for Michelle Andover three times before he finally got it right, alerting her to the WHO report. She ordered him to send it to Mr. Rothschild immediately, while she returned to the lab to review the information herself.

* * * *

Israel

Thirty minutes after speaking with his secretary, Katz was pleased to see a thick file lying on his desk. Biotechnology was such a potentially dangerous field that Israeli intelligence kept detailed records on corporations involved in it. Katz perused the file carefully, including the police report regarding the theft of the isotope and information pertaining to its production. The thieves had then torched the laboratory, or so that was what someone wanted the authorities to believe. He noted the investors in the company as well as its stated purpose to develop cell-regenerating technologies for the prolongation of human life. Katz thought about that carefully . . . prolonging human life.

He was startled by his secretary's knock on the door. Over two hours had elapsed since he had dropped off the file, and the secretary wanted to check if he needed anything additional. Katz realized that he'd been completely absorbed in his reflections on the events of the past few weeks, and in a flash of intuition, he knew who the target of the operation in Italy had to be. He immediately called the Prime Minister and arranged to see him.

* * * *

Florence

The elderly patient was not responding to the treatment as hoped, the doctor noted. His body actually seemed to be rejecting the treatment, if that made any sense, though the response wasn't exactly allergic. The doctor didn't know what to make of it, and decided to consult with some of his friends in Rome. In the meantime, he moved the patient to the ICU.

* * * *

Michelle Andover was elated to discover that Melchizedek had been found. She rushed to Rothschild's office to seek authorization for the retrieval mission. He was as shocked as she that Melchizedek had actually turned up in a Florentine hospital, shocked and deeply disturbed. The cliché that intelligence officers did not believe in coincidences was true, but Rothschild's position was beyond that of an intelligence officer. He knew that coincidences occurred all the time, but that he could not afford to treat anything as a coincidence. His solution was to call Maurice St. Claire to investigate the situation and reevaluate all security procedures, on the off-chance that Melchizedek had somehow become aware of their interest in him and had begun a counter-surveillance operation on them. Rothschild realized that he may have radically underestimated Melchizedek. He had been assuming he was dealing with a single person, but perhaps Melchizedek commanded a vast army of operatives all over the world, maybe even employing the resources of a major nation-state. But if that were true, Rothschild thought, then security at the hospital would have jumped in response to Melchizedek's admission. Yet Andover reported that her contacts at the hospital had confirmed the WHO report, and that their patient had just been moved to the ICU, without any noticeable change in personnel in the hospital. So, perhaps Melchizedek was alone, as he had originally suspected. Rothschild found it difficult to believe that someone with a large security apparatus could remain undetected; it was much easier to hide through simplicity. And so he relaxed slightly. He would let Maurice worry about the coincidence of Melchizedek's being located in Florence, while he proceeded with the planned extraction.

Turning back to Andover, he listened as she explained that she had expected Melchizedek to have been placed in a simple observation ward, making extracting him relatively simple. But for some reason the doctors had placed him in the ICU, leading to two problems. First, she had not expected the virus to create symptoms requiring that level of care, and she was concerned. And second, the ICU ward at the hospital was embedded within the labyrinth of the hospital's corridors, severely complicating the extraction plan. She recommended waiting twenty-four hours to see if he would be moved out of the ICU.

* * * *

Rosenberg's team received an alert from Janet Langley. Their target had been located in Florence, and his team was tasked to retrieve him from the hospital. They were ordered to set up surveillance around the site for the next twenty-four hours before proceeding with the extraction plan. Drexler asked her why they were delaying the operation at all, but Langley refused to offer him any explanation. Drexler was clearly bothered by the division of command, and fumed about it to Rosenberg before storming out of the room. Rosenberg then picked up the phone and dialed the number for Yaakov Katz.

Katz had known the Prime Minister for many years, and meeting with him over security matters was nothing out of the ordinary. But this case? Katz shuddered, mulling over its significance. Soon Katz found himself ushered into the Prime Minister's office, where after some brief pleasantries, he described the entire case to the Prime Minister, starting with a review of the matter since their last conversation. It was possible, he explained, that an ancient person named Melchizedek might still be alive. No, he added, he didn't know how that was possible. But his current evidence suggested either that it really was possible or that certain parties believed that it was. In any case, it would not benefit Israel for anyone claiming to be Melchizedek to suddenly show up on the international scene.

The Prime Minister knew his Torah very well, and asked why this was the case, since the Biblical story of Melchizedek showed him blessing their father, Abraham. Couldn't they use this figure to their advantage? Katz explained that even if this figure really were Melchizedek, there would be no way to authenticate him. As such, he would be believed only to the degree that what he said mapped onto what people already believed or wished to believe.

"Who was Melchizedek really supposed to be?" asked the Prime Minister.

"My best information, assuming that the Genesis reference to him is not an interpolation—something scholars never stop disputing—would make him a Palestinian king from Abraham's time," answered Katz.

"So, he might just as well legitimize Palestinian claims to the land," asserted the Prime Minister.

"Regardless of what he actually said, the Palestinians would surely lay claim to his occupation of the land prior to Abraham's arrival," offered Katz.

"And even if we argued that his blessing Abraham authenticated our claims . . ." began the Prime Minister.

". . . the fact that that authentication was required of a Palestinian king demonstrates that the land is inherently theirs. What they authorize in one time, they might revoke in another," suggested Katz.

The Prime Minister was about to reply, but paused for a moment. "Israel's status in this land is grounded in one simple fact: we are here now. Nothing else really matters. Prophecies and promises of ancient times can be debated, but we are here to stay," he exclaimed.

"Which is why Melchizedek is so dangerous," Katz said. "At best, if he were our ally, his disputed claims would be rejected by the skeptical world. At worst, he might actually support the Palestinians."

"In which case the world would find his claims perfectly believable," offered the Prime Minister ironically.

"Yes," answered Katz sardonically. "On matters regarding the state of Israel, that seems to be the usual pattern."

"And that would stir up who knows what new difficulties, wouldn't it?" asked the Prime Minister.

"That's what I fear too," concluded Katz. "Which is why I think we need to eliminate this man."

"Wouldn't it be better to apprehend him?" asked the Prime Minister.

"For what reason?" countered the intelligence chief. "We've already concluded that he cannot help us, and he might actually hurt us."

"I guess I'm just curious," admitted the Prime Minister pausing. "The operation will have to be run in Italy?"

Katz nodded.

"Well, we've carried out missions there before," recalled the Prime Minister.

"And we have someone on the inside this time," explained Katz.

"Really?" asked the surprised Prime Minister. "Well, that is good news. Presumably I'm not allowed to know how you accomplished that. I mean, Yaakov, you only drew these conclusions three hours ago!"

"I work fast?" offered Katz.

"Yes, I'm sure you do," laughed the Prime Minister. He knew that operational details would never be disclosed to him . . . unless something went wrong.

"Then the order is given?" Katz queried.

"Yes, I'll write it immediately," answered the Prime Minister gravely. Signing death sentences was far too common an affair for heads of states than most people realized.

CHAPTER TWENTY-THREE

K atz returned to Metsada, the special operations center for Mossad, and ordered the commander of the elite Sayerot Mat'kal to report to his office. Sayerot Mat'kal excelled in both anti-terrorist operations and hostage rescue. Since this operation likely involved both elements, he would prepare two complete teams, a primary team to intercept Melchizedek and a backup in case something went wrong. Both teams would be equipped with a medic prepared for radiological exposures. Given what Rosenberg reported to him, he had less than twenty hours to get his primary team in place. That would push his capabilities to the limit, but Katz was confident in his people.

* * * *

Florence
The doctor seemed relieved that his patient was showing some signs of improvement. The elderly gentleman entered in and out of consciousness, but with the gibberish he muttered, it was hard to tell the degree to which his apparently conscious state was really consciousness. He decided that he could safely move him out of the ICU.

* * * *

The nurse uploaded the doctor's orders into the new hospital management software system they had recently purchased from the United States. The Nashville based company had sent a team of two friendly and competent people to train the staff on the inner workings of the system. It permitted seamless interaction between managed care and billing. As soon as she entered the new instructions regarding her 'John Doe' (the American term always struck her as funny), a request for a room in the observation ward appeared two floors below. John Doe's bill for his daily care would reduce significantly, she knew. The nurse managing the regular care ward prepared the room for John Doe's arrival, optimistic for his chances to make a full recovery.

*   *   *   *

While the hospital management software included complete data encryption, the ultimate safety system for any network is that it be completely cut off from external access. The Nashville team had emphasized the importance of this to the hospital staff, but the system worked so well, that the administration had decided to upload the system to all of their computers, including those with access to the world wide web.

It hadn't taken long for Andover's team to break the encryption on the hospital billing system and locate the one patient with radiation sickness. As soon as he was moved from the intensive care unit, Andover again adopted the identity of Janet Langley, called Drexler, and ordered him to ready his team for the extraction. She gathered her medical team, as Drexler drove the specially equipped ambulance to pick them up and take them to the hospital. Rosenberg drove with Drexler, dressed as an emergency services provider, while Andover and her two medical assistants traveled in the rear. Once they reached the hospital, Drexler checked to assure himself that his additional three team members were in their positions, a sniper on the far roof, and two additional people dressed as civilians in the waiting area. With their communications check complete, Drexler stopped the ambulance, while Rosenberg and Andover removed the gurney. Andover's medical assistants gathered additional medical equipment, while Andover herself collected her briefcase. They entered the hospital and asked to see the managing director, who noted her professional bearing immediately. She handed him a transfer form indicating the immediate release of their radiation victim into her care. He double-checked the transfer order with the management system, and found that the order had been duly authorized by the hospital's administration. The authorization numbers on the physical transfer order matched perfectly. Andover smiled at him, as he showed them the way to the patient's room. She had placed the transfer order into their system the night before, but there was no way that the director could know that his entire system had been compromised. She laughed to herself at the ease with which the powerful could bend the good will of the common people to their own ends.

* * * *

The primary Sayerot Mat'kal team had already taken up a counter-surveillance position around the hospital. They had identified the enemy sniper fairly quickly, and an internal check on the waiting area had turned up an additional likely combatant. The Sayerot Mat'kal commander was a veteran of these kinds of hit and snatch operations from years of anti-terrorist operations against the enemies of Israel. His orders were clear: he was to neutralize the enemy combatants, capture the sick man, take a blood sample from him, and then neutralize him as well, ensuring that his body was completely consumed by sulfuric acid. Though he did not understand the need for the medical elements of his mission, he had prepared a warehouse in which to extract the needed blood and then dispose of the body. He had decided that the best time to take the enemy team would be as they were leaving the hospital, just as they entered their vehicle. They'd be experiencing a sense of relief at having successfully completed their own operation, rendering them maximally vulnerable.

* * * *

The elderly man was still quite sick, as Andover approached him. She checked his condition, and assuring herself that he was safe to move, she explained that he would be relocated to a facility equipped to handle radiological exposure. Moreover, she added, the government was interested in understanding how he had come to suffer this level of exposure.

The patient stared at her in a state of semi-delirium, but she also thought she detected a hint of alarm. She thought about administering a sedative, but decided that in his weakened condition, he would be unlikely to mount much resistance. As Drexler and Rosenberg wheeled him out of the room, Andover's assistants moved the medical equipment alongside the gurney, while Andover herself took up the rear.

* * * *

Upon entering the waiting area, Drexler's two additional men acted as they had all along. Ideally, their mission would amount to nothing more than reading a newspaper or two and then gingerly exiting the hospital. One of them grabbed an espresso and glanced nonchalantly at items in the gift shop, while the other sat among the patients awaiting treatment, feigning a cough.

As Langley and her team wheeled the patient round the corner toward the hospital entrance, their tension increased.

* * * *

The two Sayerot Mat'kal snipers had maintained their weapon sights on Drexler's sniper and the man in the hospital waiting area. The lead Sayerot Mat'kal sniper noticed his target in the waiting room suddenly tense up, indicating that the egress was about to occur. Sure enough, the plainclothes Israeli commando within the hospital waiting area rose to his feet as the ambulance crew pushed a gurney past him and out of the building. Confident that his back was covered by the over watch capability of his own sniper team, he cautiously followed his targets.

* * * *

Andover exhaled deeply as her team emerged from the hospital and approached the ambulance. She noticed that Drexler and Rosenberg were scanning the area around them like hawks, and that assured her that they were safe. Her assistants moved the gurney toward the rear, as Drexler and Rosenberg took up positions at the front and rear corners of the vehicle. But her patient suddenly tried to sit up, surprising all of them. She called to him to lie still, explaining that he was only being moved to improve his care. She then ordered her assistants to get him into the ambulance quickly.

* * * *

Watching from their own car, the Sayerot Mat'kal commander and his driver awaited the first shots, their cue to drive toward the ambulance and capture their objective. They observed their inside man walking toward the rear of the ambulance, past the medical team. Suddenly, gunfire erupted from the two rooftops, shattering the window in the hospital waiting area and killing one of Drexler's men in the hospital. The other sniper killed his counterpart on the far rooftop. The Sayerot Mat'kal commando passing the ambulance suddenly turned and unleashed a barrage of gunfire from his automatic pistol. The bullets hit Rosenberg first, and then swung in an arc toward the medical assistants. They just turned openmouthed as bullets tore open their bodies. Andover finally realized what was happening and dove for the ground next to the ambulance, the final bullets from the commando missing her by inches. Drexler jumped into action as soon as he heard the first shots, leaping into the ambulance and firing through the opening behind the driver's seat and out the back at the Israeli commando. The commando was struck in the chest, the bullets knocking him to the ground lifeless. Drexler then started the vehicle, as a car came rushing toward him.

* * * *

Drexler's other man inside the hospital noticed the rapid approach of the car, saw the passenger carrying a machine gun, and jumped into action. He withdrew a grenade from his bag, pulled the pin, and ran toward the hospital exit.

* * * *

In their heights on neighboring buildings, the two Israeli snipers continued their missions after the first kills, the one keeping an eye on the hospital itself, the other trying to get a clean shot on the driver of the ambulance. In spite of his focus on the hospital exit, the first sniper was surprised at the sudden emergence of a man holding a grenade. He instantly directed his fire at the new threat.

* * * *

As the grenade left his hand, Drexler's remaining man felt a searing pain tearing his shoulder, followed by a forceful thud in his abdomen. He then felt nothing as the world spun around him and his eyes fixed on a cloud overhead. It seemed so peaceful to him, as all sound and feeling faded from his consciousness.

* * * *

The grenade rolled underneath the oncoming vehicle and exploded, devastating the vehicle and instantly killing its occupants. In a rage the two Israeli snipers concentrated their fire upon the ambulance which drove wildly around the cul de sac at the hospital entrance in an effort to get to the open road. Drexler tried vainly to control the top heavy vehicle, while at the same time providing as erratic a target as possible. But as bullets tore into the ambulance all around him, he hit a curb near the parking garage, flipping the vehicle onto its side. Drexler kicked out the front window of the ambulance, thankful for the overhead cover of the garage. He grabbed his own assault rifle and took up a position at the garage entrance, trying to determine just how critical his situation was. He knew only that his team had been intercepted and that most if not all of them were probably dead. Presumably, their patient was still inside the ambulance. And Miss Langley, where was Miss Langley? He thought about putting a bullet into her, as he noticed her crawling from the original position of the ambulance, but then decided that she'd make an inviting target for someone else. He scanned the rooftops looking for some signs of the snipers that had shattered his vehicle, but he saw nothing, until movement in the building to his left caught his attention.

* * * *

Standard protocol for snipers is to shoot and then scoot to a new position, but never to directly engage their targets in a firefight. Their mission was silent and remote death; they were not assault troops. Nevertheless, members of Sayerot Mat'kal are chosen in part for their audacity and resolve. Seeing their friends killed in the car galvanized the snipers, and since the ambulance appeared to be neutralized, they decided to descend from their positions and move on the ambulance's location. The first sniper rapidly descended the staircase to the foyer of his building, but was unable to mentally process the glass front of the building shattering wholesale, as a stream of bullets from Drexler's gun crippled him. His partner in the next building carefully headed toward the parking garage from the opposite side of the street, guided by the sound of the assault rifle fire.

* * * *

Andover crawled toward the safety of a hospital utility vehicle, hiding underneath it as the gun battle raged all around her. She was more terrified than at any previous time in her life, and was shocked at the degree to which her limbs felt paralyzed. Her mind seemed to operate at one speed, while her body functioned in what appeared to her to be slow motion. She was unprepared for the reality of combat, the superfine focusing of the entire human nervous system on battle conditions. Soldiers could only function under these conditions for so long, but she wasn't even trained as a soldier, and the experience disoriented her. One part of her wanted to curl up into a ball and cry, while another was outraged at the disruption of her plan. Who were these people? Her mind demanded answers. But her throat was parched and her hands shook fiercely with the expectation that the next burst of gunfire might be directed her way. She finally decided to just play dead, waiting for the gunfire to subside. The Carabiniari would have to arrive eventually, and then she'd use her rhetorical skills to escape the scene.

* * * *

Inside the crumpled ambulance, the elderly man unstrapped himself from the gurney restraints and unsteadily tried to crawl out of the vehicle. He noticed the man firing the weapon near the garage entrance, so he headed toward the door at the far end of the garage's interior. He moved much more rapidly than one would expect of an elderly man, and as he went through the door and into the sunlight on the far side, his appearance differed substantially. The hospital gown was the same, but a young man had taken the place of the elderly patient. As the gunfire receded into the background, the young man re-entered the hospital through the employee entrance. He was relieved that no one interfered with him, guessing correctly that the gunfire held everyone's attention. He searched through the labyrinthine corridors of the hospital until he discovered a locker room. There he found clothes to suit his need, dressed, and headed back outside the hospital. He nearly collapsed several times, as the sickness that still surged through his body subjected him to unpredictable waves of nausea. He did not understand these feelings at all, reacting to them with both agony and surprise. Unclear on what to do next, he decided that he had to seek a place of safety, a place of sanctuary. A church would be perfect. He headed toward Santa Maria Novella.

* * * *

Drexler heard the door within the garage opening behind him and turned quickly but saw only the tail of a hospital gown fluttering through the closing door. He was about to move in pursuit of his quarry, when a powerful blow hit him from behind, directly between the shoulder blades. In spite of the force of the gun butt smashing into his spine, Drexler turned to confront his assailant with his weapon. But the remaining Israeli sniper had already readied himself to give Drexler another blow, turning the butt of his rifle this time against the muzzle of Drexler's gun. Drexler released his gun, dispersing the energy of his assailant, and instead drew his knife with his left hand and drove it into the exposed side of the Israeli gunner. The sniper writhed in agony, but managed to grab Drexler's face in his hands, squeezing with all his remaining strength. Drexler felt like his skull was about to crack, and dropped the knife in an effort to relieve himself of this new agony. He swung both his arms up and into the arms of his assailant, throwing the sniper back against the wall of the garage. The sniper managed to draw his own sidearm at this point and fired inexpertly at Drexler before his weapon jammed. The bullets only hit Drexler's leg, but penetrated his femoral artery, drenching both of them in blood. Drexler felt his conscious mind fade and tried to apply pressure to his leg to prevent the loss of blood. The sniper had by this time succumbed to the knife wound in his side and crumpled against the garage wall. Drexler took a step forward and then slid into unconsciousness himself, his body collapsing next to his opponent's.

* * * *

When the gunfire ended, Andover picked herself up and brushed off. She heard sirens in the background and decided to make her escape. She ran toward the ambulance and checked the interior, but Melchizedek was gone. She swore softly and then noticed Drexler and his counterpart huddled together like two men frozen to death in an icy but bloody wasteland. As the sirens grew louder, she noticed the rear door to the parking facility and made her own exit.

CHAPTER TWENTY-FOUR

A young woman entered the medieval church, her hands trembling as they had for the past three months when she had made the two kilometer trek to pray. She always came as early as she could, each time kneeling down in the fourth pew from the last on the left side of the church. She ignored the tourists milling about and trying the patience of the staff vainly waving off those determined to photograph the frescoes. The Prior had noticed her only three days from her first appearance. Her slender form of medium height couldn't be more than twenty-five years of age, he guessed. Her face was adorned with almond shaped eyes, slightly set apart. Blonde shoulder-length hair with wispy bangs plus the soft natural look of her skin gave her an elegant though personal, charming appearance. There was an innocent look to her eyes, full of joy and curiosity but not yet seasoned with life's ambiguities. And yet, she prayed with an urgency that reminded him of the Biblical story of Hannah, for though her mouth moved earnestly, no sound emerged.

Two months before he had gone up to her and blessed her, but the blessing did more to embarrass her. He had learned that she was an American studying in Florence for the summer, but devout on a level he had rarely seen. Saint Catherine offered her much consolation, especially the painting hanging on the rear wall of the church. He thought perhaps she was called to be a nun, and though she sought eagerly for divine guidance for her life, she was not strongly moved in this direction. The old priest watched her day after day, as each time she prayed for exactly one hour before quietly fading into the crowds that flocked what they really thought of as a museum. The church needed revenue and so catered to this attitude, selling books and postcards in the sacristy—the sacristy!—as well as charging admission to the church. The frescoes and paintings and sculptures, even the alternating black and white colored marble were not made for them, though, but for God. Ghirlandaio spent years serving God in this very church painting the frescoes that had become to the Prior the very pathway into God's presence. But this girl did not worship the paintings, something he knew in his heart was his soul's mortal danger. No, she came here to ask God something, which in her slender purity he had little doubt would be heard. This particular day was no different so far as the Prior could tell. She sat in the same pew as usual, next to an old man staring at the ceiling. So, he moved on to attend to his duties.

Anne Horn, for that was her name, noticed the change in scent first. She was overcome by the smell of roses, then jasmine, and finally honeysuckle. She sensed a radiance in the man sitting next to her . . . no, now she knew he was kneeling next to her. She dared not look in his direction, though increasingly she felt an urge to do so, attended by a shudder of fear and extreme smallness. She had always loved what the enormity of these great churches effected in her, but this feeling was rather different. It was as though the thing that the size of the church represented was in some way sitting—no kneeling—in the pew next to her. She drew up the courage to cast a glance to her right, and there she saw not the old man she expected, but a young man of dazzling golden hair, flowing like . . . . she knew the hair, she had seen it before . . . like a Botticelli, she thought, that kind of flowing hair. And his face was anciently beautiful, eternally youthful, for those contradictions were what came to mind, wise and young, experienced but fresh like the first morning of Spring.

The man was in prayer, prayer of such urgency that his knuckles were white with the force of his folded hands. Tears streamed down his face, and she then understood that the fragrance of flowers erupted from each tear drop that splattered onto the cold stone floor. All of a sudden she realized that the moment for which she had saved her life—kept her soul, her hands, her lips, and her body pure—had arrived. She would help this man.

What struck her most was that she knew she could not simply offer her help, for she was in the presence of someone far greater than she was. She had never experienced anything like this feeling in all of her life. She had read about it in the stories of King Arthur, but that didn't occur to her now. All she knew was that this man deserved her service, that it was her honor to serve him, that not to serve him was somehow unfitting. Nothing in her American political education had prepared her for this. She had known good men, she had deliberately tried to rediscover the goodness in men like Washington in spite of her professors' best attempts to encourage cynicism about all that 'romanticizing the past.' But the dignity she had come to appreciate in Washington was nothing compared to this. That was it: 'appreciate' was wholly the wrong word. All she wanted to do was bow and await his reception of her allegiance. Allegiance! That was the concept she was looking for. But not an American allegiance to flag and country. No, this was a call to allegiance to a person, to a lord, to her liege.

She was in the presence of a king. Now she knew. And for the first time in her life, she had an inkling of what her meeting the true King would really be like. Nothing in her life had prepared her for that day until this moment which shocked her with such a sense of regality and awe that she began to shake as she found herself kneeling and bowing before him.

* * * *

Melchizedek turned in surprise to the young woman kneeling to his left. He immediately realized that she was kneeling not to God, but to him. Somehow she recognized him. He determined that this must be the answer to his desperate prayer for help, and so he acknowledged her.

"Rise, my lady, and take your seat. These cold stones are not worthy to bear the honor you do me."

Anne looked up in surprise at his words. She stared deeply into his eyes, eyes so lovely, so radiant, so overflowing with justice and wisdom, and yet . . . hurt. She could see the pain and the fatigue in his features now. Her heart was filled with compassion, and she offered in a formality that surprised her, "Sir, permit me to help you, for you are weary and overcome with much pain."

Melchizedek considered her offer for a moment. Under other circumstances he would simply have thanked her for her kindness and been on his way. But these were anything but ordinary circumstances. He had no idea why he was sick, for he had never been sick a day in his life. Nor did he understand why this young woman seemed to recognize him. And he did need her help. Could his prayer have been answered that quickly? It wouldn't have been the first time, he remembered.

"Your kindness is much appreciated, my lady. I thank you," he answered.

"Follow me, Sir. I'll take you some place safe," she instructed. She offered her arm to him, and he took it. As they exited the church, she almost thought she saw an old man on her arm.

CHAPTER TWENTY-FIVE

Rothschild heard about the disaster at the hospital and was consumed with fury. What could have gone wrong? Who had betrayed them? Just then his attendant reported that Dr. Andover had arrived and requested urgently to see him. Rothschild marveled at her audacity. Surely she had to know that if she alone survived, that all his suspicion would fall upon her. Even if she were innocent, he did not tolerate failure. All this she knew, and yet here she was. He wondered if perhaps she was in shock. Taking a pistol from his drawer, he prepared to receive her.

* * * *

The secondary Sayerot Mat'kal team commander had placed his top reconnaissance soldier in an observation position. Unable to assist his comrades during the firefight, he had taken long-range digital photographs during the battle, and he now returned to send them to Yaakov Katz in Israel.

* * * *

The police inspector surveyed the shattered vehicles, shell casings, bullet damage and blood-soaked bodies around the hospital. The world press was already calling it a major terrorist incident. But the inspector was trained to deal with facts first, always the facts first, and so he began his initial review of what he had already discovered. There were two teams, judging from clothing, gear, and the locations of the bodies. One team was composed of mercenaries and people dressed as medical specialists. Their many different military tattoos together with their "soldier-for-hire" themes indicated a mercenary unit with great experience. Nothing was particularly noticeable on the medical specialists' bodies. They had died by the ambulance with perfect shots to their bodies, suggesting that they had been murdered near the beginning of the melee. The inspector discovered an empty hospital gurney inside the ambulance, suggesting that the medical team was either returning an empty gurney or bringing someone from the hospital to the ambulance. That person was nowhere to be found. He searched the medics' bodies as well as the ambulance itself but discovered no paperwork referring to any patient either, though he was hopeful that the hospital's own records would clarify the situation. As he rounded the other side of the ambulance, he noticed a pair of bloody footprints leading, no running, from the ambulance site. They faded and then disappeared as they entered the parking garage. That meant that someone, someone small and probably feminine—given the shape and size of the prints, had survived the attack on the ambulance and gotten at least as far as the garage. And, checking his notes, he concluded she had probably escaped, given that no female bodies were found there.

He walked toward the destroyed car and found badly burned bodies within, wearing the same European clothes as the members of what he currently thought was the other team, all of whom employed American weapons and none of whom had any distinguishing bodily marks or personal effects that he could find. The team showed remarkable physical strength, and their communication gear was superb. They appeared to be an elite Western special operations team, though from what nationality he could not yet determine, though he thought the Americans unlikely, precisely because all their weapons were American. He knew enough about special operations to realize that their security depended on not being obvious.

Surveying the other members of the special operations team and photographing what remained of their faces, he uploaded them to Interpol, though he felt fairly sure that they would not be found in a Western investigative database. As he walked across the street, he could see the shattered building face and the dead sniper within, his rifle still clenched in his right hand.

Returning to the parking garage, he reviewed the scene that had gotten the most attention by the police. He mused over that one, for Italians were so given to drama, and here was a crime in which it appeared that the two antagonists had nearly died in one another's arms. It quickly became clear to him that the theatrical interest was well-deserved, for a great fight had indeed occurred between these two warriors. But his examination of their bodies, clothing, and gear showed him nothing beyond what he'd already learned from the other dead.

He decided to return to the hospital, where he found another body, also hit by sniper bullets. Passing it by, he headed for the records division in an effort to determine who or what had attracted the attention of two highly professional combat teams.

* * * *

A shaken Michelle Andover approached Rothschild's office. She had considered how precarious her situation was, but decided that her best chance for survival was to employ the boldness that had marked every step of her success. She gathered her remaining courage, as Rothschild's assistant motioned her to enter her employer's palatial office. She swallowed hard as she walked beneath the imposing Medici crest. Rothschild was just finishing a phone call, and Andover noted his grave demeanor.

"Sir, I am sure you are aware that the operation failed," she began, determined to seize the initiative.

Rothschild just looked at her for a moment, and then nodded.

"We were intercepted by another team. They were professionals and very effective. They killed everyone but . . . me," she continued, faltering on the final words as she noticed the pistol lying on Rothschild's desk.

"Yes, I am aware of that fact," Rothschild answered her coldly.

"But . . ." she began before Rothschild interrupted her.

". . . you did not set up the team. You are not the traitor. Of that I am already assured," he said flatly.

"How did you come to that conclusion?" she asked in surprise, but then hastily added, "Not that I disagree with you, of course."

"I just learned that a phone call was placed by one of the mercenaries to a number in Israel," he explained.

"Israel?" she queried, still feeling very tense. "Why Israel?"

"Why indeed," answered Rothschild. "Somehow, the Israelis have discovered the value of our target, and they are interested in acquiring him for themselves. I can see the potential political value."

"Yes, I suppose so," agreed Andover.

"You did not betray me, Miss Andover, but nor did you succeed," Rothschild said returning to the point of the conversation.

"No, Sir, I admit that. But I can make it up to you," she hastily added.

"How?" asked Rothschild tiredly, his eyes glancing down to the weapon before him.

"Melchizedek is sick, far sicker than he should be," she began.

"You mean you made him sicker than he was supposed to be?" Rothschild asked, the disappointment in his voice evident.

"Yes, I screwed that up too. But I acquired his medical chart from the hospital, and this data shows that he is not responding properly to the usual radiological exposure treatment. There is something else going on. And I can discover what that is and fix it," she added.

"Only if you can find him," retorted Rothschild.

"But I can find him, Sir," she offered.

"Really?" countered Rothschild skeptically. "How?"

"Melchizedek must seek medical treatment or he may die. The treatment is very specific in kind, and we can monitor any location where he might go for help."

"But the police will likely figure that out too, so how are we supposed to match their resources and get to him first?" asked Rothschild.

"Well, for one, the police are going to need some time to ascertain what is going on here. They may not even understand that Melchizedek was the target, or that if he was, who he is. Nor may they understand that he will remain sick. These are our substantive advantages. And while the police are limited legally, we can monitor any medical system we wish."

Rothschild was impressed with her reasoning. It appeared that he still needed her. Further, if . . . no, when he finally caught Melchizedek, she was his expert on his biology.

"Very well, Miss Andover. Proceed with your plan. Do not fail me again."

* * * *

Yaakov Katz's frustration was palpable, as he spit out his gum and clawed his drawer for a package of cigarettes. How could everything have gone so colossally wrong, he wondered, staring dumbly at the packet. He had examined the digital photos sent to him by the secondary team, and now he wanted to know who this woman was, the one person who apparently survived, besides the old man. He was certainly pleased that he now had a grainy picture of Melchizedek. But while he would run his picture through their facial recognition database, he doubted anything would turn up. But the woman? Her face came through clearly in the photograph. And she was his connection to Melchizedek.

CHAPTER TWENTY-SIX

Anne led Melchizedek toward the villa where her brother was staying. As police cars raced by them, Melchizedek pulled her into an alley and haltingly inquired of her, "Where, where are you taking me, lady?"

"To my brother's villa on via Tornabuoni near Santa Trinita," she replied.

"Then we must avoid the streets. There are other ways to move through the city," he explained.

She looked at him quizzically but followed his lead further down the alley. Opening a small fourteenth century door, he led her into a darkened passage. Reaching above the door frame, he withdrew what looked to her like a couple of rocks. As the flint struck the steel, however, she realized he was lighting a torch. Soon they were beneath the city in tunnels over five hundred years old. The smell of must and stale bread struck her as her fingertips brushed against the coarse rock in the narrow passageways. Melchizedek transited the many forks and turns, diving through cobwebs filled with dust, as if he had been here many times before. Anne asked him about it.

"Yes, my lady," he answered with a gulp, biting back another wave of nausea. "I've been here before. This city has not always been safe. In times of danger, the tunnels offer refuge. Many others have been here too."

Anne wondered about that. The only time she could remember Florence being in any kind of general danger, other than the Uffizi bombing, was during the occasional serious floods of the Arno. But a tunnel would hardly offer safety in time of flood. Anne decided she would ask him about it later, for though he hurried along, the prince was tiring. She tightened her grip on his arm, suggesting that it was she who needed a rest. He turned toward her, the look of a warrior in his eyes, protection and power emanating from his form. But Anne reached up with a handkerchief and wiped the sweat from over his eyes. Here was a man whose masculinity daunted her in a way she'd never imagined possible. She thought she had never known a man at all, as his eyes stared straight into her soul. But at her touch, Anne watched the ferocity in his features soften, melting into a generous grin.

"Thank you," he offered and then turned back into the tunnel beneath Santa Trinita.

* * * *

John Horn had been napping in his villa, having enjoyed perhaps too much of the Florentine night life with his sister in the early hours of that morning. Two bottles of Chianti between the two of them had nearly reduced him to blubbering, while she just laughed, having become accustomed to Chianti the way most Americans tolerated daily pots of coffee. But he awoke groggily to echoes of what he dreamily thought was thunder. He drifted back to sleep, only to be awakened again, this time by the sound of sirens passing just beneath his window.

* * * *

Melchizedek suddenly stopped and wiped the dirt from what appeared to Anne only as an indentation in the tunnel wall. A doorway emerged as centuries of grime fell to the tunnel floor. With a grunt, Melchizedek forced the rusty hinges to give way. Following him through the open doorway, Anne found herself in the crypt of the Basilica di Santa Trinita. She followed her escort, for that is how the roles now appeared to her, as he hurriedly closed the door and replaced the dusty wall ornamentation over the doorway, concealing it. Then he mounted the stairs toward the church floor. The few tourists who bothered to look at the fourteenth century church, certainly not one of the more glamorous churches in Florence, hardly noticed them as they exited the front door and made their way to Anne's villa.

* * * *

Michelle Andover was furious at herself for having had Melchizedek in her hands and losing him. Once the combination of fear and adrenaline began to subside, she was struck by the fact that he was real. As she returned to her own quarters in Fiesole, she realized that she hadn't actually believed any of it. But he wasn't a myth. Melchizedek was a fact.

While showering and cleaning the bloody grime off her face, it dawned on her that if he had been in the ICU, they would have taken daily blood samples, and that meant that she might be able to acquire a current sample and discover what had gone wrong with the virus. She had always been aware that his blood would have mutated since 700 B.C., but she had tried to anticipate—however unsuccessfully—what those mutations might look like by comparing his blood to current Palestinian samples.

While drying herself off with a towel, she suddenly felt a cold chill run down her spine. Hurrying to her television, she saw that the firefight was all over the news, and the police had arrived at the site. She knew she'd have to hurry if she was going to acquire the blood sample before the police figured out what had really happened. Donning the outfit of a doctor, she grabbed her forged hospital security pass and hurried out the door. She knew that she was taking a great risk, for her pass might not survive critical scrutiny. But she hoped that with the confusion and ongoing needs of the hospital patients, she could still slip in and move about unobserved.

* * * *

John Horn heard the door open and called to his sister, pleased again at the opportunity to spend her academic break with her in the city. But he was surprised when he was met in the living room by a pale and exhausted old man.

"Anne, who is this?" he started and then, at the plaintive look she gave him, caught himself and directed his attention toward the frail man. "Sir, please, take a seat. Perhaps I can offer you some Chianti, or some cool water?"

"That would be most kind," replied the elderly man with an air of authority that took John aback.

Looking to his sister, he said, "Anne, perhaps you could help me open the bottle?"

Once he had her in the kitchen, he pumped her with questions faster than she could answer.

"John, John, John!" she urged. "Please, just let me explain."

John took a breath, and then answered her, "Okay, I'll go serve the Chianti, and offer some cheese and grapes. Then I'm going to come back here and get some answers out of you."

John took the bottle and glasses and headed into the living room, but his sister stayed right on his heels.

"Sir," she said to the king, "my brother doesn't know who you are. I thought perhaps we should explain that, and how we can help you."

"How we can do what?" asked John, frustrated that his sister appeared to have taken the stranger rather than him into her confidence.

The elderly man mused, "John."

Pausing, he continued, "It is a good name. It has belonged to many great and noble men of deep faith."

Again John Horn was taken aback. "Who *are* you? And what have you done to my sister?" he asked without much thought.

Anne interjected, "Let me tell you what happened in the church." And so she told him all that had happened until the time she reached the villa. John's medical sensibilities took over, and he insisted upon examining Melchizedek.

John's face grew increasingly concerned as he questioned Melchizedek about his symptoms and the failed treatments at the hospital. "It sounds like radiation sickness to me. Have you been exposed to anything radiological recently?" he asked.

"No," answered Melchizedek who then paused, "At least not to my knowledge."

"Well, we've got to get you to a hospital. Your life may be in danger."

"That is not possible," interjected Anne again. "Did you hear the explosions and then the sirens earlier this morning?"

"Explosions!" exclaimed John. "So that's what woke me . . . and the sirens too. Yes, I do remember them," he said rubbing his somewhat hung over head.

"There was an attack on the hospital where he was staying, and they were trying to kidnap or kill him," Anne explained.

"And you brought him here?" asked her brother incredulously.

"He needed me, John. Maybe he needs you too," she hinted.

"Look here, Anne, I appreciate what you are trying to do. But first, this man needs serious medical attention. Second, if there are professional killers pursuing him, he needs the protection of the police. And third, what has gotten into you? This man is just an old man, a sick old man, but that's all. I don't smell any flowers."

Anne looked hurt, reeling from what her brother had said to her. He suddenly felt guilty about hurting her feelings, but determined that feelings or not, he was right, and someone had to knock some sense into her.

"He is not who he appears to be," she said flatly.

"Then who is he?" John asked.

"I will answer that, John," said an authoritative voice behind him.

John turned and saw not an old man, but a young man with golden hair, and a face so wildly fierce as to wholly unnerve him. And yet, though the face was anything but tame, and certainly not civilized, it was nevertheless . . . good. That was the only way he could describe it. A wild goodness, a face so replete with trustworthiness that John thought that perhaps he'd better listen to his sister.

"You are wise to seek to protect her, John," Melchizedek added gently. "We can't have the ladies bringing home just anybody, now can we?"

John laughed hesitatingly, as Melchizedek continued.

"My name is M'leck-ts'dek, 'Melchizedek' in your language. In my language my name means 'the king of righteousness' or perhaps better, 'my king is righteous.' It is an old name."

"Yeah, I've heard it before," interrupted John. "Isn't it in the Bible?"

"I am in the Bible, yes," replied the king.

"You mean your name is in the Bible, don't you?" John persisted, a little unnerved.

"No, your name is in the Bible, John. I actually am in the Bible. I am the king of Salem, Priest of the Most High God. I am he who is without beginning and without ending. I never knew my parents and have no regal lineage. And I live until the end of the times."

John swallowed hard. His rational mind told him that what he was hearing was impossible. People are born and they die. That is the nature of things. Supernatural beings don't exist, or if they do, they appear as angel-like beings to people like the Virgin Mary. Not to him. And this guy was a sick old man, not an angel.

At this point in his reasoning, however, the evidentiary quality of the change in Melchizedek shocked him. The man before him might be sick, but he was no longer an old man. He had just been an old man. Now he was young and, apart from his illness, in a kind of prime of health that transcended anything John had ever seen.

"How did you change like that?" asked John.

"The only way I can explain it is via an analogy. Are you familiar with the chameleon?" asked Melchizedek.

"Yes, certain lizards can adapt to their environments, altering their coloration. But what you just did goes way beyond that."

"I grant that," answered Melchizedek. "It's merely an analogy. The only explanation I have is that my safety lies in my anonymity, and the ability to appear differently to different people aids me in preserving it."

"But if you cannot die, as you say, how could you be in danger? You would be like superman," stammered John.

"I'm not entirely sure what 'cannot die' means, to be truthful—especially given my current predicament," replied Melchizedek.

"Right, because here you are, clearly very ill. And given what you've said, you shouldn't be. Isn't that correct?" summarized John.

"Yes, I'm at a loss to explain my symptoms, as I've never been sick," admitted Melchizedek.

"You've never been sick?" John paused, musing over that information before continuing. "Then let's start at square one: how do you explain your regenerative capacity? I mean, your cells must die, just like anyone else's, right? If you scrape your arm, and some skin cells fall off, they don't survive intact forever. Otherwise, your waste product would never degenerate, right?"

"Correct," answered Melchizedek. "Perhaps I should offer you my theory on this?"

"Okay, I'm all ears," answered John, intrigued to the point of nearly forgetting about his patient's condition.

CHAPTER TWENTY-SEVEN

Andover reached the hospital and parked her car in the rear, well away from the site of the gun battle. Entering through a utility doorway, she noticed two nurses casually smoking and felt herself relax somewhat until she turned a corner and collided with a policeman dressed in full riot gear. He carried a large machine gun, and looked at her severely. He apparently took her frightened gasp as surprise, and smiled as he asked to see her pass. He casually looked at it, and then admitted her. He didn't even have a list of hospital personnel yet, Andover noted, hoping that this meant that she could accomplish her mission.

She entered the hospital's lab and logged into the computer using the false name of Janet Langley and the password that her computer specialist had created for her. Sure enough, the hospital records menu popped on the screen. Hastily, she looked for lab work requests from the ICU, silently thanking her college advisor for encouraging her not only to take a third and fourth year of Italian but also a summer trip to the country. She hoped to find Melchizedek's sample from that morning, fearing the possibility that with the transfer order, the blood work might have been discarded. Double-clicking on the ICU patient folder, she located the only 'John Doe' on the list and felt relieved to discover that her transfer order had halted his blood work. Looking more closely, she noted that some of his personal effects had been sent down to the lab too. She had not even considered that Melchizedek would have been brought into the hospital with personal items! She wondered what they might reveal about his movements and possible location.

Recording the sample number from the computer report, Andover headed toward the refrigerated containment room of the hospital's laboratory. She nearly ran over a high-ranking police officer. He surveyed her curiously and very professionally, she noted with deep unease, before heading into the very room she had just left. She walked casually round the corner before running toward the refrigerated containment room, where she found the matching refrigeration unit and retrieved the sample. But she did not see any bag of personal effects. Hurriedly, she grabbed a spare test tube and poured into it the contents of the sample tube, before corking it and shoving it into her hospital smock. Then she emptied the contents of another tube into Melchizedek's original tube and resealed it before returning it to the refrigerator. She heard footsteps and voices approaching the door, so she slipped into the laboratory wash room and hid behind a biohazard cabinet. She was still able to observe the refrigerator through a mirror located in the upper corner of the room. As she had feared, in walked the police inspector, heading straight toward the refrigerator. He retrieved what she figured had to be Melchizedek's sample tube, and returned the way he came.

After the inspector exited the room, Andover experienced a wave of dizziness, and only then realized that she had not inhaled in over two minutes. She worked her way unsteadily back around the biohazard cabinet and glanced down at the counter at a package with Melchizedek's identification number. His personal effects, she thought with exhilaration! Some lab attendant must have dropped them here during the firefight outside. Grabbing the bag, she hurried to the doorway.

* * * *

"So, how do you think you've lived so long?" Anne asked Melchizedek, while her brother checked his pulse. "You don't, I mean, do anything weird, right?"

In spite of how ill he felt, Melchizedek laughed aloud, "Oh my, oh my, my lady, do you surprise me! Only moments before you were defending me to your brother, and now you wonder if I am a vampire! Strange that your brother hadn't considered that that might be how I so easily beguiled you!"

John looked up and realized that Melchizedek was staring straight through him.

"Well, er, I mean, no, certainly not," John stammered, "but come on, sir, you have to admit it's all rather strange!"

"Fair enough," replied Melchizedek. "Let's start with what's not true. I don't drink blood, garlic doesn't bother me, I can walk in the sunlight, and silver bullets are no more lethal to me than any other metal. Oh, and before you ask, no, I don't take heads with swords, nor are there any others like me, to my knowledge."

He stared at the embarrassed though somewhat satisfied looks of his two benefactors.

Melchizedek turned to Anne and asked, "Now, as to what actually explains my longevity and health, I have a theory. Have either of you read the philosophy of Saint Thomas Aquinas or Rene Descartes?"

"No," she answered, somewhat surprised though when her brother answered, "I did, in college. I read both of them. Why?"

"Well, Rene and I discussed his theory of the preservative power of God and . . ." he started.

"You knew them?" Anne marveled and then stopped. "But why would you need them? Surely you were wiser than they were!"

"Why would you think that, lady?" he asked her.

"Because you are the king," she stammered.

"King, yes. *The* king, a bit strong . . . more like a regent, really. Priest, yes. But a Solomon? I think not," he answered.

"You knew Solomon too, I presume."

Melchizedek smiled at her, assuring her that her conjecture was correct, and then added, "I long for wisdom, and I have sought out the great philosophers to increase my knowledge. Both Thomas and Rene spoke of the way in which the power of God sustains life, and they employed the old Greek distinction between *bios* and *zoe*. Are you familiar with this?"

"No," she smiled. "But I think we're about to learn."

"Then let's begin with a question, shall we?" Melchizedek asked her.

"Oh, gosh, you're using the Socratic method! And I'll bet you even knew Socrates, didn't you? How can one ever get used to this?"

Again Melchizedek smiled and asked her, "What keeps this cup in existence?"

She answered, "Presumably a whole lot of forces holding its smaller parts together."

"All the way down to matter itself?" he asked.

"Yes," she replied.

"And what holds matter in existence?"

"I don't know . . . God?"

"Indeed, the power of the Most High God alone sustains matter in its existence without the intermediary of a whole series of forces and fields and particles and whatnot, just as by his direct power he preserves in existence the angelic intelligences, the stars."

"The stars?" she queried.

"Yes, sort of, for the stars fill the heaven above the earth, but there are multiple heavens, and the heaven above the one that you see at night is filled with the angels each of whom has a blazing star in your world."

"Oh," she replied, dazed.

"The Most High's power keeps them in existence directly, just like matter itself."

"Okay, I can see the difference. And the Greek terms?"

Melchizedek answered, "The term *bios* refers to biological life, that sustaining power of interactions that we talked about first. Biological life can be extinguished by dissolving the relationships between the parts. The term *zoe* refers to spiritual life, for the apostles of the church spoke of eternal life using *zoe aionion*, life eternal. This spiritual life is the very power of the Most High God directly sustaining something, the life of God in direct contact with something. Such a thing cannot be destroyed except that God should remove his power from its preservation. Rene and I spoke of this at length."

"But what does that have to do with your immortality and regeneration?" queried John.

"I suspect that the physiological relations in my body are sustained directly by *zoe* rather than *bios*, just as yours will be one day."

"Ours?" Anne asked in surprise.

"Why yes, in the final resurrection of all things in which this corruptible body will be made incorruptible," explained Melchizedek.

"How would that occur?" John asked.

"By direct participation in the eternal life and preservation power of the Most High God," he answered.

"But your theory does not offer any recourse as to how you can be so sick," John insisted.

"No, it does not," he admitted. "That is the problem. I have never been sick before. The interrelations of my body are apparently in distress."

"Yes, that's one word for it. Radiation either is or has disrupted some of your cells. They aren't regenerating. I'm dubious about your philosophical theory."

"Then perhaps something else accounts for my immortality?"

"Or maybe something else has maintained your physical health— something other than what has preserved your body's existence all these years!" offered John.

"The truth is," Melchizedek answered, "I don't know how it works. Rene's solution seemed reasonable enough at the time, and no counterevidence existed to render it dubious. But now . . ."

"Now you are sick. I just wonder how close to death you can come. Or if you can die by our definition, but in some sense you regenerate," John mused.

"I always wondered about that too," admitted Melchizedek.

"Did you ever test it?" Anne asked.

"What do you mean?" he asked cautiously.

"I mean, did you ever, you know . . ." she cut herself off mid-stream.

"Did I ever leap off a building or try to drown myself?" he stared her down.

"Let me guess . . . that would be presumptuous, wouldn't it? Oh gosh, I remember in Jesus' temptation that Satan suggested the same thing to him. Well, I wasn't actually suggesting it, only wondering whether you'd ever considered it."

"Yes," he laughed, "fine distinction. You are right, though, on both accounts. I always figured that my life would continue, but I could not guarantee in what form. So, lopping off an arm might not result in regeneration. In fact, I know that I can suffer wounds like any other person. In one raid many centuries ago, I took an arrow shaft to my thigh and had to tear some of my books apart to construct a bandage. It worked well enough, and I healed very rapidly."

"So, for all you knew, you might continue on immortally, but be minus a leg?" queried John.

"Exactly! So, I took good care of that leg and I avoid injuries just like anyone else. Avram the Hebrew actually discussed this with me."

"Abraham, the Biblical Patriarch?"

"Yes, you call him that, the name the Most High God finally gave to him. In his later years, we spoke often of wisdom, and I asked him about the divine order to kill his son Yitzhak, or as you call him, Isaac."

"You did? What did he say about that? I've always wondered," exclaimed Anne.

"Well, we both agreed that the test was not about murder, since the Most High God had already promised him that Isaac in particular would carry on his seed and bring forth the great Jewish nation."

"So, Isaac had to live," mused John, "even if it meant resurrecting him back to life."

"But if he knew that Isaac had to be resurrected, then how was it a test at all?" asked Anne.

"Avram explained that he did not know *when* or in what *form* Isaac would be resurrected. He knew that he must be, since only the living bear sons. But perhaps never in his lifetime. Thus, he faced the very real loss of his beloved son."

"I see," she replied, "and he also wouldn't have known what form he'd be returned in, having been all burnt to a crisp on an altar?"

"Well, no, he would not have known that either, I suppose," Melchizedek laughed, "though we did not discuss that particular aspect of the test of his faith."

"Well, it's kinda hard for me to imagine Isaac finding a bride being all crispy anyhow," she laughed.

"Indeed," he answered, laughing himself, then pausing. "I've thought of that whole situation since, in moments where my curiosity might get the better of my judgment."

"I see now what you mean," she answered smiling. "You don't throw yourself off buildings."

"Okay, so what do we really know here?" John asked, having satisfied himself that Melchizedek's current condition was stable. "We don't know about your dying, though we figure you'd come back. We don't know about your form of coming back from extreme injury either, crispy or legless. We do know that you've never been sick, and that has to be miraculous or close to it. But now you are sick."

"Which means perhaps it is not miraculous at all, but something special about my constitution, my biology," suggested Melchizedek. "Thomas and Rene might have been wrong."

"Yes, it's possible that some new technology or emerging virus might have interacted with your unique biology in such a way as to render you ill," replied John.

"John?" asked Anne. "Do you think you could figure out what's wrong with him?"

"I don't know Anne. I've never dealt with anything like this before," John answered slowly, before continuing. "I'm a doctor, Mel—can I call you 'Mel'? I can't keep calling you 'Melchizedek' and I don't think I can get used to 'your majesty.'"

Melchizedek laughed again, nodding.

"Good, then, Mel," John emphasized the name, "I work in trauma, but I have some expertise in hematology. I'd like to take a look at your blood and try to determine what is going on with it."

"You could use the lab at the university, John. That way you'd arouse no suspicion," offered Anne.

"Yes, that'd be perfect, Anne. What do you say?" John asked of Melchizedek.

"I think that would please me very much," he said thankfully.

CHAPTER TWENTY-EIGHT

As Michelle Andover wove her way through the corridors of the hospital, she again approached the heavily armed policeman at the utility entrance. She observed him checking two people waiting in line in front of her, and her heart sank as she realized that security checks were now in place for those leaving the hospital. She cursed herself for not having considered that possibility, and began frantically to think of a strategy to ensure her exit. She saw a fire alarm ten meters behind her, but thought that might just attract the attention towards her. As she moved ahead in the line, she noticed that the policeman gave her a look before awkwardly returning to cross-check a nurse's security badge. It took Michelle a moment to understand that while she was functioning on survival instincts, this man viewed her as a woman. Suddenly she became conscious of the fact that she'd hurried away from her apartment without even donning a bra, and the outline of her nipples was unmistakable under the hospital smock. Her instant revulsion at the human male's incapacity to treat women as gender neutral persons gave way to her sudden grasp of the strategy to make her escape.

The guard motioned her forward, and she approached him with a mischievous smile coupled with a twinkling eye. She handed him her security badge with a half turn of her body and commented on how strong he must be to be able to carry all that body armor and weaponry. She saw the guard grow at least three inches taller and eye her breasts lasciviously. She leaned upward toward his ear and whispered that she'd be back after lunch and got off that night at 9:00. The guard was trying to cross-check her name with her badge, and finally found the name, Janet Langley, but he was so taken by Michelle's seduction, that he failed to subject the badge itself to any serious scrutiny. Michelle knew that her name had been included on the hospital list, but she'd been concerned that the badge might not pass a thorough examination. She plucked the badge from his fingers as he checked her name, and brushing him with her breast, walked slowly out of the hospital.

* * * *

While John retrieved a syringe from his bag to draw a blood sample, Anne decided to ask Melchizedek about something that had been bothering her since she had first met him at Santa Maria Novella.

"Sir," she asked, "I'm curious about something."

"Please, ask," Melchizedek offered politely.

"Well," Anne paused, "I'm trying to understand your different appearances. Sometimes you look like an elderly man, and other times you look—at least to me—like a Renaissance prince! But if you are originally Canaanite, I'd think you should appear bronzed."

Melchizedek laughed. "Yes, that is true, lady," he paused. "I appear quite bronzed to myself," he added laughing again.

"Then why . . .?" began Anne.

"Then why do I seem to you like something fresh out of a Botticelli painting?" Melchizedek interjected.

"Yes, that's what I'm trying to understand," she explained confusedly.

"What does the Botticelli image represent to you?" he asked her.

"Why I suppose I think of youthful majesty, hearty manly laughter, boundless energy . . ." Anne offered before adding indignantly, "Why are you laughing at me?"

"Oh, the way you women view kings never ceases to amaze me," he explained to her, still smirking.

"Fortunately for you, Mister, I don't easily take offense!" Anne answered before continuing. "Also, I think of power rightly used, and a kind of grace or courtesy, I think, though that's harder to explain in a man."

"Yes, all that you think of is the nature of a true king, and when the Most High God revealed me to you, He apparently ensured that you would see an image that represented me to you. Seeing a bronzed Mediterranean might not have proved as successful," offered Melchizedek.

Anne paused to think for a moment before adding, "That would explain it, wouldn't it? People seem to see you according to some relationship between what you need at the moment and what suits their expectations."

"That is right," said Melchizedek. "But I also somehow know what they are seeing! Otherwise, I should not know to hobble about like an old man."

"Well, that is just astonishing," Anne wondered aloud, as her brother drew a second vial of blood from Melchizedek's arm.

"Looks pretty bronzed to me," he muttered, as the other two broke into peals of laughter.

* * * *

Michelle could not believe her luck in retrieving not only Melchizedek's blood but also his personal effects. Once she arrived back at her own office in the renovated convent, she ordered a full analysis on the sample, as well as a comparison with the ancient one. As she waited for her lab technician to retrieve the blood sample, her eyes fell on the frescoed crucifixion scene again. She felt a gnawing unease in the pit of her stomach, when she looked at the figure of Jesus. Melchizedek is real, she thought. What if he's not the only one? What if Jesus is real too? She stared into the eyes of the man on the cross, almost daring him to show himself, to climb down off that cross on the wall and prove himself to her.

Suddenly Michelle spoke aloud, "Oh damn it all anyway! I'm a scientist. There is no magic here. There's a reason, a fully explicable reason, why Melchizedek is alive, and I will find it. I need to find it. No magic. Only cold sober science. No magic."

She spoke the last words as whispers, trying to convince herself that she needn't worry. She'd been through hell today, so it was natural that she might be vulnerable to the pitiful state of the man on the cross. Ignore it, she told herself.

"What's that, Doctor?" asked her technical assistant.

"Excuse me?" Michelle replied, unaware that anyone had entered her office.

"I thought I heard you say something about needing to get back to work?" he answered.

"Oh, right," she explained, as she forced her misgivings to the back of her mind so she could focus on the task at hand. "We have a lot to do. Take this blood sample and run a full spectrum workup on it."

As her technician left with the sample, Michelle took one last look at the fresco, wishing for a half second that they hadn't sited her lab in a convent. Then she followed him down to the lab which they'd set up in the old refectory. While her technicians worked on the blood analysis, Michelle donned latex gloves and began to open the paper sack she had retrieved from the hospital. Peering into the bag, she saw ordinary items that might be owned by anyone, as well as Melchizedek's clothing. With a profound sense of disappointment, she asked herself aloud what she thought she'd find. A crystal ball? A secret key? Her abrupt laughter caught the rest of her lab workers by surprise, and she quickly quieted herself and began to photograph and inventory each item.

She began with his pants, feeling through the pockets but finding nothing remarkable. She was just about to examine his shirt, when she realized that a shape showed through the waistband of the pants. Feeling along the inside edge, she found a thin compartment sewn into the lining. It was sealed with Velcro, so she pulled it open and withdrew a passport. Elated, she opened it and there was the face of the man in the hospital. Now she had Melchizedek's name and picture. She looked at his age of sixty-eight years, scoffing at that, before lifting her camera and photographing each page of the document. She made a record of the entry stamps and dates, so that she could create a timeline. What surprised her the most was that the passport was Greek. She had not really considered where Melchizedek might live, but Greece would not have been high on her list.

After finishing with the passport and setting it aside for fingerprinting analysis, she felt into the waistband compartment once again and withdrew an airline ticket. She was eager to match its destination with the timeline she was developing. Opening the ticket envelope, she found a used receipt from Egypt to Florence, but also an unused return ticket from Florence to Egypt. She worked through the digital photographs of the passport stamps she had just taken and concluded that Melchizedek had flown from Athens to Cairo, spent several days in Egypt, and then left Cairo for Florence. The return ticket's calendar was open-ended, so she could not determine when he had planned to return to Cairo. But he was returning to Cairo, not Greece, she thought, which meant that he must have some kind of business there. But she couldn't find any return ticket to Greece from Cairo. So perhaps he was living in Cairo. She couldn't be sure.

Returning to his other personal effects, Andover next examined Melchizedek's money clip with its fourteen hundred Euros; since she found no credit cards, she supposed that tracking Melchizedek's passport name electronically would yield few financial records of his purchases. Disappointed, she returned to his clothing which appeared fairly ordinary for a person of his age. But when she picked up his shirt, she felt a heavy weight, followed by a loud 'clump' as something slid from the shirt and landed on the examination table. She looked in awe at the golden chain and inscribed pendant. She knew that Rothschild would be the best person to determine its age and importance, so she carefully photographed it, before placing it with the other items. Everything would be examined by her forensic team to discover what each speck of dust told her about Melchizedek's travels, while any fingerprints besides his own would indicate his possible allies. Before long, she would know how to find him. She picked up the secure telephone to inform Rothschild.

CHAPTER TWENTY-NINE

From his well-fortified office deep beneath Tel Aviv, Yaakov Katz urgently placed a call to the highly classified cyber espionage and warfare unit operating out of a location so secret that not even he was privy to it. He knew that they employed not only next generation surveillance technologies but offensive capabilities that had more than once crippled major threats to Israel. Now he needed them to work for him, and he needed them immediately.

While he waited for the secure phone connection, he mused over what he had learned. Michelle Andover was the name of the woman in the picture. She was connected to that biotech firm in New Jersey, their head researcher by all accounts. And their interest? Future regenerative technologies! There was little doubt in his mind that whoever had hired her was attempting to acquire Melchizedek for biological reasons. But who was behind her attempt to kidnap Melchizedek remained a mystery to him. Whoever it was operated in shadows and yet had the power to manage a world-scale operation that involved releasing a bioengineered strand of the polio virus all around the world. To what end? Katz had surmised that the virus was designed to incapacitate Melchizedek with symptoms approximating radiation sickness, or at least that is what his second team on the ground in Italy had managed to ferret out of their investigation at the hospital in Florence. Melchizedek had exhibited these symptoms but not responded to treatment. That much his team had determined. But now Katz needed to penetrate Andover's organization and since he knew who she was, he was convinced the cyber warfare people could help him.

The phone call finally connected and Katz heard the general in charge of the unit answer.

"Yitzhak, this is Yaakov, how are you today?" Katz began courteously enough.

"Get to the point, Yaakov, what do you want?" General Yitzhak Mordechai demanded. Mordechai envied the power that Katz wielded in the government. In a regime as small as that of Israel, every general had political ambitions, and right now Katz was significantly closer to the PM's ear than Mordechai found comfortable.

Katz knew all of this about Mordechai and that is why he proceeded as he did. "Listen, Yitzhak, I wanted to invite you to the PM's retreat on the twenty-third. He has been impressed with what I have told him of your unit's accomplishments, and I thought you might like to come along as my guest."

Mordechai frowned on his end of the phone. There would be no getting around whatever Yitzhak really had in mind, because the intelligence chief was telling him that his future connections to the PM depended entirely on his good will. Ah well, thought Mordechai, I might as well go along with him for now.

"I shouldn't miss it for the world, Yaakov. I'm pleased to hear that the PM is so interested in our unit." Mordechai knew that Katz would not miss the plural possessive pronoun, so he proceeded, "Perhaps you have an additional operation in mind that we might bring to his attention at the retreat?"

Katz's appreciation for the general increased. He had not expected such a response from the general, not that quickly. He realized that the general understood the situation perfectly and would play along for the sake of the political exposure. So, he outlined what he had in mind, and Yitzhak Mordechai assured him that it could be done.

* * * *

Florence

John Horn gathered up his blood samples and his notes and turned to his sister.

"Okay, I'm ready. Where can I find an internet-connected computer?" he asked.

"Why don't you go to the University library? You can use my ID when you log on," she offered, and then paused, searching through her purse until she found the security card.

JEFFREY TIEL

"Thanks Anne," John replied, and then turned to Melchizedek. "Now you get some rest, while I'm away. Drink a lot of this Powerade, as it will replenish your energy and help clean out whatever is going wrong in your body."

"Very well, John, and I do thank you again for your help," answered Melchizedek.

John nodded and headed out the door.

* * * *

Back in his laboratory, Rothschild looked through magnified glasses at the necklace that Andover had sent him. He had to control the nervous energy that coursed through his limbs, as he carefully handled it. Here was an object owned and touched by Melchizedek within the last week. He had never been personally closer to the man than he was right now. Of course, he thought to himself, he should have had the man in his possession. But anger would not enable him to accomplish his life's quest, and so with years of discipline under his belt, Rothschild thrust the anger out of his mind and focused on the task before him.

* * * *

John Horn took his blood samples to a local laboratory and offered his American medical identification. The Italian medical student was surprised that an American emergency room doctor would turn up at his laboratory, but he was excited about the opportunity to speak English and chat with the American. John offered to meet the dark toned, lightly built, easy-going fellow later that week at the Irish pub he had seen near Santa Maria Novella. Luigi, for that was the student's name, was so flattered at the invitation, that he offered John all he required to examine the blood sample. John was impressed with the quality of the Italian facility, especially their recently acquired electron microscope, and in just a few hours he discovered that something foreign had been introduced into Melchizedek's blood, something constructed. He had never actually seen nanites before, the little machines that swarmed Melchizedek's blood, and he wondered what they were doing there. John continued to examine the slide and watched as the still functioning nanites produced some kind of dense chemical. A thought began to form in John's mind, and he quickly took another radiation measurement. Sure enough, there was a marginal increase in the sample's radioactivity. So, he thought, the nanites are producing a radiological chemical. But how, at such a marginal level, would that result in radiation sickness?

172

John looked again at the strange chemical, as it seemed drawn to the hemoglobin protein nearby. It was then that John noticed that the protein was full of the radioactive element. John narrowed the scope of his radiation measure to include only that one hemoglobin protein. But when the indicator surged, pointing to a one thousand percent increase over what he'd predicted, he wondered if perhaps he had made a mistake. He was confident that the total radiation should be equivalent to the amount of the radiation from the chemical agent contained within the protein, so why was he finding such an extreme radiological effect? He checked and then rechecked his equipment until he was convinced that the reading was accurate.

Puzzled, he just sat there looking at the protein until a new thought formed in his mind. If the radiation from the nanite-produced chemical wasn't sufficient for the radiation reading he was getting from the hemoglobin protein, then perhaps the hemoglobin protein was itself radioactive? Searching the slide, John finally found an uninfected protein and tested its radiation level. Surprised to find that he was right, John wondered why Melchizedek's blood would prove naturally radioactive. He speculated that perhaps this was part of the explanation for his uniquely long life. John couldn't be sure, but when he looked at the radiation reading again, he was alarmed to discover that the reading from the isolated hemoglobin protein together with the reading from the isolated chemical isotope were still insufficient to account for the extreme reading he got when they were together.

And that's when it hit him. He swore softly, as he steered some of the chemical isotope toward the uninfected hemoglobin protein. He watched as the radiation within the protein began to climb exponentially as the isotope neared it. The isotope was irradiating Melchizedek's blood, increasing its natural radioactivity output to an extreme and lethal level. It was a well-planned combination effect, he concluded, sure now that he had isolated the radiological effect that was causing Melchizedek's symptoms.

He needed some additional data for comparison and decided to make his way to his sister's university library, so that he could use the primary medical database. He did not expect Luigi's laboratory to have access to the database, as the subscription cost was affordable only to major research corporations, governments, and universities.

Michelle Andover peered over her microscope in awe at the fresh sample of Melchizedek's blood. In just a few hours she had already formed a hunch about what had gone wrong with her virus. And she now suspected that Melchizedek not only would not get well, but would in fact become sicker. Something was drastically wrong with his blood, and it was getting worse. For some reason the radiological effect of the isotope on Melchizedek's blood proved more dramatic than she had predicted from the ancient sample Rothschild had acquired for her. Instead of merely disabling him for a couple weeks, she worried that it might kill him. To confirm her hypothesis, she needed a comparison with a blood disease that she thought would provide a sufficiently strong analogy to Melchizedek's condition, so she called up the international medical database at the Centers for Disease Control in Atlanta. Programming her complicated search protocol, she realized that the search would take several hours, so she returned to her microscope to run a few additional tests.

* * * *

Using his sister's identification card to enter the University library, John Horn logged onto one of the available terminals, and began his search. The library internet connection was probably one of the fastest in all Italy, and so the search time indicator showed only twenty minutes. While he watched the elapsed time meter slowly wind down, he mused over how best to treat Melchizedek, if his theory proved correct. The only thing he could imagine was an electric shock to disable the nanites, but he wondered whether Melchizedek's heart could really recover from a shock of that magnitude. Divine guarantee of health or not, John was reluctant to kill a man in order to save him. And then he had the additional problem of the effect the electrical current would have on the tiny machines. Even if disabled, they'd surely end up magnetized, and then they would attach themselves permanently to Melchizedek's iron-rich hemoglobin. And then what? Blood clots? Or something worse? John couldn't be sure. What's more, he'd still need to cleanse his blood of the radiological effect of the nanites.

While the computer continued its search, John bent his mind around the problems that faced him. How could he cleanse Melchizedek's blood in one procedure that would replace the hemoglobin, ridding him of both the nanites and the radiation? And then it hit him: plasmapheresis! Plasmapheresis was a complete blood purification procedure. It would permit him to cleanse Melchizedek's blood entirely of both the fried nanites and the radioactive hemoglobin. And with Melchizedek's enhanced recuperative powers, he hoped that his patient would be up and around in a day or so.

Reflecting on his plan, John mused that without their magnetic attraction to the iron rich hemoglobin, he would never have been able to filter Melchizedek's blood for something as small as nanites anyway. So, he would use the magnetic effect of the electrical current to good effect. If only he'd planned it that way from the outset, he sighed ironically.

One problem remained, he concluded: the blood transfusion. John could acquire replacement blood plasma easily enough, but he still calculated that he would need at least four to five units of whole blood. How would he ever find an acceptable donor? He had already discovered that Melchizedek's blood type was quite rare, but would compatibility problems arise with his ancient body? He simply did not know. The computer beeped, disrupting his reflection. The search was complete. He printed the pages and turned to rip them off the printer, before reaching to yank his sister's ID card from the activation terminal. He failed to notice the database screen suddenly include an additional entry, indicating that a correlative search was underway. As he pulled the card, the program cancelled, and the library logo reappeared on the screen. Horn headed back to his sister and her new friend, as he perused the results of his search.

CHAPTER THIRTY

The Italian Police Inspector reluctantly drew his eyes away from the pictures of his three daughters and one son to stare again at the hazy image on the office computer in front of him. Ever since the world press focused attention on the way in which the Americans tracked the activities of their Oklahoma City Bomber, police forces worldwide had begun to gather video from banks and department stores and even weddings, whatever it took to gain a better sense of the culprits and their movements. The Inspector had canvassed the area surrounding the hospital looking for whatever video footage could be found, and a bank security camera had been facing outside recording the action of the hospital attack. Initially, he found that suspicious: why would a bank camera be trained on a hospital parking lot? But further investigation revealed that a cleaning crew had inadvertently knocked the camera. And so, he now had pictures. He was most interested in the old man who hobbled away from the scene and the female kidnapper who escaped. That the elderly man left without her meant that the kidnapping failed. The Inspector mulled over the man's good fortune but also wondered at the danger that still stalked him. He asked his aid to focus the replay on the female suspect, sharpen it and expand it, and then print it. He thought he finally had a picture of the mysterious Janet Langley, the woman who had signed the release forms at the hospital. He would know for sure by day's end, when someone at the hospital identified her.

* * * *

Rothschild noted the Scythian markings almost immediately. Melchizedek's golden chain and pendent frame were clearly constructed within the first couple of centuries following Augustus' rule of the Roman Empire. The Scythians had proven to be accomplished horsemen, and scholars were now beginning to find burial sites of this enigmatic ancient nomadic people. The burial sites included masterpieces of metalwork; somehow these legendary horse archers had managed to produce highly refined golden artwork. Why Melchizedek owned a Scythian piece currently eluded Rothschild, but then in truth he knew so little about Melchizedek.

It was what lay inside the pendant's golden frame that excited him. It looked like a beautiful gem stone, amethyst he thought at once, observing its pinkish-purplish hues. But it was cut in the center unlike an ordinary gemstone; it reminded him of the keys he had seen in some of the ancient Egyptian temples. The high priests wore a symbol of their power, the gem itself, but it functioned as more than mere symbol, for it opened the temple vaults. Surrounding the stone he saw a border of lapis lazuli, the favored Egyptian glass, and it bore a very small inscription in hieroglyphs.

Rothschild disassembled the pendant, removing the stone from its golden frame. He then placed it underneath a powerful magnifying projector, so that the lapis lazuli border beamed brightly on the screen before him. Painted on the border he translated the words, "High Priest of Thoth."

* * * *

Michelle Andover's phone rang, as she again hunched over her microscope transfixed by Melchizedek's blood. She answered it angrily, but her demeanor changed abruptly as she realized that the forensic analysis on Melchizedek's personal effects was complete and available for her review. She glanced over at her computer and, noting that her database search was only thirty-four percent complete, decided she had plenty of time to read the report and consider her next course of action.

* * * *

Rothschild reflected on the significance of his find. If Melchizedek bore the ancient Egyptian priestly emblem of power, then he must in some way have been associated with the cult of Thoth, maybe even belonging to the priesthood itself. He had already known that Melchizedek's manuscript cartouche bore Thoth's symbol, linking his priesthood and kingship. He had wondered how Melchizedek, originally from Palestine, should have wound up in Egypt, and especially acquired priestly and quasi-kingly status. That had never really made sense to him, for cartouches never bore signs of service to Thoth. But then Melchizedek had never been an Egyptian Pharaoh; he was instead a foreign king apparently under the protection of the Egyptians for some undetermined length of time. And somehow he became connected to Thoth.

Rothschild tried to understand the significance of all that he had learned in the past few weeks. He had long suspected a direct connection between Melchizedek and the Book of Thoth, though he still could not predict what that connection was. But he always resisted his suspicion, because he knew it was based not on evidence but perhaps at best on what he wanted to believe. But here was solid evidence that Melchizedek was linked to the priesthood, bearing the ancient key to a temple of Thoth himself. At worst he had to know something of the Book; at best he knew its location and perhaps the real secret to his immortality lay in his possession of the Book. He would not be sure until he had Melchizedek within his grasp.

Rothschild decided that he needed to better understand Melchizedek's movements within Egypt. What was he doing there? Had he been to Khmun? Did he know where the Thoth temple lay? Rothschild pondered the questions that rolled over in his mind.

* * * *

When John Horn returned to his villa, Anne informed him that Melchizedek had been sleeping almost the entire time of his absence. John noted with satisfaction the three empty Powerade bottles.

He smirked as he turned to his sister, "Anne, you'd better wake him up, and ensure he knows the way to the bathroom."

She laughed, answering, "By the looks of it, he'll probably be in there for quite a while."

John sat on the living room sofa as he completed his reading of the medical search report. His theory confirmed, he contemplated the course of treatment he had devised and wondered whether he should not just encourage Melchizedek to see a team of specialists. But given the circumstances, he worried for Melchizedek's and now, Anne's safety. She knew too much about him. So, he'd have to proceed with treatment himself. He would need the right kind of medical facility, plenty of privacy and . . . help. John smiled at the thought of Luigi, and he wondered if he could enlist his aid.

Melchizedek emerged from the bathroom looking refreshed, and asked what John had discovered. John began with the engineered virus and its radiological effect, speculating that it was specifically created to find him, since it could not harm anyone else.

Melchizedek retorted, "But John, someone would have to have a blood or DNA sample of mine in order to create a virus specifically aimed at me. And then they would need to release it all over the world, unless they knew of my whereabouts. But if they knew where I was, then why create a virus designed to identify me? And how would they know of my existence anyhow?"

"I know," replied John. "If it was spread globally, then a fairly large organization or even a government is likely pursuing you. How they knew of your existence, I can't tell. But you can imagine what your body might offer in terms of clues to human cellular regeneration."

"Perhaps," offered Melchizedek. "It sounds like I need to recover quickly and disappear fairly thoroughly. But how will I prevent someone's creating another version of this virus and tracking me down again?"

"Well, I noticed that your blood is beginning to produce anti-bodies to the virus. So, at a minimum, whoever engineered it would have to reengineer it or start from scratch with an entirely new virus. It's the nanites that are the current problem. They are machines, and you are no more immune to them than you would be to a saw!"

"Right, I understand that. So, how do we eliminate them?"

"Well, we subject them to a powerful electrical charge," answered John confidently.

"That will kill him!" exclaimed Anne.

"That is possible," admitted John.

"But I should regenerate fairly quickly," suggested Melchizedek.

"But I thought we talked about not tempting fate or God . . ." began Anne.

John interrupted, "No, Anne, this is not some test. It's the only solution I can come up with for killing these things. If he will really regenerate, then it should work. That's faith, not temptation."

"But will my blood remain radioactive?" asked Melchizedek.

"No, because after shorting out the nanites, we'll have to give you a treatment called plasmapheresis that will thoroughly clean your blood of all radioactive contamination. You see, the nanites are producing a radioactive isotope whose energy is irradiating your unique cellular structure. Once the nanites are neutralized, we need only cleanse that isotope from your blood."

"But how can a medical filtering process like plasmapheresis screen out something as small as this isotope you are describing?"

"Great question. In my research I noticed that the isotope tends to clump together in your hemoglobin, ensuring that it will be found in large enough quantities that the plasmapheresis should filter it. Of course, you'll also need a transfusion to help with that process."

"With what donor?" asked Melchizedek, startled.

"We can use generic blood plasma, but we'll need to add five or six units of blood of your specific blood type . . ." began John.

". . . which is rather rare," concluded Melchizedek.

Anne was looking over the report from the university computer, when she suddenly exclaimed, "But John, that's my blood type!"

Melchizedek and John both looked at her in surprise. "Please tell me you are joking, Anne," John explained, "because this transfusion will be dangerous for both donor and recipient. The human body only carries fifteen units of blood. So, you'd lose nearly one third of your blood."

"No, I'm serious. And I'll do it!" she determined.

Melchizedek and John looked at one another apprehensively, as Melchizedek began the attempt to dissuade her.

"Anne, I cannot accept . . ." he started.

"No, both of you listen to me. This is why I am here. It's why you found me in the church. Or why I found you. Or why we found one another. Now it makes sense, don't you see? If I die, I die. We're all going to die anyway. Well, everyone but you, I suppose. Or at least that's what we are trying to prevent. I might as well die for something important, right? Besides, John will be there working on us both to keep us both alive and well. I'm sure you'll succeed, John! And then, I won't die," Anne answered confidently.

"I think I need a drink," was the only answer John offered her.

"Count me in," replied Melchizedek.

* * * *

Michelle Andover closed the folder in front of her. She had hoped that the forensic report on Melchizedek's belongings would tell her additional information about him, but it mostly just confirmed what she had already discovered from the passport and ticket. Melchizedek's clothes contained dust and pollens that were found in Greece, of course, as well as Egypt and Italy. She read the details of the report until she noted that one of the pollens was found only on Patmos Island. The name sounded vaguely familiar to her, but she couldn't place it exactly, so she looked up the location and discovered that it was a small Aegean island that was part of the rim of an extinct volcano. The author of the Apocalypse, the Revelation of St. John, was exiled to the island under the Roman Emperor Domitian in the 1st Century. That is why it seemed familiar to her, she realized; something from her Sunday school days about the last and darkest book of the New Testament had lodged in her imagination. St. John had received his vision while on the island, where he lived in a small cave with his scribe Prochorus. Michelle continued her research and discovered that a fortress monastery dedicated to St. John sat atop a kind of acropolis on the southern end of the island. A perfect place to hide from the world, Michelle mused. Maybe that monastery is where Melchizedek lives, she speculated, or at least he had some business there recently. She knew she must not jump to conclusions, but something about the isolation of the island and its spiritual heritage connected in her imagination convincing her that the island had some deep importance for Melchizedek. She decided to inform Rothschild of her discoveries.

CHAPTER THIRTY-ONE

Michelle lifted her secure phone to call Rothschild and noted that the computer analysis was finally complete. She was stunned to discover that someone else had recently run nearly the same search. The hematology database included a feature that created a record of any similar search criteria, so that medical professionals working on the same problem would have a greater chance of discovering their mutual interest. In this year alone researchers in Brazil and Thailand discovered that they were on the track of the same disease, when the Thai doctor used the contact information for the Brazilian researchers provided by the database to pool their resources. But how could anyone be searching for data on these particular symptoms, since they had been uniquely created by her? It made no sense to her . . . unless . . . she hurriedly clicked on the research URL and discovered that the request had been made by an Anne Horn on a computer at the University of Florence. She swallowed hard, as she realized that Melchizedek must have been acquired by another party or had found some medical ally. But she also now knew her name. Hurriedly, she phoned Rothschild's head of security, Maurice St. Claire. He promised to inform Rothschild and discover all that could be known about Anne Horn.

* * * *

John called Luigi that evening and invited him to the Irish pub across the Piazza from Santa Maria Novella. Luigi was thrilled to talk shop with the American doctor, and John regaled him with harrowing emergency situations that he had encountered in the States, including the recent Night of the Jumper. After several shots of Bushmills, John finally asked Luigi if he would like to help him with a special medical project. Luigi felt very satisfied with himself at this point in the evening, and immediately agreed. John thought he owed him some explanation, so he detailed his plan to run some advanced hematological analysis on a friend with an exceedingly rare blood type. He would show Luigi how to conduct a plasmapheresis, if he had not yet had the opportunity to see this in school. Luigi beamed with excitement at the offer, and quickly agreed. He even suggested that they use the University Medical School itself after hours, confident that he could acquire the necessary facilities. Luigi also wondered whether they should not use saline solution with sterilized human albumin protein instead of fresh plasma. John was impressed with Luigi's medical knowledge and assured him that while normally he would be inclined to use the sterilized solution instead of fresh human plasma to reduce the likelihood of infection, in this case his aim was to restore his patient to full strength more rapidly, but that yes, they would pay close attention to the infection risk.

John left the pub and walked over to Via Tornabuoni wondering whether he had been dishonest with Luigi. He certainly had deceived him, not telling him the full truth. But he could not reveal to Luigi that Melchizedek's body would resist any normal infection. John expected to take full responsibility for what he intended to do, protecting Luigi from any recrimination. Nevertheless, he was still bothered by his use of Luigi. He resolved to buy the Italian a bottle of very fine Irish whiskey whenever this affair finally ended.

* * * *

The Italian Police Inspector frowned at the results from his lab. The blood sample he had obtained from the hospital belonged to a menopausal woman, not his John Doe. Fortunately, he had acquired the medical records of the sick old man, and they indicated radiation exposure, but provided no explanation as to how the victim became exposed. The Inspector found the radiation exposure combined with the attempted extraction of the victim from the hospital deeply troubling. He doubted his ability to ferret out the likely culprits, and so he decided to take the first step in broadening the scope of his search: he would send what he had to both the Americans and Interpol and ask for their assistance.

* * * *

Maurice St. Claire called Michelle Andover the following day with a full work-up on Anne Horn. She was an art history graduate student from the States with no medical background whatsoever. Both Maurice and Michelle were puzzled, unable to figure out how she fit into the picture. Maurice added that he had located her villa in Florence through University records, and that Michelle could accompany his team as they investigated it that morning. Michelle agreed at once, and prepared for the possibility of their reacquiring Melchizedek.

* * * *

Columbia University, New York

Nikolai Borechnekov had not forgotten the curious conversation that he had had with Laurence Rothschild. Even though Rothschild was a bit of a crackpot, for an amateur he was not half bad. Borechnekov smiled at his long history with Rothschild, going all the way back to their Oxford days. Rothschild had always seemed overly wary and secretive, but Borechnekov had to admit to himself that he loved the regard that Rothschild showed him. And so, he always made himself available to assist Rothschild's latest archeological venture. Who knows, he thought, some day I might need him too.

The latest problem that Rothschild had presented to him still occupied his mind. Something about the wall relief had been bothering him. Again and again he examined the pictures of the temple, the priests, the chests with their books, the river . . . that was it! It was the river. It did not seem to be painted in the usual stylized manner of Egyptian representations of the Nile, but instead appeared to portray an actual river or part of a river. He wondered if he could locate it.

Calling up satellite imagery of Egyptian riverbeds on his computer, Borechnekov created a digital overlay of the wall relief's representation of the river and then ran a topological search program that he hoped might provide him with a match. He made sure to include not only current river courses, but ancient courses too, since over time everything changes. Fortunately, the satellite images provided him with the ancient river courses too. Strangely enough, they were easier to identify from space.

Borechnekov settled into his leather chair to wait for the search program's results. He sipped coffee and began again the task of grading graduate student papers, shaking his head in amusement at the theory one of his graduate students was proposing. When his computer finally beeped to indicate that the comparison was complete, he called up the most likely matches of the rivers in Egypt to the topography of the river painted on the tomb wall. The search program had located a possible match.

Borechnekov looked in amazement at the location. The river was the Nile of course, since it was the only river in Egypt. But the Nile around the ancient city of Khmun? That was the very city he had discussed with Rothschild already, center of the Thoth cult. Now he wondered what the odds were that of all the possible locations on the Nile as well as its many tributaries he should find one that fit his predictions as to the temple's location perfectly. Perhaps he was giving himself too much credit? He wondered. Another academic's evaluation would be the right way to go, but he knew that Rothschild insisted that his inquiries remain strictly confidential, and the cases of rare cognac that Borechnekov received from Rothschild each Christmas motivated him to observe Rothschild's eccentric requirements. Finally he decided that he would simply provide Rothschild with the data, and he could draw his own conclusions.

* * * *

John Horn fretted all day long as he prepared for the procedure that evening. He planned to return Melchizedek and Anne to the villa after the transfusion was complete, where he would nurture them back to health. He counted on Melchizedek's recuperative capacities to renew his strength quickly. His only real concern was Anne, and how long her recovery would take, but then he didn't plan to electrocute her, he thought with a smile.

He rented a van with folding seats, so that he could create makeshift mobile beds. Then he rigged up IV poles and platforms for the medical equipment. He hoped it would suffice. As an emergency backup, he knew that he could simply call the local hospital and send Anne there. Melchizedek was the person that he needed to protect, but he would only send Anne to the hospital if he was convinced that she was at risk. He actually felt more confident about her chances of recovery than he did in his knowledge of the full nature of the threat against Melchizedek and the degree to which that threat might already have involved his family.

* * * *

Anne Horn's villa proved to be as much an enigma as Anne Horn herself. The tiny apartment was fairly sparse with religious icons and impressionist and renaissance art on the walls. Michelle noted the accumulated mail and inferred that Anne had not been to her apartment in a couple of days. This raised their suspicions substantially, although still, they could not discover any clues concerning Melchizedek. Maurice found several prayer books and a rosary from Santa Maria Novella, and determined to check on the convent and church that afternoon, to see if Anne and Melchizedek might have sought refuge there. In the meantime, a frustrated Michelle decided to return to her lab to work on some antidote to Melchizedek's current illness.

* * * *

"You are sure? It's definitely Khmun?" asked Rothschild excitedly.

"Yes, at least if we assume that the river topography on the wall relief is supposed to represent the actual shape of the river and its surrounding embankments," Borechnekov replied cautiously. "It may be that the painted river's shape would have inevitably matched some feature of the Nile anyway."

"But with the rest of the tomb relief's portrayal of a temple to Thoth . . ." objected Rothschild.

". . . and with the Thoth cult centered in Khmun," interrupted Borechnekov, "it seems pretty reasonable to think that the river's shape on the wall is no accident."

"So, the temple must lie somewhere near Khmun," concluded Rothschild.

"Well, 'must' is too strong, but yes, I do think so," admitted Borechnekov. "I would send this imagery to Bartleby and ask him to conduct a survey of the region in order to assess possible locations of the temple."

Rothschild watched as the satellite data arrived electronically from Borechnekov. "Thank you, Nikolai," he offered warmly, "you have been of great help."

Borechnekov laughed heartily, "You are welcome Laurence, and good luck finding the book!"

"Sure, Nikolai," Rothschild answered with a chuckle that turned deadly serious as he hung up the phone.

CHAPTER THIRTY-TWO

As John departed to get the van, Anne and Melchizedek descended the steps from her brother's villa and waited in the foyer of the building.

"Sir," stammered Anne with a blush. "I mean, Mel, you said something in our walk through the tunnels that interested me."

Melchizedek smiled at her curiosity and said, "Please, my lady . . ."

"Oh, do call me 'Anne,' Mel," she offered.

"Very well, Lady Anne," he replied smilingly. "What would you like to know?"

"'Lady Anne' . . . it does have a nice ring to it, I suppose," she sighed. "But back to the tunnels! You seemed to know your way around them very well, and you mentioned that you'd hidden there before. What did you mean?" she asked.

"Oh, yes, the infamous Medici attack on the Florentine republic!" he exclaimed.

Melchizedek closed his eyes as he organized his memories of the ill-fated Republic. "Florence had thrown out the Medici and declared herself a free Republic. Michelangelo had switched sides away from his former patrons in favor of the new Republic. I had been observing and recording much of European history at the time, and so settled briefly in Florence. But when the Medici formed an alliance with the pope, a papal army marched toward the city from the South. They devastated and ravished a nearby town, causing a panic in Florence. During this time, prior to Florence's surrender, Michelangelo and I hid together underneath the city in those tunnels. In fact, some of his drawings down there survive. The man could not live without a chisel or brush in his hand. He also had a real flair for poetry. And his devotion to God was genuine. Michelangelo possessed an artistic understanding of the real nature of things that was exceeded only by Solomon, I think. A few Greek sculptors possessed the same technical skill as Michelangelo did, of course, and Bernini probably exceeded him, but it was what Michelangelo saw in a simple block of marble—a vision of goodness and glory unparalleled."

"Then why did his later work become so dark?" asked Anne.

"The times were dark, Anne," answered Melchizedek soberly. "All things fall into decay. Golden ages collapse into fire and sword and darkness. I have seen it a hundred times a hundred. Michelangelo watched the church tear itself apart over the evil of the Medici popes, and he grew pessimistic about the future. For many, it felt as though the Apocalypse of St. John was crashing down on their heads. You can see many of these themes in the *Last Judgment* in the Sistine Chapel."

"Yes, I always wondered why that piece, so huge, so dominating in the chapel, seems radically different in character from the earlier ceiling paintings," she replied somberly.

Poking his head suddenly through the doorway, John disrupted their sobriety with a huge smile, "Are my patients ready to go?"

Laughter greeted him, and soon they were all heading for their rendezvous with Luigi.

* * * *

Washington, D.C.

Quarston and Billings surveyed the special office that had been cleared for their joint-investigation. The recently renovated DC office complex into which they had been moved bore the fingerprints of modern bureaucracy—a motley blend of frivolity and frugality typified by the two new desks resting on a poorly installed afterthought that passed for carpet. The view was not unlike the room. The beauty of the capital was marred by several aging office buildings crowding the scene and a long smudge that ran down the window. Quarston fogged the window with his breath and rubbed at the smudge with his shirt sleeve, as Billings did a once over of the space. The room was a bit of a downgrade from Billings' office in CIA counterintelligence, though its size allowed for an additional desk—one with extra leg space, Billings noted approvingly—and any computer equipment they might need. For Quarston, the room was a great improvement over his tiny, though cozy, office at the Boston Bureau, which was largely filled with aging but neatly stacked piles of case folders. They presently finished their evaluation of their new arrangements and began unloading boxes. An assistant arrived within ten minutes with a list of additional agents that were placed at their disposal. Billings thanked her, and then turned to Quarston.

"So, now I guess we get straight with each other, right?" he pressed.

"You mean like what the CIA's interest is in Melchizedek?" asked Quarston taking the lead.

"Melchizedek?" asked Billings inquiringly.

"Yeah, what do you know about him?" continued Quarston.

"So, it's a 'him' now, is it?" answered Billings with a smile.

Quarston stared at Billings, frustrated that he'd been the one to give something away.

"Let's just call it a hunch," answered Quarston finally. "But what is the CIA's interest here?"

Billings retorted, "You know, Quarston, I've not liked you from the beginning of our little joint project. You've been holding out on me the entire time!"

"And your little counterintelligence operation isn't exactly the same thing?" challenged Quarston.

"How do you know about . . ." began Billings but stopped short.

"So, we're both on the right track, aren't we?" asked Quarston with a grin.

*   *   *   *

After picking up Luigi and making the introductions, John drove them all toward the university hospital. Once they arrived, Luigi led them down a corridor to a room which he'd already prepped with all of the equipment, monitors, and medical supplies John had requested. John was very impressed and thanked Luigi, who helped the older man onto one of the tables and prepared the catheter for entry. While John prepared Anne on the other table, he smiled reassuringly to Luigi and nodded for him to administer the local anesthetic to Melchizedek's groin. Luigi looked nervously at Melchizedek and moved to numb the area of the groin where the catheter would be inserted for the procedure. He was surprised when the old man suddenly gripped his wrist with the strength of an elephant and looked him straight in the eye.

"Aim carefully," was the message that passed between them, though Luigi was never sure whether he heard it audibly or just thought it. In any case, he then noticed a twinkle in the old man's eye, and they both burst into nervous laughter. Luigi took a moment to steady himself, since their

189

frivolity made his hands shake. Finally, he calmed down sufficiently to insert the needle and anesthetize the area using lidocaine. Following that, he slowly inserted his introducer needle into the Femoral vein which produced the expected dark red blood in the syringe, confirming that he had indeed located the vein. Luigi then removed the syringe from the needle and inserted a wire through the needle into the vein. This wire would guide the catheter for the procedure. Once the wire was in place, he removed the needle and made a small incision at the entry point of the wire before feeding the double lumen catheter over the wire and into the femoral vein. John had requested this kind of catheter, because it permitted both antero and retrograde flow of the blood through just the one catheter. Once he was confident that the catheter was in place, Luigi removed the wire and then tested the two ports on the catheter ensuring good blood flow in both the antero and retrograde directions. After John's inspection and praise, Luigi sutured the catheter in place and then put a dressing over it.

"Okay, Luigi, before we proceed with the plasmapheresis," began John as he finished prepping Anne and assured himself of her comfort, "I could use that cup of coffee."

Luigi just stared at him, puzzled.

"Didn't I mention that I'd need a little caffeine? The procedure will last several hours."

"Uh, no," stammered Luigi, mortified that he might miss the beginning of the procedure.

"Don't worry, I won't start anything without you. Could you get me a cappuccino or two from that place we passed coming to the University?"

"Sure," agreed Luigi. "Anybody else?"

Anne and Melchizedek declined but thanked him for offering.

Luigi took an extra moment in the room, and then darted away as fast as he could run.

Once John was sure Luigi was gone, he turned to his patients.

"I had to get rid of him for this part, otherwise he'd think I was killing you—which isn't far from the truth," John explained as he opened a large box and pulled out an industrial strength battery. "I calculated the amount of electrical energy needed to disrupt these nanites, and this should do it."

Melchizedek nodded and disconnected the catheter tubes from the centrifuge. John worked with him to isolate his body from any conductive surfaces, before connecting him to the battery.

John looked directly at Melchizedek and asked him finally, "Are you sure you are ready for this? It's gonna hurt like hell."

Melchizedek smiled at him, "I doubt it will prove that bad, but pain is something I can handle well enough. How will you revive me?"

"With these," explained John showing him the paddles of a defibrillator.

"So, electricity is supposed to kill the nanites, stop his heart, and then restart it?" asked Anne.

"Yeah, kinda strange, huh? What Franklin didn't know," answered John.

"Oh, he knew all right. The shock he received from that kite experiment left a serious burn scar," offered Melchizedek.

Melchizedek noticed the expectant stares he was getting from John and Anne before continuing, "Yes, I met him in France during your war with England. He had been sent there as an ambassador, for besides politics his real love was science . . . okay, maybe the French women too."

Melchizedek paused, remembering and then added, "All three occupy both mind and passion, I suppose. Anyhow, I thought his theories about electricity were remarkable. None of the ancients had any kind of decent account of what lightning was. Of course, it would require another century before the full range of applications became apparent."

"And now we're going to electrocute you," smiled John, interrupting the history lesson.

"Ah yes, you Americans are fond of doing that, aren't you? In our time we dispatched criminals with much less sophistication."

"Yes, well . . .," John began and then noticed Melchizedek's smirk. "Okay, Mel, are you ready to die?"

"I'm always ready," he said soberly. "I've been ready since the death of my first wife."

"You mean long life has a downside?" asked Anne.

"It comes with costs beyond what the human heart was created to endure," Melchizedek mused before turning to John. "John, I am ready. You may proceed."

"All right, here goes," John said as he activated the current.

CHAPTER THIRTY-THREE

Franklen Bartleby entered his trailer in the Giza desert to take the call from his chief contributor. Laurence Rothschild's dedication to his tomb excavation had occasionally drawn Bartleby's curiosity, but mostly it drew his commitment to maintaining the relationship, even if it meant leaving his dig to answer the occasional interruption.

"Mr. Rothschild!" Bartleby answered the phone cordially.

"Mr. Bartleby," replied Rothschild. "How is your excavation proceeding?"

"We are continuing to examine the wall relief, Sir. These things take time," answered Bartleby patiently, all the while wondering what new crackpot theory he'd have to endure this time.

"I'm sure," replied Rothschild with a smile at Bartleby's attempt to conceal his patronizing. "I looked over the data you sent me and I think I have found something that might help you with the location of that temple on the wall relief."

Bartleby was startled by what Rothschild told him. He had not expected such a level of intervention on the part of a contributor, but then he knew that Laurence Rothschild was no ordinary patron. When Rothschild mentioned the name of Nikolai Borechnekov, Bartleby realized that Rothschild's interest should be taken very seriously. Borechnekov was one of the world's foremost experts on the New Kingdom of Ancient Egypt.

"So, Borechnekov compared the image of the river from the tomb wall relief with the course of the Nile and its tributaries from the time of the pre-dynastic period all the way through the Roman occupation of Egypt, and he took into account changes in the river's path too?" Bartleby asked, ensuring that the search was as thorough as possible.

"Yes, exactly, and he found a spot near Khmun that seems to match the river topography," Rothschild answered.

"And I take it that he has ruled out mere luck . . ." began Bartleby.

". . . because the match turns out to be Khmun," answered Rothschild.

"Right, the center of Thoth worship, just as the wall relief indicates. Odd coincidence, otherwise," admitted Bartleby.

"I agree," continued Rothschild. "I was wondering if you might be able to narrow possible locations for the temple in and around Khmun."

Bartleby sighed. As excited as he was about Borechnekov's identification of the probable location of the temple, actually identifying the temple indicated by the wall relief was another matter entirely. It could easily take a lifetime.

Rothschild sensed Bartleby's hesitation, so he pressed the point, "Franklen, it would mean ever so much to me if you could at least take a look at the region."

Bartleby knew what that meant. A patron's gratitude was always measured in funding, so he wondered if perhaps he could venture down to Khmun in a couple week's time.

Rothschild heard the change in Bartleby's attitude, so he quietly sent a text message to his courier who had already arrived in Egypt at Bartleby's excavation. The courier acknowledged his message with a return text message, and headed immediately over to Bartleby's trailer.

"Thank you, Franklen, and please do keep this confidential," Rothschild concluded the call.

Bartleby hung up the phone, frustrated that he would have to leave his dig to undertake the beginnings of what he figured would probably turn out to be a wild goose chase. Just then he heard a knock at his door. The man at the door handed him a secured file as well as a large box. He signed for the packages, and then opened the file. There he saw the satellite imagery data that Borechnekov had sent Rothschild. He smirked at the audacity of his patron, so confident that he would undertake the survey of Khmun that he had sent the data by courier before he had even talked to him. Bartleby wondered about himself. Was he really that easy? Was there no limit to what he would do for funding for his dig? Opening the box, he pulled out a refrigeration unit. Inside the cooler he found several bottles of perfectly chilled Dom Perignon Champagne. Yes, Bartleby sighed, he really was that easy.

* * * *

A knock on the door interrupted the silence that had descended on Quarston and Billings. Quarston answered it and received the complete CDC report on the virus. It appeared that it was designed to target a specific genome and generate nanites whose function remained unclear.

"So," Billings began, "it appears that someone is after this Melchizedek figure, doesn't it?"

"They made a virus designed to kill or disable him, probably the latter given the research interests of that lab," thought Quarston aloud.

"Regenerative technologies, yeah, that's a reasonable inference," answered Billings. "If this Melchizedek possesses some special immunity or regenerative properties, then it makes sense that they'd be after him. Do you believe that he does?"

"Very possibly," answered Quarston.

"Well, since you are unlikely to tell me how you know that . . ." Billings waited for Quarston's nod, "then we have to figure that they used the nanites to disable him in a way that a regular illness wouldn't. Otherwise, why go to all the trouble to engineer a virus that employed nanites rather than merely target his specific DNA with a normal illness?"

"Perhaps a regular virus would not have infected him, so they needed to create something special," offered Quarston.

"Or perhaps they needed a way to identify him once the disabling effect began. I mean, how would they find him? What sort of disabling would yield a worldwide alert?" asked Billings.

"Ebola, small pox . . ." Quarston began.

"Except that they didn't use viruses like that. They used polio, but rendered it harmless and instead it generated these nanites whose effect we cannot figure out."

"So, it'd not be a normal illness at all," offered Quarston thoughtfully. "And if Melchizedek doesn't tend to get sick, that would make sense."

"I see where you're going with this, Quarston," admitted Billings, "but if he doesn't get sick, how do you disable him?"

"Right, and how do you disable him in a way that would trigger a worldwide alert?" added Quarston.

Both of them sat at the large table in the office in silence, until Billings suddenly picked up the phone and dialed a number. As he waited for an answer, he whispered to Quarston, "An old friend at Fort Detrick. Works at USAMRIID."

Quarston just stared at him in confusion.

"You know, the United States Army Medical Research Institute for Infectious Diseases?"

Quarston nodded hopefully, as Billings connected with his old friend.

* * * *

Luigi returned to the room with three cappuccinos, including one for himself. John was right; it would be a long night. He was curious at the smell of burned flesh. But everything appeared to be in order, except . . . the old man's hair—what little there was—appeared all frazzled.

"John . . ." he began earnestly.

"Don't ask, Luigi," John started, staring at Melchizedek's radiating hair and shaking his head, "Just don't ask. Little mishap, but all is well now."

Melchizedek added, "There are things you should touch and things you should not. I now know better the difference between them."

Melchizedek and the others broke into laughter, and though still confused, Luigi found it too contagious to avoid.

John interrupted them by asking him if he was prepared for the plasmapheresis.

Luigi found Melchizedek's catheter disconnected from the machine, so he reattached it and checked the suturing he'd done earlier. "All set," he announced to John, "He's ready."

"Anne is ready too. We'll take a unit of her blood and mix it into his returning blood together with the anticoagulant every hour, for a maximum of five hours. That'll be the length of the procedure after which time all of our patient's blood should be cleansed by the centrifugal and cleansing procedures. Got it?"

"*Si*," answered Luigi, sipping his cappuccino.

"All right, here goes," John announced turning on the machine, before sitting down with his cappuccino next to his sister.

"You'll be all right, little sister," he offered to her.

"I know I will John. I'm in the best care. And you've prepared all these energy snacks for me too, lots of fruit and juices and even some gelato, I see. You've thought of everything."

John kissed her cheek and she smiled at him proudly, before he checked on his other patient.

"Well, how are you doing?" he asked Melchizedek quietly.

"It's a bit uncomfortable is all, and I expect that I shall feel increasingly weak, correct?"

"Yes, especially at first, before the replacement cycle begins restoring the cleansed blood."

"And I'm very tired from the earlier incident. I feel . . . discombobulated."

"Yes, well, I should think so," John whispered. "Fortunately, your heart restarted after the third try. I hope we haven't done permanent tissue damage."

"Well, thank you John. Your kindness in helping me will never be forgotten, not in this world or in the next."

John was unused to hearing pronouncements of any kind, but even after living with Melchizedek for a few days, he still found them jarring. It wasn't as though he thought them presumptuous or ridiculous . . . rather, it was the sobriety with which they were offered that dizzied him. He felt in touch with something real, something grounded, and he realized that nowhere in his life had he experienced anything else like it. He wondered if this wasn't a little bit like what people must have experienced when Jesus gave his often surprising but authoritative answers to questions. John reflected on the conversation they'd had when they first met, about kings, and he realized that this was what was missing in his life. He had no king, had never wanted one in the least, but to be truthful the lack left a huge hole in his soul. He knew he was not feeling a political longing; it was something much deeper than that. There was something about the combination of goodness, wisdom, and power in Melchizedek that drew John towards him. John had initially thought this was an effect more likely to be present in his sister, young and feminine, but now he was feeling the same things she had. He wondered too if it might not be connected to service, for here he was serving this king. Yet it didn't feel like servitude at all; instead he gladly offered up his time and knowledge for Melchizedek's sake. John thought back to his emergency room patients in the States, the number of times he'd seen the same people come in with drug overdoses, the number of gunshot and knife wounds from gang-related criminality, the accident victims. He thought of how tiring it had all become to him, the faces of the patients gradually becoming mere numbers on charts. He did not feel that way now. Sometimes you just need a vacation, he told himself. And honestly, that was true; he had needed a break. And yet, there was something else here, a realization that labor and joy could be combined for the sake of a king. And if for a king, he mused, why not the subjects of a king? Weren't they all children of God? Wasn't all service for others, all loves of this kind, service to Him?

John felt Melchizedek's hand on his shoulder and heard a strange language. Turning toward him, he saw Melchizedek's eyes closed and his lips uttering ancient syllables. When he finished, John looked at him expectantly, and Melchizedek explained that he had blessed him with an ancient prayer from the time of Abraham. John thanked him and then returned to monitor his equipment. He had much to ponder.

* * * *

Quarston began leafing through the latest intelligence briefings from Italy that had been made available from the CIA. He was still keenly interested in Mr. Rothschild and the missing equipment from the NJ lab. He had begun to think that the equipment and possibly the missing Dr. Andover were together mixed up with the production of the virus, and that the arson had been designed to destroy all the evidence of the bioengineered virus in the United States.

Quarston came across a request from a police inspector in Florence concerning the terrorist attack on that Florentine hospital. Quarston had heard about the attack on the news, but had been so busy of late that he knew little of the details. What caught his attention was the request for any information related to possible causes of radiation sickness. That might trigger a worldwide alert, he mused.

Quarston read through the report that the inspector had included with his request. An unidentified person had been admitted into the hospital with radiological poisoning in his blood. That person had been removed by a fictitious transfer order signed by a woman named Janet Langley. But the transfer had been interrupted by the terrorist attack, only Quarston now learned that it wasn't a terrorist attack. The team kidnapping the John Doe had been intercepted by another combat team. However, both teams had been destroyed, and only the John Doe and Janet Langley escaped.

When Billings got off the phone with his friend at USAMRIID, Quarston asked him, "Radiation sickness?"

Billings stared at him dumbfounded, "How did you know?"

"This report from Italy. It looks like someone over there tried to kidnap Melchizedek."

The medical alarms shocked John into instant action. Fortunately, medical training from years of insane residency hours prepares trauma doctors for minute-man readiness, and John found himself acting properly while his mind tried to determine what was going on. The procedure had been running for four hours without a hitch, when the alarms on his sister's monitors began screaming. Rushing to her side, he noted that she had slipped into unconsciousness, and her breathing was shallow. He stopped the transfusion immediately—Melchizedek would just have to get by without the last couple units of whole blood—and turned his attention to Anne. Calling Luigi to his side, he ordered him to treat her for shock, while he worked to stabilize her heart and breathing. As the enriched oxygen-nitrogen mixture surged into her breathing mask, her respiration increased and the irregularities in her heart beat steadied into strong beats once again.

John then noticed fluid on the floor and realized that a small leak had formed in the IV tube that should have been providing Anne with the volume replacement for her blood loss. Quickly replacing the tube, John checked the Lactated Ringer's solution level remaining in the IV bag, and once satisfied that it was flowing properly again, turned to Luigi.

"She'll be okay," he said to Luigi, who looked scared but relieved.

John felt motion by his side and noticed that his hand was shaking nearly uncontrollably. He had never lost it in an emergency situation, not ever. But this was his only sister, and he felt as though he was about to burst into tears. Nevertheless, he called upon his training to focus his mind and suppress the emotions distracting him from his sister's needs.

"John?" he heard her say weakly.

"Sis!" he exclaimed. "You're all right. You had a little less blood in you than we might have wanted."

"I feel so weak . . . and what a headache!" she muttered.

"I'll give you something for that, and we'll get you something to drink," he began, pausing to get her a cup with a straw. He also injected thirty milligrams of Toradol into her IV line to help her deal with the head pain which he knew had to be a killer.

"What happened to her?" John heard Melchizedek ask from the other bed. Melchizedek had had the sense to remain silent until the situation stabilized, John realized with relief.

"Well, the adult human body has on average about fifteen units of blood, though it is impossible to determine its precise volume without actually pumping it out and measuring it. Anne here is fairly small-boned and probably has somewhere between thirteen and fourteen units," John began.

"You mean you took too much of her blood?" Melchizedek queried in alarm.

"No, no, that wasn't the problem," John explained. "During a transfusion you always replace the lost blood with a volume replacement such as this Lactated Ringer's solution here. Near the conclusion of the procedure, a leak formed leaving her body without the replacement solution. That in turn caused a loss of blood pressure, destabilizing her heart and respiration. She fell briefly into unconsciousness and shock, so we treated her accordingly, enriching her oxygen flow and restoring the volume replacement. I added a stimulant to her IV as well, prompting the heart to beat with greater strength, and this in turn strengthened her breathing which then increased the rate at which the additional oxygen entered her blood, quickly restoring her consciousness."

"Oh, is that all?" Melchizedek asked with relief, amused at the level of detail but impressed again by John's knowledge.

John grinned in reply, "You asked."

They both chuckled, feeling some relief after the stress of the last few hours.

But Melchizedek's face became serious again as he asked, "She'll be okay, though, now that you've stopped the transfusion?"

"Yes, I think so. With rest and nourishment," he concluded. "And as for you, Mister, you'd best keep eating those energy snacks. We can't have you going into shock too."

"Very well, doctor" Melchizedek promised before grabbing several more snacks and another bottle of Powerade. He had found that he liked the blue colored flavor the most, and by this point, his tongue and lips had turned a very dark blue color. Amused, Luigi stared at him before deciding to go back to monitoring his equipment, but as he turned he thought for the briefest instant that a young man of astonishing splendor was lying on the table next to him. Jerking his head back toward his patient, he saw nothing but an elderly man with blue stained lips. It was late, Luigi decided, shaking his head to ensure the return of clarity.

* * * *

"Michelle Andover and that medical equipment are the key to this whole thing," insisted Quarston.

"Okay, let's say that you are right," offered Billings, still suspicious at the simplicity of Quarston's thesis, "What next?"

"We talk to Rothschild," explained Quarston. "It's got to be our next move. We need to eyeball the guy, see how he reacts. With pressure from the State Department, the Italians might set up the meet. Biological attack is rather unpopular these days."

Billings considered what Quarston had told him. What bothered Billings was the apparent lack of any connection to Israel, even though it was the Israeli interest in Melchizedek that initially involved Billings in the Hentersheim murder case in Boston where he'd run into Quarston. Of course, Quarston knew nothing of the Israeli connection, or so he hoped, just as he knew nothing of whatever Quarston was concealing. But perhaps both of them could work together on the Rothschild link? Billings wasn't sure about Rothschild, but Andover had simply dropped off the earth, or had she?

Billings had an idea, "Roger, you connect with State about getting an interview with Rothschild, and I'm going to conduct an international search on Andover again. People don't just disappear, so I'll start with France where her trail ended. I've got a contact in Paris who might be able to help."

"You have contacts everywhere, don't you?" laughed Quarston.

"It's the CIA, Roger, what do you think we do?" answered Billings humorously.

* * * *

Once the procedure was completed, John and Luigi removed the catheter and monitoring wiring from their patients. Anne had recovered sufficiently to sit up, though she complained of dizziness. Melchizedek was very weak and a bit nauseous. When he added that he felt tingly sensations around his mouth, John gave him a calcium chloride booster in his IV. Then John and Luigi helped both of their patients to wheel chairs and wheeled them with their IV bags out of the room and down the hall to the elevators. Luigi stayed with them by the curb outside the university's rear entrance, while John retrieved the van. Once John opened the van's doors, he connected their IV's to the poles and asked both of them to lie down in the makeshift beds he had constructed. When Luigi returned to the treatment room to finish the cleanup, John finished packing his own supplies including the battery into the van. He decided to return to the villa, but not before a stop at Palazzo Michelangelo. He knew that recoveries depend not just on physical rest but emotional restoration, and he thought that a view of the entire city of Florence might just help with the latter.

CHAPTER THIRTY-FOUR

Quarston received a call from the State Department indicating that Laurence Rothschild continued to be unavailable for an interview. Quarston was shocked, and decided to contact the Italian Police Inspector himself. After checking the time difference, he placed a call to Florence, and Inspector Giovanni Bartoli answered the phone.

"Buongiorno," Quarston began and expended the entirety of his knowledge of Italian. Trusting to luck, he continued, "Do you speak English, Inspector?"

"*Si*," answered Bartoli. "I do. You are working on my Florence hospital case?"

"Yes, I am," answered Quarston. "But your case has intersected with the biological warfare incident that occurred recently. You are aware of that?"

"*Si*," Bartoli answered, confused. "I thought that the virus proved benign, though?"

"Yes, the polio was benign," Quarston clarified. "We have tracked the virus to a lab in New Jersey here in the States."

"You have?" asked Bartoli, still puzzled about the connection to his case.

"The lab was burned down," Quarston explained, and then added, "By arson."

"Arson," Bartoli repeated. "Why?"

"We think that whoever was behind the lab's destruction was also involved in the attempt to kidnap your John Doe. We think that the virus used in the lab was used to disable your John Doe with radiation sickness," Quarston suggested.

"But you don't have a viable blood sample, so how do you know that he was infected with the virus? My sample was a fake," objected the Inspector.

"Right, that's true. We don't have a sample. But we have independent reason for thinking that he was the target of the virus, in part because of the worldwide alert that would be created by a radiological incident. That alert would identify the viral target's location to those pursuing him. And whoever seized your John Doe has significant capabilities that match those used by the teams that deployed the virus all over the world in the first place."

"Okay, let's suppose that you are right," offered the Inspector. "Who do you think is involved? Do you have any names?"

"Your 'Janet Langley' appears to us to be an alias, just as you suspected. But we are looking for a woman here, named Michelle Andover. She led the research team at the New Jersey laboratory but disappeared following the arson."

"She wasn't burned up in the fire?" checked the Inspector.

"No, we're sure about that. There was no evidence of any human remains in the fire," Quarston answered and then continued. "Besides that, we've confirmed that she flew to France, where she then disappeared."

"I see," said Bartoli.

"But before she left, we believe she sent to Naples a large shipment of advanced bioengineering equipment which we think was used to manufacture the virus," added Quarston.

"Napoli?" asked the Inspector. "Where did the shipment go next?"

"The records indicate that it went to southern Italy, but the address turned out to be a fake, so that trail went dead," admitted Quarston.

"Can you send me a picture of Michelle Andover, as well as your file on her?" asked the Inspector.

"Sure, I'll send it to you right away digitally," offered Quarston before hesitating.

"What is it?" asked the Inspector, sensing the pause.

"I have another suspect, but it's a bit of a long shot," explained Quarston.

"Okay, who?" asked the Inspector.

"We traced the ownership of the biotech company and eventually it led to a Laurence Rothschild, a resident of Florence," said Quarston.

"Laurence Rothschild?" queried the Inspector.

Quarston detected the incredulity in the Inspector's voice and asked him about it.

"Well, Mr. Rothschild holds a significant interest in the hospital where the kidnapping occurred. I was directed by my government to pay him every consideration in my investigation. So, when he called me, I reported what I had discovered, and when I asked about his interest, he explained that he was appalled that such an action could occur at one of his hospitals, and he wished to do whatever possible to help us. So, he made available the hospital records we requested," answered the Inspector.

"Did he?" asked Quarston, intrigued.

"Yes, but you sound dubious," replied the Inspector.

"Well, I've been trying to interview Rothschild for weeks, and he has rebuffed every attempt. In fact, I requested that my State Department contact yours to apply diplomatic pressure, and even that failed. So, it seemed to us that Rothschild had little interest in helping to solve our case," revealed Quarston.

"Indeed?" asked the Inspector. "Well, we appear to have two different Laurence Rothschilds, don't we?"

"So it would appear," agreed Quarston.

"Would you like to interview him?" asked the Inspector.

"Very much," replied Quarston hopefully.

"Then come to Florence, Mr. Quarston, and I'll arrange an interview with Rothschild, ostensibly to offer him a report on my investigation. But you can come along, and then you may ask your questions too. Does that seem agreeable to you?" offered Inspector Bartoli.

"It's wonderful, Inspector, and you have my thanks," answered Quarston eagerly.

* * * *

Anne felt much better by the time John completed the ascent to Palazzo Michelangelo's large overlook area. He helped her out of the van and to the wall overlooking the Arno River valley and the famous medieval bridge, the Ponte Vecchio, with its timeless metallurgical commerce. She just sighed in awe at the sight of the Renaissance city. From her vantage point, the domes of the various churches in the city looked beautiful, especially that belonging to the Duomo. Its red tiles and marble supporting structure transfixed her. She had acquired a large poster of it for her room only the previous year. But here she was, again beholding the masterpiece of Florentine architecture. While John checked that she was nibbling the banana he'd given her, she sat atop the wall wrapped in a blanket and thought of all that had happened to her in the last few days, of who and what Melchizedek was, and of how much he had come to mean to her.

John helped Melchizedek next, but was surprised by his recovering strength.

"Regeneration," Melchizedek said simply.

"Right," answered John. "You can know it, but it's still surprising to see it."

"How much do you all know about Florence?" Melchizedek asked them.

"I know what any educated person probably knows," offered John.

"Not that much, in other words," Anne translated, laughing weakly.

John was elated at his sister's attempt at humor. Her behavior showed not only positive signs of recovery, but not even a hint of brain damage. He had been concerned about her brief lack of oxygen, but now felt confident that she would recover fully. "Well, let me give you the unofficial tour of the city," Melchizedek offered, pointing across the river to Santa Croce. "Our story begins in that church right there."

* * * *

Italian Police Inspector Giovanni Bartoli examined the picture of Michelle Andover sent by the FBI agent. He held it up to the grainy picture from the bank camera for comparison. It sure looked like her, he thought to himself. So, he now knew exactly who she was. Special Agent Quarston's information checked out, he mused. The question was whether he should pursue Andover himself, or whether he should continue to involve the Americans. Since her pursuit would require a national search, the Americans would discover that he was trying to solve the case himself anyway. So, he decided to continue the collaboration he had begun.

* * * *

John had difficulty keeping his mind on the medical condition of his patients, while Melchizedek brought the history of Renaissance Florence to life from his own memories. That this one city had brought to life the likes of Donatello, Leonardo, Michelangelo, Verrocchio, Botticelli, Brunelleschi, Galileo, Dante . . . on and on it went. What made the Renaissance possible? John decided to ask Melchizedek his opinion on that question and was surprised when Melchizedek had a ready answer.

"Golden ages occur for many civilizations, periods of peace through strength, high culture, great architecture, impressive financing, and the creation of artisan classes, but none have compared to the Florentine

Renaissance. There were two Western Renaissances prior to the one Vasari called 'the' Renaissance, one under Charlemagne and the other in the universities around the time of St. Thomas, as the ancient texts of Aristotle found their way back to the West. But the Florentine Renaissance was the beginning of a real understanding of the physical world and how it worked in participation with the true, the beautiful, and the good. You must understand that the Faith had always fostered a spirit of inquisitiveness and curiosity about the world that God created, but no one had perfected a methodology for its study. Aristotle had come close with his biological studies, but his theoretical explanations were sorely lacking. The Roman doctor Galen grasped many of the analogies between human and animal anatomy, but failed to develop an empirical method that future medical students could use to advance on his views. Heron of Alexandria came closer with the systematic similarities in his machinery, but he never offered a theory of mechanics to explain them, something which was central in Leonardo's mind. The Florentine Renaissance was premised on the possibility that the world could really be understood if you just looked carefully at it and represented it properly. So, ancient gods and goddesses as well as popes and apostles were merged in art with the most realistic representation of human experience offered since Hellenic sculpture—in the full color of fresco and then oil. All that was great in the past provided the foundation for what was to be Florence. This was a wholly new way of looking at the world, searching for ancient wisdom and building upon it. Michelangelo studied and copied classical sculptures in the gardens of Lorenzo de' Medici, for example. Now, what made this new look at the world possible?"

"I don't know," John admitted, already awed by the answer he was receiving.

"Christianity," answered Melchizedek simply.

"But if Christianity was the foundation for this new world view, why hadn't the Renaissance happened at any point in the previous fourteen hundred years?" queried Anne.

"Because Christianity alone is not sufficient. The material conditions of peace, artisan classes, scholarship, money, and others must also be in place. It's a very special and rare mix, but Christianity made it aspirationally and theoretically possible by merging the ancient Jewish monotheistic faith with all that was best from the pagans."

"Such as?" asked John a bit skeptically.

"Such as the real meaning of their gods and goddesses, as Plato used to say, not merely Apollo, but Beauty, not merely Zeus, but real Authority. The Church saw itself as the fulfillment of these two traditions."

"John!" exclaimed Anne, taking hold of his shirt sleeve, "that's what I've been seeing all through Italy. In the Sistine Chapel the Jewish prophets alternate with the pagan sibyls."

"Just so," acknowledged Melchizedek, impressed with what Anne had gleaned.

"And in Sienna at the Duomo, the marble flooring shows the same theme, with Socrates and the philosophers right in the middle," she continued.

"Yes, Moses and Socrates . . . two powerful traditions that unite together in the Christians and make possible a view of the world that encourages both the arts and the sciences in a stable and growing civilization dedicated to what is true, good, and beautiful—the fulfillment of human nature," concluded Melchizedek.

"But you'd have thought that the great empires of the past would have accomplished this, like Rome, for example," countered John.

"Yes, you might have thought that. But Florence was not even a great empire, only a little one with imperial riches due to her banking industry. It's not just empire, for empires have a tendency to conquer and seize, not really invent. The Romans were the greatest imperialists of all time but their objective was not truth and beauty for their own sakes. That is a crucial difference. They harnessed Heron's inventiveness only to construct impressive siege machinery for the continuation of war. Saint Augustine had much to say of the failings of this city of man, the city of Rome."

Pausing for a moment, John replied, "I guess I understand that Christianity might offer a unifying motivation for uniting the philosophical and Jewish traditions, but I really don't think I understand how it promotes the sciences. From what I have read about medieval science, it was actually non-existent. In fact, the church proved a barrier to the development of real science. Isn't that why Galileo was condemned?"

While Anne looked at Melchizedek expectantly, his face relaxed as he immersed himself into the past, thinking of the best way to address John's question.

"John, you are partly right, there's no doubt about that. But the full answer is more complex, because while certain elements of medieval thought inhibited new scientific advances, other elements made them possible. So, let's begin with the classical scientists, shall we?"

"Sure," John answered, his excitement mounting.

"The classical Greco-Roman natural philosophers lacked a systematic account of the sciences, something that would link them all together. The one promising contender, Aristotle's philosophy, fell out of favor fairly early, and it wasn't until the 1200's A.D. that the medieval thinkers rediscovered his work and realized its potential for offering a universal account of all things, everything from physics to biology to ethics to the nature of God in theology. But by the time Aristotle's philosophy made its way into the West, the "darkness" of the dark ages had long descended, the result of barbarian destruction of the entire Roman industrial and engineering genius, long years of perpetual war and Viking raiding, as well as horrific diseases and environmental disasters that decimated the populations. Without political stability, a scientific culture is impossible."

"Okay, that makes sense. I guess if we suffered a nuclear attack, it would take generations to rebuild. We'd probably have trouble even remembering how things worked," John agreed.

"That's it exactly!" Melchizedek continued. "The medievals had been struck by the equivalent of multiple nuclear strikes, yet they remembered that a golden age had once existed. They could see the dome of the Pantheon even though they had no idea how it had been constructed. They remembered a world of artistic excellence when they dug up Hellenistic statuary. And so they collected and systematized what they found, trying to reconstruct all that they could of the ancient world. Theology mixed with Aristotle's teleology enabled an overarching systematic approach to all knowledge. As a result, the university as we know it was born, born in the so-called 'dark' ages! Why? Because the university seeks universals, principles that order all things together."

"So, that's why the medieval world was so bookish, wasn't it? It was their only real connection to the means to reproduce the golden age of the past," asked Anne.

"Yes, they were frantic to add the knowledge gleaned from newly recovered books to what they already understood. From this obsession with systematic thought, the Western world remembered the arts and sciences of the ancients and finally began again to really understand them. So, Brunelleschi was able to figure out the mathematics of the Pantheon and then employ it himself in constructing the dome of the Duomo in Florence. And Michelangelo moved from awe at the recovered Greek sculpture in Lorenzo's garden to completing secret dissections himself to understand human anatomy, so that he finally surpassed the greatest classical sculpture in the Pieta and the David. The Renaissance greats followed in the footsteps of Donatello and Masaccio and Ghirlandaio who began the process of reconnecting fresco and architecture and sculpture with the world around them, a world that Christianity had all along declared to be good and worthy of study and emulation."

John suddenly jumped in, "But Mel, even though all this astounding art was being produced, the church still suppressed science. So, while I better understand why the medieval world wasn't capable of doing more than salvaging and unifying the remnants of the classical world, I still don't understand your contention that Christianity is the basis of the scientific revolution engendered by the renaissance."

"Fair enough," continued Melchizedek. "Let's return from the arts back to the sciences, your real love, shall we?"

Anne looked a bit disappointed, but John's eyes gleamed with excitement, "Definitely."

"Even though the medieval world produced the renaissance, its scientific theoretical basis, Aristotle's physics and teleological biology, was in fact wrong. But since it explained so much, late medieval and then early renaissance thinkers were reluctant to abandon it. Let me give you an example. Galileo proposed that the solar system was sun-centered, rather than earth centered as had been believed by the Ptolemaic astronomers. But Galileo's theory of circular planetary orbits failed to explain what was actually observed in the night sky just as much as the old Ptolemaic theory failed to explain these observations. So, it seemed silly to the vast majority of thinkers, as well as to the church, to reject the ancient Ptolemaic account when it provided a massive structure for understanding so many other things in the universe such as the natures of angels and the order of physical things in the natural world."

"Okay, I can see that," John acknowledged.

Melchizedek continued, "Yet, once Kepler used the astronomical observations of Tycho Brahe to propose elliptical orbits for the planets, a theory was finally available that explained all of the observational data. And his theory found widespread support."

John looked thoughtful as Melchizedek continued. "At the same time as these revolutionary astronomical theories were being advanced and accepted once they offered theoretical-observational integrity, Descartes was working in the realm of physics, and he made the single greatest contribution to modern science: he offered a fundamental theory about the natural world that permitted a true systematic knowledge."

John looked surprised, "Descartes did that? What was his theory?"

Melchizedek continued, "Descartes maintained that Aristotle's teleo-physics and teleo-biology had to be rejected in favor of the theory that mathematics was the underlying language of the material universe, and it could be used to understand and study all physical phenomena. And he applied this principle to optics as well as the lunar orbits and even to physics, but it was Newton who took this mathematical principle to its ultimate modern expression in what we now know as Newton's physical laws."

"And science was never the same after Newton," mused Anne.

"So, even though the medieval world sought theoretical coherence in all the sciences, they didn't really understand that mathematics was the language of the physical world," mused John thoughtfully.

"Just so," acknowledged Melchizedek. "None of us understood the full significance of mathematics in the classical world or the late medieval era. So, the medieval obsession with systematicity provided both a good and a bad result. The good effect was the pursuit of true universal knowledge first in the recovery and preservation of classical learning and then in the search for new knowledge. The bad effect was their reluctance to accept changes, since they realized that altering any one part of the universal theory would affect everything else. And this made them frown, often severely, on new theories like Galileo's, even though he was more right than the Ptolemaic astronomers."

"But that's not much different from what goes on in the scientific world back in the States, Mel," interjected John. "Take genetic research as an example. It seems intuitively plausible to think that gender and racial differences might stem from genetic determiners, but since that theory was advanced by the Nazis, scientists shy away from this kind of research. Fear of the possible result leads people to reject science nowadays just as much as in the past."

"A fine example, John," Melchizedek offered. "The causes of differences between different people, races, or genders have nothing to do with the value of those differences. That's where the Nazis went awry, in their assumption that difference in race entailed a difference in value. But human beings are all human."

"And therefore all valuable," Anne jumped in. "So, it's not the science that's the trouble, but the willingness of people to misuse science for horrible ends."

"And that causes people to be afraid of scientific theories that might lead to or be used to promote threatening policies. I guess we're not as different as the early renaissance community as I might have thought," John admitted.

"No, human beings are the same in all generations," agreed Melchizedek. "Nor should the reaction against some scientific pursuits come as a surprise, because the scientific quest is a human pursuit, and all knowledge is in fact connected. Thus, human interests might well interfere—perhaps wrongly in the long run, but perhaps not—with what scientific theories can sometimes gain traction."

"But that's where the Christian faith can prove so useful, Mel," John asserted confidently. "Not only does it motivate the pursuit of all truth, it provides moral guidance as to how we should employ what knowledge we acquire."

"Then Christianity isn't really opposed to science," offered Anne cautiously.

"No, it isn't opposed to science at all," concluded Melchizedek. "On the contrary, it motivates the examination of everything that God has created. But it also urges us to be morally prepared for the power that arises with that knowledge. And that's a lesson human beings are far from grasping."

All three of them fell into silence, staring in wonder at the glory of the city below them, Melchizedek remembering the many friends he had lost over the ages, Anne thinking of the lively artistic community of the city in the time of Lorenzo the Magnificent, and John wondering if it was possible for it all to happen again.

"Well, you two need rest," John interrupted the pause. "So let me get you back to my villa, and then I'll find us some pasta and Chianti and the healing will really begin."

CHAPTER THIRTY-FIVE

Washington, D. C.

"It's a Giovanni Bartoli, Sir?" said his assistant inquiringly.

"Oh good, put him through to me right away, would you?" asked Quarston.

Quarston ran over to his phone, "Hello, Inspector Bartoli? Buongiorno!"

The Inspector laughed on the other end of the phone. "It's nearly night here, Agent Quarston, so we say 'Buonasera,' but I suppose 'Giorno' works for your time frame."

"I have a lot to learn if I'm supposed to go to Florence," Quarston admitted.

"We'll take good care of you, do not worry yourself," promised Bartoli.

"Were you able to arrange an interview with Rothschild?" asked Quarston.

"Yes, for two days from now, so that you will be able to rest and freshen from the jetlag after crossing the ocean," explained Bartoli.

"That's very considerate; thank you," continued Quarston. "I should be leaving this evening on the redeye and should arrive tomorrow morning. I'll send you my flight details by fax."

"Good," Bartoli said and then added, "Oh, one more thing, Agent Quarston."

"Yes?" asked the FBI agent.

"I have some pictures that you will find intriguing, I think, pictures that were not part of the report I sent you."

"Oh?" asked Quarston with great interest. "Of whom or what are these pictures?"

"The John Doe and Janet Langley," offered the Inspector.

"You have their pictures?" said a staggered Quarston.

"Yes, and we have identified Janet Langley as Michelle Andover," he said proudly.

Quarston was so interested in what Melchizedek looked like that he had difficulty processing what the Inspector had told him. He now had concrete confirmation of his theory about the links between the hospital attack in Florence, the virus release, and the Hentersheim murder case.

He finally managed to say, "Inspector, that is very good news indeed. I'd like to take a look at those photos as soon as I can."

"I'll send them to you digitally right now."

"Thanks, Inspector."

* * * *

With his patients tucked into their beds and sleeping deeply for the rest of the morning and all of the afternoon, John spent the early hours of the evening at the Guelph Ristorante gathering an impressive array of Florentine foods for his soon to be starving patients. Asparagus cream risotto, ravioli with porcini mushrooms, tagliatelle with pesto, and gnocchi, as well as Florentine steaks, very rare he noted with amusement as he licked his lips. With two bottles of Chianti and another of cold Asti plus the ever-present Florentine dessert *fragola*, he knew the evening would prove rewarding . . . and healthy, he added to himself with a chuckle.

John found Melchizedek and Anne talking with one another on the sofa of the villa, and he noticed the way in which his sister looked at him. He knew that trauma could lead people into romantic feelings that proved illusory back in the real world. But he also couldn't imagine that Melchizedek could possibly feel anything for Anne, and if he did, he wasn't at all sure what he thought of that. He had heard Melchizedek's comment about his "first" wife, and he'd been wondering about that ever since.

Melchizedek leaped up when John entered the room, surprising John with his rapid recovery. Melchizedek helped him with the array of packages and the wine bottles, opening the reds immediately to allow them to breathe, while the Asti and strawberries went into the refrigerator. John checked on Anne, while Melchizedek prepared the table for their meal, even lighting candles on the silver candlesticks in the villa. Watching him out of the corner of his eye, John again wondered about this man, a former king preparing the table like any ordinary person. But how could he be ordinary? And yet, how could he not be ordinary? That's what people were, ordinary. Oh, sometimes they did truly extraordinary things, but still . . .

John's blood ran cold as he watched Melchizedek preparing to slice the bread, carefully examining the edge of the knife with what John realized was the expert eye of a warrior. Ordinary, yet hardly ordinary, he mused. He also saw that as Melchizedek's health returned to him, his full stature and life were returning to him too. John understood that he had no idea who this person really was, having only seen him as a sick patient. That was part of the problem with the medical profession, John knew, seeing people simply as patients. Well, this particular patient was a person, and John decided that he would try to get to know him, even if it meant dealing with an ancient warrior-priest-king whose knife-handling suggested just how dangerous Melchizedek might be.

*   *   *   *

Quarston waited as the images appeared in his email, and then he printed them using a high resolution printer. Soon he was staring at a worn and confused old man exiting an ambulance. It was nothing like what Quarston had imagined Melchizedek would look like, but then again he realized that his 'image' of Melchizedek was purely theoretical, so he had had little serious expectation about the real man. Maybe that was it, thought Quarston, Melchizedek is now a real person to me, not just a mythological figure. Quarston immediately called his assistant to compare the image of the old man with both FBI and CIA surveillance photographs to try to acquire additional information on him. Meanwhile, he looked at the picture of Michelle Andover also leaving the site of the stricken ambulance.

"I've   got   you   now,"   he   said aloud.

*   *   *   *

Their meal ended some four hours after it had begun, and John poured the last bit of Asti into Melchizedek's and his glasses, his sister having already retired to bed. They ascended the stairs up to the roof of the villa where a porch overlooked the city. There they talked about John's reflections on the vital connection of service to joy.

"That is the meaning of much of love, John," answered Melchizedek. "Your namesake explained this throughout his writings, but even more so in his conversations. 'Love one another!' he would say time and again, not understanding why people could not grasp this. Is the good of my neighbor so far from my view, when my own good is so close? Or is it that we do not bother to think properly of goodness at all, ours or our neighbor's?"

"I guess that's part of it. We're so busy," began John.

"Yes," Melchizedek interrupted. "Your generation is one of the busiest I have seen in all my years. Your convenient machines do not provide you with the opportunity to love God and wife, child, parent, friend, fellow citizen—in short all these neighbors. Instead, you re-invest your time to save more time, and thus fall into a bizarre regress."

"And then everything loses meaning," said John, gazing at the beauty of the buildings around him, their old architecture beckoning him toward a different kind of life.

"Not everything, for you have your sister, and your work is noble."

"But that's the trouble, Mel," John exclaimed suddenly. "I don't find it very noble. In fact, it's downright frustrating. Before I left for Italy, do you know what I did? I spent countless hours putting people's faces back together!"

"What's wrong with that?" interrupted Melchizedek in bewilderment.

"Guess how they got that way," offered John.

"Ah, now I see where you are going," nodded Melchizedek.

"Right," answered John. "Some woman jumped off a building and never thought at all about the people below her."

"And they paid the price," Melchizedek finished.

"They always pay the price," replied John tiredly. "Do you know how many children I've stitched up from knife wounds, burns, and broken bones given to them by their own parents?"

Melchizedek sat quietly, reflecting on John's description.

"And then there's the gunshots, the stabbings, the drug overdoses, the bruised and battered women. It never ever stops. I see the same faces over and over again," John cried out to the city streets below them. "Where's the nobility in that? I might as well put them all out of their misery."

"Add to that," John continued as Melchizedek listened intently, "all the people seeking freebies, coming to the ER for free health care for the slightest little things, like runny noses or contacts stuck to their eyeballs. Haven't they ever heard of contact solution?"

Melchizedek suddenly laughed and John found himself joining him.

"In spite of what you probably think, Sir," continued John between laughs, "these people drain the medical system of resources that need to be directed elsewhere."

"I see what you mean, John," Melchizedek admitted, "but that image of the lens stuck to the eyeball following your tirade against inane evil was just too much to handle."

"Yeah," John acknowledged, "you're right. It is funny, and sometimes I do just stop and laugh at it all. The things people do to themselves crack us up in the medical community. So much of it is seriously x-rated."

Melchizedek roared this time, "Okay, I get it. I've been around for a long time, and I've seen my share of self-inflicted screw-ups, I'll admit."

"I think I need a good stiff drink," John suggested while tipping the empty Asti glass for any last drops.

"You're right, we both could use one," Melchizedek acknowledged with a wink, as he returned down the steps of the villa to grab a couple of glasses and a bottle of Irish Whisky.

Once he had returned to the overlook, Melchizedek pointed to the Duomo looming over the city in its magnificence.

"How do you reconcile that, that glory, with the stupidity, inanity, insanity, and horrific evil of men?"

"I don't know," John admitted. "I suppose you've got a secret wisdom to offer on that one?"

"I wish," laughed Melchizedek. "The truth is, I don't have any idea either."

John sat quietly looking at the king, "I guess I figured that with you being a kind of religious leader or philosopher or king or whatever bundle of roles you have, that you'd have figured out the meaning of life."

Melchizedek laughed again, "Oh, the meaning of life isn't the hard part; that's obvious: God loves us."

"But how do you connect God's love with horror?" John asked.

"Right, that's the hard part," Melchizedek answered. "Or, to put it this way: why does God love us?"

"Yeah, that's the question all right," John asserted. "What can he see in us?"

"Look around you again," Melchizedek replied. "Think about the glory of this city, of Paris, of London, of St. Petersburg, or your own Savannah and New York City, and so many, many others."

"And the art," added John.

"And the churches," added Melchizedek.

"And the sculpture," nodded John.

Melchizedek smiled, "It's a paradox, isn't it?"

John reflected on Melchizedek's question, downing a shot of the whisky.

Melchizedek leaned toward him and lowered his voice, "Believe me John, I know what you are talking about. I face the same conflict, watching each new regime rise out of the ashes of those that have gone before, but do they ever change? No, the same greed, the same lust, the same corruption, the same quest for power. It's always the same."

John nodded thoughtfully.

"I remember the greatest king of Babylon, my friend, Nebuchadnezzar. He built a city of gold, his hanging gardens so astonishingly beautiful . . . words cannot express it. And yet, he was a monster, in truth. Glory in one hand, blood in the other. It's been the same ever since. Even this great city, John, matured in an age of violence and death."

"It's the same thing, I guess," John admittedly shyly, feeling a bit small.

"No John," Melchizedek suggested suddenly, "don't compare our lives. You were right. It is the same thing, the paradox of human nature. Socrates described it like this: what has the potential to be so immeasurably good has the same potential to become devastatingly evil."

"That sounds about right," John nodded, more confidently. "Maybe that's what God sees in us, that potential."

"Definitely," Melchizedek answered. "I think that we are the most interesting creation at this point, since humanity's choice is not yet fixed on good or evil the way the cosmic powers are."

"You mean the angels?" clarified John.

"Yes, they and their counterparts," Melchizedek nodded. "They've already made their choices. But human beings are free to choose between good and evil, to become all that God created them for or to reject the goodness of his love and so consume one another in distrust, greed, lust, and every sort of violence."

"So, the girl that jumped . . ." John began.

"Right," interrupted Melchizedek. "She had a story just like we all do, probably a life of agony and grief, but instead of holding on to life, to hope, she yielded to death."

"And took a lot of other people with her," John insisted.

"But we're all like her, John," Melchizedek continued. "Our whole lives are a mixture of goods and evils, done and received, that shape and construct the choice that we are ultimately making."

"I don't know," John inquired. "Are we really like her?"

Melchizedek laughed, "Okay, she made a choice to end it all early, and that's not what most people do, but we're all at once the product and the producer. We are made and we make ourselves. I think this is part of the reason that Jesus was so compassionate with people, like the soldiers dividing his possessions during his crucifixion."

"I remember that," John said. "I guess I always figured that being God he just always forgave people."

"Well, maybe that's true too," Melchizedek answered with a smirk. "But in that particular case he pointed out that they didn't have a clue what they were doing."

"A mitigating factor!" John saw suddenly.

"Right," Melchizedek emphasized. "Jesus saw how the mitigating factors always provide an opportunity to return to goodness, to choose life over death, love over hatred."

"I've never thought of it that way before," John answered.

"Jesus took the slightest potential in people and offered his love to them on those terms," Melchizedek continued. "Like what St. John told me about Nicodemus who visited Jesus in the night, or that woman of Samaria who later became a great saint."

"Jesus certainly was clever in those encounters," John replied.

"Clever in his compassion," Melchizedek corrected. "He always remembered what the person in front of him could really become, not just what they'd already screwed up."

"Oh," offered John grievously. "Now this is getting personal. I have a really hard time thinking of my patients that way."

"So did Jesus," Melchizedek laughed.

"What? What are you talking about?" John asked in bewilderment.

"Okay, I'll tell you. Jesus' hardest case to crack: who was it?" Melchizedek queried.

"Mmm . . . I'm not sure. Pontius Pilate? Or maybe Judas Iscariot?" shrugged John.

"Well, you may have me on that one. I wasn't thinking about Judas the betrayer," nodded Melchizedek thoughtfully.

"Okay," laughed John, "who were you thinking of?"

"St. Peter," answered Melchizedek.

"St. Peter?" asked John incredulously.

"Right, the guy was on the right, then wrong, then right, then wrong side of everything!" Melchizedek noted.

John just stared at him expectantly.

"Okay, you want evidence . . .," Melchizedek paused. "Try the time he walked on the water and then loses his faith and begins to drown. He was the only disciple with the potential, the faith, to actually get out of the boat!"

"But then down he went into the waves," John nodded. "And I remember some other time that he tried to talk Jesus out of his eventual death . . ."

"And Jesus actually calls him Satan and tells him off!" Melchizedek shouted exuberantly.

"Yeah, I see what you mean. And then he betrays Jesus not once like Judas, but three times."

"Which Jesus warned him he'd do, and of course, Peter arrogantly rebuked him, asserting that he'd never betray him," exclaimed Melchizedek. "But Jesus told Peter that he prayed for him that he'd not be torn apart by the events of that horrible night."

"So, he never gave up," answered John.

"No," Melchizedek replied. "People gave up on him, but he didn't give up on them. He always saw what could be, what joy was to come by their embracing the love of God."

"And yet, he definitely got frustrated with people like Peter," noted John.

"Yes, definitely. It wasn't all sentimentality and smiles with Jesus," Melchizedek chuckled. "Like the time his disciples were all arguing about who'd be the greatest in his kingdom, and he threw up his hands in exasperation and asked how long he'd have to be with that generation of people!"

"Jesus did that?" John roared in laughter, eyeing how little of the whisky remained.

"And don't forget how pissed he got at the temple that one time," Melchizedek added.

"Okay, I'm starting to see both sides of this thing. It's okay to be frustrated, because the situation is seriously frustrating," John concluded.

"Right, and sometimes we need to vent, to rage, to head out into the hills (or Florence)," Melchizedek winked.

"But when Jesus went off to the hills alone at night, he also prayed and reorganized his vision, he kept hold of the whole picture," John realized suddenly.

"Yes, if there's any great secret, that's it, what the philosophers called the theological virtue of hope, the motivation for love," Melchizedek agreed.

"So, there's no being perpetually even-keeled like an Eastern monk," John grasped.

"No, that's not human," Melchizedek agreed again.

"And God became human," John added thoughtfully.

"So, He can hardly expect us to be less. When God makes the saint, he does not unmake the man."

"I'm really grateful we had this conversation, Mel," John said after they'd reflected quietly for a few moments more. "It sounds like I need to start praying more."

Melchizedek smiled, "Yeah, I've said that on more than one occasion."

CHAPTER THIRTY-SIX

Billings returned to the joint task force office that afternoon with a large file of information on Michelle Andover. His contact in Paris had come through for him, and he was eager to relate what he now knew to Quarston. It made much more sense than this theory about Rothschild, which was nothing but a theory, so far as Billings could determine. The connection to Turkey at the very least proved geographically closer to Israel, though he knew that that connection was the weakest argument of all. In any case, he now had a solid lead on Andover.

As he entered the office, he found Quarston musing. "Roger, we've got a line on Andover," he said proudly.

"I know," acknowledged Quarston.

Billings looked confused, trying to figure out how Quarston would already know of his discoveries. But he pressed on, since how Quarston knew what he knew was still a mystery to him, but a mystery that a counterintelligence officer like himself would eventually discover. Of that there was no doubt.

"My contact in France provided me with this flight manifest. It turns out that Andover has been in France for the past few weeks, but that she recently left France for Berlin."

That broke Quarston's spell, Billings noticed. Quarston grabbed the manifest in obvious confusion. "What else did you find?" he demanded.

"From Berlin she caught a flight to Istanbul," he explained, showing the additional manifest.

"Okay," Quarston acknowledged. "And then?"

"Then our little suspect walked into a bank and withdrew about half the money in that account we flagged from the lab," Billings continued.

"Really?" asked Quarston more puzzled than ever.

"Yeah, and get this: she's altered her appearance. That's why she dropped off our radar. Take a look at this photograph."

Quarston looked at the photograph from the airport in Berlin. It showed a woman whose hardened face looked nothing like Andover but whose smaller build and sandy hair color seemed similar.

"How do you know this is Andover?" pressed Quarston.

"Well, two things: first, her name is on the manifest, and second, she accessed that bank account."

"Let me ask you something, Fred. If she changed her appearance, why wouldn't she change the name on her passport too? She had to have altered the photograph on her passport, right?"

"Yes, but perhaps she needed to keep the same name to access the funds in those accounts," Billings answered hastily, since that problem had bothered him as well.

"Possibly," admitted Quarston. "Or someone wants to make sure that we follow her trail to Turkey."

"Okay," offered Billings. "Let's say you are right. Who wants us to think that, and where is the real Michelle Andover?"

"Laurence Rothschild and Florence," answered Quarston matter of factly.

"Rothschild again?" asked Billings with frustration.

"I'm meeting him the day after tomorrow," explained Quarston.

"But we still don't have any reason to believe that Andover traveled to Italy!" pressed Billings.

Quarston reached into the folder on his desk and produced the photograph of Andover at the scene of destruction at the Florence Hospital.

Billings looked surprised, and after examining the picture carefully, admitted, "Okay, so she was definitely in Florence at the time I was thinking she was getting plastic surgery. Maybe she hit the hospital first and then returned to France to get the surgery?"

"Or maybe not. Look, we've had our suspicions about those accounts being left in that lab's safe intentionally to direct us toward Andover. It turns out that Andover was a critical part of this international criminal conspiracy, but I think that Rothschild wants to misdirect us toward Turkey," Quarston concluded.

"You might be right," offered Billings. "I suppose you got this photograph from that Italian Police Inspector?"

"Yeah, a Giovanni Bartoli, good man from what I can tell so far," answered Quarston.

"Okay, while you are in Florence, I'm going to Istanbul. At the very least, the woman who accessed the account traveled there, and even if you are correct about Andover and Rothschild, part of their criminal network is in Turkey."

"Sounds good," replied Quarston, happy to help Billings save face. "I'll see you in a few days then?"

"Right," Billings answered before trudging out of the office.

* * * *

The conversation on the top of the villa had gone so well that John decided now was probably the time to ruin it, so he asked Melchizedek, "You know that my sister is taken with you, don't you?"

"Yes, but admiration is not love."

"No, it's not. But love does admire."

Melchizedek paused, "It's been a very long time . . ."

"You've loved before. You said as much during the plasmapheresis."

"Yes."

"But the wisdom and maturity you possess must make a match very difficult," John continued.

"In part yes, but in part too, no. For the goods that the genders bring to one another exceed that of friendship. So equality is not necessary in love in the same way it is in friendship."

"You are talking about sex?"

"No, though sexuality is part of it. I mean the powers of the genders differ, and what a woman can bring to a man, that essential feminine care, nurture and intimate love that is begun by their mothers and completed in their wives, is uniquely available in marital love."

"And there is a corresponding power in the male toward the female then?"

"Oh yes, and it is quite astonishing how goodness wrapped in power, starting with her father and fulfilled through her husband, can complete a woman. Again, nothing that two female friends can experience."

John thought for a moment before asking, "Can you have children?"

"Sure, I have."

"But they die, they all die before you, don't they? Just as your wives have died."

"Yes, they all die." Tears welled up in Melchizedek's eyes, as he fell into the past, before suddenly pulling himself short and remarking, "I don't only record the effects of human evil. I experience them, over and over again. But there are unique benefits too, for I watch their generations grow and my family grow. Now there are so many, too many to count."

"Who are they?"

"Let's just say that an important strain eventually migrated to Britain. Royal blood has a way of asserting itself."

"Prince Charles!" stammered John.

"No, an earlier line," answered Melchizedek cryptically.

"You're not going to tell me anymore, are you?" surmised John.

"No," answered Melchizedek. "First, it's no one else's business, but second, I cannot take the chance that their revelation would lead to someone's pursuing them as they are after me."

"Fair enough. But your children and grandchildren . . . they all eventually die, and none have had anything like your rejuvenating or chameleon powers?"

"Correct. Either they are not genetic or they are recessive," Melchizedek paused. "My descendents are normal in every way."

"Right, well, er . . . I'm sure . . .," began John.

"It's all right, John," Melchizedek assured him. "Anne told me of your parents' death, that you are in large measure responsible for her, so these questions are appropriate. Anne is a fascinating woman, of that there is no doubt. But . . ." He paused, not sure how to continue.

"But . . . you aren't pursuing her, and yet you have thought about it, is that about it?" John asked.

"It has occurred to me, perhaps with too much wine," he answered, and they both laughed.

But Melchizedek suddenly sobered, "John, right now your safety is what concerns me most. Your connection with me is obviously dangerous, and the sooner you two return to your country, the better."

"But no one knows that we even know you. If they did, wouldn't they have grabbed us by now?" objected John.

"Maybe, maybe not," Melchizedek answered. "The truth is, we have no idea how I was initially identified or even infected. Ignorance is not security."

"Okay, you're the soldier," John admitted. "But Anne will need another day's rest before she goes anywhere. In the meantime, I'll get the tickets for a flight home."

"And we need to establish a security protocol from this point forward," added Melchizedek.

"What's a security protocol?" asked John.

"It means that if we are already under surveillance, we need an escape plan, as well as a means to communicate during any crisis."

"Okay, then I'll purchase some phones tomorrow too," offered John.

"Good, and in the meantime . . ." Melchizedek paused looking over each side of the porch, "We'll need a means to indicate that everything is safe in the villa. Do you see that window sill below us?"

"Yes, I see it," answered John.

"We'll move that one plant over by one-eighth every third hour of the day. That'll signal an all-clear for anyone who is outside the villa."

John peered over the ledge trying to determine if he could calculate and distinguish the difference between two and three eighths of the way across the sill, especially from the ground level.

"Why not just move it if something goes wrong?" asked John.

"Because if something goes wrong, you won't be able to get to the plant in time," Melchizedek replied.

"Oh, right," answered John. "When do we start measuring the day? Midnight?"

"Yes, so we move it before we go to bed, all the way to the left," answered Melchizedek. "I'm surprised I didn't think of this before."

"You were very ill, Mel."

"Well, yes, that's true. But we've got to start thinking like we're at war. That means I get you to a safe place, and then I turn the tables on my pursuers."

* * * *

John Horn awoke the next morning and headed out to buy some phones, while Melchizedek cared for Anne, nursing her back to strength with plenty of high energy drinks and as much leftover pasta as he could encourage her to eat.

As John walked through the streets of Florence, he kept wondering if he was being followed. He couldn't enjoy the scenery. He saw everyone around him as a possible bad guy. He admitted to himself that he had no idea what he was doing. How could he tell whether someone was after them? Melchizedek is right, John thought, I've got to take Anne home as soon as she's up to it.

Once he had purchased the phones, John returned to the villa by a different path than he'd left. He was pretty sure he'd seen that done in spy movies. He looked up at the window sill before entering the building, and sure enough, Melchizedek had moved the plant. That means everything is safe, he thought. Relieved, he opened the door and headed up the stair case to his villa. There he found Anne resting comfortably on the sofa sipping hot tea, while Melchizedek recited Dante's *Paradiso* to her in Italian. No woman could resist him, he thought to himself, glad that it wouldn't matter soon anyway, as they'd probably never meet again.

"How are you feeling today, Anne?" he asked his sister.

He saw the look of beaming delight in his sister, "Much better today, John."

CHAPTER THIRTY-SEVEN

Quarston arrived in Florence after an all night flight to Rome and then transferred to Florence in a quick hop. Exhausted from not sleeping during the flight and feeling quite dirty and sweaty, Quarston approached a bathroom to wash only to realize that he had to pay to get into the bathrooms. This was new, he thought in dismay. And his ever-present cleansing gel had been nabbed by airport security at Reagan National. I'm already experiencing culture shock, he laughed to himself. Dirt doesn't matter, he told himself. Get used to it.

Just then a slightly heavy set man in his mid to late forties with a face that competed with Roman sculpture for the claim to the authentic Roman look approached him. Quarston noticed that his skin was much lighter than the pictures he had seen of the Southern Italians, and given the structure of his face, Quarston guessed that perhaps he hailed from Venice, the city reputed to be the last haven of the true Romans from the old empire. Quarston was proud of what he'd already learned about Italians from his hurried study of travel books, but he was also smart enough to realize that for all he knew, maybe Bartoli looked Swiss—if this was even the Italian Inspector at all.

Inspector Bartoli noted the scrutiny he received from the tall American in front of him. He grinned at Quarston's haggard appearance and introduced himself to his foreign counterpart. Soon the two of them were comfortably settled into Bartoli's car with Quarston's luggage stored in the trunk.

"I'll put you up in our hospitality suite in the heart of the city, so that you can wash up and get some rest before the interview tomorrow. I'll call you later in the afternoon, so we can meet for dinner, and I'll show you some of the sights of our great city. You have never been here before, right?" asked the Inspector.

"No, never," muttered Quarston with a yawn. "I'll look forward to that very much."

Bartoli nodded with a smile.

* * * *

As Anne's body slowly replenished her blood supply, John thought it might be helpful for her to get some air.

Anne asked him, "John, some gelato would be just what I need right now, all that intense flavor!"

"We could go to that gelateria you told me about, the one with the huge cones on . . . where was it?" John asked her.

"Piazza della Signoria, yes, let's go there. I'm sure I'll be all right, through anticipation on the way and through gelato on the return trip!" Anne proclaimed triumphantly.

Melchizedek and John both laughed and helped Anne to her feet and out the door.

* * * *

Italian Inspector Giovanni Bartoli walked to Quarston's hotel and picked him up at the front desk. Together they walked through the pedestrian zone of the city. Bartoli showed him the beautiful Duomo, telling him of Lorenzo de Medici's dramatic escape from the assassination attempt that took his brother's life, as well as San Lorenzo, the great Medici church. Then they turned south toward the Arno River, and walked into the Piazza della Signoria in front of the Palazzo Vecchio. Quarston listened as Bartoli told him the history that occurred in just this one square, how the hand of Michelangelo's *David* was damaged during an insurrection, how Savonarola started the great Bonfires of the Vanities on the very spot where he was later burned at the stake. Quarston shook his head in amazement at Bartoli's descriptions and then looked around him at all the tourists dazed with awe as they stared at the Palazzo Vecchio and the statuary in the Loggia. Many had gelato, he noticed. A young woman stumbled near the gelateria to his left, and Quarston was about to offer his assistance when he noticed that a young man at her side quickly lifted her to her feet. He smiled as he noted the huge waffle cone in her hand that somehow survived her slip. What people would do to protect a snack! He turned back toward Bartoli just as an old man emerged from the gelateria with his own large cone of passion fruit gelato.

Bartoli and Quarston walked past the Palazzo Vecchio and through the Uffizi's arches toward the river. Quarston was struck by all the sculptures of the great men who had arisen from this one city: Galileo, Dante, Machiavelli, on and on the statues appeared. He gazed at the magnificent architecture of the Uffizi before passing on to the bank of the river Arno itself. There he looked to his right and saw one of the most famous bridges in history, the Ponte Vecchio. He thought it was even more charming than the many pictures he'd seen.

"Would you like to cross it?" Bartoli asked him.

"Oh, yes," answered Quarston at once.

They walked onto the bridge, as the crowds of tourists and artisans intermingled among the goldsmith shops now closed like little wooden chests. They crossed the bridge and entered the Oltrarno region of the city and walked down one of the streets parallel to the river toward a restaurant that overlooked the Arno itself. The Inspector gave his name and their table turned out to be located right on the river. Quarston was awestruck looking out at the Ponte Vecchio on the one hand and the Uffizi on the other.

The meal to which Bartoli treated Quarston was every bit as good as the view. Spectacular Italian wine and cheeses accompanied by an oil-drizzled focaccia, followed by a first course of ravioli in a truffle cream sauce. Then a second platter of sea bass bites with juniper berries paired with a wine that Quarston learned was called a 'super Tuscan,' and that course followed by the Florentines' famous desert, *fragole*—strawberries with lemon and sugar. Bartoli ordered a bottle of Asti to drink with their fruit, and then they washed it all down with a shot or two of a lemon liqueur known as Limoncello. Quarston decided that he was going to vacation in Florence in the future, and he slept that night more peacefully than he had slept in a very long time.

* * * *

Michelle Andover was annoyed to find her phone ringing at three o'clock in the morning. Grumbling, she stumbled out of bed and finally found the damn thing.

"What?" she growled.

"Michelle, this is Maurice St. Claire. Are you awake?"

"I am now. What is it?"

"I did some further background checking on Anne Horn starting with that church . . .," he began.

"Right, Anne Horn," Michelle muttered, crawling back into her bed, "and?"

"She has a brother, a medical doctor in the United States," St. Claire explained.

"Oh, does she?" Michelle answered groggily.

"Yes, and guess where he is right now?" St. Claire offered promisingly.

"Florence, visiting his sister?" Michelle answered sardonically.

"Right," St. Claire responded flatly.

Michelle sat bolt upright in her bed, forcing her mind into clarity. "I'm sorry, you're serious, aren't you?" she pressed.

"Quite," he answered.

"So, he used her identification to access the medical database at the University, and he must be the one treating Melchizedek. But where are they now?" Andover asked as her full sobriety returned.

"In a villa in the heart of Florence, or so I believe. His name turned up on a short term lease there, so we're going to pay them a little visit at dawn this morning. Can you be available then?"

CHAPTER THIRTY-EIGHT

The half light of early morning glowed on the horizon as the paramilitary team cautiously approached the villa. The pale red light shone on the features of Maurice St. Claire's face, darkening his austere complexion and highlighting the fierce determination and measured hope reflected in his dark eyes as they calmly scanned the peaceful surrounding villas. He thought of the neighbors quietly sleeping or brewing espresso, completely oblivious to the secret military operation next door. Seeing that no one in the area seemed aware of their presence, he turned back to his team. He had assured them that an attack at dawn had the best possibility of success, since their targets would be very groggy, while enough ambient light would be provided by the sun to avoid any mistakes in the darkness. They had planned to arrive at six o'clock but a problem with the tranquilizer darts forced a slight delay. They arrived twenty minutes late and set up a perimeter team of plain clothed men reading papers, smoking cigarettes and greeting any passersby with neighborly smiles all the while concealing their weapons under their average looking dress. Then Maurice and the main extraction team climbed the stairs of the villa after making short work of the locks on the outer Renaissance-era door with a small cutting torch rolled inside a copy of the local paper. Once at the villa's door on the fourth floor, Maurice produced a miniature camera from his backpack and slid it under the door.

* * * *

Melchizedek and Anne sat at the table drinking the morning espresso that Italians had come to rely on the way Americans take coffee or Englishmen tea. They talked deeply of Keats and beauty, of how beauty is like a ghost in our world, breaking in from the other side teasing and tantalizing us with a reality lying on the very edge of the imagination's daring. Reaching into the large terra cotta bowl in the center of the table, Melchizedek lifted the final golden croissant and, drizzling it with honey, offered it to Anne.

*   *   *   *

Seeing no movement with the camera, Maurice St. Claire's men quietly picked the lock on the heavy wooden door of John Horn's villa. His three dart men produced tranquilizer guns from under their jackets and took the lead. His weapons crew pulled several P90 submachine guns from a duffle bag, locked their fifty round magazines into place, and quickly established a perimeter in the landings and doorway. Followed closely by St. Claire and then Andover, the dart men silently rushed into the room and made for their quarry.

*   *   *   *

Melchizedek invited Anne for a stroll along the Arno, so that he could show her some of the ongoing Florentine sculptors still at work on pieces inspired by their Renaissance forbears. With her delighted smile, he called for the check at the little café where they had enjoyed their sunrise breakfast.

*   *   *   *

The action was over as quickly as it had begun, with only one person tranquilized. Disappointed, Andover realized that it was not Melchizedek but John Horn. St. Claire ordered the tranquilizer gun team and half the heavy weapons team at the villa to await Melchizedek's return, while he, Andover, and the rest of the team took John back to the lab for interrogation.

*   *   *   *

Worried that her brother would be concerned if they didn't return to his villa soon, Anne and Melchizedek turned back down Via Tornabuoni when they reached the Arno bridge. As they reached Santa Trinita, Anne was just commenting on how dreary the tunnels must have been despite Michelangelo's art, when Melchizedek seized her arm and shuffled her into the church. She was surprised by the sudden move, but the intense look on his face stifled her protest.

"John didn't move the plant," Melchizedek said with real concern.

"Maybe he forgot?" Anne asked him. Melchizedek had filled her in on their planned security precautions on the walk along the river.

"Perhaps, but he knows how important it is," he answered her. "And he's an early riser, so he'd certainly be awake by now."

"Well, maybe he just stepped out and there's no one there to move the plant," she suggested.

"That may be, but he knew to move the plant in advance in such a case. I only wish I'd grabbed a phone before heading out."

Melchizedek peered around the church door and tried to get a better look at the villa. He saw men milling around the outside chatting amicably. But something still didn't feel right, and centuries of military action had taught Melchizedek to count on his instincts.

"All right, Anne, this is what we're going to do. You are going to stay here, and I'm going to check on the villa. If anything happens to me, go to the Prior you told me about at Santa Maria Novella. I'll meet you there later," Melchizedek commanded her.

"All right," Anne stammered, bewildered by the sudden turn of events.

As Melchizedek began to leave, she grabbed his arm, and he half turned and gave her a wink before strutting out onto Via Tornabuoni in the most fashionable chic that she had yet seen in Italy. His sudden feminine appearance was strikingly beautiful, and she nearly fell over in shock. But he was gone as swiftly as he had transformed, and so she headed toward the front of the church to pray.

* * * *

As Melchizedek approached the street entrance to the villa, the men continued to chat and smoke. He noticed a hefty fellow with something behind his back staring at him. But the stare was not that of a lustful male, and that was all Melchizedek needed to know.

Melchizedek continued round the block, high heels clicking on the old stones, and back toward Santa Trinita, where he retrieved Anne. Anne was relieved to see that he was himself again and safe.

"Come on, Anne, the villa has definitely been hit, and a trap awaits us there. We have to leave the city at once. If they found John, they can find you."

"But where is John?" she asked frantically.

"I don't know where he is," Melchizedek admitted, "but I cannot find him and protect you too, so our objective right now is to get you to a safe place. I have a friend in Naples who should be able to help us with that, so we'll board a train and head there. From the safety of Naples, we can begin a quiet search for John."

"But what will we do for money? All of my credit cards were in John's villa. Can I go home and get some things?" she asked.

"No, you can't. We must assume that both you and your brother have been exposed, so we'll pick up some cash along the way," Melchizedek promised her.

"How?" Anne asked, trying to hold back tears. "You have no cards either."

"Don't worry, Anne," Melchizedek reassured her. "Money is simply a matter of knowing information, and I've had lots of time to gather information."

Anne was puzzled, but Melchizedek left no time for further conversation as he led her into the church's crypt and toward the tunnel entrance.

* * * *

Melchizedek and Anne hurried through the Medieval Florentine tunnels and emerged in an alley near the Duomo. Melchizedek led her toward a stout medieval door, but instead of opening it, he slid back a panel to reveal an old cipher lock. Melchizedek turned the knobs to the appropriate combination and then pulled the door which opened with an awful creak. Melchizedek groaned at the noise, and pushed Anne inside.

* * * *

Bartoli met Quarston at his hotel and then led him through some of the streets off the main tourist paths. While Quarston yawned, still trying to adjust to the time change, Bartoli motioned him to stop in a medieval passage and showed him the façade of Dante's tiny church. Amazed, Quarston entered the building and saw the place where the legendary bard had admired Beatrice. Before they realized it, the time for their appointment with Rothschild neared, so they headed off at a brisk pace toward the police station in the Palazzo Vecchio. They were moving so swiftly that they did not notice two people in an alley entering a building through an ancient creaking door.

* * * *

Anne found herself rushed up a narrow and turning staircase as soon as the large door slammed shut behind her. She could barely see through the stale air, as the only light shot through narrow slits in the heavy stone of the tower and illuminated the thick dust that passed for air in the passageway. After more turns up the tower than she could count, they arrived wheezing at yet another door, and again Melchizedek slid back a panel to reveal a cipher lock, only this one was digital. After he punched in the code, the door opened, and they entered a small room lit by one large window at what she surmised must be the top of one of the few remaining towers overlooking the city.

Anne scanned her cramped surroundings. She observed a small kneeling bench, a hammock suspended in the air, and a small writing desk with a very modern looking computer, she noted with a raised eyebrow.

"So, what is this place? A hideout or something?" she asked curiously.

"Something like that," Melchizedek answered, reaching underneath the desk. He pulled out a key and walked over to the opposite wall of the tower. There he felt among the various smaller stones that made up the tower wall until he found the one that moved. He pulled and tugged at it until it gave way to reveal a small hole in the wall. Reaching inside, he withdrew a small wooden chest. He placed the chest on the writing desk, and inserted the key into the lock. It clicked as he turned it, and he quickly opened the box. Anne watched in amazement as he withdrew a British passport, a pistol, credit cards, and a large stack of Euros.

"Don't worry," he assured her. "My friend in Positano will be able to get you a passport. We cannot trust your consulates, as we don't know if the Americans are involved with my pursuit."

"I wasn't worried," she stammered trying to comprehend all that he had already concluded concerning her situation. She was intensely curious about the contents of the secret box, as well as the history behind this clandestine hideout and what it told her about Melchizedek.

"You should be," he warned her seriously. "Your life is in grave danger, and you are now my responsibility. We're going to get you out of this country as rapidly as we can, but we must have travel documents to make that possible."

Seeing her eyes filling with tears, he reached for her hand and offered, "Trust me, Anne. We can get through this. But you must start thinking like a fugitive, not knowing who is pursuing you, but nevertheless learning how to spot pursuers."

"I don't think I can do that, Mel," she said before bursting into tears. Through her sobs, he could barely make out, "I'm just an American girl. I don't know anything about being a spy. And now John is gone, and I don't know where they've taken him or what they'll do to him."

Melchizedek took her into his arms and held her, as the sobs shook her body. It was bad enough that she'd just lost her brother, but her recent medical trauma added to her emotional collapse. When the sobs finally gave way to little whimpers, Melchizedek summoned all his kingly strength and reached for her chin, gently lifting her face toward his.

Anne looked in astonishment at the man before her, radiating in majestic light and authority. She felt her knees give way as her body knelt before him. Her tears faded, as the gravity and power of the man before her swallowed up her own little self and with it all her fear. She literally felt herself absorbing his strength, confident that she could trust him with her life and John's, just as he had trusted her only a few days before.

Melchizedek asked, "Anne?"

"I'm all right now, Sir," she said still facing the ground, afraid really to gaze upon his majesty again.

Melchizedek again drew her face toward his own, but this time she simply saw the man that she was now sure that she loved. She took his arm, and said, "I'm ready. Let's go."

CHAPTER THIRTY-NINE

O nce they arrived at police headquarters in the Palazzo Vecchio, Inspector Bartoli led Quarston into a gilded private office, complete with Renaissance frescoes of ancient gods frolicking with nymphs. There they found Laurence Rothschild waiting for them. Quarston saw that he was impeccably dressed, but bore a simple, almost ordinary face. Not a hint of evil showed anywhere in his features. Bartoli had instructed Quarston to remain silent until he introduced him.

Rothschild looked up at the large intimidating figure that accompanied Bartoli as they entered the room, apprehending immediately that Quarston was a foreigner. The look of displeasure that shot across his face was replaced by a warm smile so rapidly that Quarston had to respect his self-control. Bartoli greeted Rothschild and introduced Quarston as a special agent with the American Federal Bureau of Investigation. He explained that they were jointly working on the attack at the hospital.

With the accent of a British gentleman, Rothschild asked Bartoli in flawless English what interest the American FBI had in the terrorist attack.

"Well, Sir, we no longer believe that the assault at the hospital was the work of terrorists," Bartoli explained.

Quarston and Bartoli had decided to approach Rothschild on their suspect's own terms, supplying him with an update as to their progress. They intended to assess his responses to what they told him. And he didn't disappoint them.

"Indeed?" asked Rothschild. "And what makes you believe this?"

"Well, first off, there were two independent combat teams at the hospital who fought each other. Second, it appears that the hospital attack

236

is linked to an attempt by someone to release a harmful virus all over the world," Bartoli offered, halting to gauge Rothschild's reaction to their connecting two cases that one would have thought were distinct.

Rothschild played his part nearly perfectly, asking confusedly, "I'm sorry, Signor Bartoli, but I do not understand what you mean? The hospital was attacked to release a virus?"

Quarston appreciated Rothschild's acting skills thus far, so he now played his ace, "No, Sir, we believe that this woman"—he held up a picture of Michelle Andover—"was involved with both the attack at the hospital and with the production of the virus at a facility in the United States, in New Jersey in particular."

Quarston watched Rothschild's face as he betrayed a small look of surprise. He hesitated slightly in asking his next question, "Well, do you know where this woman is?"

Quarston would have expected Rothschild to ask who she was, not where she was, because people like to know who or what things are before they ask other questions about them. He felt sure that Rothschild already knew who the woman was.

Quarston decided to play the Turkey card and see how Rothschild reacted, "Yes, Sir, we have very good reason to believe that she is in Turkey. Although we think she might have altered her appearance."

The tension in Rothschild's limbs diminished slightly at that, Quarston and Bartoli both noticed at the same time. Rothschild's next question confirmed Quarston's suspicion of him, for he asked, "So, what can I do to assist you?"

As soon as Rothschild thought that they had taken his bait, he offered his help, Quarston mused, concluding that the Turkey angle was indeed a red herring.

Bartoli was prepared to ask for something concrete from Rothschild to make the meeting appear meaningful, so he asked for any hospital records relating to either a woman named Michele Andover or a woman named Janet Langley. Rothschild assured them that he would conduct a thorough search of all records and make them available by the end of the day. And with that he left.

Bartoli spoke first, "Well, he's guilty. No doubt about it."

Quarston admired his colleague's police instincts, "Yeah, but now we have to prove it."

* * * *

Rothschild mulled over the interview with the two policemen, one of them from America. He was convinced now that they were indeed on to him, that the interview had been meant to gauge his reactions to their revelations more than to inform him of the progress of their investigation.

The question now was what to do about it. Neither the Americans nor the Italians would act outside of the law, which meant that the central barrier between him and them was an evidentiary one. Years before he had embarked on this project, he had ordered Maurice St. Claire to prepare an exposure protocol, which could make the entire project disappear. He knew that file lay in his safe, ready for action should he require it.

The problem with the protocol was that it necessitated that all who knew of the project's existence be killed, and St. Claire was professional enough to have placed his own name at the head of the list. That he would be the natural one ordered to carry it out had actually amused Rothschild when he'd first read it. He had asked St. Claire whether he would carry out an order to execute himself, but St. Claire had only smiled.

Rothschild had continued in the belief that he could trust no one, ever, for the pursuit of power was incompatible with trust. Nevertheless, alliances had to be made, but they were properly secured through dependence. St. Claire knew as much as anyone about the nature of Rothschild's ambitions, but he was also aware of the risks associated with that knowledge, namely that his future—for good or for ill—lay entirely in Rothschild's security. To that end, he worked assiduously to protect Rothschild.

But Rothschild also knew that St. Claire would never pull the trigger against himself, and frankly, Rothschild needed him. If St. Claire were exposed, he was exposed, and that was the bottom line. Surely St. Claire had prepared a dossier on Rothschild that would find its way to someone inconvenient should he meet an untimely death. St. Claire's professionalism was something that Rothschild could rely upon, and that meant that it cut both ways.

So, the question was whether to invoke the exposure protocol or not. He decided to call St. Claire to discuss the matter.

* * * *

Impressed by Anne's resolve, Melchizedek led her back down the old stone staircase and into the Florentine alley. They again entered the tunnels and traveled through what Anne began to believe must be a maze underneath the entire city. After a dizzying array of turns, doors, stairs, and even an ancient ladder, Melchizedek led her to a final staircase. Telling her to wait for him there, he ascended and disappeared through a doorway at the top. Returning a short while later, he called for her to join him, and as she neared the doorway, she heard the unmistakable sounds of trains. They had arrived at the train station next to Santa Maria Novella.

* * * *

Maurice St. Claire listened with increasing interest as his boss outlined the conversation with the two police officers. He knew that he was required to offer a professional judgment on Rothschild's question, but he felt the same air of mission realization that Rothschild did. They were so close to Melchizedek that perhaps they could stay ahead of the authorities. But St. Claire also knew that much depended upon the nature of their pursuers. The Israelis had already authorized covert military action against them, though apparently without the full knowledge of who was behind the endeavor to acquire Melchizedek. If they knew of Rothschild's identity, he had little doubt that Rothschild would die. State actors, especially the Western powers, were impossible to stop. So, the question was whether the interest of the Italians and now the Americans too would either be discerned by the Israelis or shifted over to the professional military and intelligence officers of those countries.

St. Claire decided that the fact that Rothschild was interviewed at all suggested that he was not being pursued by American or Italian foreign intelligence services. Thus, they still had time. But he decided at the very least to urge Rothschild to invoke the communications and physical plant security measures that they had long ago prepared. He had evaluated all of Rothschild's central locations for possible espionage, and had constructed a detailed multi-level security plan on how to maximally prevent exposure.

Concentrating on the task at hand, St. Claire advised Rothschild against invoking the execution protocol, at least against the people he needed to carry out the project. But physical security would have to be raised to the highest level, meaning that Rothschild himself would have to have constant security and that all of their communications would have to be physically protected against any further intrusion.

Rothschild listened to his security director and nodded thoughtfully. He decided that St. Claire was probably correct. He asked him how long it would take to enact the execution protocol, and St. Claire informed him that he would have his people in position to carry out the order within forty-eight hours, so that within twenty minutes of Rothschild's activating the protocol, it would be done.

CHAPTER FORTY

Melchizedek checked the train departure board and satisfied himself as to which *binario*, or track, the Naples Eurostar Train would depart from. On the way to the track, they stopped at a vendor and purchased two bottles of water, two more of Powerade, and some fruit and cheese. Melchizedek then led Anne down the track and onto the waiting train. Escorting her to her first class seat, he headed back to the rear of the car and gathered up a pillow and blankets, fearful that the stress might prove too much for her given the recent transfusion and its complications. Anne thanked him heartily, and curled up on her seat, as Melchizedek carefully surveyed each person in the car. He then pulled down the shades next to their seats and waited anxiously for the train to depart.

* * * *

A fairly ordinary-looking Italian businessman had hardly looked up as Anne Horn and a strikingly beautiful woman brushed past him. He casually retrieved his phone and compared the photograph of Horn on its display with the young lady who walked by him. Confident in his identification, he dialed the number for Maurice St. Claire.

* * * *

As the train finally departed the station, Melchizedek allowed himself to relax marginally. He still maintained a constant surveillance on the other passengers and watched the doorways to the car with his hand never far from his pistol. He glanced at Anne curled up in the seat opposite his, sleeping peacefully. The train headed south toward Naples, the Italian countryside soon replacing the urban concentrations surrounding Florence. Looking at the cascading vineyards and green rolling hills with monasteries dotting their crests, Melchizedek relaxed for the three and a half hour trip.

* * * *

Three cars further back in the train, the Italian businessman too settled in for the ride to Naples. He kept his briefcase close at hand, knowing that its contents included a well-oiled machine pistol. His primary weapon on this trip was supposed to be the telephone, but he was prepared just in case.

* * * *

"If your agent spotted them, why didn't he stop them?" Andover asked indignantly.

"We don't know what his current capacities are, Michelle," St. Claire responded firmly. "We need to plan this out carefully. We know exactly where they are going, to Naples."

"So we pick them up there?" she queried.

"Yes, at the station, so that we don't risk losing them in the hustle," St. Claire added.

"How do we avoid making a scene at the Naples station?" Andover pressed, desperate not to lose Melchizedek again.

"The Garibaldi terminal in Napoli is known for . . . shall we say, the criminal element?" explained St. Claire. "That a group of policemen make an arrest at the station will come as no surprise."

"But won't the real policemen at the station wonder why an arrest is being made of which they have no knowledge?" Andover asked quizzically.

"They might," St. Claire admitted. "But since there are so many kinds of police officers in Italy, enough confusion might be possible that it is more likely that the other officers would help our team securing them."

"Okay," Andover finally sounded relieved. "And your man on the train will keep a close eye on them?"

"Not too close," explained St. Claire. "As I explained earlier, Anne Horn is in the company of a woman who you say is likely Melchizedek, right?"

"That's right. That chameleon gene we discovered in his DNA could definitely account for his ability to appear radically different. And your agent reported that the woman was escorting Anne Horn. It all fits."

"Yes, it does. But if he can disguise himself that easily, I do not want to risk having him transform again prior to the Napoli retrieval. So, I gave orders for my man to maintain a discreet surveillance."

"Very well," Andover concluded. "I'll prepare my team to help maintain and sedate him once your 'police officers' make their arrest."

"That won't be necessary, Michelle," said St. Claire. "My retrieval team will keep him sedated. You prepare for his arrival here in Florence, so that you can begin your experimental project. Mr. Rothschild takes a keen interest in that part of this operation."

"Fine," pouted Andover. "We'll be ready."

* * * *

Yaakov Katz had ensured that all data retrieved by the tap into Michelle Andover's communications network be sent to his remaining Sayerot Mat'kal team in Italy. He tracked her recent interest in the Horn siblings, though he was still somewhat unclear what prior connection they had with Melchizedek. And he had just received word that one of her agents had picked up Anne Horn and a woman on a train heading to Naples. Since Andover's people planned to intercept the train in Naples, Katz ordered his team to attack the train coming out of the main tunnel along the route from Florence to Naples. Their mission was simple: destroy the train and ensure that Anne Horn and Melchizedek, woman or man, was dead. His mission commander had already acquired a helicopter to take his team to the ambush point.

Katz stared at the packet of cigarettes he had bought, desperate to smoke to relieve the tension that boiled in his nerves. He hated this part of his job, waiting while others carried out his orders. Or had better carry them out, he told himself, remembering with disgust the foiled strike at the hospital. He didn't need to make a decision to take a cigarette; he only needed to get out of the way of himself. He almost felt the resolve leave his body, as he watched his hands expertly lift the lit cigarette to his lips.

* * * *

The Sayerot Mat'kal team was in a particularly feisty mood, eager to even the score for the loss of their brother team. The team commander established the parameters for the attack, deploying his men to their best weapons locations, with his two rocket attack teams stationed near the tunnel exit, straddling the train's track. Their latest information indicated that the targets would be found in the first class cabin just behind the engine, and on this particular train, the engine was leading the train, so their objective was to launch their rockets directly at the second car as it emerged from the tunnel. He placed a surveillance team on the far end of the tunnel, two men who would radio the arrival of the train and then prevent their targets from exiting the entry to the tunnel on the off chance that they survived the rocket attack. And high on the hill on this side of the tunnel, he placed his best sniper. He was determined to cover every possibility.

* * * *

Anne stirred and moved her stiff limbs awkwardly, fighting to grasp where she was and what she was doing. Then she saw him watching her from the seat across from hers, and she remembered all that had happened. She smiled weakly and pushed herself up on the seat.

"Here, drink some of this Powerade. It will help to restore your strength," Melchizedek offered.

"Thank you, Mel," she accepted the drink, and then asked, "Where are we now?"

"We are about two thirds of the way to Naples," he explained, cutting some of the cheese and fruit for her.

After she had eaten a little of each, she asked him, "Do you think we could take a walk through the train? I'm so stiff and cold. I think I need to move these limbs of mine."

Melchizedek wondered about her request, thought about whether he could guarantee her safety through the train.

"Please?" she pressed, and watched him relent.

"Very well, but let's keep it brief, okay?"

"Great!" she exclaimed and awkwardly straightened up. Wrapping herself in the blanket, she followed Melchizedek toward the back of the train.

* * * *

The Italian businessman was surprised when Anne Horn and her traveling companion suddenly burst through the door in front of him. He nearly flipped open his briefcase to grab his weapon, but managed to control himself just in time, as he saw that they were only taking a stroll. As the two of them departed his car for the next, he sighed heavily. He thought of following them, but calculated that that was the surest way to exposure. There was nowhere for them to escape on a moving train, so he decided to await their return.

* * * *

Anne opened the door of the dining car with delight, and turning to Melchizedek, said, "Well, my fine Sir, I would love to buy you something, so what'll it be? Crackers? Chocolate?"

Melchizedek laughed and assured her that some crackers would prove acceptable.

He watched her speak in fairly good Italian to the dining cashier and ask for the crackers. When the cashier told her the price, she turned to Melchizedek with an impish smile and wondered aloud if he had a couple Euros or not.

Melchizedek laughed again and coughed up the Euros. They sat together at one of the dining car tables and nibbled the crackers.

"It's good to see your face so full of color again, Anne," he said warmly.

"Well, it's a wonder what butter crackers can do for your complexion," she retorted.

"Yes, well, I've heard things on that score that would make your hair stand up on end."

"Really?" she asked and then added, "Worse than your hair the other day?"

"Well, maybe not that bad," he admitted, remembering the effect of the electric charge. "But women have been using beauty aids for millennia, and some of the formulae are . . . odd."

"Like what, for example?" she asked. "I mean, nowadays people are using botulism poison to correct sagging under their eyes."

"I had heard that," he admitted. "But how about bathing in . . ."

* * * *

The two rocket teams fired nearly simultaneously, the rockets speeding toward the first class car and crushing it between their explosive forces just as it emerged from the tunnel. The engine of the train sped ahead as its load was ripped from its back, before screeching to a halt several hundred meters further up the track. The next few cars still trapped in the tunnel derailed and crashed into the debris of the first class car, while the cars at the tail end of the train slid off the track and produced a shower of sparks and screaming metal as they ran along the tunnel interior.

* * * *

Melchizedek caught Anne's frightened gaze, as they were thrown from the table and onto the dining car's floor. Glass shattering from the car windows mixed with snack packages and soft drinks to fall upon them in a deluge. Melchizedek tried to cover Anne with his body, but then the car slid up against the tunnel wall and ran for several tens of meters further before bursting into flames.

* * * *

The Israeli surveillance team at the tunnel's entrance donned breathing masks and entered the billowing smoke, prepared to engage any two women fitting the description they had been given. At the tunnel exit all was chaos. The first class car was a burning inferno, so the Israeli commandos had to withdraw slightly up toward the two hills on either side of the valley. As dazed survivors smeared with oil and blood began to emerge from the tunnel, the commandos compared each one to the photographs they had of Anne and her traveling companion.

CHAPTER FORTY-ONE

The Italian businessman's phone began to ring, but his hand did not move to answer it. His empty eyes were fixed on the twisted metal surrounding his crushed body, unable to move as his life drained onto the broken floor of the train car.

* * * *

The faint odor of explosives mixed with the stench of carnage and burning oil brought Melchizedek back to consciousness. He forced himself to move amidst the chaos surrounding him and, ignoring his own wounds, picked up Anne's limp body and moved toward the rear of the compartment. One side of the car was crumpled against the tunnel wall, so he moved toward the door on the other side and pressed the emergency release button. Dead bodies and smoking corpses lay all round the shattered train cars. But through the smoke he saw a masked soldier with a drawn weapon warily approaching the rear of the train. Melchizedek's horror at what had happened on the train gave way to a monarchial fury that is unknown to the modern world. Gently placing Anne against the doorway of the car, he crouched in wait for the soldier.

* * * *

The Israeli commandos approaching the rear of the train were unprepared for the blurred form that engaged them. Had they been able to make a report on what they had seen, they could have said only that something that appeared to be composed of the smoke and fire that they saw around them overcame and devoured them.

* * * *

After dispatching the two soldiers, Melchizedek took their communications gear and weaponry, and then returned to the smashed dining car to retrieve Anne. She was still breathing, he saw to his relief, and so picking her up, he exited the rear of the tunnel, climbed the far hill, and hid her on some moss behind a group of tall cypress trees. Then he headed along the top of the ridge toward the other end of the tunnel.

* * * *

The over watch sniper continued to survey the faces that emerged from the train tunnel. So far none of them matched the descriptions of their targets, and his team had only five more minutes before they had to evacuate their positions. He felt nothing but surprise when his own cold knife slid through his spine and out the front of his neck. As he slumped over to one side, he looked into the eyes of a face consumed with such rage that he prayed that death might overtake him quickly.

* * * *

Melchizedek worked his way down the hill toward the first rocket assault team. From the sniper position above, he had readily identified all of the positions of his enemy. His opponents were professionally trained, so it was fairly obvious where the best ambush positions would be, and sure enough, he found the rocket strike teams wherever he would have deployed his own troops. He molded his appearance to that of the terrain around him, so that only a greenish blur appeared behind the team crouched beneath a rise on the hill. He used the knife that he had so deftly stolen from the sniper, cutting the throat of the first soldier while driving his foot into the face of his companion as he turned in alarm. Melchizedek was atop him before he could cry out, plunging the knife into his heart as he held his mouth shut with his hand. As the blood slowed to a stop within his body, he went limp and faded into unconsciousness and death.

* * * *

The Sayerot Mat'kal commander was concerned when his over watch sniper as well as his first rocket team failed to report. He expected the possibility that interference from the tunnel might affect communications, but nothing should have affected his sniper, so he raised his head for a quick look. Machine gun bullets tore his head from his shoulders, as a blurred form came rushing across the tracks toward his position.

* * * *

The remaining rocket team heard the gunfire to their left and turned to discover who was firing, but they could not visually identify anyone firing a gun. They reported to their commander on their radios, but found the channel dead. Managing their rising fear, they decided to withdraw to their first rendezvous point. They moved up the hill rapidly, keeping a constant eye around them, and relaxed a little as they reached the crest.

* * * *

Predicting their course of action, Melchizedek was already hiding on the reverse slope, and as the first soldier burst over the top of the hill, he emerged behind him kicking him full in the back and sending him sprawling down the far side. Knowing that the other soldier would not be far behind, Melchizedek aimed his captured submachine gun at the crest and fired a burst as the other soldier appeared. He crumpled into a heap as the bullets burrowed into his chest. Melchizedek then pursued the other soldier, and found him lying further down the hill, his breath knocked out of him. Fear filled the soldier's eyes as the apparition before him resolved itself into a warrior with eyes colder than death.

Melchizedek grasped the soldier's neck and lifted him bodily into the air, pinioning him against the trunk of a large tree. His antagonist's strength seemed inhuman to the veteran special forces soldier who found his legs dangling in the air, as he struggled to breathe.

"Who are you? Why did you attack the train?" Melchizedek demanded.

Defiance replaced the fear that had nearly overcome him moments before, as the soldier glared at his captor, refusing to offer any explanation. Realizing that the interrogation was useless, Melchizedek suddenly threw him to the ground. As the soldier moaned from the force of the fall, Melchizedek reached out and grabbed his enemy's head in his hands, twisting it violently and snapping his neck.

* * * *

Melchizedek carried Anne toward a farm house, where she began to revive. He placed her next to a small stream, and cupping his hands, dipped them into the cold spring water. Then he carefully returned to her and offered her a drink. As she drank, she looked at him with eyes of intense concern. He stared back at her in confusion.

"The blood . . .," she began hesitantly. "You are covered in blood."

Then she saw the weapons over his shoulder, and added, "But it is not all yours, is it?"

"No," he answered softly.

She reached up to his face and stroked it very gently, "Thank you, my king. There is such pain in your eyes."

Reaching down to her own torn clothes, she ripped off a section of the cloth and dipped it into the stream. Then she wiped the blood off his face and hands, taking special care with the numerous cuts from the glass of the train windows. Melchizedek sat there absorbing her gentle touch, feeling a sense of relief from the rage of battle that had only recently consumed him.

"Be at peace, my king," she whispered.

He asked her, "Are you injured?"

"Only bruised," she explained, "though I also seem to be covered in gelato and potato chips."

Her chuckle assured him that she was indeed okay. "Then we have to keep moving," he urged.

"Then let's go, to that farmhouse over there, I assume?" she asked pointing.

"We'll try there. I saw that they have a couple of horses."

"Horses?" she laughed. "You are going to buy me a horse?"

"Why yes, I thought I might," he laughed back, as his combat readiness gave way to normalcy. "Do you ride?"

"Yes, I took lessons as a girl," she remembered. "But I never owned my own horse."

"Let's see if we can't change that, shall we?" he asked her, pleased with her delight.

Melchizedek stashed his weapons next to the stream and took Anne toward the house. The farmhouse owner and his wife were startled by the appearance of their guests, but they soon understood the significance of the train "accident" as Melchizedek described it. When he further mentioned being interested in borrowing or purchasing two of their horses, they were surprised by the emergence of several thousand Euros. The deal was quickly reached, and Melchizedek and Anne headed to the barn with the owner where they chose two horses and saddles.

As they led them from the barn, the farm owner's wife came running from the house and called to them.

"Here, take these," she said, handing them new clothes.

Anne looked at what she'd chosen for Melchizedek, relieved that they were the clothes of a man. She couldn't always tell how Melchizedek appeared to others, and she was a bit worried that he might still appear as a woman. The clothes fit them adequately, and soon they were headed back to the stream to retrieve the weapons. Melchizedek strapped them to their horses, and they prepared to leave.

"Mel?" asked Anne.

"Yes?" he answered.

"Thank you for my horse. No one has ever given me a gift like this."

"You are welcome," he answered her. "What will you name her?"

"Well, she's a beautiful brown, Mel, so I think I shall call her Cinnamon," she answered playfully.

"Then I shall name my horse Frankincense, since we're going with spices!" he exclaimed.

"You can call him 'Frank' for short," she joked.

"Yes, but will you call yours 'Sin'?" he laughed back at her, as he kicked his heels into Frank and sped away.

CHAPTER FORTY-TWO

As Quarston packed for his return trip to Washington, his hotel phone rang. He picked it up and heard an excited Inspector Bartoli on the other end of the line.

"Agent Quarston, I just received word of another major attack here in Italy!" he exclaimed.

"What happened?" asked Quarston, his mind focusing on Bartoli's words.

"A train heading from Florence to Napoli was ambushed by a rocket attack as it exited a tunnel. Many people were killed or injured in the attack," explained Bartoli.

"And you think it is related to the attack on the hospital?" asked Quarston.

"Two things lead me to suspect this," answered Bartoli quickly. "First, we rarely have incidents like this in Italy, and this one comes too close on the heels of the other for me to consider it mere coincidence. Second, those who orchestrated the attack are all dead, just like the last time."

"At the Florence Hospital?" asked Quarston trying to understand Bartoli's breathless call.

"Yes, just like at the Florence Hospital," replied Bartoli. "So, I'm heading to the train wreck location by helicopter, and I wondered if you would join me. Could you delay your return to Washington?"

"Of course, Inspector, and thank you for including me," answered Quarston.

"Very well, get ready to go and I'll pick you up by police car in just a few minutes," explained Bartoli.

"Through the pedestrian zone?" asked Quarston puzzled.

"In times like these, the tourists can get out of my way, I assure you, Agent Quarston," answered Bartoli decisively.

Quarston believed him and headed down to the hotel entrance.

* * * *

Laurence Rothschild looked at his two subordinates with weariness, as he was still unsettled by the interview he'd had with the two police detectives. The report he received on the train derailment and rocket destruction of the first class car suggested that Melchizedek was likely dead. But then Maurice St. Claire spoke up.

"There is one anomaly, Sir, Michelle," he explained to them both.

Michelle Andover stared at him coldly; St. Claire had not mentioned any 'anomaly' to her.

"Well, what is it?" asked Rothschild impatiently.

"My man on the train tagged Miss Horn, and the signal showed movement after the train attack. But then it went dead. So, I'm not sure how to interpret it."

"Where exactly?" asked Rothschild, opening a map of the region on the ornate desk in his study.

"Right there, near where the train was hit," St. Claire pointed to the map.

"What is nearby that location?" asked Andover, figuring that she had better become involved in the conversation.

"Only a farm, from what I can tell," answered Rothschild. "Do you concur, Maurice?"

"Yes, Sir," he replied. "I'll have our people check into the farmhouse."

"Very good," concluded Rothschild. "Miss Andover, please remain."

After St. Claire exited the room, Rothschild turned to his chief biologist, "Dr. Andover, you have done well. Your tracking of the Horns was impressive. And you have discovered what from Mr. Horn?"

"Nothing to indicate any objective or destination for Melchizedek, Sir," answered Andover, pleased that Rothschild addressed her by her title for the first time. "But I do know what medical procedures he used on him. And I must say, Sir, that the boy has talent."

"Melchizedek will recover from your virus?" Rothschild narrowed his eyes.

"Yes, he will," Andover replied, momentarily stung. Just when you thought you were impressing this guy, you're on his bad side again, she mused.

"We used a virus to produce nanites that would evade Melchizedek's immune system," she continued. "But I expected his body to eventually develop antibodies against the virus, while the nanites would die out. Unexpectedly, though, the nanites effected a more intense radiological effect than we had aimed for, undermining his immune system."

"So, he could not have developed antibodies adequately? Similar to the AIDS virus?" asked Rothschild.

"That's a good analogy, Sir. Horn figured out that effect, but unlike the HIV which is purely biological and damned difficult to root out, the nanites being only microscopic machines could be destroyed by a powerful electrical current. So, that's what Horn did; he overloaded them, and they all fried. But the electricity magnetized them too, so they began to attach themselves to the iron in Melchizedek's body, located primarily in his hemoglobin. So, Horn used a blood cleansing procedure called plasmapheresis to filter Melchizedek's blood, and offered him a partial transfusion of fresh healthy blood. That procedure eliminated both the inactive nanites and the radioactive isotope that tends to collect in the hemoglobin. Horn then treated Melchizedek with immune response boosters, apparently covertly through Powerade. Melchizedek's immune system began to produce antibodies to the original virus, halting further production of the nanites, and his health returned rapidly."

"But you have a new blood sample, correct?" asked Rothschild.

"Yes, but I cannot use it to reprogram the virus for another shot at him, if he's alive," Andover explained.

"Why not?" asked Rothschild.

"Because his body has developed antibodies to the vector, to our engineered polio virus, so as soon as his immune system detected a renewed attack, his body's defenses would swarm the virus. The only reason it was able to invade his system the last time was that his body's remarkable immunity is based on the recognition of biological hazards, not mechanical ones. So, since the engineered virus posed no biological threat to him—we rendered it benign for that reason—his body did not intercept it. That permitted the production of the nanites. But now his body is producing antibodies to the virus, meaning his immune system has learned. We certainly couldn't use the polio virus again, and even if we could start from scratch with a wholly new vector, I think that his body is now responsive to the nanite threat too. If that is correct, then even if we used a new vector like avian flu for example, the nanites would likely not survive their production sequence."

"So, that's it, then?" asked Rothschild.

"It's preliminary, but yes, Sir. He will recover fully, though, so he will still provide a perfect specimen once we do recover him," offered Andover hopefully.

"Yes, I'm sure he will, and if he is alive, he will likely remain that way, so we may yet recover him," offered Rothschild.

"And what are we to do with Dr. Horn?" asked Andover.

"He has seen nothing and no one, correct?" asked Rothschild.

"That's right," she answered. "We've kept him isolated and blindfolded."

"So, his value now remains solely as a contact point for his sister?" Rothschild pressed.

"That makes sense, yes, Sir," she acknowledged.

"Then release and track him," decided Rothschild. "Oh, and one more thing, Miss Andover?"

"Yes, Sir?" she queried.

"Your communications security has been penetrated," explained Rothschild coldly.

"What?" she asked in shock.

"How do you suppose the Israelis knew where to find him, and knew to attack a moving target? Isn't it reasonable to suppose that they knew that we'd be waiting for Melchizedek in Naples?" he asked her.

"Yes, but how do we know it wasn't betrayal again, Sir?" she asked.

"First, we reviewed everyone in our employment following the betrayal of Rosenberg. Second, my own cyber-experts noted the incursion into your system an hour ago, and they've traced all that was examined," he answered.

"How bad is it?" she asked.

"Bad enough," he paused, "for you."

"What does that mean?" she pressed.

"It means that they know who you are and what you have been up to. Since we employ a secondary encryption protocol for all of my correspondence with you, they were unable to break into that material and as such have yet to identify me. So, you must be extremely careful, and you may not travel without taking all the precautions that Mr. St. Claire advises. Is that clear?" he asked.

Rothschild had elected not to reveal to Michelle the full extent of her exposure to the American and Italian authorities, in order not to alarm her to the point where her work would be affected by fear.

"Yes, Sir," she stammered, but then added, "what about Patmos Island?"

"What about it?" he asked her.

"You read my report?" she queried.

"Of course," he answered. "But Melchizedek isn't there, is he?"

"No, Sir, he's not," she admitted. "I'd best go release John Horn."

"Yes, you should," he concluded.

* * * *

Melchizedek and Anne rode together enjoying the respite from the violence they had just experienced. Melchizedek was increasingly impressed with her. He had known war throughout his life, had seen and known death intimately. But she was hitherto innocent, and yet she showed surprising and fortunate resilience.

They rode through fields of red poppies, past vineyards and through clumps of cypress trees as they continued their way toward Naples. As they came to the crest of the next hill, they could see Naples in the distance at the foot of a great but broken mountain. Melchizedek shuddered as he gazed at the monster.

"What's wrong, Mel?" Anne asked and then looked at the mountain. "It's Vesuvius, isn't it?"

Melchizedek paused before answering, "It is. We shall not tarry here long."

"Why, what is it?" she pressed.

Melchizedek turned to her with a tear in his eye, and Anne pressed Cinnamon up against Frankincense to get closer to him. "What happened, what is it? Please . . . tell me," she insisted gently.

"I was here in 79 A.D."

"Oh my God!" she exclaimed in shock. "How did you survive?"

"Through not a little luck, but also my knowledge of science," he admitted. "I used a prototype air bladder that Aristotle had designed for undersea exploration and I'd been tinkering with for a couple hundred years. It provided me and my protégé, Marius, with an ash-free air reserve facilitating our escape to the sea."

"Where were you? Pompeii?" she asked.

"No, in Herculaneum," Melchizedek answered, cringing at the name of the near-forgotten city. "I was visiting a philosophical school there. They had a beautiful villa down by the sea a little ways from the town itself. Everyone in the villa was working to remove the precious library to the ships. They managed to save all but a section of the Epicurean library. I sent Marius back to town for some last important documents, when the top of the mountain exploded. I watched the pyroclastic blast wave consume the city from the safety of my ship moored at the dock by the villa. The oarsmen hurriedly pulled us away from the dock, while I despaired of ever seeing Marius again. But then I saw his ash-engulfed form racing down the burning dock faster than an Olympian. He jumped for the ship and I caught his hand and pulled him aboard. He was the last one to escape the city."

"I don't know what to say, Mel," she exclaimed in horror.

Melchizedek paused and then admitted soberly, "It's why I avoid volcanoes now."

"Oh?" she queried.

"Yes, my job is to record the histories of the great nations of the world. Usually, each people is given one chance to rise in *imperium* and pursue justice and goodness instead of death and conquest. I usually go to live in each such regime to chronicle their deeds. But I will not go to the United States."

"What do you mean? What's wrong with my country?" she asked becoming a little indignant.

"It's not that there's anything more or less wrong with it compared to the other great powers. But the entire country is a volcano," Melchizedek explained.

"What? I don't understand. What do you mean, a volcano?" Anne pressed.

"Have you heard of the difference between a volcano and a super volcano?" Melchizedek asked her.

"No, I cannot say that I kept up my subscription to *National Geographic*," she chuckled.

"Well, I'm pretty sure they've discussed it," he laughed back to her. "A super volcano is a volcano whose blast is so enormous that it doesn't even form a cone. We're talking about a caldera—you know, that indent on the top of that volcanic cone over there—tens, even hundreds of kilometers across."

"You jest, right?" she asked with a worried look.

"No, I'm serious, and your Yellowstone National Park is a massive caldera," he answered her soberly.

She looked at him in shock. "That's what makes Old Faithful work . . ." she muttered to herself. "There's a huge volcano underneath that park? And they haven't told anyone?" she asked.

"No, no, people know about it, but what can anyone do? If the thing explodes, it'll probably destroy a third of your country."

"What are the chances it'll explode?" she asked him despondently.

"Pretty low. In geological time, we are due for another super volcanic explosion from Yellowstone, and I've been tracking the record of earthquakes and bulging underneath the ground at the park. Something is up there, but it may not erupt for another twenty thousand years."

"Right, which is where we differ. You might actually be alive in twenty thousand years, so you take geological time much more seriously than other people," she concluded.

"That is true," he laughed. "But why risk it? I can record the activities of the United States with ease from anywhere in the world."

"You're not too thrilled being here in Naples then, are you?" she asked.

"Hardly. There's been increasing activity here too," he muttered.

"You've studied volcanology, haven't you?"

"Yes, I have. Wouldn't you, in my circumstances?" he retorted.

"Well, yes, I suppose I probably would," she admitted. "What's been happening here?"

"For one thing, the smell of sulfur has been on the rise from the area's lakes and streams. There have been patches of dead trees and dead vegetation, caused by a buildup of heat underneath their roots. Then there are the increases in earthquakes, mostly minor of course. Before I travel to any region with volcanoes, I update myself. But especially here. We'll move through Naples quickly."

"You do know how to show a girl a good time, don't you, Mel?" she asked with a chuckle, as they spurred their horses toward the farms on the city outskirts.

CHAPTER FORTY-THREE

Maurice St. Claire's helicopter landed in a field near the farmhouse. Wearing the uniforms of Eurostar railway employees, he and his team discussed their search for victims of the tragedy with the farm owner who readily provided them with a description of the two people to whom he had sold a pair of horses. His wife reported that she had provided them with new clothing, because their own clothes had been tattered and soiled with blood. St. Claire asked her what she had done with the clothes, and at her puzzled look, he explained that one of the train cars had been carrying a radioactive cargo, so that it was imperative that they test those clothes. The woman awkwardly admitted that she had burned them, to destroy the disgusting human refuse. Thanking her, St. Claire returned to his helicopter and headed toward Naples. As the helicopter took off, he felt confident he knew now what had become of the tracking device.

* * * *

Another helicopter landed a few kilometers away at the location of the train wreck. Out stepped Inspector Bartoli and Agent Quarston, intent on discovering the connections between the train and hospital attacks. They arrived at dusk and quickly realized that the number of injured far exceeded the emergency personnel who could aid them. Disregarding their investigative aims, they threw themselves into the rescue effort.

* * * *

John Horn was spilled out of a van at his own villa on via Tornabuoni. These criminals had some nerve, he thought to himself, as he pulled himself up and walked into the villa. As soon as he entered the kitchen, he devoured whatever food he could find, not having eaten or drunk at all during his captivity. He reflected on all that had happened to him, how he had awoken from the tranquilizer darts in a dark room and faced a series of questions regarding his connections with Melchizedek. His captors seemed to know more about Melchizedek than he did, and from the questions he received from the woman he was convinced was a medical doctor, it became clear to him that these people knew all about Melchizedek's illness. They seemed keenly interested in how he had treated Melchizedek and then, of course, where Melchizedek was. Since John did not know anything about Melchizedek's whereabouts, he figured that there was little use in lying to his captors. His best protection of his sister lay in his ignorance. If they tortured him, he could not offer them anything anyhow. So, he answered their questions . . . for the most part. They did not ask everything about his treatment, and he did not offer anything beyond what they asked. But he thought that getting caught in a lie would increase the danger the most, and now it appeared that he was correct. They had let him go.

He yearned to climb into bed, but he wondered if he should go to the United States consulate and report his abduction. But then that would force him to reveal Melchizedek to the United States authorities. So, that was out. What then should he do? And where were Anne and Melchizedek? If he were Melchizedek, John thought, he'd get Anne to safety. And that had been the original plan, so maybe he should follow it himself.

John finally decided that he needed to get out of Italy as quickly as possible, to head back to the States. As long as he stayed in Italy, his captors might just return for him. He was about to pick up the phone to order a ticket, when it dawned on him that his abductors probably had the phone bugged. In fact, they could probably track him wherever he went. He tried to think like a spy, to figure out what their game plan would be, and what made the least sense to him was their releasing him. The gun battle at the Florence hospital proved that they didn't mind killing people, so no moral qualms barred their killing him. So why not do that? There had to be some reason that they left him alive, some reason that served their purpose.

What was their objective, he asked himself? To capture Melchizedek. What did he know that could aid that cause? Nothing. If he had known something, then they would surely have gotten it out of him in that room.

It just did not make sense to him. If he did not know anything, then of what use could he be? Why let him live?

He poured himself a glass of Chianti and sat down to eat some more cheese. He thought that having satiated his initial hunger, he ought really to try using a plate and glass. Sitting on the sofa brought back to him all that had happened in the last few days, all the joy that he had experienced with Melchizedek and Anne. How he longed for that happiness again! If only he could contact them, just talk with Anne, discover if she were all right. He worried about her post-procedural health, especially now that she must be under the stress of pursuit. He hoped that Melchizedek could protect her.

After finishing his meal, he packed his goods and called a taxi. He figured that if his phone was bugged, he could still prevent their knowing his destination. He told the taxi company that he wished to head to the Stibbert Museo, one of the greatest armor collections on public display in all of Europe. Once the taxi arrived, he instead asked the driver to take him to the airport, where he used his credit card to purchase a ticket for home. He knew that they could track his credit card too, but at this point he had little choice. They had to count on his leaving the country, and reacquiring him in an airport might prove too public, even for people of their capabilities.

While he sat in the airport waiting for his flight to Rome and thence to the States, he again wondered about Anne. He realized that she would have no idea that he had been released, and would certainly be worried sick. He wished he had left a note in the villa, but then he cursed his stupidity, because even if she were still in Florence, she'd not return to the villa. How could he give her a message, he wondered?

And then it hit him. However he tried to contact her, his pursuers would be watching. And they had to be counting on him to make the effort to contact her. He hoped that she would not try to contact him now, hoped for her sake.

* * * *

Melchizedek and Anne rode on toward Naples until they reached the outskirts of the city. They realized that they had to exchange their horses for a car or bus, if they intended to go forward. They found another farm with a stable, and asked the owners if they knew where they might lodge their horses for a while. The owners asked them how much they were willing to pay, and upon hearing Melchizedek's offer, they agreed to take the best care possible of the horses. This delighted Anne, as she had been growing forlorn at the prospect of losing her new horse so soon. The stable owners offered to give them a lift into town, so they headed to Piazza Garibaldi to find a hotel and a good meal. Their hosts suggested the Hotel Cavour, as they knew the owner and guaranteed them a superb meal, recommending the chateaubriand. Anne had never tried this dish, so she and Melchizedek booked a couple of rooms. While Anne soaked her bruised body in the tub, Melchizedek headed into town and purchased new clothes for the two of them. He felt confident that she would be safe while he was away, as there was no way that they had been tracked to Naples. He had her clothes gift-wrapped in beautiful boxes, and asked the desk clerk to have a maid leave them on her bed for her. The maid entered her room on a pretext, and Anne still soaking in the bathtub knew nothing of her real purpose.

Anne was enchanted at the gifts and soon discovered the handwritten invitation from Melchizedek to join him at the bar at eight o'clock. There she found him with two glasses of Prosecco, a light bubbling wine which served perfectly as an aperitif. After entering the dining area, he seated her and ordered the chateaubriand for two. Melchizedek asked her if he might choose a wine to match their meal, and at her enthusiastic response, he selected a superb Brunello, confident that the rich wine would match the roasted tenderloin. The chef served the meat with roasted potatoes, grilled tomatoes, cold lettuce and even a dollop of creamy parmesan, all on grilled toast. Anne wondered how these flavors would complement one another, but her face erupted in delight as she and Melchizedek found the food very satisfying. That night they stood on the roof of the Hotel Cavour and gazed at the bay in front of them. The lights of the distant islands beckoned, and Anne hoped aloud that some day she would be able to visit them. Melchizedek smiled a little deviously and assured her that she'd not be disappointed. He told her that he had spent some time on Capri Island during Tiberius's reign there, and he continued to believe it to be one of the most beautiful places on earth.

Anne returned to her room and opened the box of pajamas that Melchizedek had chosen for her. Cotton, she thought delightedly, perfect for the coziness that she longed for. Sleep eclipsed her mind as soon as she had said her prayers for John and laid her head on the pillow.

* * * *

Quarston glanced at his watch in the illumination of the emergency lighting that had been brought in by the Italian authorities. He wondered why it still said that it was only ten o'clock, until he realized that he had never actually reset his watch to Italian time. It was in fact four in the morning, and fatigue had finally begun to settle into his bones as the adrenaline that had been sustaining him faded. He noticed that someone had set up an espresso stand, so he made his way over to it and grabbed a coffee for both Bartoli and himself. They collapsed on a hill next to the shattered train and drank the coffee with sighs of satisfaction.

Looking over the scene of destruction before them, they were horrified at the extent of human suffering that continued into these early morning hours. Even now they heard the sounds of screeching metal, as rescue crews worked frantically to tear through the twisted wreckage and reach people moaning in agony.

A police officer strode up to Bartoli and greeted the Inspector, "Signor, we have identified two bodies near the rear of the train that are dressed in military gear. Per your instructions, we have cordoned off the area around the bodies for your investigation. Additionally, our people have located several more bodies dressed in the same military gear in the hills surrounding the track. I've marked each of the sites with a little flag on this topographical map of the area."

The officer handed the Inspector the map and then returned to his next assignment. Bartoli looked at Quarston, and said, "Well, if we're going to take a break from the rescue effort, we may as well begin our investigation."

Quarston nodded and lifted his weary body from the grass. Together they walked through the tunnel past the mangled cars and toward the end of the train where they found the bodies of two men outfitted for military action. They immediately noticed that their weapons and communication gear were missing. Looking closely at the bodies, Bartoli noted the way that they had died. One of them had had his nose hit with such force that the cartilage was driven straight into his brain.

"That sort of kill requires great skill," noted Quarston, as Bartoli nodded.

"And this one had his neck snapped. You can see from the bruising here and here that he was killed quickly with great force. A professional, for sure," added Bartoli.

"Yeah, one with a penchant for hand to hand kills," mused Quarston.

"So, their killer took their weapons and headed where?" asked Quarston.

"Well, from the location of these flags on the map, I'd say he probably followed a course up this hill toward the man located at the top. I doubt that he would have been able to get through the tunnel at that time, given the amount of fire damage we had to confront when we arrived."

"I agree," acknowledged Quarston. "Shall we head in that direction?"

"Let's go," Bartoli replied.

The two investigators climbed the hill along the train tracks where they achieved a much broader view of the scale of the destruction caused by the rocket attack. Quarston was still puzzled about who these men were, but as they climbed, Bartoli explained that they were dressed in the same way as the second team in the Florence Hospital attack. He would be in a better position to confirm his hypothesis, once he viewed the communications equipment carried by this team. He hoped that the killer had not taken all of it with him.

As they neared the location of the next body, Quarston suggested, "I think this is probably a sniper position, given the distance from the train and the wide view of the whole area it offers."

"Right," agreed Bartoli. "Look at this."

Bartoli held up a state of the art sniper rifle to Quarston. "Notice the heavy barrel on the gun? And look here, see this feature on the trigger? This has been custom made to fit this particular marksman."

Quarston reached down to the ground and retrieved the communications headset of the sniper.

"State of the art," he said. "Just as you thought."

"And a match to the other team. They serve the same master," Bartoli added.

"But who are they?" asked Quarston in obvious puzzlement. "Who put these two teams into the field to counter the kidnappers in Florence and then attack—our John Doe—here on the train? And how did they know he'd be on the train anyhow?"

"Good questions, but it seems clear that one group—the Rothschild group—wishes to kidnap John Doe, while the other one wishes to kill him, and . . ." Bartoli looked at the wrecked first class cabin before continuing, " . . . may have succeeded."

"Except that someone killed them all, maybe our John Doe," Quarston offered.

Bartoli laughed, "Yeah, like an old man could pull this off. It's more likely that he had his own security team, but it's odd that this time there are no other bodies."

Quarston suggested, "Well, maybe there were other casualties but the team that survived retrieved their dead and wounded."

"We'll be able to tell that in the daylight. I'll arrange a search for blood trails," Bartoli said.

"Then let's go investigate the other bodies?" asked Quarston.

"Yes, let's go. It's getting lighter, so soon we'll be able to see much better," Bartoli hoped.

CHAPTER FORTY-FOUR

Melchizedek awoke to a slight shudder, his instincts clearing the cobwebs from his thoughts. He immediately called down to the front desk, and they assured him that the earthquake was minor and nothing to worry about. Seeing that the clock already showed seven-thirty, he decided that he and Anne had best head on toward Sorrento and from there to Positano to visit his friend and acquire papers for her to leave the country.

Anne was ready with her new bag and clothes and the biggest smile that Melchizedek had ever seen on her face.

"Good sleep?" he asked her grinning.

"Oh yeeees," she said, "The best sleep I've had in days. I finally feel good!"

"Well, that is good to hear," he said warmly.

"And you, how are you doing?" she asked him with a twinkle in her eye.

"Well, except for the earthquake this morning, very well rested," he said thoughtfully.

Her countenance fell, "Earthquake? What earthquake? Is Vesuvius erupting?"

"No, no, no," he laughed, but then straightened up, "At least not yet. We'd better leave now though."

"All right," she said, "I'm ready to go."

Melchizedek asked her if she would like to walk to the station, as it was only down the street, and she agreed. Taking their bags, they headed out into the Piazza.

* * * *

Quarston and Bartoli finally located the other two bodies across the crest of the opposite hill, once the light made it possible for them to see clearly. Again, they found elite soldiers killed with perfection, one hit with a series of machine bullets directly in his chest, and the other with his neck snapped. They had discovered the soldiers with the rocket launchers earlier, and they were amazed at the expertise with which their killers employed various weapons—knives, hands, and guns. All of the kills were expertly done, and it shocked Bartoli.

"Here's what I do not understand, Agent Quarston," began Bartoli. "In the Florence incident there was a bloodbath, when the team allied to these folks attacked the kidnappers."

"Right," agreed Quarston.

"In this case these folks again launch an attack, this time on a train, a moving target. That means that either the people who killed them were waiting to ambush the ambushers—but then why permit the rocket attack—or they were on the train, right?" asked Bartoli.

"Yes," acknowledged Quarston.

"But if they were on the train, then some of them should have been killed or injured, yet we find nothing. What's more, if they were on the train, they'd have been in no condition after the crash to accomplish precision kills of the kind we're finding here. I'd expect at best the kind of running gun battle I saw in Florence."

"So, this doesn't make any sense, does it?" asked Quarston.

"No, it's a baffling puzzle," admitted Bartoli in frustration.

* * * *

Melchizedek and Anne headed into the train station and purchased tickets for the Circumvesuvius Line, the line that headed from Naples around Vesuvius and ended at Sorrento. As they prepared to descend the staircase to the Circumvesuvius tracks, a policeman suddenly yelled at them to stop. Melchizedek turned and saw not one but two policemen advancing toward them. But they were carrying tranquilizer guns, hardly police issue.

Melchizedek immediately thrust Anne down the stairs toward the underground level that led to the Circumvesuvius line. As they ran, he withdrew his pistol from his own bag and, urging Anne onward, he awaited the policemen. As they rounded the corner, he fired a number of shots into the wall to their left, causing them to drop to the ground and hug the far wall. Seeing his opportunity, Melchizedek leaped forward and followed Anne toward the train track. He hoped that the train would arrive on time, and sure enough, there it was. He and Anne leaped aboard just as it pulled away from the station.

* * * *

"Did you feel that?" asked Quarston.

"A shudder beneath our feet," agreed Bartoli. "I wonder if they've brought in some heavy equipment to work on the train."

An officer approached them and reported, "We looked all over the area, Inspector, but we found nothing. No blood or trails other than the ones around the bodies."

Bartoli suddenly stopped walking, and asked the officer, "Did you feel that?"

"*Si*," answered the police officer. "It felt like the earth moved. An earthquake?"

* * * *

"Somehow they found us again!" Anne exclaimed in fear.

"I know, but we seemed to take them by surprise at the station, as if they were waiting for us there, probably from yesterday," he said.

"You mean they waited there all night?"

"Well, it's possible; they might have figured that we were heading to Naples and the most reasonable exit from Naples is the train station . . ." Melchizedek mused.

"What are we going to do now?" Anne asked.

"They know that we are on this train, so we have to get off, fairly soon," Melchizedek concluded.

"Where?" Anne asked desperately. "What shall we do?"

"We'll have to use my emergency escape plan; I can't think of anything else."

"What's that?" Anne pressed, but Melchizedek suddenly tensed.

* * * *

The Circumvesuvius Line has a number of stops on its route, and on the stop just before Ercolano, three men had boarded the train. They moved forward between the cars, but not before Melchizedek spotted them. Drawing the captured submachine gun from his bag, he pushed Anne down behind the seat and aimed at the doors as they proceeded through them. They saw him and retreated back into the previous car. Panic ensued in the car with passengers screaming and trying to move ahead to the next car. As the train pulled into the Ercolano station, Melchizedek grabbed Anne and pulled her off the train, keeping his gun trained on the door of the other car. But the three men blew the windows out on the far side of the train and, using the car as cover, leapt from the train.

Melchizedek half-carried Anne down the steps of the train station, and out into the town of Ercolano. He ran to the first taxi he saw and told the driver to head to the *Scavi*, what remained of the ancient city of Herculaneum. As he was pushing Anne into the car, he saw the first of the gunmen emerge from the station. Aiming his machine gun in that direction, he fired a burst of against the station wall, trying not to hit the tourists fleeing in panic. At just that moment, a violent tearing of the earth occurred at the station, knocking Melchizedek to the ground, and shaking the buildings around them hideously. Melchizedek drew himself upward and into the vehicle, urging the driver, "Drive, drive, go, go!"

The taxi tore down the road toward the excavation, as the earth continued to shake the car. The road before them broke open heaving them into the air and leaving them staring at the sky. Their driver opened his door and fled, and Melchizedek and Anne did the same. As they exited their car, they saw that it lay wrenched upward on a huge section of the road that now pointed skyward. The earth continued to shake with increasing violence, and a terrible roar filled their ears.

Anne shouted as loudly as she could, "What is happening?"

Melchizedek only pointed behind her. Turning her head, she saw an enormous dark roiling cloud streaming skyward atop Vesuvius. She felt herself falling into shock, when Melchizedek grabbed her and held her face to his. Looking her straight in the eye, he yelled, "We have to survive! Come on; there's still time."

Grabbing her hand, they ran together among the splintered road sections and collapsing buildings. The roar in their ears grew so loud, that they could not hear the gunfire that erupted behind them. But Melchizedek noticed the bullets slamming into the building to their right. Drawing his own weapon again, he returned fire at the three men who pursued them only fifty meters away.

When they reached the Scavi, they ignored the abandoned ticket booth, and ran down the long ramp toward an enormous hole in the ground. Anne stopped and stared in awe at the ancient city that lay in the hole some twenty meters beneath her gaze.

"Herculaneum?" she mouthed, unable to hear her own voice in the din.

Melchizedek nodded, and again grabbed her hand and pulled her toward the stairway that led down to the ancient ruins. They could see their pursuers still behind them, as another violent earthquake knocked them to the ground. Looking into the sky, Vesuvius filled their vision, the cloud of smoke, debris, and fire surging into the sky hundreds of meters per second.

Melchizedek shook his head in disbelief and shock, mouthing in ancient Greek, "Not again, dear God, not again."

Anne pulled at his arm, and they both ran into the streets of the ancient city, Melchizedek leading the way through streets he remembered all too well. They turned right to head across the partially excavated city's four major roads. The buildings shook as they passed them, and began to collapse under the force of the earthquake. No city could stand this pounding more than once. Again, the timbers and brick of Herculaneum splintered and fell into dust.

Melchizedek felt Anne tugging at his arm, so he leaned down to her face. She put her mouth right up to his ear and shouted, "Where are we going?"

His turn toward her could not have been more fortunate, for at that moment two of the gunmen rounded the building on the corner of the main street they were taking. Melchizedek shoved Anne into the open doorway of an ancient restaurant, the old pots still half buried in the ground and the colorful marble counters longing for new transactions. Her own curiosity led her to partially lose track of their circumstances as she felt transported back into the Roman world, but another massive explosion from Vesuvius quickly returned her to reality, and she turned about to find Melchizedek again firing his weapon against their enemies. She felt as though time had slowed, for she saw the sweat and grime across his intense features, as he emptied the machine gun against the gunmen. Somehow she anticipated his need, and watched herself handing him a spare clip. He looked surprised at her, and she just shook her own head, unable quite to comprehend how she knew to retrieve the ammunition. Nevertheless, he smiled confidently, and reloaded the weapon.

This time he fired a short burst from the doorway, and then reached for Anne. Pushing her down the same road as before, he fired multiple bursts to force their pursuers to remain under cover. Emptying the next clip, he ran behind her and they turned down the road toward the ancient forum, only partially excavated. Anne saw the cliffs surrounding the city all round her and began to despair that they were trapped, when she noticed that great holes had been dug into the cliff walls in all directions by the excavators who, in order not to disturb the town above, had tunneled through the buried old city.

Melchizedek led her into one of these tunnels, just as a great darkness consumed the sunlight behind them. Dust and ash filled the entryway to the tunnel, as Melchizedek hurried her deeper into the caverns. Along the way, Anne noticed doorways, and columns, and roof tiles fixed in the solid rock around her. Anne coughed as their air supply grew increasingly foul, the smell of smoke and sulfur penetrating their lungs to their great discomfort.

"The tunnels won't protect us for long," Melchizedek assured her, "So we'll head to my emergency exit point."

"You mean you have a hideout here too?" Anne asked in surprise.

"I try to be prepared," Melchizedek explained. "I've had a long time to do so, and remember, I swore I'd never get trapped by another volcano."

"I thought your plan was to avoid them though," she answered with a hint of sarcasm.

"Yes, well, the point of volcanoes is that one never knows, and as for this particular one, I am prepared. Follow me!"

He led her toward a narrow opening in the ancient road. They squeezed through and found themselves inside the sewer system of the Roman city.

"Yes," Melchizedek explained as the tunnels muffled Vesuvius's roar. "The Romans were quite advanced and built both indoor plumbing and sophisticated sewers."

"Where will it lead us?" Anne asked.

"To the villa, where we'll find what we need," he answered confidently.

"So, it's all happening to you again?" she asked.

"No, this time I'm with you," he smiled at her.

She smiled back as he plunged ahead through the sewer system.

* * * *

The three gunmen had barely seen their quarry diving into the tunnel entrance, and were just preparing to give pursuit, when an enormous black cloud surged over the top of the excavation hole and filled it with searing ash and volcanic gasses. The men were consumed by the enraged breath of the volcano, clawing at their throats for air as their skin melted from their bodies.

CHAPTER FORTY-FIVE

Maurice St. Claire had received the reports from his policemen at the Garibaldi train station in Naples, and had ordered the attack on Melchizedek and Anne Horn. He had not anticipated a volcanic eruption, however, and his thoughts of pursuit shifted to fear for his own survival. He climbed the staircase of his hotel (the city's electricity had already given way), to reach the helicopter he had left on its roof. Along the way he called Rothschild to inform him of what was happening.

"Try to return here as quickly as you can," Rothschild told him.

"I will, Sir," St. Claire promised him.

"And what of Melchizedek?" asked Rothschild.

"My men last contacted me from Ercolano, where they were involved in a foot pursuit of the subjects. But that's right next to the volcano, Sir, and I've heard nothing since. I have to assume that they've all been killed, Melchizedek included," explained St. Claire and then added, "I'm sorry Sir."

"Yes, me too," offered Rothschild before ending the call.

St. Claire continued his run up the stair case and finally reached the rooftop door. He was surprised to see not light but darkness through the opening. Nevertheless he bounded up the last steps and through the doorway into a scene from Dante. He saw the volcano erupting in its full fury, its glow alone illuminating the sky, as all else was consumed in darkness. The city beneath him was in chaos; buildings had collapsed into the roadways that were streaming with people trying to flee toward the sea. The harbor was filled with boats making for the safety of the open bay. St. Claire shook his head in disbelief, and then turned toward his helicopter.

* * * *

Quarston and Bartoli just stared in the direction of Naples as Vesuvius continued to pour smoke, ash, hot gasses, and lava high into the sky. Quarston looked around him and realized that everyone had stopped their rescue efforts, emergency aid worker and injured party alike, and looked in shock as the great mountain rocked violently.

Quarston finally managed to overcome the dryness that gripped his throat and asked Bartoli, "Are we safe here?"

"I think so," Bartoli managed. "We're pretty far away from the volcano."

"What should we do?" Quarston asked.

"I have no idea," Bartoli admitted as tears filled his eyes.

* * * *

Melchizedek continued to move through the darkness of the sewers, with Anne right on his heels. She found it surprising that they still smelled awful, even after two thousand years had passed. She also found herself worrying about her new clothes, but then figured that they were probably so grime and soot covered, that it would not matter anyway. As she stumbled along after Melchizedek, it occurred to her that she had never cared much for clothing in any case, but then no one had ever given her anything either. She found the feminine elation with her new outfits both puzzling, because it had never happened before, and exciting, because it felt so natural to her. She had always believed in the value of beauty in art, in nature, in charity toward others . . . but she had devalued physical beauty in herself correspondingly. It occurred to her that perhaps she had gone too far. She really liked the way she felt when she was beautiful. All right, she thought to herself, she liked the way she felt when he beamed at her when she was beautiful. How much of our sense of well-being comes from the love of others, she wondered? It's not just the love that we give to others, is it, she asked herself, as she stumbled along in the darkness. Then she thought of Jesus again, how he wasn't always about doing religious work, but shared laughter and wine with good friends, like the three in Bethany, not to mention his twelve pals. He valued friendship as much as the next person, not just caring for friends, but being cared for. She thought of what it must have meant to him to look down from the cross and see not only his mother—oh, what that must have meant to him—but his friend, John. Anne began to wonder about John, why he alone of all the disciples appeared at the cross. He was young, she laughed to herself, so maybe he was just naïve about the threat to his own safety. Or maybe he just could not abandon his master and friend. No wonder that he was the "beloved" disciple, she thought. Anne began to think that her life of piety and faith had perhaps become a bit too divorced from real human experience. She thought that Jesus might have been extraordinarily human as well as divine. Maybe faith and human happiness are supposed to go together, she wondered. Maybe my feeling beautiful when he looks at me is as every bit as good as it feels, she mused.

Her reverie was disrupted by her collision with Melchizedek. She heard his laughter in the darkness, as he explained, "We've reached the end of the sewer, Anne, so now we have to climb upward into the villa tunnels. Excavators in the eighteenth century carved their way through the villa too, removing the beautiful bronzes and what manuscripts that we left behind. Those tunnels will be our escape route."

"To your next hideout?" she asked in a combination of glee and sarcasm.

"Yes, to my next hideout," he exclaimed. "You have a problem with that?"

"No, not really," she admitted, "Though because it's so exciting, it also seems kind of silly and surreal to me."

"Does it?" he asked her, smiling. "Well, I suppose it does. Anyway, here, let me help you up toward the tunnel."

She placed her foot in his cupped hand and felt the force of his strength support her as she climbed toward the sewer opening in the villa tunnel. Once there, she shouted down that she'd made it.

As he climbed upward, she shouted down to him, "Why do you suppose that adventure strikes us as silly sometimes?"

She heard him grunting with the climb, but he managed to eke out "Good question. Let's chat about it some *other* time, shall we?"

"Oh right," she answered sheepishly. "Here, give me your hand, and I'll help you through this narrow opening."

* * * *

Maurice St. Claire boarded his helicopter, while the crew ran quickly through their pre-flight checklist. As the helicopter took off from the landing pad atop the hotel, St. Claire again noticed all the people rushing toward the sea, and he wondered about something. Calling on the helicopter's intercom, he asked the pilot to head out to sea and then over toward Ercolano.

* * * *

Once within the ancient villa, Melchizedek located a torch left by an excavator and lit it with a match. Anne's was moved as she looked at the polychrome marble beneath her feet.

"Beautiful, isn't it?" Melchizedek asked her. "Imagine the entire villa with flooring like that and marble columns, and frescoes. Come this way, and I'll show you the swimming pool."

He led her through the excavated passageways of the villa toward a set of columns embedded in rock that he claimed surrounded a great swimming pool.

"I had many incredible conversations with Stoic and Epicurean philosophers here," he said thoughtfully. "I never could figure out why the ideas of Aristotle gave way to those two schools, but I was definitely alone in advocating for Aristotle's philosophy."

"You had many friends here, then?" she asked him.

Melchizedek laughed as the memories filled his imagination, "Oh yes. It was a happy time for me. The villa looked over the sea, and I had grown fond of the sea and its bounty. There was so much here, so much possibility to grow in wisdom, and yet . . ." Melchizedek paused with the grievous terminus of his memories.

" . . . and yet it ended as all things must end," Melchizedek continued. "You know, Anne, C. S. Lewis, the children's story writer, once said that Christians never say goodbye. But I will tell you the truth: saying goodbye is the essence of human pain. Everything ends. All that we do that is great ends."

Anne felt concerned at the level of despair that seemed to animate Melchizedek, "But is there no hope, Mel? None? What of love and faith and goodness? What of these things?"

Melchizedek turned toward her and spoke seriously, "Anne, these things abound in the hearts and actions of individuals, but not cultures. Were it not for the former, I'd fall into darkness. But the reality of the latter threatens my sanity."

They walked on in silence until they took a sharp turn to the right, where Melchizedek's sobriety suddenly turned to gaiety and he urged her onward, "Come, Anne, this way, let me show you my secret hideout, my lair!"

She laughed at his reference to her earlier girlish remark and caught his enthusiasm. They approached a large urn and Melchizedek reached down into it and brushed the dust away from its bottom. A handle slowly appeared amidst the debris, and he turned it. As it turned, the entire base of the urn suddenly gave way creaking open into the darkness below. Anne looked at him in surprise.

"What is this?" she asked.

"It was an emergency escape tunnel for the villa. The wealthy are always preparing for threats, and the people who owned this villa were no different. They built a few secret passageways just in case anything should change dramatically in Rome," he explained.

"Like what?" Anne asked. "I thought that Rome ruled the world."

"Well, sort of," Melchizedek explained. "Her rule was never as solid as the history books make it appear. She was always suppressing revolts in the empire, and even here in Italy the slave revolt of Spartacus made many fear for their lives. Spartacus' army roved freely all over the peninsula killing people and destroying farms and small towns, so noble families built escape routes just in case anything like that should ever happen again."

"Spartacus . . ." Anne began.

"Yes, Anne. You have to remember that the empire had a huge slave population, the result of many successful wars. But slaves remember their own freedom and grandeur, when they were once soldiers, bakers, nobles, and even kings. And sometimes those memories and their current despair galvanize them into action. The Romans finally crushed the revolt, and as was typical of their tactics, they made such an example of the captured rebels, that no serious slave revolt ever occurred in the empire again."

"So, where does this secret passage lead?" Anne asked.

"Follow me, and you'll see," he said.

Anne climbed into the darkness after him and down a ladder that was smooth as modern steel. She thought that odd enough to ask him about it.

"Mel, how come this metal feels so modern?"

"Because I replaced the old ladder with this one. I've added a few upgrades for my own purposes," he answered.

"Can't wait to see those," she exclaimed.

"Well for one . . ." he paused blowing out his torch.

Anne yelled aloud in the darkness, just as the entire cavern filled with light. There stood Melchizedek next to a generator. She gave him a look that could kill an ordinary mortal, but then Melchizedek was no ordinary mortal, and he did have a flair for the dramatic.

"You just have to make it into a theatrical performance, huh?" she taunted him.

"Well, I learned an awful lot from Heron in the old days and then Leonardo more recently, about the use of machines in theatre," he stated deadpan.

"Did you?" she asked and then added, "How do I compete with you?"

"You don't," he pressed on chuckling, "Allow me to reveal my real baby. Follow me."

Anne followed him to a ledge overlooking a large pool of dark black water, down a metal stair case and toward a small wooden dock. Melchizedek ripped a tarp off a large object next to the dock to reveal a small submarine.

"What do you think of her?" he asked Anne.

The submarine's cockpit reminded Anne of an ice planet speeder from the first Star Wars trilogy, but the similarity died there, as the greater bulk of the body of the vessel occupied significant depth under the water. Anne walked up the dock toward the coned nose of the submarine, imagining what a fright a fish might feel on encountering this monster rising from the depths. Heading back to Melchizedek, Anne admitted to herself that she really was impressed, but telling that to him was another matter. A little more fun seemed in order.

"I'm speechless, really, I don't know what to say," she paused for a moment and then continued. "Okay, let me get this straight. In case you ever got caught in a volcanic eruption, you put a mini submarine here?"

"Almost, though you must remember that I love scientific exploration, especially under the sea, so I occasionally come back here to explore the bay. It's large enough for two people, so we should stow our gear and then head out," he explained.

"Every time I think I begin to understand you a little more, you just show me how much more there is to know!" she revealed.

"And you think it's hopeless?" he asked her.

"No, I kinda like it," she said, grinning.

* * * *

Maurice St. Claire's helicopter made its way toward safety over the Bay of Naples, while the volcano continued to pour ash and debris into the sky. He ordered his crew to turn the aircraft to a course parallel with the mainland and head toward Ercolano.

* * * *

After Melchizedek had stowed their gear in the cargo compartment of the mini sub, he began to fuel it from a large diesel tank he had installed inside the cavern.

"It doesn't do to leave fuel sitting inside the submersible tank," he explained.

Once they were fueled, he removed the battery charging cables, confident that the batteries were ready, and then invited Anne to enter the submersible. She began to climb into the rear seat, when he pointed to the front.

"I get to ride in the front seat?" she asked.

"Oh yes," he answered. "The view is remarkable from there, and I can pilot the craft from either location."

"The seats are staggered in elevation, aren't they? That way I won't block your vision?" she asked once she had taken her seat.

"That's right," he answered. "And from the front position you have windows covering almost three hundred degrees."

"Well, that should make for a spectacular view . . .," Anne began and then, staring in to the black water, added, "Once we get into the sunlight."

Melchizedek's huge grin unnerved her somewhat, so she asked, "What? What'd I miss? What's so funny?"

Leaning in close to her, Melchizedek croaked in his finest pirate accent, "Well, Dearie, the worrrrrrrrrld in the dark crrrrannies of the sea is every bit as beautiful as the worrrld in the open waterrr, only much much morrre . . . stimulatin'."

Anne laughed uncontrollably, "All right, all right, I can't wait. Let's go before this cavern collapses on top of us."

Her remark reminded Melchizedek of the dire straits his secret harbor was really in, so he fastened her into her seat and then jumped into his own.

As he checked the mini-submarine's systems, Melchizedek began his pre-cruising briefing.

"Because we have one unified cabin, we will share our oxygen supply. Since you are facing forward, communications could prove problematic, so put that headset on and we'll be able to hear one another."

She laughed again, as he talked her through what to her were completely obvious points. Nevertheless, at the end of his brief description of emergency procedures, she could not help but add, "Aye, aye, Sir."

She received a playful swat on the head for that remark followed by the sudden drop of the submersible vehicle beneath the icy black waters of the tunnel harbor. Anne screamed in terror as they continued their descent into the blackness, unaware that Melchizedek had a sonar that provided him with a virtual representation of the cavern walls. After he felt that he'd scared her sufficiently for her sarcasm, he asked her if she'd like to see where they were.

"Yes, I'd love that," she said with a gulp, as her stomach slowly returned to its place.

Melchizedek told her to push the button next to the round display, and upon doing so her own sonar screen lit up giving her a visual representation of the tunnel they were traveling through.

"How fast are we going?" she asked, somewhat alarmed by the speed at which they were negotiating the craggy turns.

"Only about three knots," he explained. "Would you like to really see where you are?"

"Well, sure, but how . . ." she began.

"Then behold!" Melchizedek proclaimed in his best showman voice.

The tunnel lit up, as the submarine's external illumination filled the cavern with glowing light. All sorts of bizarre creatures darted away trying to avoid the bright lights. Anne stared in awe at the world around her, convinced now that Melchizedek was right about the deep crannies of the sea.

After they traveled a bit further, Melchizedek told her to watch the next ridge. As they neared it, the standard illumination suddenly went out, replaced instead by florescent light. The cave luminesced with the glowing colors of phosphorescence, reds and yellows, greens and blues, not only on some of the fish, but in the fissures between rocks and even in the rock itself. Again Anne marveled at the incredible display of aquatic beauty. Her seatbelt prevented her attempt to turn and thank him, but not before Melchizedek saw the tears that were streaming down her joyful face.

CHAPTER FORTY-SIX

Maurice St. Claire's helicopter approached the Ercolano coastline but the increasing turbulence caused by the great heat of the volcano buffeted the aircraft.

"This is as close as we dare approach, Sir," began the pilot. "And I'm concerned that the dust, soot, and ash in the air are going to clog up our systems if we don't leave quite soon."

"Very well," St. Claire answered, "but I need to take pictures of any boats that are emerging from the smoke."

"Well, Sir, I see only one," he answered, "that fishing boat at about two hundred meters at thirty degrees off our nose."

St. Claire shifted to the other window of the aircraft and zoomed in on the boat. No life appeared to have survived, as the boat was drifting over the swollen sea. Nevertheless, he took pictures. In case Melchizedek escaped, he was determined that they would have something to use to find him.

"We've got to go now, Sir," called the pilot urgently.

"All right, let's go," St. Claire answered.

* * * *

Melchizedek and Anne continued cruising through the underground waterway until they finally broke into the open water of the bay.

Anne spoke up at once, "It certainly is dark for this time of day, isn't it?"

Melchizedek nodded, before remembering that she could not see him. "Yes. It's probably volcanic ash darkening the sky."

"Can we take a look?" she asked him.

"No, not yet," he answered. "We're still probably not clear of any debris material that might be falling back to earth from the eruption. Vesuvius can hurl enormous stones into the air, and we do not wish to be caught underneath one of those."

"But couldn't we get hit by one of them down here?" she asked.

"Yes, but only if we didn't take precautions to move out of the way," he began and then continued, "Debris falls much slower through the water than through the air, so I've set one of the sonars to search over our heads. If anything suddenly appears in the water, we'll know about it, and I can take evasive action. But if we get near the surface, we would be unable to detect any falling rocks and still have time to evade them."

"Because sonar works only under the water, right?" Anne asked trying to ensure she understood.

"Correct," Melchizedek replied.

"Then why not use radar on the surface?" she asked.

"Well, if we surfaced and used radar, the rocks would still be falling so rapidly through the air that I couldn't avoid them. And we cannot use radar while underneath the water."

"Okay," she acknowledged feigning grumpiness, "I guess I'll just have to wait and enjoy the sights down here."

Melchizedek laughed and pushed the submarine to an increased speed of twelve knots. They ran along the seafloor to give them maximum time to avoid any unwelcome boulders from overhead.

"Mel?" Anne asked.

"Yes, Anne?" he replied.

"I've been thinking about what you said about how C. S. Lewis said that Christians never say goodbye, and I've been wondering if maybe he wasn't right, after all," Anne explained, wondering how Melchizedek would react.

"What do you have in mind, Anne?" he asked, interested.

"Well, we do say 'goodbye' to our friends and loved ones who pass into death, right?" Anne asked.

"Yes," answered Melchizedek.

"But then we all die too, and pass through death into love itself, where there are no more goodbyes," Anne explained.

"Right," said Melchizedek, not a little puzzled.

"It's you who are different, Mel," Anne said gently. "You never pass through death; it never ends for you, so it's always another goodbye. Your experience may not be all that human."

Melchizedek was silent for a few moments, as he thought through what Anne was suggesting to him. Then he replied.

"But Anne, human nature was made for immortality, not death, so isn't my experience closer to human nature?" he asked her.

"Perhaps, in a way, but not when everyone else dies it's not, because human nature is what belongs to us as a species, right? Not just an individual. So, when everyone else dies, your immortal experience, even if technically right, does not produce the joy that it should, because you are isolated in your immortality, and we were made for one another."

Melchizedek again sat in silence, pondering the wisdom that rose from Anne's lips.

"You experience many more goodbyes than were ever meant for any normal human being," she concluded.

"You may be right, Anne. I cannot say that I've ever thought of it quite like that."

* * * *

Israel

Yaakov Katz crushed a second empty cigarette packet and threw it against the wall, as he watched the news reports about the volcanic eruption. Something must have gone tragically wrong, he thought, because the volcanic eruption should only have affected an area to the south of the planned ambush site. Yet he had heard nothing from the team, not a peep. Nor had there been any news reports on the ambush. It was as if it had never happened. Had his team been intercepted prior to their set up point? Or had they carried out the attack? But with all the destruction caused by Vesuvius, perhaps not even a rocket attack on a train could compete for either media or police resources. But if they had carried out the attack, what happened to them? They should have communicated their success. If they succeeded in the attack and made it to their rendezvous in Naples, could they have been killed there? No, that seemed inconceivable to him. Something must have gone wrong before the attack, he concluded grimly, something so serious that no one from Sayerot Mat'kal survived to make a report.

Katz put in another call to General Yitzhak Mordechai, wondering if their tap into Andover's communications might have revealed anything about the outcome of the attack. But General Mordechai only delivered more bad news.

"The tap is lost to us," he explained coldly. "And we cannot tell whether it is due to the communications disruption throughout Italy caused by the volcanic explosion or whether it was discovered. In either case, it's done."

"Can't you reengineer it? Or enter their system by some other means?" asked Katz.

"We have been unable to do that," replied Mordechai.

"Then doesn't that make it likely that the tap was discovered and their communications security upgraded to prevent future attacks?" asked Katz.

"We do not know that, and military officers do not trade in supposition," answered Mordechai flatly.

Katz cringed and squeezed the phone so hard, he thought it would crack under the pressure, but he nevertheless managed to reply, "Well, thank you for your help, and I'll look forward to seeing you at the PM's retreat."

Katz was now convinced that Andover's people had not only plugged the communications leak but had also somehow intercepted and killed his second team. He realized further that he was out of options, in no small measure because the PM would never approve his deploying another team. He stood and began pacing the room. He downed three more cigarettes, as he reflected on every detail of the operation, scrutinizing them for any possible trail back to Israel. Nothing, he thought with relief. He looked at his watch and realized that his mistress would be awaiting his arrival in no more than thirty minutes. He'd made her wait before, but what was the point now? He looked pensively at the lower drawer of his file cabinet, the one reserved for closed—failed, he thought bitterly—operations. With one final look at the Melchizedek folder, he shrugged and opened the drawer.

* * * *

"Do you think it's safe to surface now?" Anne asked after they had not seen any evidence of boulders crashing through the surface for a while.

"I think so; let's take a look," answered Melchizedek.

He moved the submarine toward the surface but before breaking through raised a small antenna.

"What's that for?" Anne asked him.

"It's a radar antenna; it will enable us to determine whether any ships are nearby. Best to avoid surfacing in front of them," he said smiling.

"Yeah, I guess so, but can't we just see under the water to tell if any ships are nearby?" she asked looking through the crystal clear water.

"Yes, if the water is clear enough, but visibility is never perfect and never as far as you can see either from the surface with your eyes or with radar, so I use this as an extra precaution," Melchizedek explained.

Melchizedek scanned the surface and said, "Well, I don't seem to pick up any ships but something very small is moving and moving fast. Could be a low flying aircraft."

* * * *

The helicopter made one final pass along the coast of Ercolano, before beginning its long turn out to sea. The pilot was intent on getting into completely clean sea air, in order to relieve his air filters from the stress he imagined they must be straining under. Neither the pilot, nor his navigator, nor St. Claire noticed a bubble of water emerging from the sea beneath them, a bubble that soon took the form of a small submarine.

The helicopter veered away from the coast and hugged the water line to avoid as much of the soot that filled the air as possible. Once clear of the volcanic radius, they rose to an adequate cruising altitude, flew as far as Positano and then headed North back toward Rome and Florence.

* * * *

The submarine broke the surface right into a seagull, whose surprise at their sudden appearance left them both howling with laughter. But as Melchizedek turned the boat back toward shore, the awful horrors that they had narrowly escaped plunged them both into grievous silence. Vesuvius continued billowing masses of hot gasses and molten rock high into the air, while Ercolano itself, and with it ancient Herculaneum, was covered over by a pall of thick black smoke.

"We'd best head to Capri now, Anne, and we'll move faster underneath the water than on top of it," Melchizedek said finally.

Trying to turn her emotions away from the volcanic destruction, Anne replied, "Yes, and we can get underneath these awful swells; they are making me a bit sick."

Melchizedek dove the submarine back into the depths of the bay and headed toward Capri Island.

* * * *

"There was no sign of any survivors from Ercolano, Sir," explained St. Claire from the helicopter now safely outside the volcanic destruction radius.

"The town itself?" asked Rothschild.

"Completely destroyed . . . again," added St. Claire soberly.

"Everything comes full circle," pondered Rothschild.

"What's next then?" asked St. Claire.

"Well for one, we have Miss Andover study our newest blood sample. She may yet learn something in spite of her preliminary report," Rothschild answered.

"And your Egyptian project?" asked St. Claire.

"It continues," began Rothschild, "slowly."

"Is there anything else, then?" asked St. Claire.

"There is one loose end. Talk to Miss Andover about Patmos Island. Once things settle here and international travel is again possible, I want you to visit the island and identify its relationship to Melchizedek," Rothschild paused before continuing, "You may find the Book there."

"Indeed?" asked St. Claire.

"One never knows," Rothschild explained. "Melchizedek was a high priest of Thoth from what I can tell."

"A high priest?" asked St. Claire quizzically. "How is that possible? I thought he worshipped the Jewish God."

"Well, I cannot explain it, only tell it as it seems to be," answered Rothschild.

"Then Patmos it is," determined St. Claire.

"Get some rest first, you and your men. Take a week and then go to the Island," offered Rothschild.

"Thank you Sir," replied St. Claire appreciatively.

* * * *

As they approached Capri Island, Melchizedek rose to the surface again, giving Anne a view of the island's astonishing cliffs. She was awed at their beauty.

"I really wish I had a camera, Mel, but I doubt the pictures would record the magnificence of these natural wonders," she told him.

"No, I agree with you. This place always gives me such peace," he said pausing, "Hey, have you ever heard of the Blue Grotto?"

"You mean the underwater cavern that Capri is famous for?" she asked. "Sure, I have."

"What would you say if I told you that there is another Grotto?" he asked.

"And you found it, I suppose?" she asked him.

"Oh yes," he explained. "I've dived all around this island, but the entry to this other Grotto is much further from the shore line, and much deeper, accessible only to divers. That's why no one else knows about it. But the sunlight still reflects off the ocean bottom to create a remarkable color scheme in the cavern. Would you like to see it now?"

"Definitely, aye, aye, Captain, take us away!" she said before adding, "Dive, dive, dive!"

Turning slightly toward him, she said, "I always wanted to say that."

Melchizedek sent the submarine into a steep dive at flank speed. Anne screamed in delight as they dived toward the bottom of the bay. Turning the submarine away from the shore line, Melchizedek headed toward a deeper channel. The beautiful blue waters of Capri are just as sensational below the surface as above, and Anne found the experience enchanting.

Driving the submarine into the channel, Melchizedek headed back toward the island when suddenly Anne exclaimed, "I see an opening in the cliff up ahead! Is that it?"

"That's it!" he replied, slowing the submarine down to negotiate the low overhang covering the entrance. Soon they were heading upward again into a large cavern. Melchizedek used the sonar on the submarine in order to leave Anne's eyes prepared for the ghostly blue light that she would soon encounter. When they broke the surface of the water in the cavern, Anne's speech turned to exclamations of "oh" and "ah" as she absorbed the beauty all round her. The sunlight reflected through the water to create dancing blue light that illuminated the cavern. As their eyes adjusted, they could see more and more of the cavern's features. Melchizedek brought the submarine completely to the surface and piloted over to a dock, where he secured it with ropes fore and aft.

Turning to Anne, he said, "Would you like to swim?"

The sparkle in her eyes told him her answer, and after removing her safety harness, she plunged into the glowing blue water. The refreshment of the cold water brought her senses back to life, and aroused the realization of how much her limbs ached with the stress and injuries of the past few days. While Melchizedek attended to the submarine's maintenance and unloaded their gear, she swam all around the cavern, diving deeply and then rushing to the surface with shouts of joy.

Melchizedek called out to her, "You remind me of a dolphin that Aristotle and I once found in the Aegean Sea. That little guy played with the same zest for life that you display right now!"

"Well, we're alive, Mel! We made it," she hollered back.

"Yes," he answered her, "we did. And tonight we will get some much needed rest. Our pursuers must think that we died in Ercolano, so we'll stay here for a while. I imagine that the transportation network in Italy will be tied up for days responding to the eruption anyway."

Anne swam over to the dock and looked up at Melchizedek. "I'm going to have to get out of these wet clothes too," she muttered somewhat embarrassed.

Melchizedek produced a towel from behind his back. "I'm all ready for you. Here's a towel, and there is your clothes bag. Somehow you managed not to lose it in all that chaos."

"Well, we girls have a way of hanging onto our bags," she explained chagrined.

"Yes, I've gathered that over the years. Listen, I'm going to go up to the surface using that staircase over there, while you can go into that room over there and dry off and change. We'll get you a hot bath soon enough, okay?"

"Okay," she answered, still keeping herself submerged in the water.

Melchizedek turned toward the staircase and headed straight up toward the surface, as Anne listened to his footsteps to be sure that he was out of sight. Once she was sure she was alone, she drew herself out of the water, and quickly wrapped herself in the towel. As she dripped along the dock toward the room Melchizedek mentioned, she found it odd that she was so intent on covering herself in her wet clothes even when she was sure no one could see her. She laughed again when she noticed that she shut the door behind her and then began to change.

CHAPTER FORTY-SEVEN

Melchizedek hurried up the ancient stairway. He had discovered this Grotto many centuries before and actually cut the stairway into the stone himself over a period of about seventy years. He was proud of the achievement but kept it a closely guarded secret. He had built a villa over the point where the staircase broached the surface, high up on one of Capri's grandest cliffs with a view of the open sea. He checked the villa carefully to be sure that no one was waiting for them when they arrived. In spite of what he had told Anne, he was not completely sure how much of his life had been exposed to those who were chasing him. And he was unwilling to take any chances. Once he was assured of the villa's security, he picked up the phone and ordered a full set of groceries and then ran here and there cleaning, opening windows, and organizing, as he had not lived in the villa for several years. He walked down to the small wine cellar he had installed and chose the perfect bottle for that evening. After placing the bottle on the kitchen counter, he went upstairs and checked the condition of the guest rooms, choosing the best one for Anne, a room with a portico that hung right over the cliff face. He ran out to the garden, picked some wild flowers, and placed them in a vase on her night stand. Pleased with the look of the place, he found fresh towels and bath supplies for her, and then returned to the cavern.

Anne had dressed in dry clothes and was exploring the underground cavern. She found several ancient marble busts but could not make out the names in the low light. Most of the cavern was filled with nautical and diving equipment, and she wondered if he could teach her how to dive. She selected a pair of the fins and tried them on, and then found a weight belt which proved quite heavy out of the water. She next picked up a face mask and fastened it to her head. Anne turned around toward the staircase as she heard footsteps and watched Melchizedek momentarily paralyzed with puzzlement as he noticed this aquatic monster that had crawled into his lair. His confusion turned into laughter, as she ripped the mask from her face with a huge smile and lumbered toward him, her flippers flapping on the cold stone floor of the cavern.

"Are you a seal or a person," he asked lightly.

"Both," she answered mischievously.

Melchizedek helped her remove the diving gear and then took her up the long staircase to the surface. She was quite out of breath by the time they reached the villa, but its beauty and her interest in his Capri home soon overtook her exhaustion. She sped with relish from room to room on the main floor complimenting him on his artistic choices and decorating capabilities until she stopped in astonishment.

"These Monets are real, aren't they? They're not copies?" she asked him. "And this small Greek sculpture is an original too, isn't it?"

"Everything is authentic," he admitted. "Unknown to the world but part of my soul."

"They are beautiful," she said admiring the sculpture of the boy discus thrower. "This place is beautiful, too. You built it, didn't you? I can tell."

"I learned architecture in Egypt. They know a thing or two about building. But I love Italian villas most of all, and I tend to pattern my homes on those models if I can. Of course," he added, laughing, "I don't build an Italian villa in the heart of Damascus!"

"No, I shouldn't think so," she answered laughing.

"Shall I show you your room?" Melchizedek asked her, picking up her things.

"Sure, I can't wait to see it," she replied eagerly.

Melchizedek took her up a spiral staircase that led up to several rooms, one of which he entered. She followed him, saw the open doors leading to the veranda, smelled the fragrance of the freshly cut flowers, and saw the plush bed that he had made for her. She noticed that a bath was already hot and filled with bubbles, but her eye was taken with the small portrait of a girl that lay on the night stand next to the flowers.

"Who is she?" she asked him.

"My daughter," he answered.

"She is lovely," Anne said. "When did she live?"

"In the sixteenth century, the last time I was married," he said thoughtfully.

"You have been alone that long?" she asked thoughtfully.

"Well, er . . . yes, I suppose so," he admitted, a bit embarrassed.

Anne had not intended to embarrass him, so she shifted the subject to the veranda. "Can I look?" she asked.

"Sure, let's look," he offered enthusiastically.

The view from the veranda took Anne's breath away. Capri's famous sparkling blue sea beckoned to her like the sirens of Homer. She looked at the cacti and flowers growing in the crags of the rocks all the way down to the white water battering the rocks below. She pointed at the birds below them and laughed aloud.

"I've never seen birds from the top before, Mel!"

The doorbell rang from below them, but as Melchizedek turned to answer it, Anne asked him, "Is it all right if I just stay here for a while longer?"

"Of course, Anne," he replied. "Come down when you're ready. And don't forget your bath."

"I had completely forgotten it!" she answered him, "And oh how my body could use it. Thank you so much for bringing me here."

Melchizedek smiled before leaving her room and pulling her door closed behind him. He quickly descended the staircase and reached for his pistol before answering the door. He was relieved to see the grocer with his order. The grocer helped him take the groceries into the kitchen and then handed him the prize, a large fresh sea bass. As Melchizedek placed the fish in the refrigerator, the grocer noted Anne's shoes on the floor, and pointing to the fish wrapper added, "Perfect for a lady, no?" Melchizedek grinned and handed him an extra fifty Euros for his trouble.

"*Grazie mille,*" he replied with a slight bow, before heading out the door.

While Anne bathed, Melchizedek attended to the meal he planned for her. Soon the fish was prepared to be baked, and before long the smells of his succulent choices wafted their way up the stair case and into Anne's room. She chose a simple cotton dress to wear for the evening but added one of the cut flowers to her hair. She came down to find Melchizedek surrounded by freshly cut tomatoes, risotto, asparagus, basil, and rosemary. He was just taking the fish and the bread from the two ovens, when she entered the kitchen.

"Don't you look lovely this evening, Miss Horn?"

"Why thank you, Mel, I feel so refreshed."

He grinned at her, as her curiosity got the better of her, "So, what have I been smelling for the last half an hour?"

"You shall soon see, but why don't you go out to the veranda now?" he offered.

"Okay," she said and headed toward the large open door way to the portico. There she found a table set for two with ancient jeweled goblets and a bottle of very fine Bordeaux. She prepared to seat herself, when she noticed that Melchizedek had somehow appeared behind her and held her chair. He poured her some of the wine and then brought the risotto. She waited in anticipation as the candlelight illuminated the gorgeous fish that Melchizedek carried on a large silver tray.

"A toast?" he asked her, once he was seated across from her.

"Sure," she answered.

"To truth," he offered.

But before he could get the wine to his lips, she added, "And love."

"Always," he replied.

The meal proved every bit as tasty as it looked. They had not eaten since their morning breakfast at the hotel in Naples, so they made quick work of the delicate fish and steaming risotto.

As they gazed at the sea below them and the stars above, Melchizedek decided to take up the conversation they'd begun earlier. "Anne, remember what we were talking about before, about how saying 'goodbye' at our friends' deaths is part of the tragedy of human experience, but that in our own deaths we finally enter into perpetual love, yet I am blocked from this because of my immortality?"

"Sure," Anne replied.

"Well, I've been thinking about Him, the true King. He gave up his own life in an act of love, trading his immortality for the sake of the most amazing good, the redemption of the world. My problem and my despair is that I often feel like I am trapped by the demands of justice never to achieve love."

"What do you mean?" Anne asked.

"Well, my immortality was given to me so that I can witness the deranged nature of human empire, how human regimes always fall into corruption and evil. I presume that in the final judgment, I will be called as one of their own to rebut the justifications that kings will make for their conduct. Thus, my role is essentially one of the enforcement of justice. But I often feel the same darkness as a prosecutor, always bringing down the sword of judgment, yet realizing that in the end it makes no difference, because more wicked men appear in the next regime. It just never ends, so where is the joy? Only for me, it's worse, because I don't even have the satisfaction of executing justice; I only record the deed for a future judge."

"That is a tragic situation," Anne admitted, pausing. "Yet you find joy in other areas of human experience, like friendship and inquiry and art and culinary delights, right?"

"Yes, but those friends die, so inquiry becomes my deepest pursuit. But even Aristotle knew that one needed friends for fulfillment in the pursuit of knowledge."

"But you do find friends, presumably, in each generation?" Anne asked.

"Yes, always, and I consider that a divine mercy," he replied.

"Yet you still face the dramatic problem of finding job satisfaction, don't you?" she asked.

"Well, yes, that is one way to put it," he admitted.

"And men really need job satisfaction," she muttered more to herself. "John has mentioned as much to me."

"I suppose so," he sighed.

"All right, then you need to rethink your job, because I don't think that justice excludes love!" she exclaimed suddenly.

"What do you have in mind?" he asked her.

"I mean that if you turn over the coin of justice you will find love," she asserted confidently.

"Meaning what, exactly?" he pressed her lightly.

"For whom is the justice that you seek?" Anne asked him.

"So, it's to be a Socratic conversation, is it?" he joked with her. "Well, the justice is ultimately divine, so it must be for God."

"Okay, sort of, I mean, in part that has to be right," she admitted thoughtfully, "but it must be more than that, because you are the voice of all those people who suffer injustice and tyranny. The reckoning that God will bring upon those vicious tyrants must in some way be matched by a restoration to all those people for their loss."

"Yes, it must be, if justice is to be complete, fully taken up within love," added Melchizedek.

"Then you must be a part of that redemption, that restoration, too, Mel, for otherwise how will all that you have seen be fulfilled within you?" Anne asked.

Melchizedek sat silently, thinking over what she was saying.

"Consider this, Mel, didn't God tell Daniel that after all that he had seen in his apocalyptic visions, a place of rest would be prepared for him?" Anne asked him.

"Why yes, indeed, and that provided him with rich comfort, because he became deeply depressed about the future for Israel," Melchizedek answered.

"Then here's my theory," she concluded. "First, you must see that to record the evil of men is a record of love for the sake of the victims of that evil. You are loving on a vast scale, and if you really are called to testify on their behalf, you will be carrying the weight of real people whose hopes and dreams were shattered by the raging insanity of men bent on war and destruction. So, it isn't merely justice, but love too. Second, when God makes all things right, that will include healing those wounds, but since you also carry those wounds, that healing must extend to you too. So, you can participate in the same faith and hope that we mortals do, only on a much grander scale, for in the end all is swallowed up in love. I think that God will make you a part of their restoration."

Melchizedek just stared at her in amazement. Finally he spoke, "Well . . . your wisdom is truly astonishing."

"Out of the mouth of babes, eh?" she asked laughing.

"No, my lady, not a babe," he said bowing his head toward her.

CHAPTER FORTY-EIGHT

The next morning after a light breakfast of fruit and croissants, Melchizedek asked Anne if she would like to see Capri. Her delighted response soon saw the two of them on a scooter zipping along the sheer cliffs toward the town of Capri. They parked the scooter and walked among the various bars, shops, and hotels that lined the streets. The tourists and natives were all abuzz about the volcanic eruption, the shopkeepers worried that their profits would plummet because all ferries had been redirected toward the evacuation effort. Melchizedek and Anne learned that the eruption's main blast had been directed toward Ercolano, but that from Naples to Sorrento ash and falling rock continued to disrupt life. All of Naples was being evacuated in a massive migration into Northern Italy. Aid was pouring into the country from all over Europe as well as from the United States who joined NATO in supporting the Italians' relief effort.

In spite of the horror on the mainland, life continued for the tourists trapped on Capri as well as for the shopkeepers, lemon growers, and wood workers. Melchizedek and Anne walked through the shops until he found a dress maker and a lovely linen dress that he thought she might try on.

"I do find it agreeable," she laughed as she twirled in the shop's mirrors, admiring the way the dress flattered her natural beauty.

"Me too," added Melchizedek.

Anne looked down at the price and her face fell, "But it's far too expensive. I would never spend this much on a dress."

"I would spend that much on a lovely woman," Melchizedek rebutted.

Anne blushed, but persisted, "It's just too much, Mel."

"Anne," Melchizedek began, "I've not spent money on a woman in over five hundred years, so imagine what my holdings must now be assuming even the most marginal interest rate?"

Anne was not sure whether to hit him or just accept his offer, but in the end decided on both, clubbing him with the words, "So, women are that expensive, are we?"

"It's better to spend one's wealth on wives and daughters, than on war," Melchizedek replied just a bit too soberly.

Anne nearly asked him, "So which am I?" but thought better of it. Instead she just replied, "Well, call me flattered."

As Melchizedek turned to pay for the dress, Anne whispered to him, "Of course we'll need some shoes . . ."

His grin told her that all was well.

* * * *

After a day visiting the beautiful gardens and delights of Capri and Anacapri, the smaller town at the very heights of the Island, Anne and Melchizedek retired back to his villa for a quiet evening. After changing her clothes and locating a most comfortable pair of slippers, she returned down the stairs to find Melchizedek. But as she passed a partially opened doorway, she thought she heard a clicking sound. Quietly pushing the door open, she found Melchizedek seated in a small office surrounded by electronic gear and typing away into a laptop computer. She couldn't help but notice the symbol for the Red Cross on the screen, and then realized that Melchizedek was entering a donation for their disaster relief efforts in Naples. She found the amount of twenty-five million Euro staggering, struck at once not only by the resources available to a man who had lived over a thousand lifetimes but by his compassion.

Anne thought her intrusion inappropriate and so backed quietly out of the room, when Melchizedek turned and spotted her.

"Anne!" he said delightedly.

"Um . . . hi, Mel," she stuttered. "I didn't mean to intrude. I heard the computer and wondered if I might use it too."

"Why do you need it?" he asked her puzzled.

"Well, I haven't checked my email in days, and I wondered if perchance John had tried to contact me," she answered hopefully.

"But you are dead," Melchizedek said flatly. "Anyone tracking us will keep a close eye on all of your accounts, and it is important that there is no activity on anything, not your finances, not your email, nothing at all."

"Oh, well, then can I at least check on John, even if I can't write to him?" she asked.

"Does he have a website?" Melchizedek asked her.

"Yes, so I can go see if he's updated it with his trip to Florence. If so, then he is obviously alive and free," she answered.

"Alive, likely; free, not necessarily," he answered her. "You must expect the possibility of a trap."

"Okay, so if I link up to his website, will anyone know it was me?" she asked.

"No, all they would be able to tell is the general location of the one looking at the site, but we can use a scrambling technology which will make it appear that we are using a different server in a location on the other side of the world."

"Sounds good. Let's do it," she affirmed.

Melchizedek activated the scrambler, and Anne brought up her brother's website. She frowned quickly, as she realized that nothing had changed since she'd last looked at it before his trip to visit her. Her fears for her brother intensified, but when she was about to close the browser, Melchizedek pointed to the "last updated on . . ." message at the bottom of the screen.

"Look at that date," he said to her.

"It's only yesterday," she exclaimed. "But he didn't change anything on the site. That doesn't make sense."

Melchizedek thought through the implications of this discovery, and suggested, "Perhaps they released him, and he is aware that they are going to try to use him to track us. So, he only updated the date of the site, making it clear that he is alive."

"And possibly free, because if someone were forcing him to make changes, wouldn't they require him to put pictures of the Palazzo Vecchio and an account of how much better gelato is than American ice cream and things like that?"

"You may be right," he replied, amused at her examples. "John is proving very clever. I like him more all the time."

Anne beamed at him, and added, "Well, can we contact him somehow?"

"I don't think that we have to," Melchizedek surmised. "I think we just did."

"What do you mean?" she asked.

"Look at this counter over here. It shows how many visitors have been to the site since its inception," Melchizedek said.

"Right, and I'm afraid not many have visited. It's mostly just me," she admitted. "Really, there's not that much interesting there."

"So, since you just visited the site, the counter will increase by one, and who other than you would likely have visited it?" Melchizedek explained.

"So John will think it was me, know that I'm okay, but realize that I couldn't send him a message!" she exclaimed.

"Right," Melchizedek answered, relieved that John was safe.

*   *   *   *

The next morning Melchizedek knocked gently on Anne's door, awakening her to a hearty breakfast with fruit, croissants, coffee, eggs, sausages, and potatoes.

Anne laughed when she saw the tray, and at Melchizedek's confounded look, she jested, "Couldn't decide on Continental or English, eh?"

"If you are going for a dive this morning, you'll need the energy," he taunted her.

"A dive?" she asked excitedly. "You mean with tanks and masks and . . ."

". . . and fins!" he finished for her.

"Wonderful!" she began. "What will we see?"

"Fish, lots of fish," he joked.

"Well, I like fish. That sea bass was very tasty," she complimented him.

"And a wreck, an ancient Roman wreck that is caught in that crevice we saw as we approached the deep channel entrance to my cavern. I don't think anyone has found it yet," he continued.

"Wow! How'd you find it?" she asked.

"I saw it sink," he retorted flatly.

"And the crew?" she asked with concern.

"Well, they'd all be dead by now anyhow, wouldn't they?" Melchizedek explained.

"I suppose so, but what an awful thing to watch," she said distantly.

Melchizedek admitted, "You're right, watching men die in the sea is no easy thing. I suppose I've become used to death, too used to it. The crew all drowned in the storm. The ship was supposed to deliver supplies to the Emperor who was ruling from Capri. You'll find some fascinating things on the wreck, I'm sure."

"I've never dived before," Anne explained quietly. "You'll teach me?"

"Of course, and you'll be quite safe, okay?" Melchizedek assured her.

"I'll be ready in half an hour," she started and then stopped, "But . . ."

"You'll be needing this," he finished for her again and handed her a brightly wrapped package with a large silver bow.

She took the package happily and opened it to find a beautiful navy blue bathing suit. She smiled at him admiringly.

"A half hour then," he concluded, and left her to finish her breakfast.

* * * *

Quarston and Bartoli had returned to Florence as quickly as they could wrap up their investigation of the train attack, all the while trying to clean up the track to provide rail support for the relief efforts in Naples. Their report would not measure up to FBI investigative standards, Quarston knew, but in times of national crisis, the people always take priority.

Once back in Florence, Quarston reviewed all that they had learned from the train attack and reread Bartoli's own report on the foiled kidnapping at the hospital. Something was bothering him, he realized, but he could not quite place it. He decided to get some fresh air to clear his aching, tired brain, so he walked down to the Arno River just past the Uffizi museum. No sooner did the Ponte Vecchio come into view than a number of powerful black men ran past him at high speed, carrying rolls of what looked like . . . posters! As they turned the corner, he noticed a police car speeding after them. A Nigerian outfit, he remembered Bartoli telling him, had cornered the black market on souvenirs. Bartoli had explained how they were generally tolerated by the police, though every now and again, a few raids were conducted to keep them on their toes and prevent them from shifting their illegal activities toward bullying tourists. Crime that tourists enjoyed was crime that Florence could wink at.

And then it hit him. Quarston found himself running back to the police station not quite as fast as the Nigerians, but fast enough that the tourists wondered what he was running from and began to stare.

Melchizedek took Anne back down the long stone stair case to the cavernous harbor far beneath his villa. There he showed her how each piece of the diving apparatus functioned and taught her dive theory. Once she felt comfortable with the explanations, he illuminated the cavern and encouraged her to try out the gear. She took to the water like a fish and about fifteen minutes later she surfaced and spit out her regulator with a huge grin on her face.

"Let's go to the wreck!" she shouted to him.

"Come on back to the dock and we'll suit up for the dive and get a fresh tank for you, okay?" he asked her.

Once they were suited and tanked, Melchizedek dropped a brightly colored orange rope into the tunnel. Anne asked him why the rope, and he explained that in an ascending tunnel, divers could become disoriented, so the rope with its directional arrows could be counted on to lead the way to safety.

"Ready?" he asked her. In answer she stepped off the dock and into the water. He joined her and soon they were working their way down through the tunnel toward the sandy bottom. Anne enjoyed the glowing blue water even more than she had in the submarine, because this time she felt as though she were bathing in sunlight.

*　*　*　*

Quarston rushed into the police station and up to Bartoli's office. Bartoli looked up in surprise at Quarston's red face and asked him ironically, "Freshened up then?"

"Oh sure," Quarston laughed, trying to regain his breath. "How did our John Doe, an old man sick in a hospital bed, recover sufficiently to make his escape on a train toward Naples? And all in less than a week?"

"Assuming he was on the train," Bartoli murmured and then added with sudden realization, "You assume that he must be the target of both the hospital and train assaults!"

"It seems reasonable," Quarston acknowledged. "Michelle Andover was sent by Rothschild to kidnap him at the hospital where he was suffering from radiation poisoning or something similar, right?"

"That's right," answered Bartoli.

"So, we know one set of the pursuers and we know the target," explained Quarston.

"Yes, we know the target, but we don't really know why, do we?" asked Bartoli.

"No, we really don't," Quarston deceived Bartoli. "But we know that our John Doe is the key. He possesses something that Rothschild wants badly enough to have gone to this much trouble to acquire him. And someone else wants it too, someone who initially discovered the kidnapping at the hospital and tried to intercept . . . not protect him."

"Right, and we know that, because the attack on the train was carried out only by one side, namely the professionals, all of whom were killed. And now you are wondering how our old John Doe managed suddenly to become so healthy?" asked Bartoli.

"Exactly," answered Quarston. "How did he get better if he was moved out of the hospital and then escaped on his own feet? Why didn't he just collapse a few blocks from the hospital?"

"He had help," nodded Bartoli.

"He had help," repeated Quarston.

CHAPTER FORTY-NINE

Melchizedek and Anne reached the seafloor and followed it out into the deeper channel. Anne looked in awe at the huge sea turtle that lumbered across her path, barely batting an eye at the intrusion of the two bubbling mammals. They followed the sea turtle into a school of fish that darted around them zealously. As they emerged from the fish, Anne noticed Melchizedek pointing toward the seafloor, so she followed him until he suddenly vanished behind a series of coral encrusted rocks. She swam around the outcropping and then realized that the coral had grown over the prow of a ship, not rock, and she stared in amazement at the splintered timbers beneath her of what had once been a Roman cargo vessel. Melchizedek motioned her toward the hold, and there she saw multiple pots filled with olive oil, as well as wine amphorae still sealed with their imperial seals. A wine fit for an emperor, Anne thought with wonder. She then saw the chests, and with Melchizedek's help, opened the lid on the closest one. It was filled with finely crafted jewelry, in pristine condition. She picked up an ancient cameo of the imperial couple with a ruby backing, and looked inquiringly at Melchizedek. He depicted the act of placing the object into his wetsuit, so she knew it was okay to take it with them. They closed the lid on the chest and then opened the next chest, but it was filled only with the soggy remains of scrolls.

Melchizedek pointed to his underwater watch, indicating that they needed to return to the cavern. They swam out the rear of the ship and upward so that she could see its full outline in the crevice of the channel. She nodded to Melchizedek and they swam back toward the cavern.

*　*　*　*

Quarston and Bartoli carefully reviewed the information on their John Doe's illness. Several times Quarston had to bite his tongue so as to not identify John Doe as Melchizedek. Keeping information compartmentalized was something he had become accustomed to in his job, but for some reason Melchizedek had taken such a life of his own in Quarston's imagination, that he kept wanting to refer to John Doe as Melchizedek.

"You know, Roger," began Bartoli, "there is another question here."

"What's that?" asked Quarston as he reviewed the medical data from the hospital.

"How did an old man defeat an elite assassination team on a train? How did he survive the initial attack on the train, get off the train, and then kill the attempted assassins?" Bartoli pressed.

"Yeah, I wondered that too," Quarston answered, and then again deceived Bartoli, "It looks like he has his own security detail?"

"No, because when he was admitted to the hospital, there is no record of any security attending to him," answered Bartoli.

Quarston frowned, realizing that Bartoli was eventually going to figure out that Melchizedek was more than a mere old man. Quarston himself was not exactly sure how Melchizedek had done it either, but he assumed that someone who had survived for several thousand years probably had a few tricks up his sleeve. Still, Quarston mused to himself, his killing an entire hit team by himself seemed a remarkable feat, especially for an old man. Quarston's thoughts slowed down appreciably as he reflected on that paradox, and then it hit him: why think that Melchizedek was an old man? If he regenerated, he should be young perpetually, not old. That was exactly what the professors had told him when they'd discussed the paradox of Eos. If Melchizedek were in prime physical condition, then that would at least answer Bartoli's query. But then why did the hospital records as well as Bartoli's photograph show an old man?

Quarston decided to acknowledge the direction of Bartoli's questions, "Then our John Doe is not as old as he appears."

"Right," answered Bartoli with satisfaction. "Who is he and how does he appear so old? If he were wearing a disguise, then hospital personnel would have noticed it, but there is nothing in their records to indicate any such thing."

"No, there isn't," Quarston paused. "Yet he must be younger than he appears, so he has the ability to alter his appearance. I guess we have to acknowledge that, even if we don't know how he does it."

"And that means that tracking him must be extremely difficult," added Bartoli.

Quarston nodded, impressed with Bartoli's thinking, "So how did the second hit team find him on that train?"

"Especially if he recovered from the radiation sickness," explained Bartoli.

"There'd be nothing to identify him," admitted Quarston.

"Unless he's not alone, and they tracked whoever he was with," wondered Bartoli aloud.

"And so we come full circle: who helped John Doe recover? Where was he in the days between the hospital attack and the train attack?" asked Quarston.

"I'm not sure how we can discover the answer to that question," confessed Bartoli.

"I've got a hunch," explained Quarston. "That's why I ran back here!"

* * * *

As they approached the seafloor with its reflected sunlight, Anne noticed the orange rope hanging from the cavern above them. Following it, she took the lead up into the tunnel, still aglow with the blue light. The rope provided her a constant reference point until the tunnel opened up into the cavern and its electrical illumination. They surfaced and swam over to the dock, where Melchizedek helped her out of the water. She smiled, though her teeth chattered from the cold, and Melchizedek wished he had taken her onto a boat in the warm sunlight. Quickly wrapping her in a towel, he stowed their gear, and carefully took the cameo from her wetsuit. He wrapped it in a silk cloth and placed it into a small wooden box.

She was eager to return to the warmth of her bath, so they quickly ascended the staircase, their bare wet feat smacking the cold stones. Once in the villa, Melchizedek motioned her to the veranda and opened the box. Withdrawing the cameo, he held it up to the sky, and the rays of the sun illuminated the ruby glass backdrop to the white glass etching.

"These cameos are very rare," Melchizedek explained. "They were popular in Rome for about fifty years around the time of the rule of the August Gaius Julius Caesar Octavianus. You have chosen well."

Anne blushed as she accepted his compliment. "I've never seen anything like it," she explained.

"Well, Queen Elizabeth owns one," he said smiling.

Anne's eyes widened, as the realization of the likely worth of the piece grew in her mind. She started to return the cameo to the wooden box, but Melchizedek held her arm and shook his head.

"Anne, jewelry is for adornment, not storage. Wear the cameo. No one will believe it to be an authentic Roman piece anyway, so you needn't worry about thieves!" he added laughing.

"But it must be worth . . ." she began.

"Yes," he interrupted. "More than you have ever seen."

Melchizedek paused for a moment in reflection and then asked her, "Anne, do remember the story of the young woman who approached Jesus with a costly ointment?"

Anne looked embarrassed, but admitted sheepishly, "Yes."

"Things are made for people, not people for things. Things are mortal, but people are immortal," he explained. "So, it's perfectly appropriate for you, an immortal being, to wear a merely mortal cameo, don't you think?"

"But I am not as worthy as he was," she explained.

"No, you are not a king," he paused. "But you saved one, so accept this with my royal gratitude."

Anne looked up at Melchizedek, into those dazzling eyes, took the cameo from him and clutched it to her heart.

* * * *

Quarston and Bartoli sat at the computer in Bartoli's office and ran a search cross-referencing the hospital data describing Melchizedek's symptoms together with their location in Florence.

Within minutes two local searches appeared, one at the University and another at an undisclosed remote location. Bartoli pointed at the username associated with the remote search, Janet Langley.

Quarston nodded, "Michelle Andover again."

"Right," answered Bartoli. "So the other one must be the people who helped John Doe."

"Anne Horn," read Quarston. "She has a university identification and logged on . . . look there. It appears that she logged off before Andover completed her search, so . . ."

Bartoli interrupted him, "So, Andover picked up her trail!"

"But it wasn't Andover's people who attacked the train; it doesn't make sense," offered a puzzled Quarston.

"I think it does make sense," answered Bartoli suddenly. "Rothschild's operation has been penetrated. Someone is tracking his movements, watching his plans unfold and either thwarting them or leaping ahead of him."

"Then we need to examine his communications carefully," offered Quarston. "I have some technical experts who might be useful."

Bartoli noted the sudden sensitivity in Quarston's voice. He merely shrugged, "You Americans are the best in the electronic surveillance business. Bring in your people."

"Ok, I'll ask them to start from within the United States, and then send a team here if necessary," Quarston answered.

"And I'll find out everything there is to know about Anne Horn here in Florence," concluded Bartoli.

*　*　*　*

After her bath and a quiet dinner, Melchizedek invited Anne to another of the rooms at the top of the spiral staircase. In deference to Melchizedek's showing her only her own room in the upper floor, she had barely managed her driving curiosity to enter it. She likened her situation to a child who having just finished *The Lion the Witch and the Wardrobe* wondered whether the wardrobe in the next room might not just lead to a magical realm. When Melchizedek opened the door, she noticed the scents first—strong smells of leather and tobacco followed shortly by those of brittle, ancient books. A man's world, she thought, as she followed Melchizedek inside. The sharp sizzling of a match drew her attention to the small but vibrant light of a single candlestick in the center of the room. Melchizedek then drew a candle lighter from near the doorway, and proceeded to solemnly light the multiple lamps that surrounded the perfect circularity of the room. Above her head Anne noticed that a gold-mirrored dome reflected the candlelight downward. Her eyes were drawn to the dark spot at the top of the dome with tiny dots of sparkling light. Suddenly she understood that it was an oculus, and she was staring into the stars of the night sky. She smiled and returned her gaze to the room itself, now aglow with candlelight.

All round the room's circumference were acacia wood shelves filled with books and even some scrolls, she noted in amazement. At the point where the shelving gave way to the curve of the dome above, she observed small sculptures reflecting many different cultures. She was sure that she saw one from China, another from Egypt, still another from Assyria or Babylonia. At the junctures of the shelves were panels with attached candle lamps, but above each lamp she now noticed swords, one per lamp, and each sword from a distinct time in history. Her knowledge of ancient weapons was not good enough to confirm the hypothesis that now entered her mind, namely that the swords and sculptures matched cultures. She decided to check the books, wondering if perhaps there was a threefold match, and sure enough, underneath the Chinese figure, she saw Chinese books. So, this room was a repository of the greatest literary works of several of the most magnificent cultures in history. She spiraled around the room and saw Roman and Greek works as well as Persian and British and French texts.

Melchizedek motioned her across the floor toward the French doors at the far side of the room. She began to cross it, when she noticed the floor itself and stopped abruptly. Beneath her feet lay the most beautiful mosaic she had ever seen. It was a scene from the work of Josephus, she realized, when Alexander the Great approached the city of Jerusalem with his army. The Jewish High Priest came from the city and met the general, and showed him the Biblical book of Daniel the Prophet. The Priest explained that Alexander was one of the figures mentioned in the prophecy, and Alexander spared the city. She remembered from her class at college that Josephus also reported that Alexander had long experienced a repeated dream of a messenger of the gods wearing a funny hat, and that when he saw that the High Priest in his priestly head gear wore exactly that hat, he alighted his horse and bowed down before him—to the consternation of his generals! She laughed at the memory, while her mind continued to examine the picture. Something about it seemed familiar to her, so she asked Melchizedek.

"This mosaic is by the same artist who created the Pompeii mosaic of Alexander, so you probably notice some similarities. You have to understand that such artworks were commonplace in Rome. You now hang on a museum wall what we walked upon. I often smirk at the way in which your scholars depict the ancients. But if I were in their place, I suppose I would draw the same conclusions they do."

"But you are also a historian, so why don't you correct their inaccurate portrayals?" Anne asked puzzled.

"Well, for one, my observations would be thought of as mere speculation, unless I revealed that I lived in these cultures, and so occupied the status of an eye-witness. Second, my actual histories are not meant for human eyes. They are saved for the future, for the ears of those who would justify themselves before the Most High God. Few men have read them, and those that did have rarely fared well. I showed them to Daniel, of course, my truest friend over the passing millennia. Solomon was wiser, naturally, but Daniel was the greatest man I think I ever knew. He was certainly my closest friend. But even he found them difficult to read. But come, Anne."

Anne followed Melchizedek as he opened the doors to yet another portico. The fragrance of the jasmine flowers that surrounded it began to intoxicate her with their sweetness. Melchizedek lit another series of candlesticks which illuminated both the flowers and a table with . . . she looked again, and then realized that yes, it was a chess board. The board itself was beautifully colored marble. She'd seen a similar use of color in the Medici Capella in Florence, she realized. The pieces were made of solid gold and silver.

"Do you play chess?" he asked her.

"Actually, I do," she replied. "Care for a game?"

"I'm eager for it," he answered her, motioning her toward the large leather chair at one end of the table.

He opened a small drawer in the table and withdrew a pipe and tobacco. "Southern tobacco, from your United States," he explained. "Really, the best there is. I must say too that during your War Between the States it was nigh impossible to acquire."

When Melchizedek lit the pipe, Anne closed her eyes and took in the aroma. She had long loved pipe tobacco, for it reminded her of her father. She still missed him after all these years, and that memory made her miss her brother all the more. Melchizedek noticed her eyes and asked her gently, "The tobacco brings you memories of past loved ones; would you prefer I put out the pipe?"

"No, no," she answered quietly. "These are people I want to remember. Some memories we'd prefer to forget, but others though painful should never be forgotten, because they are all that we carry of the people that we love."

Melchizedek nodded and rose from his chair. Passing back through the French doors, he opened a cabinet built into one of the shelving units and soon returned with a bottle and two tulip shaped glasses. She realized from their shape that he was bringing her Port, one of her true loves. She looked at the bottle in surprise at the date, 1945. "I've always heard that that was a great year for vintage Port, but of course I've never tasted it," she said admiringly.

"I buy multiple cases of each vintage year, but I buy crates of the best years. You are right about this year. It and the 1963 were wondrous vintages, and the port is still developing in the bottles, even this long after bottling. 1977 was very good too," he began.

"Yes, I once drank a glass of 1977 Fonseca—it filled my mouth with an intensity of aromas and flavors, and the finish lasted three minutes," she exclaimed.

"Then you are in for a treat tonight," he told her, opening the bottle and decanting it. "We'll let it breathe, of course."

"They say that wine is alive, so it must breathe," began Anne, "but I've always thought that this is most true of Port."

"Port has a way of developing quite unlike any other fortified wine, I agree with you," Melchizedek added smiling.

"I suppose you have a crate or two of the 1994 vintage?" she asked with interest.

"Your supposition is correct," he acknowledged, "though with the explosion of interest in Port over the last couple decades, the price was surprisingly high as soon as it was released."

Anne looked lovingly at the Port in the decanter illuminated by the dancing firelight. Its deep ruby color almost enchanted her. She had felt that effect with wine and candlelight before, she thought to herself, noting with amusement that this time the effect was prior to her having drunk anything. She turned to Melchizedek and asked him, "Do you think that enchantments are real?"

He started at that question and then turned away in thought. "What do you mean, exactly?"

"Well, I find that beautiful things seem to slow down time itself."

"You mean as if eternity can break into time through the beautiful?" he asked her.

"Yes, that's a great way to put it. Then you do know what I mean!" she exclaimed.

"I know what you mean. I feel that way when I hear Beethoven, when I gaze at the stars or the sea from these porticos, when I . . .," he paused and then continued, ". . . look at the happiness of wonder in your eyes."

Anne blushed and answered, "I suppose I am curious, kinda like that little monkey, George. Do you know about him?"

"Oh yes," he laughed. "I love George too. Quite a monkey!"

She paused, then added seriously, "Thank you for the compliment."

"You are most welcome to it, Anne, for it fits you well," he answered. "Rarely do I meet people animated by such a spirit of inquisitiveness coupled to an appreciation of beauty."

"Well, you sure have described little ole me," she answered. "I think I'm going to need that Port soon." Anne felt as if she might swoon.

Melchizedek laughed, "I suppose a little taste won't hurt, but we'll allow most of it to mature further with the air."

He poured her a little of the wine and watched her hold the glass up toward the flames behind her. When she had finished observing its coloring through the candlelight, Melchizedek watched as she next swirled the wine and then placed her nose right into the glass and sniffed once, then paused, sniffed again, and finally a third time. She sat back to appreciate the scent's complexities. Forcing her mind to remain intellectually disengaged, she allowed the Port to dazzle her senses. Finally she took some of the wine into her mouth, and Melchizedek stared in wonder as her face broke into expressions of intense appreciation and pleasure. Our greatest experiences of pleasure lie on the border of pain, so the facial responses are not all that distinct. Anne definitely appeared enchanted, as the wine swished up to her palette, over her tongue, around her gums, filling her mouth with the most intense flavors that she had ever experienced. Finally, she swallowed the wine, and the taste buds in her throat delighted in the last bit of that mouthful, before the aftereffect of the wine began, the finish. She placed her glass on the table and sat quietly as the flavors danced throughout her mouth like echoes in a canyon, slowly, ever so slowly, fading away. After eight minutes she looked up at him, glowing.

"That was the greatest sensible experience in my entire life," she said simply. "Thank you."

He smiled at her again, and they began their game. After a few moves, he looked at her in surprise and said, "The Scottish Gambit, eh?"

She flashed a devilish smile back at him, and the battle commenced.

CHAPTER FIFTY

Quarston listened to the telephone call from the United States. The FBI's initial examination of Rothschild's personal communications security showed only that it had just been radically changed. The agent leading the investigation spoke with admiration about how Rothschild's system was inaccessible, since all important information was housed on servers that were now physically cut off from the outside world. But that had only recently changed, the agent explained to him.

"From what I can tell, Agent Quarston," the agent continued, "Rothschild had a security plan prepared. The changes that went into effect are too well thought out and far too expensive to be implemented as quickly as they were without extensive preparation."

"So, he expected possible penetration?" asked Quarston.

"He must have," acknowledged the agent. "We do have data from before the changeover, but most of it appears to be philanthropic and business related material."

"Well, bundle all that you have and I'll plan to review it," Quarston concluded.

Bartoli looked up from the report on Anne Horn that he was reading, "Nothing?"

"Yes, but the kind of nothing that tells you something," he offered with a twisted smile.

"Ah, yes, so I was right?" Bartoli asked him.

"Yes, Rothschild appears to have recently upgraded his security, so it would appear that someone had penetrated his networks," answered Quarston.

"And from what I've got here," Bartoli pointed to the file he was holding, "it appears that Andover's people were tracking Anne Horn."

"Is she a doctor?" asked Quarston.

"No, she's an art student . . . from the States," added Bartoli.

"She's an American?" asked Quarston, adding quizzically, "and an art student?"

Bartoli nodded. "What's interesting about her is her brother, a John Horn. He's a doctor, an American doctor, works in emergency services and hematology in the States, in Washington, D.C."

"Well, it's certainly becoming a small world, isn't it?" asked Quarston in amazement.

"John Horn was recently in Italy, right here in Florence," Bartoli continued.

"Visiting his sister?" asked Quarston.

"Looks like it. He rented a villa a few blocks from here, and his rental agreement doesn't expire until next week," Bartoli pointed out.

"Then we can interview him there?" asked Quarston hopefully.

"Let's go find out," Bartoli said and headed toward the door.

* * * *

Bartoli and Quarston ran up the steps of John Horn's villa and knocked on the door. Bartoli was about to go find a key, when Quarston pushed on the door and it opened.

Bartoli looked at him in amazement, "How did you know it was unlocked?"

"I always check . . . you just never know," offered Quarston smiling.

The two investigators entered the villa and noticed immediately that someone had left in a hurry. Horn's suitcase and clothes were gone, but little things were left behind. A toothbrush in the bathroom, some migraine medicine in the kitchen . . . Quarston watched as Bartoli noticed the same things that he did. More and more Quarston liked and respected the Italian investigator.

But it was clear that Horn was gone. Bartoli grabbed his phone from his pocket and called someone at his office.

"By the time we return to my office, we should know whether he left the country," Bartoli explained.

"Good," Quarston said. "It doesn't appear that we're going to find much here. But I've got another question for you."

"Oh?" asked Bartoli.

"Yeah, this medicine made me think of it," began Quarston. "If Horn aided in John Doe's recovery, then how and where did he do it? There's no evidence here of any medical procedures."

"You're right," admitted Bartoli. "I hadn't even considered that. He would have had to have worked secretly, I suppose, which means that perhaps he made special arrangements."

"You mean illegal arrangements?" laughed Quarston.

"*Si*, those kinds of special arrangements," laughed Bartoli.

* * * *

Melchizedek returned the phone to its cradle and smiled at Anne.

"All right, everything is prepared. We board our ship tomorrow and then on to Patmos!" Melchizedek exclaimed.

"Where we meet your old friend at the Monastery of St. John, but he is definitely not St. John, right? Only you live on and on?" Anne asked with a twinkle in her eye.

"Right, he's an 'old' friend in the usual manner of speaking. I've had a special relationship with each Archimandrite, the superior monk at the Monastery. Each one passes down to the next the knowledge relating to my existence, and the monks have always offered me comfort and brotherhood. They spend a great deal of their time preserving ancient records, so we share much in common."

"Except that they have no women, right?" Anne asked and then bit her lip for her forward response.

"Uh . . . well, of course, that's one of the differences. It's certainly one that you'll notice right away!" he answered laughing.

"So, what do I do about papers? My passport is still in Florence," Anne explained.

"We wouldn't want you traveling under your real name anyhow, so I've got a friend coming here this afternoon to deliver some new travel documents for you," he answered.

"Well, a cruise does sound awfully relaxing," she began, but then hastily added, "Not that the last few days here haven't been wonderful."

Again Melchizedek laughed. "No need to worry, Anne," he answered. "Freud's ego is not particularly strong in me anyhow."

Anne looked as though she'd just stepped on a baby bird. "But Mel, that's not what I meant. I've really loved it here. It's just that a cruise sounds exciting, and I've never been on one before."

"I know, really," he assured her. "I was kidding you with the ego reference."

"Is that supposed to be a pun on my age?" she asked with feigned defiance.

Melchizedek laughed again and shifted the subject. "Anne, I've got one final surprise for you this evening, but we'll wait until it's quite dark, okay?"

"Sure, what is it?" she asked with delight.

"Oh, you'll see, after dinner and the rest of that port from last night."

*　*　*　*

As they entered Bartoli's office, Quarston watched as someone ran over to the inspector with another report on Anne Horn.

"It looks like Miss Horn has gone missing. Only she did not take any of her belongings with her. She has just disappeared. And her passport remains in her villa," Bartoli explained, reviewing the report.

Quarston frowned. This investigation had already led to many murders, and he did not relish yet another one. "What about her brother?" asked Quarston.

Bartoli nodded and headed down the hall to check with one of his colleagues. He returned a few minutes later.

"He's left the country, only days ago. And get this: he purchased the ticket just before he left, ignoring his own return ticket with its reservation for another week from now."

"So, he paid more and got out fast," thought Quarston aloud. "He returned to the States?"

"Yes, back to Washington," Bartoli nodded.

"Then I guess it's time for me to go home, isn't it?" asked Quarston.

Bartoli glanced at his watch. "You can still make the flight to Washington if you leave in the next half an hour."

At Quarston's wide-eyed look, Bartoli offered, "Perhaps a police escort would be useful?"

*　*　*

After a sumptuous dinner of beef filet with demi-glace topped by fresh black truffle and accompanied by an outstanding Brunello di Montalcino, Melchizedek and Anne poured themselves glasses of port and stared out at the moon-lit sea so far below them.

"Mel," she began, "I think this must be the loveliest time in all my life. I don't know if the fear from Florence and the train and the volcano makes this joy stronger—I almost think it must, but this villa on this island overlooking this glorious water is the most beautiful place I've ever seen."

"That's why I call it home, and return here every few years. I have traveled over most of the earth, and there are places of exquisite beauty quite unlike Capri, but Capri captures my heart."

"What other places do you mean?" she asked curiously.

"Well, there are places in China that will shock you with their grandeur, and then there are the Swiss Alps, the Scottish Highlands, the African Savannah, on and on it goes!" he exclaimed.

"You'll take me there, to these places, then too?" she asked him.

"Once I ensure the security of my books, and am confident of your long term safety, then yes, I'd be happy to take you to all of these places . . . if you'd like, of course," he offered.

"I would Mel, very much," she answered warmly. He then noticed that her face grew drawn and she added, "But do you think we'll ever really be safe?"

"I have known danger throughout my life, but it alternates with abundance and joy, so yes, I think we will be. And don't forget that if we really must hide, you're with the expert! I've been doing it for thousands of years," he laughed in answer.

Anne felt much relieved and turned the conversation toward the surprise she had been awaiting all that day.

"Yes," Melchizedek answered her staring at the stars, "I believe it is dark enough. Come, let's pour the remaining port into our glasses and ascend through that wall."

Her confused look only compounded as he pointed to the fireplace inside the villa. He walked over to it and as he reached up into the flue, Anne heard a click. At the sound the fireplace swung outward revealing a spiral stone staircase.

"A secret passage!" she shouted with girlish glee.

Melchizedek pulled a torch from the fireplace mantle and proceeded up the staircase with Anne in close pursuit. When they finally reached the top, they both stood panting in front of a strong wooden door.

"Pity the Romans never invented elevators," she offered.

Melchizedek nodded and reached into his pocket to produce an ancient key which he slid into the lock. It creaked but finally clicked with his sharp turn. Anne's eyes were wide with wonder as the door opened to reveal a large shape underneath what looked like a veil.

THE SEARCH FOR MELCHIZEDEK

Melchizedek led her into the room and proceeded to turn a switch on the wall as he blew out the torch. The room was engulfed in eerie red light which Melchizedek explained was the same light used in old submarines to prepare the watches.

"I actually purchased these lights from the Italian Navy when they decommissioned several of their Second World War submarines," he explained to her.

Anne looked around her and saw that the walls were covered with painted star charts. Below them on low shelves all round the room were books on astronomy, both modern and ancient. She looked up and saw that like the chess room, this room had a dome, but there was no oculus at its center. Somewhat disappointed by that, she turned to Melchizedek and asked him, "So, what's under the tarp?"

Instead of answering her, he moved to the other side of the door and began to turn a crank. To her astonishment, she heard the movement of heavy metal grinding against metal and saw that the dome above her had split apart and was beginning to open. Ever so slowly, the dome retracted until she found herself staring at the stars of the night sky.

Melchizedek then said to her, "Come."

Taking her by the hand, he lifted one side of the tarp and placed her hand on something cold and metallic. With a great tug, he then hurled the rest of the tarp to one side to reveal a large reflecting telescope. The room was in fact a small observatory.

Anne's earlier disappointment now gave way to enthusiastic wonder. Melchizedek showed her how to direct the telescope and fix it on a 'moving' star or nebula. She stared in awe at the bright shapes that danced before her vision.

"You said in Florence that each star is an angel in the heavens?" she asked him.

"Each angel has a star in this world, yes," he answered. "Incredible, isn't it? A universe this vast offering an eternity of exploration."

"Some day when the true King returns and death is finally ended, in that day we'll be able to fulfill our longings to venture into the heavens?"

"Yes," Melchizedek promised her. "The divine hope answers the deepest longings of man."

After viewing various stars and nebulae, Melchizedek showed her a comet. She then asked him, "So, Mel, where did you get this telescope?"

"I built it," he answered her.

"You built it?" she asked him. "How did you learn to do that? Don't tell me you studied with Galileo?"

"No, he studied with me," he replied.

"But I thought that he invented the first telescope," she rebutted.

"That's what everybody thinks. But as with the first human flight, it was Leonardo da Vinci that first invented the telescope," he explained.

"I thought that Leonardo's wings couldn't fly," she replied mystified.

"They fly just fine when built to his precise specifications. Leonardo's works are enjoying renewed interest by scholars and engineers who are finally building his machines correctly. And guess what?" he asked her.

"They work, right?" she answered.

"Correct. The wings were marvelous too, but Leonardo became fearful about their use, just as he did with the telescope," he answered.

"What was his worry?" she asked.

"He realized the power that flight would give to man, and he just did not believe that human beings were ready for that kind of power. Man will always try to fly too close to the sun," he answered.

"The legend of Icarus," Anne murmured.

"Yes, the old legends still have much to teach," Melchizedek answered. "I actually didn't think that he was correct about ceasing his research into flight, but that's because men are the same in each generation. They don't really get much worse. But Leonardo didn't know that. Each generation thinks that his is far worse than the prior golden ages. I tried to convince him otherwise, but he was actually a fairly stubborn guy."

"So, tell me about his telescope?" Anne asked.

"Ah, yes, he left no notes about it," Melchizedek replied. "When he was living in Rome, he ordered a number of glass lenses, and he would run them upstairs into this laboratory which he always kept locked against any intruders. He only allowed me to enter. And he built a very fine telescope. I was surprised to watch the stars and the planets grow so large."

"But why did he fear revealing it to the world?" Anne asked.

"Oh, the telescope fears were quite different. The fellow who ground his lenses got into a dispute with him about payment and reported Leonardo's secret dissections of corpses to the authorities. I always told Leonardo that doing those in the dead of night would eventually attract the wrong kind of attention, but he assured me that the night would keep his research safe."

"So, the authorities came after him? During the Inquisition?" Anne asked.

"Yes, they did. Leonardo was ordered not to continue those experiments, but the whole incident was sufficiently frightening to him that he really worried what the response would be to his telescope. So, unlike Galileo, Leonardo dismantled the thing," Melchizedek explained.

"What did he do with it?" Anne queried.

"It's here, in this case," he said pointing toward a large case built into one of the shelf units. "Leonardo knew of my fascination for the sciences, and so he offered the telescope to me on the condition that I not show it to anyone for 200 years."

"Oh, so he knew about your long life?" Anne asked.

"Oh sure, we were close friends. I agreed to his terms, but in the end Galileo's telescope showed up only a few years later. Nevertheless, I've kept Leonardo's secret to this day."

"What a story!" Anne exclaimed.

"I've got lots of them," he answered, chuckling. "But we'd best get to our beds, because we leave early tomorrow for Patmos."

CHAPTER FIFTY-ONE

Back in Washington Quarston looked bemusedly at the boxes and boxes of transcripts from the data recovered in the Rothschild investigation. He then remembered that he was operational leader of a task force. He had nearly forgotten that working in Italy, so he smiled and called for some of his assistant agents to review the material. He was pleased that the viral release was sufficiently important for agents to be assigned to the case round the clock. He glanced out of his window and saw that the morning sun had yet to rise. Feeling his face tighten into a yawn, he decided that the coffee machine was the best remedy.

Returning to his desk with a hot cup of American coffee, Quarston tried to adjust his expectations to how much weaker it would taste compared to Italian espresso. He picked up the report on John Horn that another agent had prepared for him. Everything he read showed a man dedicated to his medical profession. Nothing suspicious or remarkable about him. And yet . . . somehow he was mixed up with Melchizedek. Quarston was not sure if Melchizedek had a prior relationship to Horn, or if he met Horn in Italy, and if so how? He had many questions for Horn, and he decided to interview him from the standpoint of omniscience, namely that he already knew everything, so Horn had best just tell the truth. By cleverly mixing fact with his own conjecture, he could discover whatever additional information Horn might be hiding. Assuming he had anything to hide, Quarston mused. But people always had something to hide, Quarston knew. It was human nature.

* * * *

Anne looked wistfully at the morning sun rising over the sea from her room's veranda, took one last longing look at the exquisite lion foot tub, and finally picked up and kissed the picture of Melchizedek's daughter. Putting everything back in its place, she sighed and then headed out of her room and down the staircase with her bags.

She found Melchizedek putting some fruit, coffee, and pastries out for a light breakfast, so they ate together and then proceeded out the door of the villa. A taxi awaited them, and soon they found themselves on the ride of their lives as the taxi driver raced toward the harbor below, the sheer cliffs only inches from their tires.

After tipping the driver, Melchizedek met a man who handed him an envelope for Anne and directed them to the launch that would take them to the cruising ship anchored off shore. Melchizedek took Anne aside and opened up the envelope. He showed her a new American passport with her face but a new name, as well as an American driver's license, and American credit cards. She looked up at him in surprise.

"It's important for you to appear to be the person whose identity you are assuming. An American does not travel without credit cards and usually can't bear to leave his driver's license behind. In this way nothing will stand out for an immigration officer's notice."

Anne nodded, "So, I need to know all the information contained here, my new address, my new name . . ."

"Right," he replied. "You cannot even hesitate. I chose the same first name for you, because it's just too easy to get caught not answering to a new first name."

"Okay," she replied. "I'll have this memorized by the time we get to the ship. They will check our papers there?"

"Yes," he answered. "Let's go then. Our launch is over there."

Melchizedek pointed the way to the launch and handed the pilot his fee. Soon they were speeding out of the harbor toward the ship that waited to take them to Patmos. Anne wondered how it was that a ship was traveling to Patmos from Capri.

Melchizedek answered, "Actually, this ship is on a general Mediterranean cruise, but several of the stops have been cut short due to the eruption in Naples. Patmos was on the original itinerary, so we should be there in about a week."

Their launch approached the large cruise ship, and an effusive steward met them at the door by the waterline. Taking their gear aboard, he led them to their cabins and asked for their passports which he promised would be protected in the ship's safe. Melchizedek thanked him with a generous tip, and then arranged to meet Anne once they had both stowed their gear.

* * * *

Quarston knocked on the door of the apartment and a tired man in his early thirties answered.

"Hello, Mr. Horn?" asked Quarston.

"Yes?" Horn answered, blinking his eyes trying to bring himself to wakefulness.

"I'm Special Agent Roger Quarston with the Federal Bureau of Investigation. I'm the Bureau's liaison with my Italian counterpart in our joint investigation of the recent terrorist attacks in Italy."

Quarston watched Horn's eyes registering both the Italian and the 'terrorist attacks' references. "I understand that you recently returned from Italy yourself?"

"Yes, that's right," Horn acknowledged still standing in the doorway.

"Well, I'd like to discuss your time there, if you don't mind. May I come in?" Quarston asked him.

John hesitated, very unsure what to do, but finally admitted Quarston into his apartment. He offered the FBI agent some coffee and headed to the kitchen to prepare it. Quarston noted both the delay at the door and the display of hospitality. As Quarston looked around the apartment, he saw Horn's bookcase. There he saw the same wonderful books that had grabbed him as a young college student, worn and used. Plato, Aristotle, Thucydides, Polybius, Seutonius, Epictetus, Sophocles, Euripides . . . that was just the first shelf. He glanced down to the second and third and saw books by St. Thomas, St. Augustine, Chaucer, Mallory, Shakespeare, Donne, Swift, Locke, Descartes . . . all of these clearly read as well. Looking at the art on the walls, he saw a man deeply in touch with his humanity. He saw splendor and joy and hope and longing and grief and hunger and yearning. Quarston found himself longing for this man's friendship and though professionally he pushed that aside, he nevertheless wondered if perhaps he should alter the way he planned to interview Horn. Rarely did one interrogate a good man.

* * * *

Anne and Melchizedek explored the ship from bow to stern and finally settled in on teak wood chairs with some books in the afternoon sun of the upper deck.

"Mel?" asked Anne, dropping her book face down in her lap.

"Yes, Anne?" he answered, looking over to her.

"I've noticed that people aren't responding to you as an older man, nor as a woman, so I take it you appear as a younger man?" she asked.

Melchizedek blushed slightly before answering, "Well, yes, er . . . I just thought that we would be able to enjoy ourselves more without constantly waiting for me to shuffle along . . ."

"Yes, that's right," she broke in, confident that her intuition had been correct, and eager now to agree completely with his rationale. "What's more, the kinds of conversations that we have might sometimes seem odd coming from two people with such a dramatic age difference."

Melchizedek stared at her, blinked once or twice, and then smiled at her. "Right."

She then leaned in very close to him and whispered, "Of course, they have no real idea, do they? I mean, about just how dramatic the age difference is?"

Again he blushed, but this time her face was so close to his that she could feel the heat rising with the color. Awkwardly, he replied to her, "Age does make a difference, but not always for ill. Like aged Scotch, for example. Perhaps I'll go get a glass. Would you like some too?"

"No, that's okay. None for me, though I thank you very much for asking," she answered.

Once he was out of earshot, she burst into laughter and then quickly tried to smother it as heads all round her turned in her direction. After containing her outburst, she sat in her chair looking down the direction he'd taken with a knowing feminine smile.

* * * *

John Horn tried to relax in his kitchen, but he shook worse than when he had first touched a scalpel to living human flesh. He barely managed to place the coffee cups onto their saucers before making such a mess of pouring the coffee that he had to begin again. After he had poured the new cups and placed the saucers on a tray, he opened a cupboard and withdrew a box of butter cookies covered in chocolate. Perfect with the butternut coffee, he decided. He turned with the tray to exit the kitchen and nearly dropped everything. The FBI agent was standing there watching him.

CHAPTER FIFTY-TWO

Quarston watched John Horn nearly jump out of his skin. He reached to steady the tray just in time, and then noticed that Horn didn't seem nervous they criminals usually were. Maybe it was something else? Worry for his sister? The more he saw of Horn, the less he wanted to play him the way interrogators usually do.

As they entered the living room together and prepared their coffee, Quarston began with a question, "So, John . . . can I call you John? Good. I can see that you also are a man who believes in goodness, beauty, and truth."

John nodded slowly in amazement at the obvious reference to Plato's great transcendentals.

"Then you'll understand why Melchizedek might need my help. I need you to help me find him."

John looked like someone had just appeared to him from the other side of the grave, as Quarston so nonchalantly mentioned Melchizedek's name.

"You do know Melchizedek, right? I mean, he told you his name when you treated him in Florence?"

John was so shell-shocked from the way the interview was going that he merely nodded his head.

Quarston smiled inwardly and pressed John for the details of his experience of Melchizedek. But he was surprised when John quite suddenly pulled himself together and counterattacked.

"Exactly who do you represent, Agent Quarston? The American Justice Department or yourself or . . .?" pressed John.

"I represent two individuals murdered in this country in an effort to get the secrets to Melchizedek's long life," Quarston explained, seeing in John's eyes the acknowledgment that his hunches concerning Melchizedek were right after all.

Quarston paused momentarily before lowering his tone of voice and fixing John with his stare. "And I am heading a task force aimed at finding those responsible for re-engineering the polio virus as a vector to locate Melchizedek and recklessly releasing it all over the globe. Your government does not take kindly to biological weaponeering. We call that 'building weapons of mass destruction,' regardless of the allegedly benign nature of the final product. To many of my colleagues that virus was a prelude to a real WMD first strike, an attempt to gauge our responses to an attack."

"But not to you, since you know it was used to target Melchizedek," John continued, not missing a beat.

Quarston paused for a moment again, realizing that John was not intimidated in the least. His earlier reaction must have been shock at the level of Quarston's knowledge rather than fear, as Quarston had suspected. Quarston decided that he would have to try to win John's trust, something that in this instance at least he could do genuinely.

"All right, my interest is different than that of my colleagues," Quarston admitted. "In my investigation of these murders here in the states, I uncovered some ancient manuscripts that were written by Melchizedek."

John's eyes grew wide in wonder, "Really? Wow."

"Yes, well, I didn't know that your friend had written them at the time, only that they were written by the same person, who had lived for a very long time."

Quarston was pleased with himself as John tried to correct him, "No, no, Melchizedek is not my friend . . . I mean, not . . . well . . ." he paused, trying to figure out just what it was that he was saying. "I mean that I only just met him in Italy, through my sister, Anne."

"You didn't know him before going to Italy then? But Anne did?" Quarston queried.

"No, Anne just met him in a church, when he was suffering from the radiological effects of the virus. She brought him to me, and I conducted a hematological analysis and discovered the virus and its effects. Then I treated him to eliminate the virus from his system."

"So, you took in a complete stranger and treated him in a foreign country where you presumably have no license to practice medicine?"

pressed Quarston, before adding, "Not that I'm here about medical licensure issues, of course."

"That's fortunate. I did worry about that, but my oath requires me to help those in medical need, and Melchizedek was vulnerable in an ordinary hospital, obviously, so I was able to acquire some work space in the university hospital and conduct the procedure."

"But what is your sister's interest in Melchizedek? I mean, it just seems odd to me that she'd bring him home like a sick bird and expect you to treat him," explained Quarston.

John paused to sip his coffee, mulling over his own experience of meeting Melchizedek for the first time. "It's difficult to explain, actually, but I know what you mean. Initially, I had the same reaction that you are having. But he's not like an ordinary person, not at all. I mean, he's a king. He's actually kingly. You find yourself literally wanting to serve him. Not that he's some kind of task-master or something. It's not like that at all. There is just such majestic bearing in him, such raging goodness and power. It's hard to explain to Americans, I think."

Quarston listened carefully to John, and an image struck him from his childhood. "You make him seem like Aslan, the lion in the Lewis Narnia stories."

John looked up sharply, "Yeah, that's not half bad. I think that's a great description. What did the beavers say to Lucy?"

"That Aslan is neither a safe nor tame lion . . ." Quarston began.

". . . but that he's good," finished John. "Right, imagine meeting Aslan! You'd bow before him. You'd have a sense of hugeness, literally in his case I guess, of that for which monarchy was made, in whose image it was made. And that's Melchizedek. He is himself an image of the true and great King, and so when you see him, you feel drawn to that element that is missing in our time, the love of and for a good king."

Quarston found himself admiring John far more than investigative impartiality permitted. But then he had to admit that John was not a suspect. Still . . . still, Quarston suddenly realized that his own commitment to Melchizedek was greater than his commitment to the FBI. He now knew that he would never allow Billings to get his hands on him. So, maybe he and John were far closer, more on the same side of things, as it were, than Quarston would have hitherto believed.

"Okay, let's say that I understand you about Melchizedek's importance and why you helped him. But where is he now? And where is your sister? She seems to have disappeared from Florence," Quarston continued.

"We got separated after the transfusion . . ." John began.

"Transfusion? You gave him a transfusion?" asked Quarston.

"Sure, it was part of the procedure. Anne donated some of her blood to him, since she happened to have the same rare blood type that he had. But during her recovery, I was snatched by some people who want very badly to capture Melchizedek. I was supposed to take Anne out of the country, so with my disappearance, I have no doubt that he took Anne and left Italy immediately."

"You were interrogated then? By the people who were after Melchizedek?" queried Quarston.

"Yes, they had a myriad of questions, mostly about the medical procedure I had done. Most of the time I was in conversation with a woman, and it was obvious to me that she knew all about the viral structure. I figured she'd constructed it. They told me that if I didn't answer their questions, the consequences would be severe. And since I couldn't figure out how answering them would threaten Anne or Mel, I decided just to answer them," John explained a little sheepishly.

"Good," Quarston acknowledged. "You would have told them everything eventually anyhow. People don't resist prolonged torture these days, John. And since you knew nothing as to Melchizedek's location, you couldn't offer them anything that would harm your sister. As a result, you are alive and well, aren't you? Don't feel guilty about it. You did the right thing."

John looked like someone had just lifted a safe off his back. Quarston realized that the American hero complex was indeed alive and well. There were times when heroism was appropriate, but there were other times when brazen action was just that, brazen and foolish.

"When they were finished questioning me, they let me go. I returned to my villa, gathered my things, and went straight to the airport. I had to get out of Italy and back here. But on the plane over here, I thought about why they'd let me go," John explained.

"And you figured that they were watching for Anne to contact you?" asked Quarston.

"Right, so I've continued on the assumption that I'm always being watched, that my mail is being read, that my phones are tapped, etc." John answered.

"Well, I've got a friend in the CIA that you should meet," Quarston said bemusedly. "Maybe he'd try to recruit you."

John realized that Quarston was joking with him and eased up considerably, laughing. But while John was himself convinced that Anne was safe, he didn't dare reveal that fact to Quarston. He still believed that

Melchizedek's and Anne's safety lay in their not being found. Only if he was convinced that they were in great danger would he reveal to the FBI man how possibly to use his website to leave a message for Anne.

"John, I have some potentially bad news," Quarston continued.

"What do you mean?" John retorted.

"Well, there was a second attack, like the first one at the hospital, but this one on a train, and we're convinced that your sister and Melchizedek were on that train," Quarston began.

"You mean the terrorist attack on that train near Naples?" asked John nervously.

"Yes, but we didn't find their bodies, and what's more, the attackers were the ones who were killed, if you can believe that."

"Oh, I can believe that, easily enough. You have to remember that Mel is an ancient warrior too. He's fought more battles than anyone alive, and from what I could tell from my conversations with him, his knowledge of tactics and weapons is impressive," John told him.

Quarston logged that information away in his mind. He realized that he still had not fully come to grips with the fact that Melchizedek was a real modern-day person, not an ancient Biblical patriarch-type wearing a robe and escorting some sheep near a burning bush. Melchizedek was instead a serious player, fully capable of killing when necessary—ruthlessly and efficiently.

"So, what's the bad news, if you think they survived? Just that they were attacked?" asked John.

"No, the bad news is that we believe that they headed south toward Naples, just before Vesuvius blew. The trail ends there, but since everything is still pretty much chaos in the city, we just don't know what happened to them," explained Quarston. "Did Melchizedek give you any indication of where he might go if he left Italy?"

"No, nothing," answered John. "But I can't imagine he was too thrilled being caught by Vesuvius again."

"What do you mean, 'again'?" asked Quarston.

"He mentioned something to me in Florence about having been in Herculaneum when the volcano erupted in 79 A. D.," John answered.

"If Herculaneum was destroyed, how did he survive?" asked Quarston with curiosity.

"He apparently used a tunnel under a villa where he was studying philosophy, a tunnel that led to the sea. I think he mentioned something about using a prototype air tank to avoid the toxic gases and ash," John revealed.

"Well, that's a place to start, isn't it?" asked Quarston.

"What do you mean?" asked John.

"Well, if it turns out that he and Anne made it to Ercolano—assuming that is where they were headed—then I can check the tunnels of the old city to see if they have been recently used."

"But wasn't Ercolano one of the cities completely destroyed by the eruption?" asked John.

"Yes, it might be a while before I can continue the investigation," admitted Quarston waiting to gauge John's reaction.

"Oh, well, that's too bad. Hopefully, you'll be able to pick up their trail soon enough," John said with just a tinge of relief instead of hope.

Quarston was now convinced that John knew more than he was telling about Melchizedek's and Anne's whereabouts. But he also knew that John's kidnappers would have torn him limb from limb if they believed that he possessed any such knowledge. So, it must have come to him since his captors had released him. But how, he wondered. How had they contacted him? Well, Quarston thought to himself, at least he now knew that John Horn believed that they were alive. And that information was crucially valuable to him. The next question was who else was aware of it.

328

CHAPTER FIFTY-THREE

Halfway through their journey to Patmos, Melchizedek sat at the breakfast table and watched as Anne emerged from a staircase from the deck below. Her slow gait aroused his notice, and as she neared him, he perceived that she was pondering something weighty. Melchizedek offered her some espresso, and then asked her what she thinking about.

"Well," she began, "I've been doing some reading in the Bible about you."

"Oh you have, have you?" he asked, chuckling. "Checking me out, eh?"

"Let's call it doing some background research," she answered and accepted the hot coffee graciously.

"I've been reading the Epistle to the Hebrews," she said but paused when she noticed Melchizedek's face turning slightly pink.

"What is it?" she pressed. "You already know what I'm going to ask?"

"No, not really," he answered with what she took for weariness. "Go ahead and ask your questions."

"Well," she began again, "I've been reading the section where it talks about you as a kind of model for the true king, both priest and king."

"Right," Melchizedek explained. "No Jew could be both King and Priest under the Law, because the Law placed the priesthood in the tribe of Levi and the monarchy in the tribe of Judah. You might remember the story about Saul, the first Israelite King, who tried to collapse the priestly role into the kingly role, and what happened to him as a result."

"I remember that," Anne acknowledged. "So, the Messiah would have to have his kingship under the Law but his priesthood outside the Law. And that's where you come in, a priest prior to the Law."

"That's right," Melchizedek answered her. "A priesthood in perpetuity."

"But here's my question," she explained. "I don't understand why the text says that you have no descent, no descendents, since you obviously have children."

Melchizedek paused for a moment, before answering her with a strange grin that made her wonder about her earlier thought that he was tired. "Well, what do you think the author had in mind when he said that?"

"I don't know. It seems like you shouldn't have any kids," she answered, perplexed.

"Well, consider this: you agree that I am a model or forerunner of the true king, correct?" he asked.

"Yes," she admitted.

"And you agree that he has a bride?" he asked.

"A bride?" she hesitated. "You don't mean all that stuff about Mary Magdalene is actually true, do you?"

Melchizedek laughed so hard he nearly burst. "No, no, no, the bride of Christ is the Church, isn't it?"

"Oh, right," she recovered herself quickly.

"And do you suppose that that marriage, the marriage that all loves in this world bespeak, will remain fruitless?" he asked.

"I'm not sure I get what you are asking," she managed finally.

"Well, I mean a true love always bears fruit, right?" he asked.

"Yes, I suppose it must," she answered.

"And the ultimate fruit of love is person?" he asked again.

"Yes, I think I see what you mean," she responded. "Like in our world love bears the fruit of children."

"Yes, and divine love bears sons of God, children of God, persons loving in the image of their creator, right?" he asked her.

"Right," she said.

"Then when Christ unites with his bride, that union must also bear fruit," he said.

"Well, what could that fruit be?" she wondered.

"I don't know, actually, but I think it must be something pretty extraordinary, perhaps wholly outside our imaginations. But my point isn't to guess at the nature of that fruit, but merely to point out that the person for whom I am an image will have descent, fruit. So, it's not reasonable to think that the text of Hebrews means that I'd never have children," he explained.

"Oh," she answered. "I see what you mean now. Then what does it mean?"

"It means that I will not have monarchial descent, no king will replace me, just as no king will fill the shoes of the true king, since his kingdom will be an eternal kingdom without end."

"So, you could have children, but not of your royal monarchial line in Palestine?" she asked.

"Exactly. I had no children during my reign as king in the time of Avram," he admitted.

"How do you know that's what it means, though, Mel?" she pressed. "It seems like a bit of a stretch to me."

Anne stared at him as he again showed that embarrassed look. Then it hit her, "Oh, you knew the author? Of course, so you asked him what it meant!"

"No, er . . . not exactly," he answered even more awkwardly with the same look he had expressed earlier.

"Then what is it? Out with it, man," she pressed him again. "I really want to know."

"I am the author," he admitted sheepishly.

"You? You wrote the Epistle to the Hebrews?" she asked in astonishment.

"Yes," he said.

Anne began to think about the book, how it referred to events and details that no one could know except one who had actually lived in the past. She thought of the great chapter on faith, and how Melchizedek must have so loved writing about the faith of good men rather than his usual record of imperial evil. And she thought about the difference in depth between the Epistle to the Hebrews and its most complicated Biblical rival, St. Paul's Letter to the Romans. She had often wondered about the complexity of the argument of Hebrews, how it demonstrated . . . an ancient wisdom, she thought finally. That was it, as though someone who had been there in the beginning and lived on through so much trouble was conveying what he had learned to urge a people not to lose heart, to maintain their faith in order to enter the promised rest.

Anne turned to Melchizedek and smiled. Then she grew closer to him and kissed him on the cheek.

At his surprised look, she explained, "That makes sense to me, actually, now that I think about it and I think about you. It must have been such joy for you to write. But even though I'm no New Testament scholar, I've never heard anyone put forward the theory that you wrote it!"

"No, since no one knows that I am alive, or rather that I was alive at the time the book was written," Melchizedek nodded. "You're right. It'd be a very strange theory to publish!"

As Melchizedek headed to the buffet table to prepare a plate full of fresh fruit for her, Anne watched him closely, wondering what lay in his mind. She thought that if all that was happening to them were really just some novel, how she would covet the chance to see his thoughts. But then, she thought with frustration, the author would probably never reveal Melchizedek's thoughts anyhow, leaving her with the enigma of a man for whom she felt nearly irresistible attraction.

CHAPTER FIFTY-FOUR

Quarston reviewed the hefty report that his analysts had compiled for him on Rothschild's communications prior to the security upgrade. He had learned from his cyber-warfare team leader that since Rothschild's server was no longer accessible, they had spent days tracking the communications to the myriad of people he and his companies talked to. They then grabbed the messages from those publicly accessible servers, for the most part legally, he had added with a smirk.

Quarston was always impressed with the sort of information that the FBI could gather on people, and Rothschild, for all his discreet secrecy, was no different. He looked over the general layout of the report. There were intercepts based on his various businesses, others on his philanthropic efforts, others that appeared personal, and still others that were encrypted and currently unbreakable. Quarston looked through the business interests first, noting that his analysts had merely summarized the gist of the intercepts since none of them stood out as particularly important to them. Quarston observed that while varied, Rothschild's businesses showed an overarching interest in biology and regenerative research.

Quarston next looked at the philanthropic report, and he nearly swore as he saw just how much funding Rothschild annually made available for charities. It was more money than he even thought Bill Gates possessed. Yet Rothschild moved in shadows, barely acknowledging his ownership of these companies. Quarston also noticed his funding of various research projects at universities, many of them focused on regenerative research. Quarston wondered if Rothschild was primarily interested in immortality, when he came across the Egyptian digs funding. The connection within his imagination between immortality and Egyptian mummies, however bizarre from an investigative standpoint, made him stop and take a closer look. His analysts reported on several conversations between Rothschild and American archeologists, one exploring Hermopolis, ancient Khmun he saw, not a city of any familiarity to Quarston. He glanced at the report and saw that the intercepted communication regarded locating a new temple site devoted to the god Thoth and some further discussion about holy books. After what the Boston College professors had indicated to him about the meaning of the parchment cartouche, the reference to Thoth caught his attention. Quarston glanced through the remaining intercepts for any additional references to Thoth, and sure enough, he found a call between Rothschild and a professor at Columbia University regarding a Scythian artifact that bore Egyptian hieroglyphs referring to Thoth. Quarston tried to remember where Scythia used to be, and felt pretty sure that it was nowhere near Egypt. There was just too much that Quarston did not yet know. Rothschild, Melchizedek, Thoth, the manuscript fragments, the life-prolongation technologies . . . somehow all these pieces fit together. He closed the file and laid it on his desk, trying to picture how the finished puzzle would appear.

* * * *

"We'll be in Patmos in just a couple more days, Anne," said Melchizedek with his eye to an ancient nautical device.

"That's a sextant, isn't it?" she asked.

"That's right," he answered. "You use it to chart your position against the locations of the stars."

"And then you can set your course and navigate to your destination," she finished.

"Right," he replied smiling.

"Why don't you just look at the position board over there?" she asked, pointing to a large board that gave their exact position, updated by global positioning satellite every fifteen minutes.

Melchizedek looked her straight in the eyes, "And when your precious satellites fail, then what?"

"Back to the old ways, I suppose?" she asked with a twinkle in her eye.

"Right, and though I know the old ways, it pays to keep one's skills up to par," he answered.

"That's a curious expression for you to use," she interjected.

"Which one?" he asked.

"Well, the phrase 'up to par,'" she replied. "That's a phrase from the game of golf, a fairly recent game. It doesn't make sense to think that you could keep up with all the new colloquialisms."

"I don't see why not," he answered her. "As long as I live in a culture or with many people from a particular culture, I tend to adapt to their linguistic usage. You might have noticed that I'm quite adaptable."

This time Melchizedek had the twinkling eye, and Anne laughed heartily. "Yes, I have noticed that, you chameleon!"

"Moreover," Melchizedek continued, "golf is actually a fairly—using contemporary standards, of course—old game."

"Really?" Anne asked. "I would not have guessed that."

"Well, the Scots were playing it in the 1400's. Caused quite a stir," Melchizedek remembered.

"Why?" Anne asked him.

"Because people became more interested in the game than in practicing their archery skills!" he replied.

"Oooooooohhh," Anne answered with feigned gravity. "Mustn't have that."

"It's kind of like the poker craze sweeping your country," Melchizedek continued. "Poker is an intriguing game, but one mustn't forgo the deeper practice of strategy in Chess or Go."

"But poker is the challenge of human nature, Mel," she replied.

"Anne," he began, "do you suppose that Chess and Go do not equally challenge human nature?"

"But you can always see what your opponent is doing in those games!" she answered.

"Almost true," he rebutted. "What you can see is where your opponent's pieces are, but not what he is doing. What he is doing is entirely in his mind."

"So you can bluff in chess?" she asked.

"Oh sure," he answered. "Don't you remember the other night when . . ."

Anne interrupted him with her piercing eyes. "Oh yes, I remember all right. I never saw that flanking attack coming," she confessed. "You liquidated my castled position, while I expected the main attack to occur in the center."

"A bluff, then?" he asked her.

"Touché," she answered. "A bluff."

JEFFREY TIEL

* * * *

Quarston heard the phone ringing in his office and barely caught the call coming from Turkey.

"Hey Roger," the voice began. "It's Billings in Istanbul."

"Well, hello there, Fred," he answered. "How are things in Turkey?"

"Turkish," replied Billings mournfully. "Turkish and slow. Getting this investigation going has proven nearly intractable."

"Well, what have you found so far?" Quarston asked.

"Remember when I mentioned the woman I thought was Michelle Andover was heading to a bank here, to access that account?" he asked Quarston.

"Sure," Quarston replied.

"Well, it seems she didn't withdraw all the money, after all," Billings continued.

"What did she do with it?" Quarston asked.

"She wired some of it to a holding company here, and guess what sort of companies they own?" Billings asked him.

"Genetic research? Life-prolongation technology?" Quarston answered.

"You guessed it!" Billings answered. "There's got to be a connection here to the attack. But I'm having a devil of a time convincing our NATO ally to work with us to penetrate this holding company. Seems the family that owns it has a rich history here."

"So, the CIA has its limits?" Quarston asked him.

"Yeah, right. We'll get this case opened up soon enough!" Billings replied confidently and then paused.

Quarston waited through the silence but thought he could hear muffled voices, when Billings suddenly added, "Hey, I gotta go. It looks like we may have found a way into one of those companies."

"I'll fill you in on what I learned when we talk again," Quarston offered, relieved that he'd not yet have to divulge anything he had discovered.

"Okay, thanks. And bye," he concluded.

Quarston returned the phone to its cradle slowly. More and more he felt as if the Turkey connection was merely a red herring, Rothschild's emergency net. In fact, he predicted that a raid on one of those research companies—probably a rival to Rothschild's anyhow—might well yield vials of the very virus released at airports all over the world. But what would that prove? Rothschild's reach was extensive, and he had little doubt that his organization could plant the virus anywhere he ordered. But Quarston

336

knew that Rothschild had to be behind the virus, because Rothschild alone had both the means to engineer it and the motive to kidnap Melchizedek.

CHAPTER FIFTY-FIVE

Rothschild approached Michelle Andover bent over her microscope.

"Well?" he asked, startling her.

"Nothing new," she answered with frustration. "I mean, the sample is obviously up to date, but as with the original, it tells me nothing about how his cellular regeneration works."

"So, we must find him again," Rothschild announced.

"Yes, Sir," she conceded. "I'm afraid so."

"And what of using this sample to generate a new virus to locate him?" Rothschild asked her.

"I've confirmed my preliminary results. Both the polio vector and the nanites will be attacked by the antibodies in his blood. I used a sample of Melchizedek's blood and ran it through the same procedures that Dr. Horn did. Then I tested our original virus on one half of it. They were subject to attack almost immediately. I then injected our nanites into the other half, and they too were recognized as threats."

"So, to employ the same strategy to find him, we would have to reengineer an entirely new vector as well as produce an alternative nanite system?" Rothschild asked her.

"Yes, and that will take time," she admitted.

"Very well. Begin the new project," Rothschild ordered.

After a pause, he turned back toward her and asked, "Did you brief Mr. St. Claire on your data from Patmos Island?"

"Yes, Sir."

"Good," he acknowledged. "Hopefully that will yield some results."

* * * *

The ash from Vesuvius had by now spread over much of the Mediterranean Sea, and it resulted in a truly stunning sunset that transfixed Anne, as she sat at their table on the foredeck of the ship, gingerly making its way toward the Greek Islands.

"Mel?" Anne asked.

"Yep," he said, straining to crack the leg of the giant king crab that lay on his plate. It finally gave way, but hot water under pressure within the leg sprayed all over him. Anne burst into laughter, as he dowsed himself with ice water from her glass.

He looked up at Anne, bemused, "This had better be good now!"

"I'm sure it will be," she answered. "My rock lobster dish is wondrous."

"Mmmmmm," Melchizedek sighed with delight, as he chewed the succulent crab meat. He followed it with a swallow of an aged chardonnay, before adding, "So, what were you going to ask me?"

"Oh, right," Anne remembered. "I was wondering what the plan is for Patmos, exactly."

"Well, I told you about the monks who live on the island in the Monastery. They care for the sacred site of St. John's receiving the revelation that he recorded for the New Testament. I knew John very well, and after he left the island an order of monks eventually settled there. It wasn't until much later that the Emperor, Alexios Komninos, ordered the monks under the leadership of Christodoulos Letrinos to build the monastery," Melchizedek explained.

"But other than your special relationship with the head monk, what else do you do there?" asked Anne.

"Oh, I enjoy the library, of course!" he laughed. "But I keep many of my things there, including my spare keys."

"Your spare keys?" she asked in astonishment.

"Yes, you must imagine that I have keys to doors all over the world," he said.

"I can imagine that, a huge ring filled with keys," she laughed.

"Not far from the truth, except that ancient keys sometimes took different forms what you see now," he answered.

"And you are after one of these ancient keys?" she asked him.

"Yes," Melchizedek replied. "I had just come from my Repository—the place I keep my Record's original books—to Florence in order to hide one of the new digital copies that I finally completed. I managed to conceal it, but my illness caught up with me and someone in the hospital relieved me of my key."

"The key to the Repository, you mean?" she asked.

"Right, that key," he answered.

"And that key is one of those very old ones that differs from keys nowadays?" she continued.

"Yes, it's an ancient Egyptian temple key, and I'll need it to enter the temple without setting off its defenses," he laughed.

"Its defenses?" she asked in alarm.

"Oh yes, and they are formidable. Heron of Alexandria and I upgraded the temple significantly in the first century A. D. Ancient Egyptian tomb defenses amounted to little more than subterfuge in their design, so it needed a great deal of work."

"Who was Heron?" she queried.

"He's little remembered now, but actually very important in the history of science," Melchizedek began. "Heron was an expert at building machines! Would you believe that he built the first fully mechanized theatrical performance?"

"In the first century?" Anne asked. "Roman times?"

"Oh yes," Melchizedek answered. "The Romans were far more advanced technologically than most people know. And Heron made major contributions toward their advances, especially in weaponry technology. He figured out how to double the power of the usual ballista, developing a twin torsion spring engine for firing the bolt. The bolt was a large arrow that could slice through multiple rows of infantrymen, whether armored or not. It was a fearsome weapon, and that is part of the reason that Heron spent so much of his spare time building entertainment machines."

"Kind of like Leonardo?" Anne asked.

"A lot like Leonardo!" Melchizedek answered nodding. "Both were mechanical geniuses, both used their minds to develop incredibly advanced weaponry, and both were fearful of the consequences of those weapon designs actually being used. They compensated for their anxiety by displays of mechanical theatre that dazzled audiences."

"What else did Heron invent?" Anne continued.

"Well, let me try to remember. He built a coin-operated water dispensing machine, the world's first steam engine . . ." Melchizedek began.

"The first steam engine?" Anne looked at him in shock, as Melchizedek nodded. "Then why didn't the Romans start the industrial revolution?"

"Yes, good question," answered Melchizedek. "Looking back on it now, one certainly wonders. But you have to try to understand what the world is like when you cannot imagine the future at all. Throughout history, knowledge has been learned and lost, over and over again. The primary reason it is lost is that it isn't used. You see, the Romans needed mechanisms of war, so they invested money to support their construction. But who needed a steam engine?"

"But an engine can do work," Anne said in surprise.

"Yes, it can," Melchizedek answered her. "But you need to remember that this particular engine was rather inefficient, so it couldn't do all that much. It was really more of a cool toy. No one thought of it as a machine. Moreover, why does one need engines when one's entire economy is based on slave labor, as the early imperial economy was?"

"I had not thought of that," Anne answered.

"Well, I remember once that Emperor Vespasian was offered a machine to reduce manual labor, and he ordered it destroyed. Can you think why?" Melchizedek asked her.

"No, since he was a politician, not a businessman," she answered.

"Political power," Melchizedek said simply and then closed his eyes remembering, "*Sine me pascere plebeculam meam.*"

"What does that mean?" Anne asked.

"It means that the emperor is the one who feeds the masses, for therein is his power. No machine that any commoner could use would be allowed to interfere with the imperial power gained by feeding the people of Rome their bread," Melchizedek replied.

"So there are complicated economic and political reasons, as well as visionary reasons for Heron's devices not starting the industrial revolution eighteen hundred years earlier," Anne concluded.

"Right," Melchizedek answered, "but Heron did help me design the defenses in my Repository, and so I'll need my key from Patmos to disable them."

"But they don't use steam power, right?" Anne asked.

"Correct. They use beans and sand," Melchizedek said with a huge grin.

Anne looked at him in shock. "What?"

"Actually, the power source is gravity, but we activate that power by slowly releasing the sand or beans underneath huge stones. As those stones fall, they perform all kinds of work in the temple," he explained before adding, "Heron was a genius at the use of such gravity systems. He used them in his mechanical theatres."

"But why do you need to return to the Repository?" Anne asked.

"Because I need to be sure that my texts have not been harmed," he answered. "I'm still unsure how we were tracked throughout Italy, and though I feel much safer now, I did lose that key. If my intended kidnappers have it, they may be able to deduce its use and the location of the Repository."

"Can I go with you?" Anne asked.

Melchizedek shook his head. "Once I know that the Repository is safe, I'll return to Patmos and then I'll take you there, but first I'll show you the glory of ancient Egypt!" he promised her.

"Sounds good," Anne said but then looked a little bit gloomy.

"What is it?" Melchizedek asked.

"I think I shall be rather lonely with a bunch of monks," Anne said.

"Don't worry, Anne," he assured her. "You'll find plenty to do. And I won't be gone too long in any case."

She didn't look completely reassured, so he added, "And I have a small surprise for you in the Monastery's tower."

Anne perked up noticeably, "Oh really? What is it?"

"You'll just have to wait, won't you?" he said.

"Oh just a clue? To whet my appetite?" she begged him.

"Okay, just one. It's something of Leonardo's."

* * * *

Maurice St. Claire packed his bags for the journey to Patmos Island. He'd miss Paris, he knew, remembering the previous evening he'd spent with Bridgette. But work was work, and he was a professional. He laughed at that thought. Bridgette worked for him too. Okay, so he was a professional in matters of love as well. He was a Frenchman, after all. Love and work walked hand in hand.

St. Claire closed the door to his room at the inn, and headed down the steps to greet the inn keeper. He gave her a fine bottle of Bordeaux as a parting gift. He planned to fly to Athens where he would rendezvous with his combat team. Then they would take a ferry to Patmos. Once on Patmos they would head to the Monastery in the hopes of learning what they could about Melchizedek and the Book of Thoth. But before all of that, St. Claire decided that a quick stop at his favorite café was in order.

* * * *

Rothschild peered at the old maps the Renaissance cartographers had made. He loved old things, maps were no exception. But their notions of things Egyptian left much to be desired, he thought. He heard a knock at his door, and his aide informed him that he had a call.

Rothschild answered the phone to hear Franklen Bartleby's voice.

"Mr. Rothschild?" he asked.

"Hello, Mr. Bartleby," he answered. "I assume you received the Nile River data I sent to you from Borechnekov at Columbia?"

"Yes, yes," he answered. "The satellite imagery of the river matched the temple wall relief perfectly."

"You mean you've confirmed that Khmun is the city indicated on the tomb wall relief as the location of this new temple of Thoth?" Rothschild asked.

"Better than that, Sir," replied Bartleby. "I'm in Khmun now."

"What did you find?" asked Rothschild excitedly.

"Well, I used some of the other data from the wall relief to estimate the distance of the temple from the river," he explained.

"What data?" inquired Rothschild.

"Well, there are water carriers indicated in the relief," he continued. "But they are all carrying the water by hand, not by pack animals."

"So, the temple must lie within walking distance of the Nile," Rothschild speculated.

"Exactly," answered Bartleby. "I also noticed that on the tomb relief, the temple lies at a point where a tributary feeds into the Nile, putting the temple nearly into the river."

"Similar to an isthmus?" asked Rothschild.

"Yes, but with the tributary running parallel to the river," answered Bartleby.

"And you compared that with the satellite imagery?" asked Rothschild.

"I found it!" exclaimed Bartleby.

"The tributary?" asked Rothschild.

"Better than that, Sir!" exclaimed Bartleby again. "I found the temple itself."

CHAPTER FIFTY-SIX

Rothschild reviewed the report that Bartleby had just faxed to him, containing pictures of the Thoth temple site at the ancient Egyptian city of Khmun. The Romans had renamed the city Hermopolis Magna in honor of Thoth whom the Greeks identified with Hermes, the messenger god. Looking at the map that Bartleby sent, he could see the tributary river from Lake Qarun.

The temple site itself looked like nothing but a lump of sand in a landscape dotted with hills of sand. But then he looked at the picture of the excavation that Bartleby had secretly undertaken, and there on the far side of the site lay a partially uncovered pylon doorway, an entry point into the temple between two large objects jutting outward from the wall. Rothschild looked closely and saw that they were two massive baboons. Just like the tomb relief.

Quickly, Rothschild dialed Bartleby again, "Hello, Mr. Bartleby?"

"You received my fax then?" asked Bartleby.

"Oh, yes, an impressive discovery," answered Rothschild.

"We are very excited, Sir," replied Bartleby.

"Whom do you mean?" asked Rothschild curiously.

"My team, I mean. We followed your instructions to report any finds to you first. But we must report this site to the Egyptian authorities," explained Bartleby.

"There will be time enough for that later," answered Rothschild. "Right now, your first priority is to ensure that you have the funding for a full excavation."

Bartleby paused at the mention of money, making Rothschild smile.

"Of course, Sir, we would appreciate your recommendations on possible sources," offered Bartleby diplomatically.

"Well, I would like to see the site firsthand," explained Rothschild. "And if I like what I see, I'll provide the funding."

Rothschild heard the phone drop on the other end of the line before Bartleby managed to recover it. "All of it?" he asked like a school boy. "Sir, it will cost a small fortune."

Rothschild smiled again, "All of it, Mr. Bartleby."

"Then I'll arrange for your arrival. Two days? Will that work for you?" he asked.

"Yes, I'll fly by jet to Cairo, and meet you there," answered Rothschild.

"Good, good," replied Bartleby.

"Oh, and Mr. Bartleby?" Rothschild added.

"Yes?" he asked.

"Tell no one about the discovery. Ensure your team keeps the secret. I would like to arrange a world-wide announcement if you don't mind," said Rothschild.

"Okay," replied Bartleby. "We won't file the discovery with the authorities until you have seen it. We already camouflaged the entry point, so keeping it secret should not prove difficult."

"Then I'll see you in a couple of days in Cairo," Rothschild concluded the call.

* * * *

Quarston found himself up to his ears in paperwork, now that he alone was running the joint task force. Billings' absence had its benefits, but also its negatives, Quarston mused. He stood up to stretch his aching legs. This wasn't what he joined the FBI for. He always felt the need to beat the streets. But he was also getting older, and maybe it was time for him to consider a desk. Quarston stared out the window missing his old partner but also kind of missing Inspector Bartoli, he thought with a smile. His ringing phone jarred him. It was his cyber warfare team leader, the agent who had written the intercepts report.

"Sir?" asked the Agent.

"Yes, go ahead," Quarston answered.

"The NSA just forwarded to me a priority intercept on the Rothschild case. He made a call to some archeologist in Egypt and indicated that he would be leaving the country to meet him in Cairo. We thought you would want to know that right away."

"Boy, do I ever," Quarston answered him eagerly. "Send me the transcript now, would you?"

"It's on its way, Sir," the Agent promised him.

Quarston hung up the phone and watched as a new document appeared in his email. He opened the attachment and the transcript of a call between Rothschild and a Bartleby—Quarston recalled the name of the archeologist working on a tomb in Egypt—and read through it with increasing curiosity. Rothschild was interested enough in this new temple not only to promise complete funding for its excavation but to demand total secrecy concerning its discovery. Quarston thought about the motive that Rothschild offered to Bartleby, namely that he wished for a grandiose announcement to the world. That did not jive with the conception he had formed of Rothschild, a man protected by layers of misinformation and shadowy connections. Quarston concluded that Rothschild had an alternative motive, but was it connected with Melchizedek or not? He could not be sure, but he could not pass on the opportunity to trail Rothschild beyond the borders of Italy either.

Quarston made the arrangements for his own flight to Cairo and noticed that he would be stopping in Rome. He thought of Bartoli and all the help that the Italian Inspector had already provided. They had worked extremely well together, and truth be told, Quarston could use the Inspector's help. He phoned Bartoli and relayed to him the contents of the telephone intercept and invited him to join him in Rome for the flight to Cairo. Bartoli warmed to the idea immediately, eager to work again with the FBI agent and finally resolve his own cases in Italy.

* * * *

Melchizedek and Anne stood on the forward deck of their ship and watched the prow cut through the water, as they approached the rocky coastline of the island of Patmos. Anne glanced up at Melchizedek and noticed his eyes, rich with memories. She wondered what life must be like for a person for whom every place was laden with meaning. She felt that she was beginning to discover the answer. Somehow just being with Melchizedek made new places feel familiar, comfortable, almost homey, she thought.

Their boat slowed its approach, and Melchizedek pointed out the monastery fortress sitting atop the acropolis of the island.

"St. John's cave is over there," he added, pointing further along the island.

Anne squinted, but couldn't really make out the location, when Melchizedek continued, "We'd best go below and gather our gear. Our next adventure awaits!"

Anne grinned broadly, eager for what awaited them and pleased with his use of the plural possessive pronouns.

* * * *

Quarston decided that before he traveled to Egypt he had best converse with his old professor, Beaufort, and relay to him what he could of what he had learned so far on his case. He never could tell what additional insight the professors might provide him. Since he did not have time to fly to Boston, he hoped that he could speak discreetly enough by phone so that no one listening in on the conversation could determine his intentions. So, he dialed Beaufort's number and heard the pleasure in his old prof's voice at again talking to his former student.

"Ah, Roger, how good it is of you to call," Beaufort offered warmly. "My colleague and I have been interested in your progress."

Quarston appreciated Beaufort's cryptic reference, and responded, "Hello, Sir. I am preparing for a little excursion to Egypt, actually."

"Are you, now?" asked Beaufort with obvious interest.

"I may go check out an archeological site, for a bit of fun," he continued.

Beaufort thought for a moment and asked him, "Do you have a guide?"

Quarston realized suddenly that he had simply planned to tail Rothschild in Egypt, but that to accomplish such a pursuit, he would obviously need local assistance of some kind. But it could not be official, given the sensitive nature of his case.

"I don't, actually," Quarston admitted to Beaufort. "Do you have someone in mind?"

"I do, in fact," continued Beaufort, "an old graduate student of mine. He is currently working on a first century Roman cemetery near Giza. I assume you are flying into Cairo?"

"Yes, that's right," Quarston answered.

"Then maybe he can meet you at the airport," offered the professor.

"I'll have one traveling companion," Quarston thought it important to include that information.

"That shouldn't be a problem," Beaufort added quickly.

"We might wish to travel through some rough terrain," Quarston continued.

"I'll tell my former student—his name is Michael—to be prepared to guide you even through deserts, if you wish. Will that do?" asked Beaufort.

"Can he supply the equipment we might need?" asked Quarston.

"Can you supply the cash he might need?" Beaufort retorted.

"Then I guess we have a deal," Quarston added with a smile. "Oh, and professor . . ."

"He's quite discreet," Beaufort finished for him. "No need to worry on that score."

* * * *

Melchizedek and Anne departed the cruise ship for the small launch sent from shore to meet them. Two monks with broad smiles greeted them, speaking in Greek to Melchizedek who answered them in kind. Anne listened to their laughter, gleaning what she could of the content of their conversation from their body language. She noted a robust sense of manly love, the kind of camaraderie that exists between soldiers or athletes long used to working together in stressful situations. She noted that Melchizedek seemed to make pointed references to specific details of each monk's life, and they in turn questioned him about his trip. Since they did not show any shock or surprise at what Melchizedek related to them, Anne inferred that Melchizedek must already have informed the monks by telephone of at least the most disturbing elements of what had befallen them in Italy.

Once their gear was secured in the launch's tiny 'hold,' Anne seated herself in the bow and enjoyed the spray of the water as the boat surged toward the rocky shoreline of Patmos Island.

* * * *

Maurice St. Claire landed in Athens and took a taxi near to the rendezvous point he had arranged with his team. He paid the driver, and then took a roundabout path toward his destination to ensure that he wasn't being followed. Once he felt safe, he walked to a garage door and knocked twice. The door opened and there he found his team, a mixture of mercenary soldiers and a couple of experts on ancient Egyptian culture that had been briefed by Rothschild on what they should look for. Both of them had rather unscrupulous pasts, having been jailed for export violations in the antiquities markets. So, St. Claire could trust both that they would not alert the authorities to their mission and that they could be trusted only so far.

As St. Claire checked their supplies, he smiled at the memory of a conversation that he and Rothschild had had many years before. Rothschild had called it a 'trust' paradox. When St. Claire had asked what that meant, Rothschild had explained that people who are willing to bend the law, or better—in Rothschild's vocabulary—destined to make the law, such people could not really be trusted, since there was nothing to count on except that they would do anything to fulfill their interests. Yet any operation of significance required something akin to trust. So, the paradox forced one to wonder how anything could really be achieved outside the law. Rothschild had then laughed, and when St. Claire asked him why he was laughing, he exclaimed that it was like the famous paradox of the halved distance: if a distance can be halved infinitely, then it seemed that one must cross an infinite space to reach the other side. Yet, people routinely walk across distances of any length. In the same way, the trust paradox suggested that criminal activity was incoherent, yet there was never a time in history when it failed to flourish.

As St. Claire looked at his crew, he remembered the one thing you can count on: people will remain faithful to their tasks, so long as the reward of doing so and the risks of not doing so are sufficiently high. Opening a case he had retrieved from an airport terminal locker, St. Claire showed his team the multiple thousands of Euros it contained. He withdrew all the money, ten thousand Euros a piece, and then distributed it, reminding them as he did so, that three times that much awaited them upon their mission's completion. Seeing the look of satisfaction in their faces, he proceeded to brief them on the specifics of the night's operation.

* * * *

Quarston boarded his airplane and lumbered past the comfortable first class passengers sipping their champagne toward the coach class that FBI regulations required him to use. He knew that many agents believed that trans-Atlantic flights were sufficiently strenuous that the agency would be better served by making its employees comfortable during travel. But the American people would not splurge for perks that they themselves forsook. His fellow citizens packed like sardines all around him reminded him to focus his attention on something he could change, namely himself. And so after buckling himself into his seat, he pulled out his worn copy of Plato's *Republic* and returned to the dialogue that so many years before had changed his life.

CHAPTER FIFTY-SEVEN

Once they had arrived in the harbor of the island, one of the monks offered Melchizedek and Anne a ride in a small truck. Soon they were speeding up the island toward the monastery fortress that towered over the island.

At the monastery, the monk carried their bags and showed them to their rooms, cells really. Anne noticed that Melchizedek's cell looked very much like the cells of the other monks, but the one to which they introduced her was decorated with religious art and several holy icons. It also included a dresser and private bath. She thanked the brother for his kindness and hospitality, realizing the relative opulence they were affording her.

While Anne refreshed herself before dinner, Melchizedek walked toward the office of the Archimandrite, the superior monk at the Monastery.

"Father Bartholomeos!" Melchizedek said warmly, as he greeted the aged man.

The old man gripped the edge of his small writing table and stood up and looked at Melchizedek. Swifter than Anne could have believed, he bowed himself before him.

"Rise, dear old father, you are not subject to me," Melchizedek recited what had by now become a ritual between them.

"But I am subject to the King, and he is in you," the Archimandrite answered.

"But he is in all of these," replied Melchizedek pointing to the brothers.

"And I serve them all," replied the monk with a final bow and a smile. The Archimandrite then kissed both of Melchizedek's cheeks in the customary greeting of the East.

Then the Archimandrite turned to face the wall where an eighth century icon of the true king crowned in his glory hung. Melchizedek joined him on the floor bowing before their sovereign. They said prayers together before rising. Then the Archimandrite hugged Melchizedek close to himself, thanking the man-befriending God for protecting him through his recent travails.

Melchizedek next relayed to Bartholomeos the full story of what had happened since he last left Patmos. Bartholomeos was relieved to hear that the digital copy of the Record was safely stored in Florence, but his face turned to pure joy as he heard the tale of Anne and her brother, John, and all that the two strangers had done for Melchizedek.

"She actually saw you as a king?" Bartholomeos asked him.

"Yes, right in the church, just as I was praying," he answered.

"Happy coincidence," Bartholomeos replied winking his eye at him.

"Indeed," Melchizedek answered.

"And she gave you her own blood?" Bartholomeos asked.

"Had I allowed it, she would have died for me," Melchizedek explained, noticing Anne's arrival and conversation with some of the brothers. "It was truly remarkable. I have watched over her ever since."

"Yes, I saw the two of you come in together. Her smiles told me how you've watched over her," the monk probed.

Melchizedek refused to be baited, answering only, "She's a lovely young woman, Father, pure of heart and earnest in goodness."

"Then I should meet her, shouldn't I?" Bartholomeos asked, before adding slyly, "Perhaps I can recruit her for the church."

"She is already of the church, dear Father," Melchizedek answered deadpan.

* * * *

Maurice St. Claire and his team drove their van down to the ferry site for the trip to Patmos Island. Fortunately, the ferry could carry vehicles, so their weaponry would remain concealed. St. Claire nevertheless armed himself with an automatic pistol. He never took chances where he could avoid doing so. His men were silent and professional, except for the two Egyptologists who talked animatedly with one another. St. Claire caught the raised eyebrow of one of his veterans.

* * * *

"Miss Andover?" Rothschild called to his subordinate.

Michelle Andover looked up from the specimen she was studying, her face goggled and her hands clad in surgical gloves. Rothschild felt the oddest feeling looking at her. Then he realized that she appeared 'cute' to him. Repulsed at the dangers such feelings could ultimately generate, he turned toward the lab itself as he spoke to her.

"How would you like to take a trip?" he asked her.

Pulling the goggles up to her hairline, she answered, "Where? I thought I was supposed to stay here out of sight."

"You are," he smiled, "but not out of my sight."

She looked at him in confusion, so he continued, "I'd like you to come with me on an expedition in Egypt. We may have a direct link to one of Melchizedek's facilities. I need you to be prepared to collect forensic evidence and possibly DNA samples, anything that might provide us with an enlarged picture of his life and network of other locations around the world."

"Oh sure, I can do that," she answered enthusiastically. "It'll be great to get out of this lab. Egypt, huh? I'll be sure to pack plenty of sunscreen."

"You do that, Miss Andover."

* * * *

Anne and Melchizedek sat with the brothers for their evening meal, simple fare received with thanksgiving and joy. They all ate in silence, as was their custom, and only began to converse once their wine rations were poured at the conclusion of the meal.

The Archimandrite then spoke to Anne, "So, Miss Horn, you have had enough adventures in the last couple of weeks to last a lifetime."

"Oh my, how right you are, Father," Anne acknowledged. "But somehow I knew when I was praying and first discovered Mel at Santa Maria Novella that whatever came of my helping that poor old man seated next to me was something that I was prepared to endure."

"He is difficult to endure, isn't he?" asked the monk deadpan.

Without missing a beat, Anne replied, "Oh yes, all those walks down memory lane to exotic places! They become tiresome, don't you think? How much beauty can a girl tolerate?"

Melchizedek and the monk laughed at Anne's riposte. The Archimandrite talked for about half an hour with Anne, learning of her life in America, the loss she endured in her parents' early death, the devotion that she showed her brother, and her hopes in traveling and studying in Italy.

"It sounds as if your brother means the world to you. I'm relieved that he is safe," the monk offered.

"I was terrified and nearly inconsolable in Florence when we realized that he had been kidnapped at the villa. I nearly came apart, but Mel encouraged me. I pulled myself together, so that we could escape."

"What sorts of things do you and your brother do in the States for recreation?" the monk asked her.

"Well, in the little time he has available in his medical career, we have enjoyed outdoor activities like hiking and canoeing," she replied, a little bit curious as to where the conversation was heading.

"Ever do any hang-gliding?" asked the monk catching Melchizedek's eye.

Melchizedek showed no apparent interest in the question, so Anne's puzzlement grew, as she answered, "Yes, actually, my brother taught me. How did you know?"

"I didn't know," he answered. "Just curious."

Before Anne could press the monk on his curiosity, he turned to Melchizedek and asked quietly, "When do you return to the temple of Thoth?"

"As soon as possible, Father," Melchizedek replied. "I need to be sure that the temple is safe. But first I needed this key."

"I wonder who has the other one," the monk mused, staring at the key that now hung about Melchizedek's neck.

"I wonder that too," Melchizedek answered with concern. "That's why I need to leave here as soon as possible."

"I don't think it's likely that any markings on the key itself would reveal the temple's location," offered the monk.

"I agree," replied Melchizedek, "though it's obvious that it's the key of the high priest of Thoth."

"Which could lead someone back to you," answered the monk, as Anne's eyebrow arched in curiosity.

"I know. But the Record is now encrypted and safely stored in three locations around the world. If I have to destroy the temple, Heron and I prepared for that."

The Archimandrite smiled at the reference to Heron. His monks had benefited from their association with Melchizedek, possessing some of the only copies of works of Heron that Melchizedek had safeguarded over the years. They also owned an additional codex of Leonardo's work, again thanks to Melchizedek, and they devoted themselves to copying, maintaining, and studying these old texts.

"Do you need help? I could send some of the brothers with you," the monk offered.

"No, if I'm alone I'll be able to disguise myself completely, adapting to whatever circumstances require," Melchizedek answered confidently.

"Then go with God, my son and most holy priest and king," the holy man blessed him. "May Thoth whom you serve protect you as always he has."

"Thank you, Father," answered Melchizedek.

The Archimandrite dismissed the monks from their post-meal conversation, and then turned to Anne. "The hour has passed when the tourists attend to the holy places on this isle. Would you like to visit the Cave of the Apocalypse of St. John?"

"Oh yes, Father, very much," answered Anne.

"It's within walking distance from here, so since you like to hike, shall we go?" the monk motioned them toward the door.

* * * *

Maurice St. Claire's team arrived at Patmos Island by ferry. Their Egyptian specialists had quieted considerably, now that they were green with seasickness. St. Claire's men smiled at that, as they readied themselves for the drive up the narrow streets to the white houses of the town of Chora that lay just beneath the fortress monastery. St. Claire gazed at the hills surrounding the town, thinking how much they reminded him of the Scottish highlands, when he noticed the look of dismay in the face of one of his younger men.

"How are we supposed to assault that?" he asked, pointing to the massive medieval towers and walls of the monastery's defenses.

"The monastery was designed to protect it against pirate attacks in the middle ages. Though the defenses are formidable, when do you suppose was the last time that anyone actually assaulted the monastery?" asked St. Claire in reply.

"Maybe World War II?" asked another of his mercenaries in answer.

"Right, at least that long ago. We have the element of surprise, and I doubt the monks have any working weapons," answered St. Claire. "But if they do, your training is superior to theirs. Who ever heard of a bunch of old monks defeating a crack combat team?"

One of the Egyptologists suddenly piped in, "Well, the Knights Templar were warrior monks . . ."

He stopped cold at the looks he received from the soldiers.

CHAPTER FIFTY-EIGHT

As they walked toward St. John's cave, Anne found the opportunity to ask Melchizedek the questions that had been plaguing her since dinner.

"Mel, there's so much that I don't understand here. Why did Father Bartholomeos bless you in the name of Thoth, an Egyptian god? And why is your Record stored in a pagan temple? And how can you be the servant of Thoth, a false pagan god? I thought that there is only one God."

Melchizedek smiled thoughtfully for a few moments before answering her. "Where to begin?" he mused to himself.

Finally, he turned to her and asked, "Anne, do you know the name of the God whom I knew in the time of Avram?"

"Yes, you always refer to him as the Most High God," Anne answered.

"Right, good. Now pay close attention to that name: 'most high' God."

Anne thought for a few moments, staring at the beautiful sunset that had begun to overtake the island, and then her eyes opened wide, "You mean that there really are other gods?" And before Melchizedek could answer her, she blurted out, "And you serve the highest of them all, the most high?"

"Yes, exactly," he answered her.

"But how does that square with the Bible?" she pressed.

"Right, good question. What is meant by the term 'god'?"

"I don't know," she admitted. "I guess I never thought about it."

"The gods are the beings of spirit," he explained. "The Biblical Psalms refer to the Most High speaking to the other gods."

"So, the gods of ancient Egypt were real?" she asked in amazement.

"Of course, some of them were, and are," he explained. "That's what the ten plagues of Moses were all about. The Most High God was demonstrating his supremacy over the gods of Egypt."

"So, that's how the wizards of Egypt were able to duplicate Moses's first plagues?" Anne asked, as she began to see the implications of what Melchizedek was telling her.

"Right," Melchizedek explained. "It was a contest of the deities. In fact, in the text of Exodus, the Most High God tells Moses he is determined to acquire glory from the gods of Egypt, because they were refusing to show him proper honor."

"Okay, let's say that you are right," she conceded, "then explain why these other spirits are in conflict with the Most High God in the first place."

"Because one of their number originally decided to take the place of the Most High," Melchizedek answered.

"You mean Lucifer. Oh, now I understand! The gods are the angelic beings," Anne realized aloud.

"Yes, and angels are spirits. Evil spirits are called devils or demons, while good spirits are called angels. When Lucifer fell and took a third of the angels with him, some of them became the false pagan deities," he continued.

"But then how can you serve Thoth, a demon?" Anne asked in increasing frustration.

"It's a bit more complicated than that," Melchizedek explained. "When the Most High God created the angels, they were all given tasks in accordance with their various powers. But when Lucifer challenged the Most High God, saying, 'I shall ascend to the position of the Most High,' he was answered not only by his judgment and fall, but also by a reordering of the angelic authorities. Michael was elevated to defeat Lucifer, his name being an answer to Lucifer's proud defiance."

"What does Michael's name mean?" Anne asked.

"It is a sarcastic question directed back at Lucifer: 'who is like unto God?' Don't ever say that the Most High lacks a sense of humor," Melchizedek chuckled before continuing. "But the spirits who sided with Lucifer did not lose their original capabilities, and that created a competition throughout the universe."

"How?" asked Anne.

"Well, there are angels responsible for oversight of almost everything that you can imagine, including things regarded as holy by the ancient peoples," he explained.

"Like what?" Anne asked again.

"Like the harvest, fertility, art, war . . .," Melchizedek began.

"Oh, I see now," Anne answered confidently. "So, there are angels responsible for all these areas. Like when poets talk about the muses, or . . . love. So, there really is a goddess, or angel, of love then?"

"Oh yes, absolutely, but there is also a fallen angel who masquerades as the goddess of love, trying always to sow corruption in her name."

"So, if I were an ancient Roman and worshipped Venus, I might just as well be worshiping a false goddess, a demonic being masquerading as the true Venus?" Anne asked.

"If that so-called 'Venus' demanded from you the worship deserved only by the Most High rather than the honor truly due her station, then you would most definitely not be worshiping the real Venus, but her false image."

"So, the ancient pagans were partly right and partly wrong," Anne mused.

"Oh yes, and that's why even though the earliest Christians railed against paganism in their sermons, as the Church grew in wisdom, the fathers realized that the pagans were not completely wrong," Melchizedek answered.

"Then your Thoth must be a true angel," Anne continued.

"The real Thoth—that's only his Egyptian name—does exactly what the Egyptians always thought. In the next world he records the judgment given by Osiris in the evaluation of the deeds of a man after his death. Anubis weighs the deeds of the man against justice itself, represented by the goddess, Maat. I serve Thoth here in this world by recording the deeds of regimes against the time of their judgment."

"Only those angels' real names aren't Anubis or Thoth, and they don't have heads of a dog or an ibis, right?" Anne asked recalling her college class on Egyptian mythology.

"I don't know," Melchizedek answered her. "I never met Anubis."

"But if they are spirits, then how can they have the heads of animals?" Anne demanded, as they reached the halfway point to the Cave.

Melchizedek laughed so hard, he could barely contain himself, "Oh, right, right, right, Anne. We're not talking about their essential spiritual form, but how they are represented on the earth when (if ever) they descend. Haven't you ever noticed how strange some of the angelic beings appear that serve the Most High at his throne? My dear friend St. John wrote of these beings in his vision of the Apocalypse."

"Oh, yeah, I do remember that. One was all covered in eyes, right?" Anne announced.

"Yes, much stranger than merely having the head of a dog!" Melchizedek replied still laughing.

"All right, Mel, enough laughter, let me see if I understand this. You were in Egypt, serving as a high priest of the true Thoth, the holy angel of the Most High God. But a false demonic being calling itself Thoth often tried to corrupt the proper honor due Thoth as well as the worship due the Most High God. Moses came along and . . ."

". . . announced the name of the god he served," Melchizedek interrupted her in order to tell her more of the story.

"What do you mean?" she asked.

"When Moses met God in the wilderness by the burning bush, God presented to Moses his own true and essential name," Melchizedek explained.

"I remember that: the most holy name that devout Jewish people still won't pronounce," she said.

"But as with all true names, this one carries important meaning," Melchizedek continued.

"Yeah, it means, 'I am,'" she said cautiously. "I never really understand that. It always seemed kind of distant and impersonal."

Melchizedek smiled, "It is at once most personal and most abstract. The 'I' is deeply personal, that God is person, supreme person. The 'am' means that God is being itself. His existence lies within himself."

"So, he does not depend on anything or anyone else in order to exist," Anne realized.

"That's right," Melchizedek acknowledged. "And what do we call independent existence?"

"Omnipotence," Anne said at once. "Infinite power, the only way to truly be independent from every other thing."

"Well done, Anne," Melchizedek praised her reasoning. "Moses had just met the Supreme God, one God in whom lies all knowledge, all power, and all goodness."

"And we now call those properties omniscience, omnipotence, and omnibenevolence. Only, I never really understood why an omnipotent being would have to be good," she confessed.

"An omnipotent being possesses within himself maximal reality, all possible power, all that is, all being, right?" he asked.

"Yes," she answered.

"And evil is the lack of goodness, its negation, its 'privation' as the philosophers like to say?" he continued.

"Oh, I see now," she exclaimed. "Evil is a lack and if God is omnipotent, he possesses no lack at all, so an omnipotent being cannot be evil!"

"Right," Melchizedek answered. "So, when Moses showed up in Egypt and I heard the name of the God he served, I realized immediately that the Most High God that I worshipped had just revealed himself to Moses as *Adonai*, the name we use to represent God's unspoken most holy name. I had already figured out that my God was most high because he is supreme. And the supreme deity had just announced himself."

"To rescue his people from slavery," Anne offered.

"Yes, for this people, the Israelites, had descended from my friend, Avram. And I knew that the Most High had blessed him through me. But now I also knew a more accurate name for the Most High."

"What did you do?" Anne asked.

"Behind the scenes I pled with Pharaoh to give in to Moses's demands, knowing what would happen if he did not. The demonic spirits masquerading as the true angels had dominated Egypt by this time, offering all kinds of power and magic to the priests. So, when I learned that the Most High planned to wage war against these rogue spirits, I knew that Pharaoh's confidence was misplaced."

They walked quietly for a while, as Melchizedek remembered the panic of that time and Anne processed all that she had just learned. They continued to follow Father Bartholomeos on the trail toward the sacred cave.

"But Mel, if the Pharaoh thought of himself as a god, then wouldn't he have demanded that you worship him?" she asked thoughtfully.

"Oh sure," he answered.

"And you did?" she asked again with widened eyes.

"Not a chance. When I initially came to Egypt, I arrived as a foreign king and priest to my own god, and the Egyptians quickly gained an appreciation for my authority and power. They gave me a name and title, and the Pharaohs were given to understand that I would continue while they departed to the afterlife."

"They knew of your immortality then?" she asked.

"Oh yes, definitely," he answered. "It served to offer me great protection."

"They must have thought you were a god," she wondered aloud.

"Yes, that was a problem too, actually," he laughed remembering. "But once they understood that I served Thoth, it was clear that I was not a god."

"And so you recorded the deeds of the Pharaohs?" Anne asked.

"Oh yes, I have piles upon piles of records of the actual conduct of the Pharaohs. Their heart scarabs won't protect them," he exclaimed.

"What is a heart scarab?" she asked.

"When an ancient Egyptian was mummified, little stone scarab beetles were placed at various points in the mummy as amulets, magical stones," he explained. "The heart scarab was placed over the location of the heart."

"Why?" Anne asked.

"So, that when the deceased person reached the judgment on the other side, where Anubis, Thoth, and Osiris waited, the person's heart would not testify against him," he explained.

"Well, that is surely convenient," she scoffed.

"Yes," Melchizedek conceded. "The Egyptians were both foolish and wise. They knew that a man's heart will always condemn him; in this lay their wisdom. But their false gods convinced them that through magical spells they could somehow cheat the Most High; in this lay their foolishness."

"It sounds like the Egyptians were a mixture of goodness and evil, truth and falsehood," Anne mused.

"Yes, as almost always occurs in this world, man is indeed a mixture of good and evil. Were it not for this, he would not be redeemable," Melchizedek agreed.

"And yet the Egyptians were a truly great culture," Anne offered.

"One of the greatest in magnificence, in duration, and in knowledge," Melchizedek answered thoughtfully.

"What do you mean, 'knowledge'? I didn't realize that we learned very much from them," Anne answered.

"We may not have," Melchizedek explained. "But the ancient Greeks certainly did. The Egyptians made major advances in sciences such as mathematics, architecture, physics, biology and astrology."

"Astrology?" Anne asked. "You mean 'astronomy,' right?"

"Are they different?" Melchizedek asked.

"I should think so," Anne replied in shock. "Astrology is the attempt to read divine purpose out of the stars, whereas astronomers treat the stars as what they are, physical bodies."

"Is that all they are, Anne?" Melchizedek pressed her.

"Well . . ." she began but stopped. "I guess I don't know. If they are something more, then what are they?"

"Do you remember the conversation we had about the connection between the angels and the stars?" he asked her.

"Yes, that the stars are representations of angelic beings," she answered.

"And the planets were sometimes thought of as the bodies of great intelligences, powerful gods," he explained.

"Which is why they were named after ancient deities, right? Like Mercury or Jupiter?" Anne asked.

"Yes, that's right," he answered. "The bodies in the heavens—what space used to be called—have always been associated with the divine. If you read the beginning of the Hebrew book of Genesis carefully, you'll see that the stars were given as signs of the intentions of God."

"But isn't astrology just hocus pocus? That's why it is forbidden in the Bible," she objected.

"You think it is forbidden because it is merely superstition?" he asked her in amazement.

"Well, yes, I guess I do, or did?" she began to wonder about her own conclusion.

"It was forbidden for the Jewish nation not because it was superstition, but because it worked!" he explained.

"What? Well, how can that be?" she demanded.

"If it didn't work, then why did the Most High God place the star of his own Son in the sky so that my Magi observed it and recorded the birth of the true King?" he asked her. "They then followed that star right to his cradle."

"Okay, you got me there," Anne acknowledged, pausing for a moment to try to come to grips with this massive enlarging of her universe. "But why were the Jews forbidden to practice the art?" she finally asked.

"Because their guide was supposed to be the Most High himself. He was their God; they were his people. They were supposed to follow the column of raging fire he provided by night, not the faint light of the stars."

"So, it was about faith . . ." she began.

". . . and love, as always," he concluded for her.

"But astrology just seems like a bunch of nonsense today. I've read the horoscopes. They are just vague pronouncements that are true of most people anyway," she added with concern.

"That's right, it doesn't work like it used to," he admitted.

"What?" she asked in surprise. "What do you mean?"

"Well, once the true King arrived, died, and rose again and ascended to the heavens, all authority was given into his hands. It was a huge shakeup in the spiritual world," Melchizedek explained.

"And he deactivated astrology?" she pressed him.

"It would be better to say that the representation of the intention of God was now incarnate, in this world, no longer in the heavens," he explained.

"But if Jesus ascended, he was no longer here," Anne objected.

"But his body remained," Melchizedek answered.

Anne's initial confusion gave way to sudden understanding, "Oh, you mean the church, the Body of Christ?"

"Yes, do you remember how St. Paul describes it in his Ephesian letter?" he asked her.

"Not really," she admitted tiredly, with wonder at the intellectual ache that had begun in her head.

"All authority was given to him, the true King, upon the completion of the great atonement. And he in turn gave that authority to the church," he explained.

"So, the church represents God's will on earth, and we do not need the stars for guidance anymore," she concluded. "But that means that the church possesses incredible power."

"Yes, Anne, beyond comprehension," Melchizedek paused, watching her closely to see if she really understood. Her face showed first fascination, then alarm, then determination and finally realization.

"It's the power of love, isn't it, Mel?" she said finally. "It's like any other power in a way; you have to use it properly, and that means love."

"Yes, Anne, the greatest power that ever has been or ever will be," he nodded.

CHAPTER FIFTY-NINE

Maurice St. Claire stopped the van on the outskirts of the town of Chora. The acropolis and the monastery fortress loomed menacingly above them. Motioning for his men to mount up, they checked their gear one final time and hid their weapons in large duffle bags or underneath loose-fitting clothing. Any sign of the worry that he'd seen earlier had vanished, as their professionalism turned them deadly serious. The pair of Egypt specialists they had brought along were another story. They still chattered between themselves, until one of the mercenaries told them to shut up and not open their mouths again until they were needed. St. Claire smiled grimly at their chastened faces. He decided his team would walk from here, waiting for darkness before launching their assault.

* * * *

After reaching the convent built around the holy site, Father Bartholomeos led them toward the sanctuary. Anne looked at the literature on the Apocalypse of St. John and mentioned half under her breath that she never did understand that book. She was surprised when Father Bartholomeos agreed with her.

"Neither have I, Anne," he said. "Its meaning is a mystery to me."

"What do you think, Mel? Surely you understand the meaning of the Apocalypse," she hoped aloud.

"Nope, I haven't a clue. At best that text is highly idealized, and at worse it is cryptically symbolic," he answered.

"But many people in America think that they've got that book figured out," Anne retorted.

Suddenly looking mischievous, Melchizedek asked her, "Wouldn't they be surprised to learn that not even St. John, the author, knew what it all meant! If he did, why wouldn't he have just written the meanings, rather than all the symbols?"

Father Bartholomeos nodded, adding, "Each generation interprets the Apocalypse in light of its own circumstances."

"And maybe that's the point of the book for now," agreed Melchizedek. "The letters to the churches at the beginning of the book are warnings of impending judgment, and then the apocalyptic vision itself is the despair of apparently unending judgments. Each generation has a lot to think about in that regard. I should know, since I've been recording their acts for years."

"At least there is hope in the end," Anne replied quietly as they approached the entrance to the Cave of the Apocalypse itself.

"Yes," Father Bartholomeos answered her. "Without hope, we should be undone."

As they walked quietly through the cave, Anne whispered to Melchizedek, "I guess it must look a lot different from back then, huh?"

He smiled at her, nodding. "All of these sites now have churches built around them. But it gives it all a solemn feeling, and that is important."

Father Bartholomeos showed them where St. John had slept in the cave and where he had received the vision that he recorded as the Apocalypse.

Once they had exited the holy cave, the Archimandrite left them alone so he could speak with the nuns.

Anne asked, "Mel, did you visit the Apostle here?"

"Yes, we were quite close. That man taught me more about love than any other person that I have ever known. He was consumed with it, convinced that the perfection of love was the purpose of God's becoming man."

"Sounds like he changed a lot from the young man the gospels record," Anne said.

"What do you mean?" Melchizedek asked her.

"Well, didn't he and his brother once ask Jesus to rain down fire from heaven on a town?" she asked.

Melchizedek laughed aloud, "Oh yes, John told me about that day too. Jesus just shook his head in frustration at that one. It wasn't like the days of Elijah anymore." Melchizedek paused before adding, "But John's zeal never left him, you know."

"What do you mean?" Anne asked, as the Archimandrite returned to them.

"We should return to the Monastery. The sisters have agreed to watch over Anne until your return from Egypt. But she can stay with us for this evening," he told them.

"Thank you Father," Melchizedek said, before turning to address Anne's question as they followed the monk out of the convent and back toward the monastery. "Well, the story goes like this. Once in Ephesus, I think—if I am remembering correctly—John was enjoying the baths. And in walks one of the heretics against whom he had been preaching."

"Heretics, that early?" Anne interrupted him.

"Oh yes, from the very beginning of the church there were people who decided to use the new faith to their advantage, using it to control people rather than liberate them to a life devoted to truth and love. They changed little things or emphasized certain doctrines to the exclusion of others and ended up leading little upstart groups all over the Empire. The Apostles and Bishops had a hard enough time trying to iron out what the new Christian faith really meant from all they had experienced with Jesus, without additionally trying to protect the new believers from these cult leaders who wanted only power or sexual domination or the money of the people they deceived. You'll find that the letters and sermons of the Apostles and Bishops of the first few centuries of the church are full of warnings against these people many of whom endorsed Gnostic versions of Christianity."

"Gnosticism . . . I've heard that term before, but I'm not sure what it means," reflected Anne.

"Gnosticism makes the aim of religion something called *epignosis*, or super-knowledge. In other words there is common or ordinary truth for the regular people, but special or higher knowledge, spiritual wisdom, secret truth, available for the truly extraordinarily faithful. St. Paul rejected these ideas in his letter to the Christians at Colossae. He was always saying that everything he taught, he taught in public, there being no distinction between what he said in private and what he taught out in the open. Christian truth was supposed to be given to all people, not parceled out so that certain special people received mystical enlightenment," Melchizedek explained.

"So, Gnosticism is an esoteric or otherworldly take on Christianity?" Anne asked.

"Right, it's an attempt to merge Christianity with the mystery cults of the pagans in which extreme measures are used to put the mind into a state fit to receive this secret wisdom," he explained, pausing to gaze at the pink glow of the sunset bouncing off the wispy clouds just above the horizon.

"And the heretic Christian groups went for this too?" Anne asked.

"Oh yes. Simon Magnus followed the Christian apostles in order to acquire the power of the Holy Spirit. He cared nothing for love, as though the power of God can be separated from his love. He actually offered the apostles money for the power. It's bizarre, really," Melchizedek answered. "What Gnosticism does is offer to human beings an alternative destiny, to shed the human body and become something else, an ascended being, a pure spirit. Everything of this world, the physical earth, human relationships, green plants, warm blooded creatures, food, drink and even sex, are all looked upon as trapping the Gnostic, keeping him from reaching true enlightenment. So, Gnostics tend toward asceticism, trying to rid themselves of earthly desires and physical interests in order to reach their conception of God. They create all kinds of additional rules and observances for their cult groups designed to create an alternative community to the original church, and to restrain the physical for the sake of the spiritual."

"I remember finally realizing that the physical and the spiritual are not opposites," Anne offered.

"That's exactly it, Anne," Melchizedek answered her. "When the Most High God created this world, he said that it was good. When he made man, he said of all his creation that he alone was not good—not because he was a physical biological being, but because he was without a mate, a woman. So, to complete man, he did not create a special otherworldly esoteric knowledge for him to try to reach, but instead created a woman for him to love."

"I see what you mean now. The Gnostics confuse spiritualism with spirituality. Everything that God made is good, is spiritual. But not everything he made is spirit, since some things are physical. But when you confuse those things, you could actually become contemptuous of this physical world, rejecting it in favor of a so-called 'spiritual' but really merely non-physical life," Anne summarized the discussion before concluding, "That wouldn't work very well for a human being."

"No, it wouldn't, because the Gnostics really wish to become angels instead of human beings. God became man to make men true men, not angels. The incarnation was a huge demonstration of God's approval of his having created a being made of both spirit and matter. Granted, the fallen spirits didn't like it at all, thinking that such a half-breed mutation—their view—was disgusting and repulsive. But they are completely wrong. For only in human nature can we see exemplified the ultimate divine relationships of love, father and son, as in the divine trinity, or husband and wife, as in the love of Christ and his church. All of human life is an opportunity to love and thereby participate in divine love. Christians are supposed to be the greatest lovers on earth, the most fully human beings possible. The Gnostics reject all of this, aiming instead for a non-human destiny. And so they reject the good things that God made in the world which should be received with thanksgiving, things like wine, and food, and sex, and laughter, and poetry, and sculpture, and . . ."

Anne interrupted him, "But Mel! That kind of thinking is still around. I mean, back home in America . . . America was started by the Puritans, people who hated everything of this world, even colorful clothing."

"Yes, I know, Anne. The Apostles and Bishops failed to win the battle with the Gnostics," Melchizedek admitted.

"But why?" Anne asked.

"Because of what religion does to people, what it has always done. People think that being religious is being something other than what is normal. So, they try to fashion a religious life that is somehow distinct from ordinary living. And they almost always tend toward this kind of Gnostic repudiation of human nature," Melchizedek answered.

"But being a religious person is supposed to change you," Anne objected.

"Yes, you are right, Anne," he acknowledged. "But into what is it supposed to change you?"

Anne stopped and just stared at him, processing all that they had spoken about before answering. Father Bartholomeos stopped walking when he realized that they had fallen behind and headed back toward the two of them.

"Love," Anne said finally. "That's the answer, isn't it?"

Melchizedek nodded. "Faith is supposed to transform people, all right, but not into angels. It's to make them into lovers of God and their neighbors. They aren't supposed to be freaks who hate everything around them, but people who fully enjoy all the goods of the world to which the Most High God has appointed them."

Father Bartholomeos broke in, "My daughter, think how many of my monks come to their vocation thinking it is a rejection of the world in order to acquire closeness to God?"

"I can imagine many," she answered.

"Yes," he admitted. "But the faith is not about escape from the world to God, for God came into the world to redeem the world, to bring it back to himself as a realm of joy and love."

"And yet you monks wear alternative clothing, and you have special rules, and you live unmarried," Anne replied.

"Yes, we do, and you can see how the Gnostic confusion can creep into the monastic life! Here is the key to understanding the difference: the life of a monk is not more spiritual than your life," the Archimandrite explained.

"Every kind of life is holy to God, then, none being better than any other," Anne thought aloud. "I was struggling with this in Florence."

"The life you are equipped to live is the right life for you. If to be a nun, then a nun. If to be a wife, then a wife. Both are holy and beloved of God," the Archimandrite continued.

"So, bishops and priests and pastors are not closer to God than everyone else," Anne answered.

"Not in virtue of their vocation, no, and unfortunately, too often, their vocation misleads them into being further away from God's love. For with great power comes great temptation," the Archimandrite said softly.

Anne realized that he was remembering, probably the loss of friends who had turned after the life of power and their own glory rather than the life of love and their neighbor's glory.

Melchizedek put his arm around the old monk's neck and whispered something to him. The old man's voice cracked, as Melchizedek held him close to his heart. Anne edged away from the two of them feeling suddenly terribly intrusive. But Melchizedek held up his hand toward her, motioning for her to stop. Father Bartholomeos slowly recovered his composure and then suddenly knelt down before Melchizedek who placed his hand on the monk's head and said something in Greek. She thought she caught the word for 'peace.'

The monk arose and turned toward her. "There is much loss in this world," he began, pausing, "but those losses are not justification for rejecting it. I myself have felt the lure of isolation and rejection of the world around me. But our community here on Patmos is not meant as a refuge from the world, but as a service to the world and to the church. Our brothers take special vows and observe special rules, as you saw at our meal, but they have more to do with the unique mission we perform than any secret spirituality or enlightenment that we hope to gain by being monks. You might think of it more like being a soldier, whose life takes on unique disciplines because of the mission he serves. But soldier and civilian alike are all citizens, just as monk and lay person alike are all equally Christians and equally loved by God."

Father Bartholomeos then turned back toward Melchizedek, "Thank you, old friend." And then with a twinkle in his eye, he added, "I think you still owe us that story of St. John in the baths!"

"Right, I'd forgotten," Melchizedek answered with a laugh, resuming their walk back toward the monastery.

Anne too had almost forgotten what had led them into the conversation about Gnostic heretics, so she said, "You had told us that St. John was in the bath in Ephesus, when a heretic he'd been preaching against actually walked into the bath."

"Okay," Melchizedek acknowledged before continuing. "So, the heretic walks in, and John jumps out of the bath, naked of course as everyone in the baths would have been, and runs out of the complex as fast as he can yelling for everyone to escape while there was still time."

"Escape from what?" she asked, as Father Bartholomeos chuckled aloud.

"From the wrath of God!" Melchizedek answered, laughing himself. "Apparently, John was concerned that the entire bath complex might be brought down on the heretic's head!"

"So, he was warning them to get out," Anne realized.

"Right," Melchizedek finally caught his breath from his own laughter. "Of course, it was more of an object lesson as to what heretics deserved than a warning about God's likely judgment on bathing heretics."

"But I'll bet people didn't forget the naked apostle running out of the baths, did they?" Anne asked smiling.

"No, no, he never lived it down," Melchizedek added, laughing again. "Nor did I ever let him forget it."

The three of them finally reached the monastery as the last rays of the sun disappeared over the horizon.

CHAPTER SIXTY

Maurice St. Claire watched as the light diminished in the west. It's nearly time, he thought. He wondered about his employer's obsession with this ancient book. But he'd learned over the years that Rothschild was a realist, who invested in projects that paid off. He didn't have to understand it. He just needed to carry out his orders.

St. Claire took a final look at his watch, and then again at the horizon, as the last rays of light vanished. Satisfied, he walked back to his assault troops. As his soldiers put the finishing touches on their face camouflage, he ordered them to move into their positions to begin their assault. One by one they checked their guns and then slipped into the darkness.

*   *   *   *

As they entered the Monastery's refectory for a snack after their trek to the Cave, Anne said, "So, Mel, you'll head to Egypt tomorrow, and I'll go stay with the nuns. That's the plan, right?"

"That's right," Melchizedek answered her.

"But aren't you forgetting something?" she asked.

"What do you mean?" he looked at her in puzzlement.

"My surprise, the 'Leonardo surprise'?" she asked eagerly.

"Ooooooooooooohhh, right," he answered with a smile. "That surprise."

"You might as well show her now," Father Bartholomeos offered. "You can have your snack later."

"Okay, Anne, follow me. But we've got another climb ahead of us, to the very top of the Monastery," Melchizedek ordered. "Think you're up for it?"

"Am I ever!" she answered confidently.

* * * *

A brother had been pouring waste water over the side of the fortress when from down below he heard a curse. No one was supposed to be along the wall at this point, he thought, worried about the danger the steep cliff posed to a pilgrim. Peering over the ledge, he saw several men in black clothes, but he could not make out who they were. Calling down to them proved to be the last mistake of his life.

* * * *

Father Bartholomeos, Melchizedek, and Anne heard the gunfire at the same time. Within minutes, two brothers ran into refectory.

Father Bartholomeos called out to them, "What is it?"

"Several men have entered the compound, Father. They have guns. And they are shooting anyone who resists them," one of the brothers said, as more gunfire echoed through the walls of the monastery.

"Our guests must escape," the Archimandrite ordered.

"Through the tunnel at the bottom of the well?" the brother asked.

Anne heard herself say, "Not another tunnel!" though later she could not quite understand whether it had been voluntary.

The other brother agreed with her, however. "I don't think we can make it to the well. The intruders are already within the walls and the well lies in the center."

Melchizedek broke in at this point, "I'll take her by air. It's the only way, Father."

Anne looked confused, as Father Bartholomeos nodded his agreement. Grabbing Anne's arm, Melchizedek whisked her away through the hallways of the monastery as gunfire closed in on them. The bells of the monastery began to toll their pirate warning, when another burst of gunfire silenced the bellman.

* * * *

Maurice St. Claire had cursed his luck when the water spilled over the wall and landed on one of the academics, but cursed his man more for shooting the monk. That action had forced his hand, so he had ordered a rapid assault. He and his men tore into the monastery firing on anyone who moved and loudly ordered all the monks to cease resistance and assemble in the square. As the gunfire waned, the monks cautiously appeared one or two at a time.

One of his men brought an old monk to him, "This is the head monk, I think, at least from the way the others look at him."

"Hello, old man. You and I are going to have a conversation," St. Claire said to him, before turning to address his Egyptian experts, "Go through the compound and seize whatever you can find related to ancient Egypt. We'll try to sort it later. Take one of my men and a monk with you to ensure that you don't miss anything or stumble into a hostile reception."

* * * *

Melchizedek led Anne to the highest point of the monastery and to a locked door. He lifted up the ring of keys that the Archimandrite had pushed into his hand before their flight. Selecting the key for the door, he opened it and pulled Anne inside. Once safely inside, he relocked the door.

Anne thought that the room smelled musty, but she could not see anything around her. But the room filled with light, as Melchizedek lit a lantern. She looked in amazement at the wooden devices that stood before her.

* * * *

"I take it you are Father Bartholomeos, the leader of this band of monks, right?" St. Claire asked the old monk.

When he received no reply, St. Claire smashed his fist into the old man's face, shattering his nose and lip in a spray of blood. The monk fell to the ground but remained silent.

"I want you to tell me about Melchizedek, everything you know about him. We know he lived here, and we want the Book of Thoth!" St. Claire demanded.

Father Bartholomeos tried to think through the pain that engulfed his face. He realized that his captor had spoken of Melchizedek in the past tense. That meant, as Melchizedek had hoped, that his pursuers believed that he had died in Ercolano. Relieved, Father Bartholomeos said a prayer and resolved to uphold his oath to protect the secret of Melchizedek's life.

Raising his bloodied face, the old monk looked at St. Claire and said, "Thoth? What do you mean? We are Christians here."

St. Claire hit the monk again, this time shattering his jaw with the force of the blow. Father Bartholomeos crashed to the ground as unconsciousness relieved his pain.

* * * *

What Anne saw took her breath away. There before her eyes were two gliders constructed exactly like what she had seen in pictures of Leonardo's designs.

"You said you can hang glide, right?" Melchizedek asked her.

"Sure, but . . . I mean . . . how do you control these things? They really fly?" Anne asked.

"They fly all right. And we've got to take them down to the harbor so that we can get off this island as fast as we can. Here, let me help strap you underneath one."

Melchizedek showed Anne the control surfaces for her glider. She looked up at the delicate white fabric that was drawn tightly over the wooden bat-winged shape frame. She gulped at the idea that she would soon be soaring into the darkness of the night with nothing but this contraption to hold her in the air.

"You *do* know how to fly, right?" Melchizedek repeated to her.

"Yes, Mel, I do. Don't worry."

"Uh-huh," Melchizedek answered, hearing the sound of her words. "Well, we have little choice. So, follow me."

Opening the large hanger doors at the far end of the room, Melchizedek checked Anne's glider one last time, and then strapped himself into the lead glider.

"Okay, ready?" he turned back toward her with a smile. She nodded affirmatively, and then pulled the goggles attached to her helmet down over her eyes.

"Here we go!" Melchizedek said and jumped into the darkness.

Anne hesitated for a moment, when a blast of machine gun fire tore the door behind her from its hinges. She ran for the opening and leaped, as the blackness of the night swallowed her.

* * * *

As the entry door splintered into fragments before his gunfire, the mercenary, followed by the Egyptologist and a monk, broke into the room and observed the open hanger door. Running toward it, he stared out into the darkness and could just make out the white form of what looked like a large bat. Raising his gun, he aimed just ahead of the white form and squeezed the trigger.

* * * *

The monk that followed the invaders into the upper tower room was astonished to see the large room concealed so well behind a door that he had been told was merely a closet. It took him a moment to realize that their guests had left through the hanger door at the far end, and only a moment more to understand that his captor was now aiming a machine gun at one of them.

Without another thought, the monk threw himself at the mercenary.

* * * *

The Egyptologist was surprised to see what he took to be a docile monk suddenly lunging at the mercenary preparing to fire on the escapees. He reached out to stop the brother's assault, but managed only to trip the monk who fell hard against the mercenary's leg. The mercenary drew up in agony as the bulky monk's weight shattered his right knee. His aim went wide of the mark as he turned the machine gun on his tormentor.

* * * *

Seeing the muzzle of the gun drawing toward him, and feeling the other man grabbing him from behind, the monk decided that his only hope lay in the open hanger door. Pushing with all his might, he forced the tangle of men toward the opening. Though he heard no sound, he saw the gun buck in recoil again and again, as its bullets drove into his body. The monk lost consciousness as he reached the night air.

* * * *

The Egyptologist tried desperately to draw back against the weight of the monk and pushed forward to prevent his falling over the edge. But though his action threw the monk and the mercenary with him out the hanger door, the specialist tangled his hand in the monk's bullet torn cassock and found himself pulled along toward the opening. Frantic to keep from being pulled into the darkness, he screamed for help.

* * * *

Maurice St. Claire looked above him at the sound of the gunfire and screams, barely leaping out of the way as the screams turned to cracking bones in a horrifying series of thuds. Slowly St. Claire pulled himself from the ground to survey the open doors high above him. He began to form some idea of what had happened, when two of his soldiers called for his attention.

He followed the men into the monastery's living quarters and into a room that was decorated better than the ordinary cells. There they showed him a bag containing women's clothing. St. Claire looked at the contents curiously, wondering why monks would have a woman staying with them, a woman who had presumably escaped through the hanger door. He looked at the tags on the clothes and realized that they were from Naples and Capri. St. Claire's mind worked rapidly to form the astonishing conclusion that Melchizedek and Anne Horn were very much alive.

CHAPTER SIXTY-ONE

A nne concentrated on keeping her glider stable, trying to get a feel for the strange controls as the glider repeatedly surprised her with its sudden dips and turns. With great effort she managed to control her descent, though by now she had no idea where Melchizedek had gone. She decided that her best course of action was to aim the glider toward as soft a landing as she could muster. Looking around her, she realized that she was already far from the monastery and Chora, though because she knew little of the island, she had no idea where she should go to head toward the harbor. Using the lights from the buildings beneath her as a guide, she began to head toward darkness, so that she would not land dangerously on a building. But as she continued to descend, she heard the sound of water, and realized that the darkness was in fact the sea, and that she would drown long before she escaped from her harness in the water. Deciding that she could not get the glider back over the land, she unfastened herself while still in the air and as soon as her feet hit the cold water, she released the glider and plunged into the menacing blackness.

* * * *

Melchizedek heard the gunfire behind him as he launched his glider and turned hoping to see that Anne was following. She finally flew out of the hanger and soared away just as a flash of gunfire erupted from behind her. Melchizedek watched in horror as part of her rear stabilizer disintegrated as the bullets tore into it. Turning his glider over and back toward Anne's crippled craft, he watched her descend rapidly beneath him in jarring turns and dips, until her glider seemed to acquire some degree of stability. He continued to fly over and down toward her, until he realized that she was heading for the open sea. He shouted to her to turn back toward land, but his words were swallowed up by the distance between them. Frantic for her safety, he aimed his glider nearly straight down toward her stricken plane only to find that she was no longer aboard. He pulled his plane up over the water, as her glider rose dizzily in the air and then swung over and plunged into the waves.

* * * *

Anne felt herself pulled beneath the water over and again, as her wet clothing dragged her down. She finally managed to release her helmet, and clawed for the surface, desperate for air. When she again felt pulled underneath the water, she suspected that she was trapped within a dangerous current. She knew better than to fight the water, so she pulled herself to the surface one last time, took a huge breath of air and then allowed the water to pull her into its depths.

* * * *

Melchizedek continued to soar over the water, searching desperately for some sign of Anne. He knew that his remaining time in the glider was measured in seconds, as he continued to lose altitude. Without the sun to warm the air, there were no thermals that he could use to gain altitude like the birds.

* * * *

Anne felt as though her lungs were going to burst inside her, when the pressure of the water rushing around her eased, indicating that she was headed back toward the surface. No sooner had she noticed the pressure change, than she burst through the surface and rose nearly a foot above it in a surge of water and bubbles. She coughed and sputtered as she tried to breathe and swim through the choppy surf.

* * * *

Melchizedek finally saw the whirlpool that had engulfed Anne. It was so dark that he almost missed the swirling water. He tried to determine where it might have taken her, but realized that he was only seconds from crashing into the water himself. Releasing his own harness, he dove straight into the center of the whirlpool, figuring that that was his best chance of finding Anne.

* * * *

Anne slowly worked her way through the strong currents back toward what light she could see on shore. She knew that without the bit of light that she had spotted there, she would have had no idea which way to swim. Her limbs were already exhausted, so she found each stroke agonizing. Finally, she realized that she had to shed her clothing, or she would certainly drown. Pulling her blouse over her head, she released it into the sea. Then she pulled off her shoes and her skirt and let the water take them as well. She noticed the change immediately and found that she could pull herself toward the shore with greater ease.

* * * *

Melchizedek shot to the surface like a missile after the whirlpool's currents released him. He was gasping for air, but he could finally breathe again. He tried to call out to Anne, but the noise of the water and his own exhaustion made him realize that he needed a moment to catch his breath or she'd never hear him. Seeing lights on the shoreline, he surmised that that would be Anne's destination too, and so he swam for safety and a hopeful rendezvous.

* * * *

Anne continued to fight for her life, tiring even more in her bid for the shore. Wondering if another current was pulling her in the opposite direction, despair and fear gripped her heart. She recognized that if she gave into the fear she would die, so she imagined her brother's strong arms holding her when she was a young girl, and the image of strength and warmth gave her hope.

Anne wondered if she were losing her mind, the image becoming reality, because she actually felt like John's arms were wrapped around her. She felt far more buoyant than she had expected to be, and she thought that the shore was approaching more rapidly than her furtive kicking could produce. It slowly dawned on her that the reassuring voice she was imagining was not her brother's voice at all, but someone else's, and that the arms around her were real. Sensing that she was nearly naked, and startled at the proximity of another person, she kicked away frantically.

Melchizedek kept soothing Anne in his arms as he feather-kicked for shore. He heard her calling her brother's name, and thought that she may have slipped into a semi-delirious state. His hope at her suddenly increased strength was dashed when she heaved herself away from him. With the possibility of losing her forever in the murky waters, Melchizedek shouted at her, "Anne! It's me! Mel! Stop fighting me!"

* * * *

Melchizedek's voice snapped Anne back to reality. She called out, "Mel, I'm here," as she swam back in the direction of his call.

Melchizedek kept talking to her and swimming toward her answering calls until he felt her body collide with his. Wrapping his arms around her, he offered some warmth to her shivering hypothermic form. Through the starlight, he could see the tired smile on her face and the glimmer of hope that had returned to her listless eyes.

"Don't worry, Anne. I've got you now. And the stars are with us too," he said soothingly.

* * * *

As he swam for shore, Melchizedek shared Anne's worry that the current was drawing them away from safety. Thinking back to his knowledge of the island, he concluded that their best course was to let the current take them rushing around the island. Saving his strength, he continued to hold Anne above the water, providing her with warmth, and soothing her with reassuring words.

Melchizedek fought the guilt he felt over his decision to escape with the gliders, knowing that recrimination could give way to panic. He needed his mind alert, and so he began to recite Euclid's proofs to himself. He had been shipwrecked in the water many times before, but this was the first time that he had been with someone he cared for this much. He found himself surprised at the depths of his concern for Anne, but he forced these thoughts out of his mind, so that he could again focus on the conditions necessary for survival and escape from the sea.

CHAPTER SIXTY-TWO

Despite the early morning hours, Maurice St. Claire called Laurence Rothschild. He knew that his employer would be interested in what had developed at the monastery. St. Claire decided to omit the details of the botched assault and focus on the positives.

"Good morning, Mr. Rothschild," he began.

"Yes, Maurice, what is it? What did you find on Patmos?" Rothschild asked him, realizing from the hour that St. Claire must have discovered something important.

St. Claire decided to start with the best news first, "Sir, I think that Melchizedek and Anne Horn are alive."

"What?" exclaimed a shocked Rothschild. "Why? How do you know that?"

"We found bags belonging to a man and a woman that had recently been in both Naples and Capri. But the two people themselves were nowhere to be found. Nor did any of the monks prove willing, despite motivation, to disclose anything about their identities."

"So, you think they escaped Ercolano for Capri?"

"That's my best guess. My helicopter just couldn't cover that much water when we were searching," St. Claire tried to deflect what he feared would be criticism from Rothschild.

"Where did they go?" asked Rothschild.

"They flew out of the monastery on makeshift gliders and they haven't been seen since, so I am afraid I have no idea where they are," St. Claire admitted.

"But we now know that they are alive," Rothschild returned to that startling bit of news.

St. Claire appreciated the way the conversation was going, so he decided now to mention his other news, "Sir, we had no luck locating any Egyptian texts, let alone the Book of Thoth. We tore this place apart too."

"Don't worry about that," Rothschild answered, to St. Claire's surprise.

"Why's that, Sir?" he asked curiously.

"Because I'm following a new lead on the book. How would you like to meet me in Cairo later today?" Rothschild asked him.

"Okay, I guess I can do that. Do you need my team too?" St. Claire asked him.

"Yes, bring the mercenaries, but release the Egyptologists. We won't need them," Rothschild answered.

St. Claire acknowledge Rothschild's order, knowing very well what fate awaited the remaining specialist.

* * * *

Melchizedek continued to hold the increasingly limp form of Anne as his own strength waned. She occasionally sank into delirium, but at Melchizedek's gentle coaxing, she recovered enough to add a bit of her own strength to their increasingly desperate situation. He had lost track of the time and tried to calculate using the movement of the earth's rotation against the stars. But he began to feel sluggish mentally and wanted very much to rest. He remembered the silks of the East, how soft and luxurious they could be, the perfumes and aromas wafting through the air, intoxicating the senses.

Melchizedek suddenly awoke and just kept from losing Anne in the water. Bitter with himself for falling asleep in the water, he called upon his military experience and began again to rigorously work through Euclid. He also began to pray.

* * * *

Quarston looked at his watch and prepared for the next meal on his transatlantic flight to Rome. He had always wondered how people were supposed to sleep on these flights, when so much effort was made toward fattening them up. But to what end, he wondered. Probably to prepare us for the jet lag to come, he thought with misery.

As the current whisked them around the island, Melchizedek could see light in the east, surprised at how much time they had already been in the water. Fishing boats were departing the harbor, and Melchizedek saw that one of them was heading directly for them. As the boat approached them, Melchizedek shouted weakly to the crew who only just heard his cry. The boat slowed and soon the two freezing and exhausted travelers were being warmed with blankets and hot fish soup.

* * * *

The fishing boat turned back toward shore at top speed, but as the boat neared the land, the captain noticed Melchizedek motioning for his attention. Melchizedek's strength was returning, so he was able to articulate a brief account of the attack on the monastery the night before, and on the captain's need for discretion if Melchizedek and Anne were to escape.

The captain knew the brother who maintained the monastery's launch, since nearly everyone on Patmos knew everyone else. He drove the boat toward where the launch was tied up, and sure enough, there was the brother carrying out his morning maintenance, oblivious to the disaster that had befallen his brothers the night before. He was often ordered to sleep down near the water to maintain the boat for arriving or departing guests.

The brother was perplexed to see Melchizedek on a boat approaching the dock, since he had thought that he was supposed to be taking Melchizedek to a ship heading for the mainland that very day. But once Melchizedek related to him what had happened at the monastery, the brother thanked the captain for rescuing them, and then brought them up onto the dock. Instead of taking them to the launch, he showed them to a powerful cruiser, which belonged to a wealthy benefactor of the monastery. The benefactor graciously offered them his boat and provisions as well as a pilot, but the brother wanted to drive them to the mainland himself, and soon had them bundled up in warm blankets, their hands gripping mugs of steaming hot tea, as the cruiser surged toward Greece.

* * * *

Quarston awoke to the flowing sounds of the Italian language and realized that his plane was preparing to land in Rome. He was surprised that he had fallen asleep, and pleased until he tried to move. Once landed, he pulled his aching body from his seat, grabbed his bag and stuffed his precious book into it. He then made his way a bit unsteadily toward the exit and out toward customs where he found Inspector Bartoli waiting for him.

The contrast between the two detectives could not have been more marked. The Italian was immaculately dressed and impeccably groomed, while the American's clothes were shabby and wrinkled, and he looked and smelled like he needed a minimum of one bath as well as a barber. But Inspector Bartoli was not a man who allowed such superficial trivialities to interfere with his work. He had already seen the measure of Special Agent Quarston, and besides, he knew what redeye flights did to people.

Bartoli greeted his friend warmly and escorted him past the curious customs officials and directly back into the Rome terminal. Bartoli stopped for some cappuccino and a bit of refreshment, enabling Quarston to regain his senses as the hot coffee and chocolate-filled croissant strengthened him.

Bartoli glanced at his watch and realized that their flight for Cairo would soon be leaving. He excused himself for a moment and found a location with good cell phone reception. He then placed a call to his officer responsible for the surveillance of Laurence Rothschild. Bartoli looked pleased, when Quarston saw him returning.

"What is it?" he asked his Italian counterpart.

"It seems that Mr. Rothschild is right on schedule. He just arrived at the airport."

"Oh, good," answered Quarston, before noting the look in Bartoli's eye. "There's something more! What is it?"

"He has a traveling companion," Bartoli offered cryptically.

"And that would be . . .?" Quarston played the game with his friend.

"Michelle Andover," Bartoli announced, very satisfied with himself.

"Well, now, that is interesting, isn't it?" Quarston replied. "You don't think we should stop them here?"

"If we only want the little fish," answered Bartoli, "since we still have nothing definitive on Rothschild."

"And I'll bet she'll suddenly up and die on all of us, if we try to stop their plane," Quarston added, as Bartoli nodded in agreement.

"We need to arrest her when we can guarantee her safety," Bartoli concluded. "Shall we go?"

"Sure," Quarston answered, stuffing the remainder of the croissant into his mouth and swallowing the last gulp of coffee.

Quarston and Bartoli approached the Alitalia counter, bypassing the huge line that had formed. Bartoli spoke to one of the attendants after flashing his Inspector's badge, and a manager soon met them with a congenial greeting. He led them around the security cordon and directly toward their gate and waiting plane. Quarston prepared his ticket, but Bartoli motioned for him to put it away. As they entered the plane, the steward invited them to sit down in the First Class cabin. Quarston began to object to Bartoli that his seat was in coach.

"No, no, you are in Italia now, my friend. These seats are complimentary, so please, please feel at ease."

"How did you manage this?" Quarston asked him after the steward offered them each a glass of Prosecco.

"I did some work on a case a few years back. Someone kidnapped one of the children of the owner of Alitalia!" Bartoli answered.

"You found the child?" Quarston asked.

"Si, and the owner's gratitude knows no limitations. If he discovers that I try to purchase a regular flight, he will call the Prime Minister of Italy himself and complain. So, I've been ordered to accept his hospitality. Naturally, I am willing to endure my share of such hardships," Bartoli added with a smile.

Quarston stretched his legs into the wide open space in front of him and relaxed to the feeling of the bubbly wine coursing through his body. After the squashed conditions of his trans-Atlantic flight earlier that morning, Quarston was soon sleeping in peaceful comfort.

CHAPTER SIXTY-THREE

By the time they reached the mainland, Anne had warmed up and regained some of her strength. Melchizedek watched her in amusement as she devoured yet another large bowl of hot soup in the harbor boat house that the Monastery owned on the mainland.

Not until she lay back in the bed the brother had prepared for her did she finally notice her ill-fitting clothes. Barely a second passed before she bolted upright, pulled the sheets around her up to her neck, and looked in embarrassment at Melchizedek.

"What is it?" he asked in surprise.

"My clothes," she said. "What was I wearing when we were rescued?"

"Less than you have on now," Melchizedek answered, smiling.

"Oh, my!" she answered softly.

"Anne," Melchizedek began, "a half-freezing, pale and soaked woman does not usually catch a man's eye. The sailors bundled you up as soon as you were out of the water."

"But Mel," she elongated his name, "I'm missing some other things."

"Your underwear, yes, I know. You were soaked to the bone, and we had to remove your wet clothes," he explained.

"Who? The sailors, you mean? Or you? Who's 'we'?" she asked in confusion.

"The fishermen pulled us on board, and immediately put blankets over us. They took us below and that's where I removed your remaining soaked clothes," he said agreeably.

"Oh you did, did you?" she said with feigned anger.

"Yes, I did," he answered straightforwardly with an awkward grin and a pause, before adding, "You were under a blanket the entire time, of course."

Anne let the subject hang in the air between them before finally saying, "Thank you for saving my life, Mel. I'll never forget it. I really began to lose it in that water."

Melchizedek smiled soberly at her, remembering his own plight in the water, and then turned to the brother and thanked him for his help. The brother called for a taxi, providing them with enough money to get them to a bank.

Once they were in the taxi, Anne asked, "Mel, where are we going?"

"Egypt," he answered her. "I'm taking you with me. I've got to get to the bottom of what's happening here, and the first step is to check on the temple."

"But how can we get to Egypt without our passports?" she asked.

Melchizedek lifted his shirt and she saw the personal documents pouch still hanging on his side. "The whirlpool didn't pull that off of you?" she asked in astonishment.

"Nope. So, we have our papers. A bit wet, but they'll do. We'll go to the airport, grab cash at a bank, get some proper clothing, and then we'll head to Cairo. Any remaining chill you have will evaporate in the desert in no time at all," he added with a smile.

"Sounds good to me," she said with a final shiver.

* * * *

Quarston and Bartoli stepped off the Alitalia flight onto Egyptian soil and went through customs under civilian passports, so as to not alert Egyptian authorities to their presence. Bartoli thought this a bit odd, but Quarston assured him that the less the Egyptians knew about their objectives, the easier it would be for them to accomplish them.

As they exited the airport's secure area, Quarston noticed a sunburned face staring at him from behind a small sign that read "QUARSTON." Laughing, he introduced himself to the young man of medium light build, with dark closely cut hair, a neatly trimmed light beard, dark brown eyes and a narrow mouth on an oval face. Dropping the sign, he extended his hand to Quarston, grinning hugely, "Mike Adams, Mr. Quarston. I guess we share a certain professor?"

Quarston laughed, "Oh yes, I guess we do. Mike, meet Giovanni Bartoli; he's working with us out of Italy."

"Nice to meet you too," Adams offered, before ordering, "Okay, gentlemen. Follow me."

As they passed out of the airport, Bartoli's phone rang. After a few moments of rapid Italian, Bartoli closed the phone and informed Quarston, "Rothschild's plane is set to land in about twenty minutes. He's to be picked up curbside by private car, so if we have a car, we can follow him."

Both of them looked at Adams who grinned again and said, "Let's go. Car's this way."

*   *   *   *

Maurice St. Claire's remaining combat team members nonchalantly boarded the aircraft for the brief flight to Cairo. Minus the academics, the mercenaries felt much more comfortable. Their work was supposed to remain narrow in scope, requiring precise professional technique. Civilians, especially academics who spent most of their time with their heads in the clouds, compromised the safety of the team. So, when St. Claire put two bullets into the back of the head of the remaining academic, not a murmur of dissent arose among the group. In fact, when St. Claire passed out the specialists' shares of the monastery mission payment, laughter erupted between them.

*   *   *   *

Expecting Rothschild to emerge from the airport terminal at any time, Quarston and Adams watched from the front seat of the car, while Bartoli surveilled their rear from the back seat. Suddenly, Adams spoke aloud, startling his focused guests.

"Beaufort hinted pretty strongly that this mission might be dangerous, so Giovanni, reach into that bag on the floor back there."

Bartoli picked up the heavy rucksack and unfastened the belts that held it shut. He pulled out several handguns, all taking nine millimeter ammunition, and several boxes of bullets. He selected the Beretta for himself and handed the other guns to Quarston in the front seat. Quarston whistled in surprise, as he picked up the Glock and checked that the clip was properly loaded, before beginning to load the spare clip.

"And where did you get these?" Quarston asked after his whistle subsided.

Adams laughed and answered, "In Egypt having friends makes a real difference."

"The rest of our supplies?" asked Quarston.

"Beaufort told me to prepare for the worst, so the trunk is full of desert survival gear, including lots of water. And he mentioned something about your having enough cash if our supplies ran out," Adams spoke as delicately as he could about the money Quarston already owed him.

Quarston reached underneath his belt and felt for his passport and money belt. Withdrawing a blue slip of paper, he handed it to Adams. "This should keep us amply supplied for now. And there's twice that when we're through."

Adams looked at the five thousand dollar check and chuckled. "Federal Bureau of Investigation, eh? Okay, call me interested. I've got to hear the story of how Professor Beaufort got himself mixed up with a G-man with the authority to issue five thousand dollar checks."

Quarston was about to answer, when a sleek black Mercedes sped up to the terminal in front of them, and two serious looking men emerged and carefully scrutinized everyone to be seen, before dashing into the terminal and returning with Michelle Andover and Laurence Rothschild. Quarston and Bartoli both just stared at her, stared at the woman who was responsible for so much of the death and mayhem of the past few weeks. As usual, she failed to look the part, appearing as ordinary as anyone else that day. That was the problem with evil, thought Quarston, it failed to leave distinctive physical marks on anyone but its victims.

No sooner had Andover, Rothschild, and his security team entered the Mercedes, than the car sped away from the curb. Adams nearly collided with another car in his efforts to maintain visual contact with the fleeing vehicle. Quarston watched in a mixture of admiration and curiosity as Adams pursued the car with enough discretion to remain undetected. The Mercedes headed for the center of Cairo and suddenly pulled into a hotel's parking lot. Quarston's team watched as Rothschild, Andover, and the two security men exited the car and entered the hotel. Quarston asked Adams to keep the car ready, as he and Bartoli walked into the hotel after their quarry.

* * * *

Since Rothschild had already left the lobby, Quarston spoke with the desk clerk to ascertain his location. They learned that he had taken a room, so they decided to sit at the bar and wait to see what transpired. As they ordered a pair of club sodas, Bartoli pushed a small but sophisticated piece of communications gear over to Quarston who picked it up and examined it carefully.

"Where . . .?" he began.

"Our friend, Adams," Bartoli said matter of factly.

"He's a pro, then," Quarston admitted aloud to himself.

"Yeah, but he's certainly not trying to hide the fact from us, is he?" Bartoli asked.

"Not with the way he was driving earlier," Quarston agreed.

"Nor with his choice of weapons," Bartoli smiled, patting the large gun underneath his shirt.

Quarston nodded, noting the familiar feel of the Glock against his side. "He knew what we shoot, didn't he?" he asked Bartoli, who nodded his agreement.

"And that earpiece and hidden mike presumably put us in contact with Adams?" Bartoli asked.

"Let's find out," Quarston answered, donning the earpiece and clicking the mike.

"Adams here," came the voice through Quarston's earpiece.

"So, you know who we are . . .," Quarston began.

"Yes, I do," admitted Adams. "I work with Billings."

"Small world," said Quarston.

"Yes, very small," answered Adams. "Billings is on his way here. He apparently agrees with you now that the Turkey angle is a wild goose chase. Not that he'll admit that to you, of course."

"I see that you do know Billings, then," Quarston laughed in reply.

"Oh, yes, indeed I do," answered Adams. "He was involved with my training."

"And Beaufort doesn't know?" asked Quarston.

"Not really, though he's not stupid. I'm sure he put you onto me for a reason here in Egypt," Adams continued.

"We're glad to have you aboard, Mike, but I'm afraid that we're having too good of a time in this nice air-conditioned bar drinking scotch on the rocks," Quarston needled him.

"Age has its privileges," was Adams' reply.

CHAPTER SIXTY-FOUR

Anne changed out of the clothes the monk had given her, and out of respect for his kindness, stuffed them into her new bag, intent on returning them herself with all the heartfelt thanks she could muster. She continued to worry about Father Bartholomeos, about what had happened to him. She left the women's rest room and saw that Melchizedek was using one of the airport's pay phones. She watched the emotions of first gravity and then relief and finally determination flash across his features. Hoping that he had heard good news from Patmos, she ran up to him as he returned the phone to its cradle.

"Father Bartholomeos?" she asked hopefully.

"He's going to recover, but he took an awful blow to his face. Several of the monks were killed, many of them people that I have known since they were children. I am really beginning to tire of this," he said forcefully.

Anne had seen that look in his face before, and while it frightened her, it also provided her with a sense of hope. Melchizedek struck her as an anachronism, a man living at the heights of civilization on the one hand but still possessed of an ancient monarchial sense of authority and justice that bordered on the barbaric. It occurred to her that perhaps he was not the oddity at all. Though civilization always rested on the determined will of men like Melchizedek, its softening effect on the sentiments of the civilized sometimes made them incapable of acting in their own defense. Yes, she concluded to herself, perhaps the odd ones were the people of her own time.

Anne looked again at Melchizedek's face and realized that he was now watching her. His face had turned from its outward watchfulness to sheer delight. She felt the heat rising in her cheeks again, and heard herself say, "I'm hungry."

Melchizedek laughed and said, "Come on, Anne. I'll show you a little place that is sweeping the Mediterranean. Food from my old neck of the woods."

"What is it?" she asked inquisitively.

"Mr. Kebab!" Melchizedek answered her. "Lebanese food to die for."

* * * *

Maurice St. Claire looked through the window of his aircraft and saw that they were descending toward the runway over Egypt. He had never been to Egypt before and marveled at how drab the colors of the land were. How could a desert country survive, he wondered? But then he spotted the Nile and the rich land on its banks. He understood now what the flight attendant had meant when she'd mentioned that ninety-five percent of all Egyptians lived within five kilometers of the Nile. But somewhere in that desert, well away from most prying eyes, lay a temple buried in the sands. He was becoming Indiana Jones, he thought to himself. Well, maybe he and Rothschild together made up the famous Dr. Jones, he corrected. In any case, it couldn't be long now. He glanced at his watch to confirm that he was right on schedule for his rendezvous with Rothschild.

* * * *

After lunch Melchizedek and Anne headed toward their gate for their flight to Egypt. As they stepped aboard, Anne was surprised to see that her seat was first class. She looked at Melchizedek inquiringly, and he motioned her ahead. So, she sat in her seat and waited for the stewardess to pass on before asking, "First class?"

"You've been through a lot the last couple days, Anne. I thought the relaxing setting might be more comfortable for you," Melchizedek replied to her.

"Well, that is too kind, but don't think that I'm going to lighten up on you," she laughed.

"What do you mean?" he asked, feigning fear.

"Get me a glass of wine, and I'll tell you," she promised.

Melchizedek asked the stewardess for a pair of Pinot Grigios and then looked to Anne expectantly.

"Okay," Anne began and then sipped the crisp cold wine. "A hint of citrus?"

"Yes," Melchizedek answered approvingly. "I find it refreshing."

"You'll need it to answer the question I've got for you," she pressed him.

"Whenever you like," he said indifferently, as he reached for a magazine, and then cast a quick wink in her direction.

"It's about astrology and what we talked about on our trip to the Cave of St. John," Anne said.

"Ah, I see. Okay, what's your question?" Melchizedek asked her, relieved that her focus had shifted away from the earlier topic of how she had become dressed after their ordeal.

"Well, you said that the magi who visited the Christ child saw his star and followed it, right?" Anne asked.

"Correct, and they knew to look for his sign because of their astrological understanding," Melchizedek added.

"And it was permissible for them to use the stars, because they were outside the Jewish Law and prophets?" Anne continued.

"Right," Melchizedek answered her.

"And you were good friends with one of those prophets, Daniel, right?" Anne asked.

"Yes, very much. Daniel was one of the wisest men I have ever known and was also one of my closest friends," Melchizedek explained.

"But he refused to break the Jewish Law to eat the king's Babylonian food when he was a boy, right?" Anne said, recalling the Biblical story of Daniel's capture and attempted brainwashing by King Nebuchadnezzar of Babylon.

"That's right, because the king's dietary regimen included foods prohibited by the Jewish Law," Melchizedek answered.

"But if astrology was also against the Law, then how could he become a magi, and not just a magi, but a leader of the magicians?" Anne asked.

"Oh, I see what you are wondering. How did Daniel avoid astrology, when astrology was at the core of his job?" Melchizedek clarified the question.

"Right. I'm trying to understand the kind of relationship he could have had with you too," she confessed. "Wouldn't your dabbling in those arts have offended him?"

"Well, Daniel did study all of the knowledge and wisdom of Babylon, as it was part of his curriculum during his training. But knowing Babylonian myths and deities did not require him to worship Babylonian gods. Knowing things didn't constitute a violation of the law. Performing prohibited actions did. That's why he refused to eat the King's meat," Melchizedek explained.

"But how could he have avoided performing the astrological arts?" she pressed him.

"Well, Daniel was a master of dreams and interpretations," Melchizedek explained. "The Most High God opened his mind to understand what was asked of him by his superiors and at the same time prevented the stars from revealing these things to the other magicians. This ensured Daniel's promotion. God was with him, obviously."

Melchizedek paused, remembering. "Daniel and I actually got along handsomely. We even shared some of the same depression about the world, him mostly about the future of Israel, me mostly about the future of the pagan realms. His visions showed that the exilic judgment on Israel would not be the end of her travails. And it really bothered him, to the point of illness, actually."

"So, you were doing for the pagan regimes what Daniel was doing for the Jewish people, recording their acts and lives?" Anne asked.

"Sort of, though mine were histories of past conduct, while Daniel's were visions of the future and thus deeply symbolic," he explained. "But Daniel talked them over with me extensively, trying to understand their meaning. That's what he was doing when Nebuchadnezzar built that insane golden statue."

"You mean the story of the three youths in the fiery furnace?" Anne asked. "And Daniel wasn't there—everyone in my Sunday school class wondered about that!"

"Well, he was with me, I can assure you of that," Melchizedek answered her laughing.

"But surely the decree applied to everyone all over the Babylonian Empire!" Anne emphasized.

"Well, to tell you the truth, we didn't even know about it!" answered Melchizedek. "Daniel was helping me with the Record in a secret location far from the usual trade routes."

"And he had no problem with your study of the stars?" Anne asked.

"No, he didn't," Melchizedek answered. "Look, Anne, the Most High God can reveal things to people as he sees fit. With Moses it was a burning bush. With Daniel it was through dreams and visions. With Abraham it was with a voice from the darkness. With the philosophers it was with arguments about the cause of all goodness. With the pagan sibyls it was with little clues about the eventual incarnation. With you it was through showing you a vision of me that was incommensurate with the old man you should have seen."

Anne stopped short at the inclusion of herself in the litany of kinds of revelation of God. She had not even thought of her experience in those terms, and was taken aback. "Oh!" was all she could muster.

"The fact that some people abuse the gifts of the Most High, use knowledge for the sake of evil, doesn't mean that those gifts don't, or better, didn't have a proper use. You've just seen the horrible abuse of astrology in the way in which its present day practitioners manipulate and control the people who come to depend on them. But manipulation and control occur in many other venues too."

"I suppose you are right, Mel," Anne conceded. "I just thought that Daniel being a good Jew must have felt the same revulsion toward astrology as I do."

"Daniel didn't need astrology, Anne, because the angels themselves spoke to him directly," Melchizedek added.

Anne nodded slowly, "I guess I see that. If the angel, of whom the star is only a sign, himself appears, then who needs to study the sign?"

"Makes sense to me," Melchizedek answered her with a chuckle. A slight elbow in his right rib cage was the only reply he received.

CHAPTER SIXTY-FIVE

Quarston and Bartoli looked up from their drinks, as several highly toned men strode into the hotel and immediately headed up the central staircase. Once they were gone, Bartoli said, "They have a familiar look, don't they?"

Quarston nodded, "Seems like you saw quite a number of them dead at the hospital in Florence."

"Why does Rothschild need a merc team here?" asked Bartoli.

"I don't know," confessed Quarston cautiously.

"Let's just make sure that we remain on the tailing end of this group," Bartoli warned.

"Agreed," said Quarston.

* * * *

"We've arrived, Anne," said Melchizedek gently.

Anne awoke with a yawn and that feline look of satisfied sleep, but soon had her nose pressed against the window to get her first look at Egypt, the ancient land of the pharaohs.

As the plane taxied off the main runway, a series of busses arrived to take the passengers from the plane to the terminal. Anne was struck by the monochrome sandy color scheme that greeted her as she stepped out onto Egyptian soil for the first time. After the bus dropped them off at the terminal entrance, she felt that same foreigner-self-consciousness that she'd felt the first time she entered Italy. Only here the internal dissonance was more dramatic, because she could not discern even the letters of the Arabic language that surrounded her. The smell of the place struck her too, an odor of spicy heaviness, reflecting the differences of diet and hygiene between Egypt and the West. But she was also moved by the friendliness of the smiles around her. As Melchizedek paid for their visa stamps, she felt a tugging on her leg and looked down into the wide dark eyes of a young Egyptian girl. The girl's mother beamed in pride at her daughter, as Melchizedek motioned Anne through the passport control station and on toward the terminal exit.

"Mel?" Anne asked, as they moved into the stifling heat to hail a taxi.

"Yes, Anne?" he answered, motioning for the car.

"Am I supposed to wear a head covering like that woman in the terminal?" she wondered.

"No, Anne, though it is good of you to notice. If you need to blend into your surroundings, then yes, a scarf and long dress will prove essential. But as a matter of culture, only the more conservative of the Muslim women wear the scarves over their heads. Christian women as a practice do not do so, something that in less secular times clearly delineated the Coptic Christians from the Muslims," Melchizedek explained.

"Because the more religious governments of the past tended to encourage or require the head covering for Muslim women?" she asked.

"Right," Melchizedek smiled at her. "Feeling the effects of the cultural differences already, eh?"

"Definitely," she replied. "I always find new cultures fascinating to explore, but each time I have to overcome the discomfort caused by those differences."

"Indeed," he answered as a taxi pulled up the curb. "I've been through my share of cultural makeovers!"

Anne laughed, as Melchizedek approached the black and white colored taxi. She marveled as he slipped easily into what sounded to her unskilled ears as perfect Arabic. Anne realized that he probably knew nearly every language that had produced a civilization.

Climbing into their taxi as the driver stowed their new bags, Anne spoke aloud, "I'm sure glad that you urged me to keep that Roman cameo in Capri."

"It would probably be in our pursuer's hands otherwise," he answered her with a grin. "In spite of losing your passport and with it your name and nationality, as well as losing nearly all of your clothing and gear twice, you're doing rather well, aren't you?"

"All things being equal," Anne congratulated herself, "I'd say I'm not doing half bad! I don't feel like I need a shrink, and I do have the cameo still."

"Yes, you do," Melchizedek began, "but we mustn't forget about Cinnamon, your horse! You will see him again too."

"Oh yes, how I loved him, Mel," Anne remembered, but then her face turned sour, "We won't be riding camels into the desert, right?"

"No, we shouldn't need camels," he laughed. "They do take some getting used to, though. Where we're going we should be close enough to roads to finish the trip by foot. Speaking of which, I'd better let our driver know where to go."

Once he finished giving his directions to the driver, he turned to Anne, and said, "Well, we're off. We'll follow the course of the Nile on our trip, so that you can see the heart of Egypt."

"Can we see the pyramids?" Anne asked him.

"I'll show you the pyramids and all that remains of the greatness of Egypt once I check on the Repository. But we should head there directly," he answered.

"Where is it?" she asked.

Melchizedek looked at her for a moment and hesitated.

"It's not like I'm going to tell anyone," she said smiling.

"Old habits die hard," he said.

"You give that phrase whole new meaning," she added with a laugh.

He nodded with a smile and then answered her question. "We're going to an ancient city that the Romans called Hermopolis Magna, but in the most ancient time we called it Khmun."

"How far away is it?" she asked, settling into the back seat of the cab.

"Oh, not more than an hour and a half, I should think," he calculated.

"Kinda wish we had another one of those kebabs," she murmured.

"Your wish is my command," he answered her, before giving another series of directions to the cab driver who smiled hugely when he heard the request.

* * * *

Quarston watched as two of the mercenaries returned down the stairs to greet four men who were just entering the hotel. Quarston observed that these four looked more like academics than either mercenaries or businessmen. What Rothschild was up to was becoming less and less clear.

As the mercenaries took the men up the stairs, Quarston wished he had some means to overhear their conversation. Three distinct groups were meeting together for something important.

He had just ordered another club soda when his earpiece sounded. It was Mike Adams.

"Heads up. Something's going on out here. Four cars are pulling around to the front of the hotel," he reported.

Sure enough, no sooner had Adams contacted them, than Quarston and Bartoli watched as the entire group came bounding down the stairs, Rothschild and Andover and the new fellows flanked by the mercenary entourage. They headed out the door and into the waiting vehicles.

* * * *

As they drove out of Cairo, Anne licked her lips enjoying the last bit of the kebab that Melchizedek had bought her. Their driver was thoroughly amused with his two passengers by this time, as Melchizedek had also kindly purchased a kebab for him. Pointing to their right, the driver recommended the Pyramids of Giza to their attention. Anne leaned right over Melchizedek to get a look at the tops of the incredible structures that dominated the West side of Cairo.

She looked longingly at Melchizedek who nodded assuringly that they would indeed come back and see them.

* * * *

As soon as the cars had left the hotel, Quarston and Bartoli ran for their car. Adams must have had a great combat driving instructor, Quarston thought, as the car raced up to the hotel door. Bartoli again jumped into the back seat, while Quarston briefly looked to the roads to see which way the vehicles had gone.

"I've got them, Sir," called Adams, "Don't worry."

No sooner had Quarston closed his door, than Adams had the car moving in pursuit of Rothschild's party. Adams took several back alleys, turning this way and that. Quarston hadn't yet seen the vehicles they were chasing and was just about to ask Adams about it, when he suddenly zipped out onto a broad street and there ahead of him were the cars.

Quarston patted Adams on the shoulder, "Not bad for a young kid."

* * * *

Anne watched the Nile River as their car drew ever closer to Khmun, noticing the people driving everything from modern motor craft to reed hulls driven by sail. She pointed them out to Melchizedek who nodded, "Hasn't changed in thousands of years."

He paused before adding, "Well, there are a lot less crocodiles! Because of the Great Aswan Dam, all of the Nile crocodiles are now confined to Lake Nasser—not a place you'd want to swim in, I can assure you."

Anne observed in fascination the shift from modern to ancient Egypt as they continued away from the industrial hub around Cairo. She saw little children riding donkeys laden with harvested crops, houses of roughly constructed mud bricks, and women covered from head to toe in dark black clothing. She felt as though she had entered another time.

Melchizedek pointed out a huge field of sugar cane, "The Egyptians are well known for their national sweet tooth, especially at the end of the Ramadan feast."

"I see small mountains or hills a few kilometers further back from the river, Mel. Is this the extent of Egyptian agriculture?" she asked, curious at the hints of wild deserts only a short distance away.

"Pretty much, Anne," Melchizedek began. "Almost all of the population of Egypt occupies just four percent of the land, right along the Nile River. But a few kilometers to the East or the West of the river, and the deserts swallow you up."

Anne nodded thoughtfully, trying to imagine how different the character of a people must be whose lives depended entirely on one great river and its occasional tantrums. She wondered how strange her own country would be if the whole population lived within a few miles of the Mississippi River, the rest of the land being nothing but desert plains.

Turning back toward Melchizedek, she noticed him staring into the desert too with a distant, almost protective gaze. She heard him speak softly to no one but himself, "The desert . . . it was always the perfect hiding place. We'll soon see if that remains true."

CHAPTER SIXTY-SIX

"What's our game plan here?" Mike Adams asked Quarston, as they followed Rothschild's party.

"We want to know what Rothschild is up to. He's brought a significant force with him," Quarston replied.

"Yes, I noticed that," Adams answered, "and that's what's got me concerned, frankly. We don't have the combat support to confront these guys."

"I know," Quarston answered. "We'll watch and see what they do. We can arrange a team to intercept Rothschild once his plane returns to Italy, if we have to."

Bartoli nodded his agreement, "But we want to know what his interest is in this temple of Thoth."

"Temple?" asked Adams. "Nobody told me anything about a temple."

Quarston sighed before filling Adams in on the intercept that indicated that Rothschild was traveling to Egypt to meet an archeologist named Bartleby, whom Bartoli and he assumed was the leader of the academic team who met with Rothschild in the hotel. Quarston left out any reference to Melchizedek.

"I wonder why he cares about an ancient temple," Adams wondered aloud.

"So do we," answered Bartoli. "The full range of his interest and criminal activity is part of what we are trying to ascertain."

"They are accelerating," Adams said presently.

"Can we still follow them discreetly?" Quarston asked.

"Only if I give them some lead time on us, but that will likely put them beyond visual contact for a bit," Adams said.

"So be it," answered Quarston. "If they make us, our mission is over anyhow, so it's worth the risk."

* * * *

"All right, Anne, here's where we stop," Melchizedek announced suddenly, ordering the driver to pull over along the highway.

The driver appeared mystified as his two passengers exited the vehicle in the middle of nowhere, but the generous tip that Melchizedek offered him offset the notion he had formed that just maybe his fares were insane.

* * * *

Bartleby sat with Rothschild in the lead car, directing the entourage toward their destination.

"How much further?" Rothschild demanded, unnerving Bartleby who had always thought of his benefactor as a kooky nerd.

"Maybe twenty kilometers," Bartleby answered.

Rothschild sat back in his seat and relaxed. So near to the culmination of his life's twin quests, he found it surprisingly easy to control his nerves. Melchizedek and the Book of Thoth! The power of life itself would soon lie in his hands. He would allow nothing to stand in his way.

* * * *

Melchizedek and Anne crossed the desert sands on foot, Anne now understanding the directions her escort had given her for her apparel choices in the Athens airport. Her boots were high enough to keep the sand out, and her broad hat provided enough shade that she could see. The dark sunglasses didn't hurt either, she thought. But she couldn't beat her thirst. Glad that Melchizedek had filled their knapsacks with bottles of ice water, she nevertheless felt some competitiveness with him not to drink them.

Melchizedek slowed suddenly and turned to wait for Anne. He mentioned too that he wanted a drink. Happy to stop, Anne ripped open her knapsack and pulled out an icy bottle. As the water poured down her throat, she thought about just how potent a life force the Nile was, surging through the lifeless desert. She finished the entire bottle and only then noticed that Melchizedek had hardly touched his water. He was smiling at her with that same pleased look she'd seen when she fell for his center feint in their chess game.

"So," she scolded, "you stopped for me, didn't you? You didn't really need a drink?"

"Try to remember where I grew up, Anne," he laughed. "I'd probably not do so well in the arctic."

After her experience in the frigid waters around Patmos Island, she shuddered to think what the Arctic Circle would do to her. But truth be told, she knew she was feigning her irritation. His concern touched her.

"How much farther?" she asked after a few minutes rest.

"Follow me," Melchizedek answered.

They mounted a long hill with rocky terrain at its crest. Breathing hard in the intense heat, she finally made it to the outcropping, when Melchizedek suddenly stopped and announced, "We're here!"

"What? Where?" asked Anne in surprise looking at the sandy hills in every direction. "There's nothing here at all."

"That's what it's supposed to look like," said Melchizedek with a twinkle in his eye. "Natural camouflage is the best kind. Heron and I designed it this way, and no one has ever figured it out."

"But where is the Repository?" Anne said. "I still don't understand."

Melchizedek climbed the final steep angle of the hill past the sand and onto the rocks. Reaching his hand into a crevice, he pulled out several handfuls of sand before straining hard to reach a switch at its bottom. As he turned the switch, the rock facing gave way and swung outward on internal hinges. Anne looked on in amazement at the brilliantly colored, ibis-headed figure of Thoth who guarded the doorway.

"How do we open it?" she asked.

"With this," he answered her, pulling the ancient high priestly key from around his neck.

Anne watched as Melchizedek inserted the key and twisted it to the right. She heard several cracks and sand began to pour out from two holes bored into the lowest part of the door frame. As the sand continued to pour out, the door slid to the right and the two of them entered the darkness.

* * * *

"Where are they?" Quarston demanded as they sped southward along the highway.

"I don't know," answered Adams in frustration. "We should have intercepted them by now."

"But there was nowhere for them to have gotten off before this point," objected Bartoli.

"Then they still must be ahead of us. Maybe they made us and just took off," suggested Adams in embarrassment.

"No, wait!" Quarston motioned ahead of them. Just over the crest of a hill far in advance of them they saw one of the four cars they were pursuing. "Okay, hang back a little now, we've got them."

Adams breathed easier and focused his attention on maintaining visual contact with their quarry.

* * * *

"Pull over here," Bartleby ordered Rothschild's driver.

The caravan of vehicles left the highway for a small road that headed away from the river. Rothschild looked out his window, as their four vehicles approached a large building. Parking at its front, the passengers exited and looked to Bartleby for instructions.

"We'll take off-road vehicles from here," announced Bartleby. "I've got them in the back along with some camels in case we have any trouble with the Hummers."

Rothschild nodded, impressed with Bartleby's thoroughness.

"Where is the temple?" he asked.

"About two kilometers from here around that large hill over there," Bartleby explained, handing some binoculars to Rothschild.

Looking at the mound of sand through the binoculars, Rothschild nodded to Bartleby and then noticed Maurice St. Claire emerging from the tail vehicle.

"Status?" Rothschild asked him about security.

"Clear," answered St. Claire and then nodded to their 'guests.'

Rothschild nodded affirmatively and approached his confidant before saying quietly, "You take one of the men and escort our guests away, once we reach the temple entrance."

"Understood," St. Claire replied.

* * * *

"Where'd they go?" Quarston asked as they crested the hill and saw not a single one of the cars they were following.

"I don't know," answered Adams. "They should be here."

Adams accelerated, when Bartoli suddenly yelled for them to stop, pointing frantically to the little road they were passing. Adams slammed on the brakes and moved to the side of the highway, finally stopping some thirty meters past the road.

"I think they took that road," explained Bartoli to Adams and Quarston's incredulous stares.

"Why?" they asked in unison.

"Dust," answered Bartoli. "Like in the Westerns."

Quarston nodded, but wondered if maybe his Italian friend was just a little bit mad. But he then said to Adams, "Well, it won't hurt to take a look."

"Okay, boss," Adams answered and slammed the car into reverse back toward the intersection.

* * * *

Melchizedek reached into his satchel and removed a lighter. He then bent to the ground and opened a small door in the wall and produced a torch. Once lit, the torch filled the room with light, and Anne exclaimed at some of the most vibrantly colored Egyptian art that she had ever seen.

"Where are we?" she asked in confusion.

Melchizedek smiled as he replied, "We are in a small room on the roof of an ancient temple of Thoth. You might call this the doorway to heaven!"

"So the temple is beneath us, underneath the hill we just climbed?" Anne asked.

"Right. This is the uppermost part of the temple. The ground floor is several meters beneath us," he explained. "The main entrance to the temple lies at the base of this mound on the opposite side of the hill. The entrance, as well as the temple itself, is completely covered in sand."

Melchizedek walked across the small room toward what Anne realized was another doorway, this one flanked by the figures of Horus and Osiris, Egyptian deities governing day and night. He slid his key into the slot of the door and twisted it to the left. But instead of the door opening, a panel slid open on the wall. Anne walked over and saw a series of knobs like the knobs on a combination key lock, but instead of numbers, there were figures that she could not decipher.

"It's Hittite," Melchizedek explained. "But do you see the hieroglyphic inscription over here?"

"Yes," she answered puzzled.

"It's a riddle, written in Egyptian, but the answer must be entered in Hittite," he explained.

"So not only must someone solve the riddle, he must first be able to read it and then know how to answer it in the correct language!" Anne observed.

"Right. Rather a good security system, don't you think?" he asked her.

"I cannot imagine that anyone nowadays could solve it," she agreed. "What is the riddle?"

Melchizedek answered her, "Okay, I'll translate it for you. You know, Anne, back in the day riddles were huge."

"Entertainment for the lower classes?" she chuckled.

"For everyone, actually!" Melchizedek replied. "Kings were judged wise based in part on their ability to construct and solve riddles. They sent them to each another all the time. Politics through wit. Solomon was renowned for his ability to resolve them."

"Maybe we should pose riddles for our presidential and congressional candidates," Anne mused with a big grin.

"Maybe you should," Melchizedek answered. "I don't follow your politics as well as you do, but it's been a long time since I heard anyone ask a ruler whether he was wise, and if so, how he would demonstrate that."

"I can't imagine if someone tried that these days," Anne answered, laughing. "It'd probably be the end of that reporter's career!"

"Okay, you ready?" Melchizedek asked.

"I sure am," she answered eagerly.

Melchizedek translated the riddle in its poetic form:

I never was, am always to be,
No one ever saw me, nor ever will,
And yet I am the confidence of all
To live and breathe on this terrestrial ball.

Melchizedek watched as Anne's face twisted into a look he could only thereafter describe as a cute intensity. He waited two minutes and then glanced at his watch, making sure that she caught the look. She fixed him with an evil glare that caused him to smirk with the mirth of it all.

Finally, she spoke, "Well, it's something in the future, that's for sure, given the first line. But it's something future that one can never really get to. So, let's call it the continuous future?"

"Okay," he nodded to her.

"Moreover," she continued, "the line 'I am the confidence of all' seems to imply something like hope . . ."

". . . but hope is something one can possess now," he interjected.

"Right, so it must instead be the terrestrial basis for hope, its material condition," she concluded firmly.

"And what would the material condition of hope be, Anne?" Melchizedek smiled broadly at her.

Anne was about to confess her ignorance, when she lit up and answered somewhat nonchalantly, "Why Tomorrow, Mel, whatever else?"

"Bravo, Anne," he encouraged her. "One pharaoh took three weeks to solve that riddle."

Anne beamed with pride at her accomplishment until Melchizedek offered, "Now, why don't you go ahead and key in that answer?"

Glaring at him again, she responded, "Hittite wasn't offered at my high school."

Laughing, he twisted the dials to the proper sequence that answered the riddle and then firmly twisted the key all the way to the right. As the sound of huge stones moving against one another reverberated around her, Anne watched as a hidden door slid open on the floor in front of her to reveal a ladder that descended into the darkness. Grabbing another one of the torches, Melchizedek lit it and then re-crossed the room to shut the door behind them. Anne gasped as the room was plunged into darkness except for the two torches, one of which suddenly disappeared. She turned quickly and realized that Melchizedek had taken it down the ladder.

"Shall I follow you?" she called from above, hearing echoes from the cavernous rooms below her.

"Yes, Anne, but first let me get some light down here," he called back to her.

Anne waited a few moments and then caught the smell of myrrh wafting from the passage below her as the red glow of torchlight cast shadows below. She climbed over the side of the hole and began to descend just as Melchizedek yelled to her that it was okay to come down.

CHAPTER SIXTY-SEVEN

Rothschild and his men climbed into the Hummer vehicles that Bartleby had prepared for them and drove off. Bartleby's team accompanied by St. Claire took the lead vehicle, guiding the caravan to its destination. Rothschild took Andover with him and asked her why she was laughing.

"The camels, Sir," she admitted. "I was really worried we'd have to ride them."

"You're right," he conceded. "That would not have been very pleasant."

Rothschild's stare at Andover lingered a second longer than he wanted, and he was afraid that she noticed. Irritated with himself, he couldn't understand how insignificant biological drives could obscure his moment of triumph. Thrusting himself fully into his task, he crushed his feelings.

* * * *

"Look! There are the cars!" Quarston exclaimed as the four cars came into view next to a large building.

Adams slammed on the brakes and drove off the road. He then pulled the key from the ignition and said, "I hope they didn't see us."

"Me too," answered Quarston. "But there's only one way to find out."

"Right," answered Adams. "Let's break out our gear. I've got everything we could need for desert travel."

They climbed out of the car, and walked to its rear, where Adams waited with a number of packs. Quarston opened his and saw water, sunglasses, sun block, binoculars, and food before he closed the pack and looked up smiling at Adams. "You're all right," he said agreeably to Adams before adding, "for CIA."

The three men crept up a hill that gave them a good view of the cars and the building. Quarston peered through his binoculars, and was about to speak when Bartoli whispered, "Nothing. They've gone somewhere."

Adams agreed and the three of them advanced toward the building.

* * * *

Anne stared in wonder at the wall that greeted her when she reached the room at the bottom of the ladder. She observed a long series of raised relief cartouches each topped with the royal double crown of the pharaohs of Egypt. Inside each double crown she found a red circle, symbol of the sun god. Reaching in front of her, she felt the cold metallic surface of the cartouches and confirmed her suspicion that they were inscribed into pure gold.

She looked up at Melchizedek expectantly. In answer to her unspoken question, he replied, "I call this the Cartouche Room."

"Makes sense," she nodded, pointing at the wall. "The record of the pharaohs of Egypt? I think I've seen pictures of these records in other sites in Egypt."

"Yes, you are correct," he paused before continuing.

Realizing there was something more than met the eye here, she pressed him, "And?"

"Look closely at the royal crowns," he offered, holding a torch to her.

Grasping the torch, she moved close to the nearest cartouche and held the flame near its surface. She saw that the light reflected from within the red sun symbol. "It's transparent glass," she exclaimed. "They're hollow!"

"Right," Melchizedek acknowledged. "It's part of the defensive system of this Temple. If someone were to enter the temple without entering the proper code, sand would fill up one of these circles, telling me where the breach had occurred."

"So, this is an ancient security system, isn't it?" she asked.

"Exactly," Melchizedek answered. "I placed it here in the innermost part of the temple, the 'back' of the temple given where the entrance lies. I could access it from the entryway in the roof or use that door as an escape if someone breached the security."

"So, the main part of the temple is through that doorway?" she queried, trying to look around him at the beckoning hallway.

"Yeah," he laughed. "Follow me."

No sooner had they left the cartouche room for the short corridor that connected it to the Repository's archive, than Anne stopped abruptly and stared in astonishment above her. The roof over head soared some ten meters, but it was the scene on the wall that stunned her. Torchlight danced off the golden relief of an enormous scale with Egyptian deities on all sides. She saw Thoth, the god with the head of an Ibis, holding a reed pen and writing palette, recording what another god was saying. She recognized the dog headed god, Anubis, weighing the heart of a man, the pharaoh she guessed, on the scale against a feather. The feather belonged to Maat, the goddess of order, justice and truth and sometime wife of Thoth. Anne smiled at that, thinking how appropriate it was that the companion of the recorder of judgment should be truth, and that against the truth, against justice itself, the heart of the king would be weighed. Next to Anubis stood the goddess Ammit, distinctive for her crocodile head and lion body, waiting to devour the heart found wanting, the heart of the unrighteous.

"And there is the pharaoh, standing before the judgment?" Anne asked.

"Yes," Melchizedek confirmed. "There stand the pharaohs, each one of them, standing before the divine tribunal, where Thoth will take my record and present it to the Most High who will judge each one according to his deeds."

"Against the feather of truth," Anne mused. "A heart would have to be quite light to balance against a feather, wouldn't it?"

Melchizedek smiled approvingly at Anne, "Yes, Anne. Who can stand against the truth? Who will be found righteous? Our hearts only condemn us."

"And yet the pharaohs thought that they could cheat?" Anne asked. "With their heart scarabs and special incantations?"

"They thought that the gods were themselves ruled by magic, a magic that they, as the incarnate gods on earth, could master," Melchizedek answered with a shrug. "But look over there, Anne."

Anne turned toward the opposite wall of the corridor to another raised relief again covered in pure gold. This one showed Thoth holding two objects, an ankh and what looked to her like an eye. "It's Thoth, I can see that," Anne answered. "But what is he holding?"

"He bears the ankh and the utchat. The ankh is the symbol of life and the utchat, the all-seeing eye of Ra. There is no escape from the gaze of the gods, Anne. Eternal life is inseparable from the judgment of the Most High, who sees all," Melchizedek said with a sigh.

"Something is bothering you about all of this, Mel?" Anne asked, still spellbound by what she'd seen.

"I tried to tell them, to tell them all, that there would be no use in the spells of the Book of the Dead, for there is no deceiving the Truth," Melchizedek answered. "Anne, look back at the judgment scene. Do you see the song above it?"

Anne looked above the scales and saw a series of hieroglyphic expressions, but she could not have told whether they indicated a song or a grocery list, so with a light hearted smile she answered, "Yes, but would you translate?"

Melchizedek grinned at her, and then lifted up his head and opened his mouth in song such as Anne had never heard in all her days. He was not reading, but singing it, singing the song as he remembered it sung in the days of the Pharaohs!

> *The west is the abode of him who is faultless,*
> *Praise God for the man who has reached it!*
> *No man will attain it,*
> *Unless his heart is exact in doing right.*
> *The poor is not distinguished there from the rich,*
> *Only he who is found free of fault*
> *By scale and weight before eternity's lord.*
> *There is none exempt from being reckoned:*
> *Thoth as Baboon in charge of the balance*
> *Will reckon each man for his deeds on earth.*

Melchizedek suddenly looked more regal than Anne could remember, and then she realized that his song complete, he was speaking to her in a loud voice, "Welcome, Anne, sister of John Horn, to my realm, for this land was given me by the Pharaohs into perpetuity. I alone am king here, lord of this temple, keeper of this divine Record of the deeds of men, which in the final hour I will present to the Most High King, who is blessed forever and ever."

Anne found herself on her knees bowing before her lord and king, the man she realized represented all the good that she had ever loved. She knew that her heart belonged to him alone and in her obeisance she knew she was giving him all that she had.

"Rise, Anne," she heard a quiet voice calling to her. Anne looked up to see the Melchizedek she had come into the temple with smiling at her kindly. "Let me show you what I've been doing all these years."

JEFFREY TIEL

CHAPTER SIXTY-EIGHT

"There it is!" exclaimed Bartleby excitedly.

Maurice St. Claire looked at the camouflaged entrance to the tomb at the bottom of the hill, confident that the archeologists had fulfilled their purpose. He keyed his lapel microphone and alerted Rothschild to the temple entrance's current visibility. Rothschild acknowledged and St. Claire nodded to his driver who turned the Hummer away from the temple site.

Bartleby waved frantically in the other direction, thinking that they were going the wrong way. Then he sat still and paled, before suddenly clutching at the door release to escape the vehicle.

*   *   *   *

Rothschild, Andover, and the remaining eight mercenaries exited the other three Hummers at the temple's entrance and quickly removed the netting and camouflage that the archeologists had used to hide the partial excavation.

Rothschild surveyed the temple entrance and found the two lunar obelisks lying horizontally, the sand obscuring most of their form. He proceeded toward the pylon doorway, noting how the large stone baboons were in exactly the location that the tomb wall relief had indicated. He walked up to the stone door painted with the ibis-headed god, Thoth, and saw the key slot that only a priest bearing the key to the temple could open.

Retrieving the key stolen by Andover from Melchizedek's belongings at the hospital, he pressed the key against the wall and it fit perfectly. So, he thought, you really are a high priest of Thoth!

He twisted the key slightly to each side and realized that it could turn either to the left or to the right. Not knowing which way to turn it, he selected the left and turned the key. He heard a crack as he did so, and noticed a spout of sand erupt beneath his feet. And then the door opened before him.

* * * *

Quarston, Bartoli, and Adams crept up to the four cars and examined them, quickly ascertaining that no one had been left behind to guard them. They next approached the building and found it empty too. Looking at one another dumbfounded, they circled round to the rear of the building and discovered the corral with the camels as well as a number of fresh tire tracks.

"It would appear that Rothschild and company switched vehicles," Adams remarked.

"Off road vehicles by the looks of these larger tracks," Quarston added, as Bartoli nodded and headed to the camels.

Bartoli opened the door to the corral and, grabbing a bridle from the fence, began to prepare one of the camels for riding.

"You know how to saddle and ride camels?" Quarston asked him.

"I've seen a lot of Westerns," Bartoli answered dryly.

"Uh-huh," was the only reply Quarston gave him.

"Necessity is the mother of . . .," Bartoli began.

". . . insanity," Quarston finished for him before adding, "but I don't know any other way for us to follow them. None of the cars can drive through this sand."

"Well, then, I guess we use the camels," Adams conceded, grabbing a saddle and helping Bartoli prepare the first camel.

* * * *

Bartleby realized too late that the driver had already set the door locks, so his frantic efforts at escape were futile. St. Claire just looked at him with a coldly amused smile, now covering his team with a pistol.

"Why?" asked Bartleby. "Why are you doing this? Mr. Rothschild and I have an arrangement. He'll be very angry over this breach in our relationship."

When St. Claire just continued to stare at him with the same detached smile, Bartleby realized the full extent of his predicament. St. Claire was not running rogue, but carrying out the orders of his superior, Rothschild. So, Rothschild must have ordered their . . . their what, Bartleby wondered with deep anxiety.

"What are you going to do with us?" he asked St. Claire finally.

St. Claire had been waiting for Bartleby and his team to discover the gravity of their situation, and he now ordered the driver to stop the vehicle. Once men realize that they are dead anyway, they will stop at nothing to kill any and all whom they believe are behind their deaths. So, it was imperative for St. Claire not to deny Bartleby's people hope, for he knew that the hopeful will always prove compliant.

"Out of the car," St. Claire ordered softly. "You are free to go."

St. Claire watched the looks of relief flood the faces of the doomed men who grabbed for their doors as soon as they heard the locking mechanism release. St. Claire rolled down his window and threw a satchel full of water bottles to the men who accepted them gratefully and then began to walk away from the Hummer. St. Claire kept his window rolled down and accepted the submachine gun that his driver had kept hidden in one of his bags. Once the archeologists were far enough away that they would not be able to rush the vehicle, St. Claire opened fire.

* * * *

Rothschild ordered two of his men to enter the darkness first and light the way. They grabbed several electric torches and plunged into the temple. Rothschild then heard over his earphone that St. Claire was on his way back. Ordering St. Claire to take up a rearguard position outside the temple, Rothschild called to Andover and the six other mercenaries, and they walked through the doorway.

* * * *

Melchizedek led Anne from the short corridor adjoining the Cartouche Room into a cavernous space, filled on all four sides and throughout the interior with shelves full of books, tablets, and scrolls. The walls were lined with the myrrh incense torches that Melchizedek had lit, and Anne noticed their construction was designed to prevent sparks from escaping and igniting the library. There were too many stories from ancient times about great libraries going up in flames, so she imagined that Heron and Melchizedek had gone to great lengths to protect the Repository from accidents.

"So, this is the great Record?" Anne asked.

"This is it, my Repository," Melchizedek assured her, staring himself at the thousands upon thousands of volumes that he had written over the centuries. They found themselves shaking their heads in unison, her at the staggering size of it all, him at the staggering effort it had taken him to write it.

* * * *

Quarston painfully lifted himself off the sand for the second time and stared at the camel who continued to defy him. Bartoli and Adams were howling in laughter and urging him to show that camel who was boss, so Quarston gathered up his courage and what little remained of his pride and made for the camel's back once again.

The animal realized that his rider was apparently determined, and so with what Quarston swore years afterward was a shrug, the camel set off after its companions.

* * * *

"I don't know what this is, Sir," observed the mercenary soldier to Rothschild who came at once to the man's side. They had entered the main gate of the temple, called a pylon, and no sooner had they exited it, than they had run into another door.

"It looks like some kind of combination locking mechanism," answered Rothschild. "Let me see. This is a riddle written in hieroglyphs which I can read, but the answer keys are in a script I don't understand. This doesn't make sense. Why ask the question in one language and expect to be answered in another?"

"I don't know, Sir," answered the soldier without realizing that Rothschild was consulting only himself, not the hired help.

Rothschild concluded that he would not be able to decipher the text without consulting experts, and that would take days that he did not have. So, he ordered the soldier, "Blow it."

The mercenary soldier could deal with that order readily enough, and in moments, he and his partner had wired the door with a small amount of plastic explosive.

* * * *

St. Claire and his driver pulled their Hummer in next to the others and took up positions to guard the temple against any intruders. Both of them checked their machine guns to be sure that no sand would interfere with their firing. Then they checked their radios and grabbed several water bottles apiece.

* * * *

The three camels continued along the tracks that the trucks had made, leading away from the corral. Quarston's camel continued in its ornery ways and soon Quarston found himself trailing the others from quite a distance. He watched as the Adams and Bartoli stopped their camels. Adams dismounted, checking the ground, before saying something to Bartoli who pointed in one direction. Then they both looked back at him, waving in the other direction and calling to him before remounting their camels and heading off.

Quarston urged his camel onward, trying to catch up with his friends.

* * * *

The explosion inside the temple startled St. Claire who quickly radioed Rothschild. His employer assured him that the explosion was planned, but St. Claire couldn't help feeling that using explosives on ancient architecture was a recipe for disaster. Nevertheless, St. Claire and his remaining soldier maintained their vigilance watching the hilltops around the entrance to the temple.

Within the temple, the doorway was blown open and the mercenaries worked to clear the way of rubble, before the two lead soldiers headed forward once again.

CHAPTER SIXTY-NINE

Melchizedek looked up in alarm at the muffled sound and small vibration that he and Anne felt.

"What was that?" she asked.

Melchizedek rushed back to the Cartouche room and checked the series of red circles on the cartouche wall.

"Someone else is here," Melchizedek announced. "They have entered the temple through the main entrance. They must have cleared away tons of sand."

Melchizedek continued to examine the wall before adding, "But they did not use the key properly, if they used one at all, because this circle here has been occluded with sand. This means that the defense systems have gone active."

"Are we in danger from them, Mel?" Anne asked with concern.

"No, not here. But the intruders certainly are. But what puzzles me is that explosion," he added.

Melchizedek strode over to a series of ceramic dowels that protruded from one of the walls, and then he pointed to a large hammer. He explained that should something unfortunate happen to one of them, the other had to reach this position and shatter the ceramic dowels. That would release the sand gravity system that Heron and he had devised to seal up the temple forever deeply beneath the sands of Egypt.

"Why Heron?" asked Anne curiously. "I mean, wasn't this temple built long before Heron? Surely, the Egyptians themselves designed their own defensive systems."

"Actually, no," answered Melchizedek. "Their real strengths lay in subterfuge, not defense."

"What's the difference?" she asked.

"Well, take the pyramids as an example. There are false passage ways, designed to convince you that you'll find nothing further in the pyramid, because they lead you to a dead end," he said with a twinkle in his eye.

"Even in danger your wit and flair for puns continues," she observed deadpan.

"Yes, that's right," he admitted. "A defensive system consists of something designed to stop the intruders, maybe pin them down, or outright kill them. At best, the Egyptians created wells in the floor that an intruder might step into and fall twenty meters to his death. But they really were not that inventive at architectural tomb or temple defenses. Heron, on the other hand, was absolutely brilliant. He and I completely renovated this temple with up to date designs and weapons systems."

"Weapons? There are weapons here?" Anne asked.

"Oh, of course. The intruders are in for a most unpleasant surprise," answered Melchizedek.

"Mel?" Anne asked suddenly. "How do we know that they aren't just archeologists conducting an excavation?"

"Since when do archeologists use explosives?" he answered with a question.

Nodding back to him, Anne took another look at the hammer, trying to imagine herself swinging it and shattering all those dowels.

Finally she said, "You know these people aren't going to stop until they kill us."

"I know, Anne," Melchizedek answered gravely. "That's why we're going to finish this here and now."

* * * *

Rothschild's two scouts led the way into the darkness illuminated now by the powerful beams of light that emanated from the flashlights attached to their submachine guns. As they entered the room beyond the pylon, they lit flares and tossed them on either side of the corridor. But what they saw took their breath away. Still walking through the pylon's gate herself, Michelle found the spectacle of hardened soldiers staring around them with their mouths open quite silly . . . until she entered the hypostyle hall herself.

Egyptian temples all have a similar pattern to their construction, a series of four inner rooms along one axis, with the floor set at a slight incline and the ceiling at a slight decline. This creates a horizontal pyramidal or sun-ray effect coming from the holy shrine at the temple's core. The first and largest room after the pylon is called a hypostyle hall, so called because of the enormous stone papyriform columns that fill the room, each usually capped with a carved lotus or papyrus flower. The next couple of rooms functioned as offering rooms, providing the priests with a location to prepare sacrifices and incense. And the final room, the holy of holies, housed the divine barque and the golden image of the god.

As Michelle stepped into the hypostyle hall, she was immediately overwhelmed by eight huge, brightly painted statues of the god Thoth that flanked both sides of the central corridor. He was presented in the usual formal style with his left leg extended in front of the right, a papyrus scroll clutched in the hand of his left arm hanging rigidly at his side, while his right held a great spear thrust slightly forward, its shaft aiming toward the roof. She followed the spear points to the ceiling at the center of the corridor, where a row of images of the goddess Maat were painted, her great multi-colored wings drawing together the two sides of the hypostyle hall.

Michelle next noticed the enormous columns, sixteen on each side of the central corridor, though instead of the usual representations of lotus and papyrus flowers, the columns took the shape of great limestone scrolls, each one some fifteen meters in height. Her gaze drifted toward the base of the columns, where they sat on the darkly painted black floor of the chamber, the black paint representing the dark sediment of the land of Egypt along the Nile after its annual flood. And where the columns reached the soaring ceiling, she saw brightly painted five-pointed stars on a dark blue background, representing what she figured must be the night sky.

On the four walls of the hall, she observed beautifully painted raised relief images surrounded by hieroglyphic text. She had seen pictures of Egyptian art before, of course, but none could have elicited the wonder she felt at these brilliant colors and precise eighteenth dynasty mastery. For unlike the many excavated temples that dot the course of the Nile, this temple had lain hidden from the ravages of time.

Michelle glanced over at Rothschild who was eagerly reading the inscribed texts, "Sir, what is it? What do these hieroglyphs say?"

Rothschild took a few more minutes to finish reading and then replied scornfully, "It is only a warning, not the book itself."

Concerned, Michelle pressed him, "A warning about what?"

"On the left wall is the story of Nefrekeptah, and on the right, the story of Setna, two great magicians of ancient Egyptian legend," he answered.

"And what are these stories?" she asked.

"Nefrekeptah and Setna both sought the wisdom of the Book of Thoth," he replied warily.

"And?" she asked again, "what happened to them?"

"The myths suggest that upon finding the Book, the wrath of the gods fell upon them, and their happiness was consumed. Nefrekeptah lost his wife and son, and Setna very nearly lost his family too. He managed to return the Book just in time to avoid the full fury of the gods, after being warned in a horrible vision . . . but it's all nonsense, of course," Rothschild answered confidently.

"If the book is real, why are you so sure that the warnings are false?" she asked with concern.

"Ancient curses?" his mocking eyes penetrated straight to her soul. "Come on now, Miss Andover, let's be realistic. Every time anything important is hidden, there's some great curse attached to it, right?"

When Michelle's worried look didn't change, he added sarcastically, "Besides, I've no wife and child to threaten, do I?"

As Rothschild brushed past her, Michelle looked thoughtfully at the reliefs of Nefrekeptah's young son, Merab, and beautiful wife, Ahura, drowning in the Nile. Then looking at the opposite wall, she shuddered in horror at the image of Setna's vision in which he clutched the withered corpse of Tabubua, for whom he had traded the lives of his wife and children. The lesson was unmistakable: one might exchange one's dearest loved ones for the knowledge of the Book of Thoth, but in the end it could offer nothing but death.

In spite of her misgivings, Michelle followed the others into the first offering room.

*   *   *   *

Quarston's camel rounded the next hill when he saw the two empty camels of his friends standing next to three of the Hummers used by Rothschild's party. Wondering where everyone had gone, his eyes followed the footprints up the next hill. He urged his camel onward as Bartoli and Adams worked their way up the hill that led to the small valley containing the temple's entrance.

*   *   *   *

As Rothschild's force made their way ahead into the first of the offering rooms, the painted reliefs that had covered every wall and column in the hypostyle hall suddenly gave way to reliefs covered in pure gold. As they continued to advance, his two lead scouts were transfixed by the beauty and value of what they saw, and failed to notice the subtle difference in the flooring beneath their feet. One of the soldiers shouted in surprise as the two of them suddenly found themselves falling, falling, and falling into a shaft of darkness and death.

Rothschild, Andover, and his remaining six men rushed forward to assist their scouts, only to find the fallen weapon of one of them illuminating the dark hole that had swallowed them. Using a series of ropes, they quickly constructed a bridge, and soon all eight of Rothschild's party were across the gap.

They took much greater care as they advanced this time, constantly on the lookout for new holes or any other ancient booby traps. But as they were about to pass into the second offering room, Andover noticed a stunningly beautiful lapis lazuli vase in a niche. Generations of pharaohs had supported trade routes all the way to the Afghan mountains, the only place where lapis lazuli could be found. Andover was transfixed by the same attraction that gripped them, but when she reached out to pick it up, Rothschild shouted to her to stop. But it was too late. The vase was already in her hands. All of them held their breath waiting for the inevitable booby trap to hit them.

When nothing happened, Andover said, "See? Nothing to it," and carefully placed the vase in her bag, convinced it would be worth a fortune on the black market. The troop continued to advance, penetrating further into Thoth's lair.

CHAPTER SEVENTY

What Rothschild's party did not know was that ancient ballistae cannot be maintained in the firing position for long, so Heron and Melchizedek had devised a gravity-based cocking mechanism for them. When Andover lifted the vase, the weight shift activated a small avalanche of sand deep within the temple. As the cavity from which the sand emptied grew larger, a half ton stone began to drop. The stone's weight pulled two heavy chains attached to twenty ropes that slowly drew back the arms of the ballistae in the room to come.

* * * *

Rothschild approached his crouching lead soldiers.

"What is it? Why have we stopped?" he asked them.

"I don't like it, Sir," answered the first.

"Me neither," agreed the second.

Rothschild peered into the corridor before them and noticed that it was filled with cobwebs—a stark contrast to the brilliant gold of the previous room—but other than that, he could not identify any discernible threat. Finally, he turned to the first soldier, "Tell me it's not the cobwebs, please."

"It's the cobwebs," he admitted. "They don't belong here. Why not in any other corridor?"

"You think that they are some kind of trap? Like a huge spider?" Rothschild asked him, puzzled.

The soldier laughed aloud, "No, no, not a big spider. I think that they are disguising the trigger of some weapon up ahead."

"Ancient trip wires? Are you serious?" queried Rothschild.

"I'm not sure that they are ancient, Sir," explained the commando.

At Rothschild's confused look, the soldier continued, "Let me show you something."

Rothschild followed the big commando back down the corridor to the hole that had swallowed his lead men. The commando pulled a powerful light out of his haversack and pointed it into the hole. Far down below Rothschild saw one of the bodies of his men with a spear point protruding through his back.

"What do you see?" asked the commando.

"A dead soldier with a shiny though bloody spear through him," answered Rothschild grimly.

"Right," replied the commando, before continuing, "and does anything seem strange to you about that?"

Rothschild looked again into the hole, trying to determine what the commando was talking about. He looked carefully at the body, and then again at the spear point. As the commando's light moved, it glistened brightly, and then Rothschild understood.

"Ancient metallurgists could not have produced a metal that pure," he announced.

"Which means that someone else has been here within the last fifty years," explained the commando.

"Hence your worry about tripwires," realized Rothschild. "But if we only just excavated the entry, how could someone else have found and then fortified the temple?"

The commando shook his head, and then looked puzzled at Rothschild's suddenly enlightened expression.

"What is it, Sir?" asked the commando.

"We're closer to our quarry than we might ever have realized," Rothschild answered cryptically, confident now that only the original builder of the temple would have known of its location and could have upgraded its defenses. He was confident now that Melchizedek had been here, recently.

Rothschild and the commando returned to the web-laden offering room to rejoin the group. "What do you suggest we do?" he asked.

"Burn it," answered the commando to the agreeing nods of his colleagues.

"Then fire the corridor," ordered Rothschild who then withdrew with the others to the safety of the hypostyle hall.

Within minutes only the lead two mercenaries remained at the front of the cobweb infested corridor. They each grabbed a phosphorus grenade, pulled the pin, and threw their ordnance, before rushing back to the scroll columned hall.

A roar of flame and blinding light overwhelmed Rothschild's senses as the firestorm swept through the advance corridor, burning the webbing to ashes. After the fires died down, the two lead soldiers returned to examine their work and found a significant number of huge iron darts that had been fired through the corridor as the thin tripwires that the cobwebs had disguised were burned apart and set off.

The first mercenary brought one of the meter long darts to Rothschild.

"Roman," he muttered. "This temple was built long before the Romans, but obviously someone from that era fortified it."

"It should be safe to proceed, Sir," replied the soldier, returning to his lead position.

* * * *

At Quarston's repeated order to stop, his camel finally lurched forward onto its front knees throwing him directly into the horn of the saddle. With a moan he awkwardly dismounted the beast and, as fast as he could move through the deep sand, tried to catch up with Bartoli and Adams who were already nearly to the crest of the hill. But the quiet of the desert was transformed by the unexpected sound of machine gun fire, as the form of Adams was hurled back down the hill toward Quarston.

Quarston watched as Bartoli drew his Beretta and made for the hill crest to return fire on their attackers, but he had barely managed to get off a few shots before he too slumped to the ground as bullets sprayed the sand all around him. Quarston tried to manage the disbelief and horror that bent round his intestines, as he drew his own gun and drew back the bolt. Climbing the rest of the way up the hill, he stopped for just a moment to stare down at the lifeless form of the Italian detective who had lately become such a good friend. Filled with a rage that consumed any thought of his own safety, Quarston tore over the crest of the hill.

* * * *

The fire that swept through the corridor did trigger the ballistae to fire their deadly darts, darts capable of penetrating multiple ranks of soldiers in full battle armor. But one of the ballista triggers caught momentarily.

As the group walked through the still smoldering offering room, the unfired ballista's twin torsion springs suddenly released. Rothschild heard the sound that forecasted the defeat of many of Rome's enemies, their machines of death unleashing their lethal cargoes. A powerful dart rushed toward the advancing soldiers, passing right by the lead two, through the chest of the third and into the head of the fifth before lodging itself and its two passengers in the wall behind them.

Andover screamed in horror as the remaining mercenaries dove to the ground, desperate to avoid any more bolts flying from the wall ahead. Pulling Rothschild and Andover down next to them, they sprayed the wall with bullets, in the hopes of releasing any further darts.

*　*　*　*

Melchizedek heard the gunfire and watched the cartouche wall, as more and more of the red circles were replaced by golden sand. His face grew increasingly grim as he reached for a pair of dazzling bronze swords overhead. Ordering Anne to hide in the Cartouche room, he returned to the Repository room, crossed to the far side, and listened at the other doorway.

*　*　*　*

Outside the temple, Maurice St. Claire and his driver had left their firing positions and were advancing on the hill crest where they had felled the intruders, when another man screaming in holy fury roared over the top firing his pistol. St. Claire watched as his fellow soldier went down in the sand before overcoming his own surprise and aiming his submachine gun at his crazed attacker.

Quarston saw the submachine gun's muzzle flash but heard no sound, even as his own gun barked back in reply. Time seemed to slow down for Quarston, as he observed the expression on St. Claire's face switch from determination to disbelief that Quarston was still charging toward him. Finally, Quarston watched as two of his bullets tore into St. Claire's chest, spinning him around and knocking him to the ground.

*　*　*　*

Rothschild and Andover crouched in the smoldering debris of the offering room, as the mercenaries examined the holy of holies for booby traps. Finding none, they invited their employer ahead. When Rothschild entered the holy of holies, the smallest room of the temple, Michelle noticed a dumbfounded look emerge on his face.

"There's nothing here," he sputtered.

"You mean, the Book of Thoth should be in this room?" she asked.

"No, no, not exactly . . ." he stammered. "It's more that an intact 18th dynasty temple should have a holy barque as well as an altar and a shrine containing an image of the patron deity."

"You mean a boat?" Michelle asked again, her own confusion mounting.

"Yes, exactly," Rothschild explained. "All Egyptian temples were connected by causeways flanked by sphinxes that connected with the Nile River. During special religious festivals, the images of the gods would be sent along the Nile on these special reed boats, barques."

"Why?" Michelle asked. "Where were they going?"

"Oh, right," added a recovering Rothschild, as he walked toward the false door at the end of the room. "The god's image would very likely join the image of a consort deity in her temple."

"Holy matrimony?" Michelle joked.

Rothschild smirked at her, "Something like that, yes."

"So, where is the barque and the statue of the god?" she asked.

"I don't know," Rothschild confessed. "And this false door seems to be made of wood rather than stone . . . very strange."

"False door?" Michelle asked again.

"Yes, on the back wall of the holy of holies in Egyptian temples you often find doors carved into the stone—inoperable spiritual doors, hence 'false' doors," Rothschild offered, feeling the wood of the door before him.

As his mercenaries stood round, Rothschild slipped a small knife between the panels of the door and exclaimed, "It's a real door; there's no stone wall behind this!"

"But I thought this was the final room in the temple," Michelle objected.

"Yes, usually that's true," Rothschild began, "but occasionally you'll find dramatic variations, like the temple at Abydos, for example, where there are a series of additional rooms beyond the seven shrines to the many gods worshipped there."

"It's certainly a clever piece of subterfuge, isn't it?" Michelle asked. "I mean, there are no handles or evidence of hinges on this side at all. It's easy to miss."

"You're right," Rothschild acknowledged. "We need to remove these doors."

Two of the mercenaries had removed their packs and pulled out tools. The men worked as efficiently as they killed. Soon the door panels were stacked up against the side wall of the holy of holies, as the gods in the colorful stone wall reliefs stared down their disapproval. Michelle couldn't help but feel awkward and increasingly uneasy as she stood waiting for the opening to be enlarged. The temple's secrets were soon to be theirs, but the warnings about the Book of Thoth weighed on her mind. Even the lapis lazuli vase in her sack seemed heavier than it had before.

Telling herself that this was all nonsense, Michelle shrugged off the strange feelings that occurred to her. It was at that point that she called out, "Do any of you smell something?"

They all ceased their labors and sniffed the air.

"Incense," offered one of the mercenaries.

"Yes," Rothschild answered, taking in the fragrance, "but stronger than before. I noticed a faint odor in the offering rooms, but it's stronger here."

"Could it be left over from ancient times?" asked another of the mercenaries.

"I suppose it could," answered Andover, her scientific bearing returned. "But did you notice that it got a lot stronger once we began to open that door?"

"Yes, you're right, Michelle," replied Rothschild, forgetting his formality and moving toward the small opening that had already emerged.

"Much stronger, definitely," he added. "Smells like myrrh to me."

"Yes, that's it!" exclaimed Andover, "a sweet heavy smell! I think that's what was affecting me before, almost like an enchantment. I felt like the gods in this room were looking down on me."

The men around her all eyed her strangely, but one of them admitted, "Yeah, I kinda felt the same way—something heavy and oppressive."

"Well," began Rothschild staring into the enlarged opening, "finding incense in a holy place isn't surprising, but finding it beyond the holy place surely is. So, what lies beyond this doorway?"

He aimed a light through the opening but saw only a narrow passageway, so he motioned to his four remaining soldiers to proceed. One by one they passed through the doorway, ever deeper into Melchizedek's lair.

CHAPTER SEVENTY-ONE

Quarston stared at his opponent, dead in the sand, still trying to understand what had just happened to him and his friends, when he felt his own feet give way beneath him. As he fell to his knees, he looked down at his own chest and saw the blood soaking through his clothing and dripping to the sand where it was absorbed in little crimson pools. Feeling his breathing stop and his remaining energy dissipate, Quarston looked curiously at the sand which rushed toward his face as death consumed him.

* * * *

The mercenaries suddenly stopped, pulled their weapons upward, and cut out their lights, as their lead man motioned to them. As their eyes adjusted to the sudden darkness, Andover noticed the unmistakable glow of firelight ahead in the room to come.

Rothschild motioned his four remaining mercenaries ahead. Moving out of the narrow corridor from the false doorway in the holy of holies, they found themselves in the Repository room and immediately identified the flaming torches. Their senses maximally alert, they communicated with their eyes and fanned out, seeking those who had arrived before them.

Rothschild and Andover entered the room behind the four and saw shelf after shelf of tablets, scrolls, and books, and on the walls, displays of Thoth, Anubis, Horus, and Osiris in the judgment over the pharaohs. Rothschild had just begun to speak to Andover, when he noticed a blurred shape move from the corner of the room to its center and overwhelm one of his mercenaries. The man simply disappeared in a hazy spray of blood, as the other soldiers turned to determine what had befallen their comrade.

Rothschild tried to warn his men, when the second mercenary was overcome by the blurring mist of blood, and he too disappeared from view. Realizing that Melchizedek had to be in the room, Rothschild ran for the other side and into the Cartouche room, seeking refuge, as the third and then fourth of his men screamed in agony as they too were cut down by their unseen assailant, their advanced weapons clattering to the ground useless.

As Andover crouched to her knees in terror of her impending death, she heard a shout and saw that Rothschild had returned to the Repository Room with a woman whom she recognized from her file picture as Anne Horn. His pistol drawn and aimed at her head, Rothschild shouted out for Melchizedek to reveal himself.

* * * *

In the Repository Melchizedek appeared suddenly, as if he were stepping right out of the ancient books. Covered in the blood of his enemies, his grimy swords fell to the ground with loud metallic clangs.

"Good, good, good," exclaimed Rothschild feeling himself finally in control of the man he had so long pursued. He tightened his grip around Anne Horn's neck and pressed the pistol to her temple before continuing, "Don't make any sudden movements; you know I will kill her."

Melchizedek just stared at Rothschild, showing no emotion, a sign of his defeat so far as Rothschild could figure. Rothschild looked down to the floor at the bloodied hulks of his dead mercenaries and thought of the dissection he had planned for Melchizedek. But then his years of discipline took over once again, and he settled his mind on his real objective.

"The Book of Thoth, it's really here, isn't it? All the esoteric knowledge and wisdom of the ages! The secrets of the stars! The mystery of eternal life, and I alone possess it all, or soon will," he declared, glaring at Melchizedek.

"You are gravely mistaken, Mr. Rothschild," Melchizedek spoke to a startled Rothschild. "No man possesses the Book; it will possess you. Flee now or you will be consumed."

"No, you would prevent my knowing what you know, how you have lived forever. Well, it's time to share, Melchizedek. It's time for the world to know what you have kept for yourself all these years," he answered.

"The world? Is that really your concern? Not all knowledge is meant for everyone, Laurence," explained Melchizedek, trying to reach the small bit of boyhood that Rothschild had long sought desperately to suppress. "Do you not remember the serpent's lie in the garden? Sometimes we are asked to wait. Sometimes what we would know now would be too great a burden."

"Yet you deign yourself worthy of this knowledge!" retorted Rothschild.

"Hardly," sighed Melchizedek. "I was chosen; the choice was not mine."

"Well, I choose my own destiny, and I choose to live, to escape death, to know eternal power," answered Rothschild.

"All power is given for the sake of those under it, Laurence," explained Melchizedek sadly. "How is it that with all your education and experience you have learned nothing?"

"Child's lies. No one believes in all that fairy tale, noblesse oblige nonsense anymore. You are from a bygone era."

"Few people in any era can resist the fruit that cheaply offers the knowledge of good and evil, can they? For what is power but that ability, to do good or evil? What have you done with the power you already possess, Mr. Rothschild? What is the character of your life? Where is your virtue?" asked Melchizedek soberly.

"*Virtu*? I know *virtu*," Rothschild replied, substituting Machiavelli's homonym for the ancient moral category, "but I reject your inane teachers. Socrates, Aristotle, Augustine, Aquinas . . . where did their virtue get them? All of them buried and gone. There is another *virtu*, and you know that of which I speak."

"Yes, for I know its author and he is truly said to be the son of the devil, for anyone who looks goodness in the face and mocks it, casts himself far from the Face of life and instead submits himself as a slave to the dark one."

"A slave! Hah," laughed Rothschild. "There is nothing in this world greater than man, and you know it. Even if there were others, those ghosts of the night, where are they, and what can they do except scare silly children? As Solomon of old, I shall now command them all, for the wisdom of Thoth is not bound by materiality."

"You revile the intelligible ones, whose domain is eternal light. You despise majesties far greater than mine. You reject the authority of Love itself, so what shall become of you except slavery to hatred? You are a fool, Rothschild, for you have given yourself over to your own deceit."

Anne looked in amazement as Melchizedek began to change before her, his modern clothes replaced by a tunic of increasingly bright light. She saw that his head bore a great crown and that in his left hand he held a sword and in his right a scroll. But then the scroll gave way to a crook and the sword a flail, while a golden collar appeared round his neck. No sooner had that image stabilized, than she saw that the image of a large bird, an ibis she realized, now dominated Melchizedek's head. And his hands now carried stylus and writing tablet.

Melchizedek, or Thoth—she could not be sure—began to speak in a language that Anne could not comprehend, and as he did so, his face and hands and feet blazed like fired bronze. She heard his voice as if it were the sound of many waterfalls but still she did not recognize his speech. Suddenly she understood why she thought he looked so much taller, for her face had finally touched the stone floor as she bowed before him. And then she understood his speech.

"Be it unto you even as you have asked. The request of your heart is granted."

CHAPTER SEVENTY-TWO

Rothschild stood spellbound by the transformation of Melchizedek but failed to comprehend its meaning. And as suddenly as it had begun, both Melchizedek and Anne were gone. He found himself alone in possession of the Repository, alone with the greatest wisdom known to the universe, the Book of Thoth. Laughing at Melchizedek's stupidity in abandoning the Book, Rothschild picked up the first volume he could lay his hands on and began to read.

Michelle Andover slowly rose from her slumped position against the room's entrance, watching her employer reading faster and faster. She realized that he must be reading a few pages per second but then noticed that it was more like hundreds per second, and then faster and faster until he seemed to be taken up into a great blur. Volume after volume flew off the shelves and opened themselves before him before joining the whirlwind of books that encircled him. He looked mesmerized, then astonished, and finally confused. His face began to tremble and he fell to his knees as the books sped all around him.

Michelle watched as Rothschild suddenly screamed with a cry that she could only thereafter describe as the agony of all the hearts of men. He slumped forward as the books fell to the ground around him. She ran over to him and found that he seemed incoherent and deeply disturbed. She worried that he might be experiencing a seizure, but then changed her mind and thought that perhaps he had succumbed to some form of psychosis. She tried to lift him, but he thrust her away and crawled to the corner of the room where he shook violently and babbled incoherently.

It was then that she realized that Rothschild was not the only one shaking. The entire temple shook too, as shelf upon shelf toppled over and the ceiling above her began to give way. Abandoning any hope for Rothschild, she ran from the room and headed back toward the holy of holies.

* * * *

While Rothschild was transfixed by the curse, Melchizedek had grabbed Anne's arm and run into the Cartouche room to retrieve the great hammer that lay against the wall. With a mighty blow, he had shattered all the ceramic dowels, beginning the chain reaction that he and Heron had planned for so many centuries before.

Pushing Anne toward the ladder they had first descended, he urged her to climb as quickly as she could. As she pulled herself up the rungs, she heard the sound of massive stones moving and sliding in the bowels of the great temple. She sensed the entire edifice beginning slowly to sink beneath the sand.

Once Anne reached the top of the ladder, she grabbed the torch from the wall of the little entry room and held it over the hole, so that Melchizedek could see his way up to Anne's smiling and then suddenly inquisitive face.

"What is it?" he asked her when he reached the top.

"What happened to that man? You called him Rothschild. You knew him?" she asked.

"Not until today, I didn't," he admitted, climbing out of the ladder hole. "For some reason his name simply became clear to me in my mind. So, I used it, and fortunately, it was correct."

"You must have some experience with that happening to you to be so confident," Anne pressed him.

"A bit," he admitted with a grin.

"What happened to him?" she asked, as they headed toward the outer door.

"He thought that possession of the book would provide him with secret knowledge and ultimate power, just what the Gnostics have always sought, esoteric magical wisdom. The Egyptians were frantic for it too; hence, all the old stories about the dangers of pursuing the Book of Thoth."

"Your Record is the Book of Thoth?" she inquired.

"Yes, but it contains no secret wisdom—only the dark truth of human nature gone horribly wrong," Melchizedek explained, as they headed toward the upper temple entryway. "And no man is fit to behold that story. When we see what we have really become, it drives us to insanity."

"But you aren't insane, and you said that the prophet Daniel helped you work on it too, and he wasn't insane either," Anne countered.

"Aren't I, Anne?" Melchizedek looked at her soberly for a moment and then suddenly winked.

"Oh, you're scaring me, Mel!" she exclaimed.

"Only divine grace enables any mortal man to read the book, for the book was not meant for mortals at all, but instead is the divine record that Thoth—Melchizedek—will one day open and set before the eternal scales of the Most High God," he explained, motioning her toward the doorway.

Anne stopped, looked at Melchizedek gravely, and then asked him, "Then, are you a god? Are you Thoth?"

"Not really, though at times I seem to become the body of the god, the great angel of justice, Thoth to the Egyptians. I am his eyes, his hands, his servant. I am immortal and endowed by the Most High with special gifts. But I am not to be worshipped, for I serve the Most High God," Melchizedek answered her and then paused at the doorway.

He continued, "But if you mean to ask am I a man, the answer is that I am man, not angel, not god. I am man—king, and priest, and keeper of the great Record, the chronicle of mortal evil, but also as you rightly pointed out, the promise of hope and love for its many victims."

Melchizedek looked at Anne softly and asked her, "Can you accept that I am all of these and still a man?"

Anne answered him more swiftly than he could have expected. "These do not diminish but instead establish your masculinity for me."

Melchizedek looked at the resolution and joy that had filled her face and smiled broadly at her, before the floor under their feet again shook violently.

"Come on, Anne, we have to get out of here, right now!"

CHAPTER SEVENTY-THREE

After abandoning Rothschild to his fate in the heart of the temple, Michelle Andover steadied herself against its increasingly unstable architecture. The floor swayed, throwing her to the ground. Forced to resume her way on her hands and knees, she choked on the dust and sand that seemed to be filling up the temple's corridors all around her. Desperate to escape, she tried to climb up and over the top of the sand and find her way back through the offering rooms and back into the hypostyle hall.

* * * *

As Melchizedek and Anne sped out of the upper temple door at the rocky outcropping, they heard the far off sounds of machine gun and pistol fire. They stopped and stared at one another, trying to comprehend its meaning, since they had thought that they alone were the targets of Rothschild's gang.

"Come Anne, let's go round the crest of the hill and find out what's happening at the temple's main entrance," Melchizedek urged her. Together they scrambled up the rocky crest, soon reaching the top. Looking down from the heights, they saw the figures of five men lying prone as the sands beneath them absorbed their blood. Seeing no movement, Melchizedek began to descend, but turned at Anne's query.

"This temple is my realm, Anne, given to me by the Pharaohs of Egypt as a gift into perpetuity. I alone have the authority to give and take away life here. Remain here if you wish, but I must go," Melchizedek answered her.

Realizing the political realities of her partner, Anne shrugged and replied, "Then we shall go together."

They climbed their way down the far side of the rocky outcropping until they came to the sandy hill that led down to the great baboons guarding the temple's entrance.

* * * *

Michelle Andover coughed and wheezed, trying to breathe as the air around her continued to fill with sand. It seemed to be coming from the ceiling and walls together, and she despaired of escape. As she struggled for her life, her thoughts drifted back to Rothschild, the man she had thought had the world at his feet, the man upon whom she had come to depend for her security and hope. Yet now she knew that the entire quest was a massive illusion. She had given her life to this man, had taken lives for him, and yet he could now only babble the incoherent speech of a babe.

* * * *

All Quarston could remember thereafter was the face of a large bird hovering over him. But then the bird's face transformed into that of a man bearing what Quarston felt was regal kindness. The man stared at him before saying something in a language whose sound was as ancient as his eyes. Quarston recalled seeing a hand move over his chest, and then nothing at all.

* * * *

Andover thought that she could see the light of the entry way to the temple ahead of her. She crawled now with the starry ceiling of the hypostyle hall right above her head. Desperately, she clawed for the pylon door way and pulled herself down toward it with all her remaining strength.

* * * *

Quarston felt himself gulping down air, when he suddenly coughed violently. He opened his eyes and sought mental clarity. Remembering the gun battle, he looked down and grasped for his chest, but though his clothes were tattered and stained with blood, his body was completely whole.

Hearing voices from the other side of the hill, he grabbed his gun and rushed over to where he expected to find the bodies of his friends. But instead he found them quite alive, the clothing where the bullets had entered them still torn and bloody, but their bodies intact. They looked up at him dizzily, and Quarston, overwhelmed with joy, ran down to them. All three fell to their knees trying to comprehend what had happened to them.

"A dream," Adams began.

"Of a bird," continued Bartoli.

"No, it was a bird man," Adams corrected.

"Yeah, a bird man, with ancient Egyptian clothing, like one of their gods or something," Bartoli remembered.

"It squawked and touched me," Adams continued.

"No, it spoke something, but I couldn't understand it either. It touched me too," Bartoli added, amazed that their dreams were the same.

"You too?" Adams asked of Quarston.

Quarston thought of the face of the man that had appeared over him in his dream, sure now that it was Melchizedek. He reflected on his conversations with John Horn and his professors back in the States before answering, "Yeah, same dream."

Hearing a tumultuous roar over the crest of the hill, the three agents trudged back toward the temple just as a huge torrent of sand erupted from the pylon entrance. The rest of the temple had already succumbed to the desert sands. The two great baboons guarding the temple toppled over and swirled into the vortex, as the uppermost columns of the now visible rooftop colonnade tumbled over and landed with muffled thuds before they too were drawn into the swirling sand. Several more fountains of sand erupted from the temple's now submerged entrance, as the sand below the temple was sucked into and through its openings.

The three agents looked in surprise as a creature barely recognizable as a person emerged from one of these fountains, dazed and nearly incoherent. Quarston ran up to her and dragged her clear of the tumult. The two of them lay in the sand exhausted from their exertions, until Quarston realized she had to be Michelle Andover. But instead of a criminal he saw a muddied face streaming with tears. Quarston pulled a cloth from his pack and wiped the dirt from her eyes and face. Slowly the woman emerged from the grime. Quarston felt none of his usual compulsion for cleanliness and order. Instead he felt pity for Andover who unexpectedly reached forward and hugged him.

Bartoli and Adams ran over, thinking that she was assaulting Quarston, but he motioned them away and held the stricken woman in his arms.

Tears poured from Michelle's eyes as she described what had happened in the temple, "I trusted him! I gave my life for that man. And he was nothing but a fraud. Everything he told me was a lie."

"What happened to Rothschild?" Quarston asked her.

"I left him in Melchizedek's Repository, huddled in the corner. He didn't even seem human anymore, more like a scared animal."

"Melchizedek did this to him?" Quarston queried.

"I don't know, it's hard to say," she explained, still whimpering. "It was sort of Melchizedek, but not really. He looked like that bird god that I felt looking down on me all through the temple. Thoth, I think."

Quarston nodded thoughtfully, thinking back to his dream. He knew exactly what she meant.

"You know, Michelle, you've made some pretty bad choices here . . ." Quarston began.

"I know, you don't have to say anything more," she confessed. "I shouldn't have survived the temple's destruction."

Looking up at Quarston's face, she added, "You know, I looked into Anne Horn's eyes when Rothschild grabbed her. I saw her fear. I felt it for her. We should not have done that to her, to any of the people we hurt. I'm disgusted with myself."

"You know you'll be arrested," Quarston said after a few minutes pause.

"I know," she sighed. "I'll help you in your investigation, whatever you need. I'm not asking for any special treatment. I know what I deserve."

Quarston admired the change that he found in her. In spite of her tears, he saw beauty in her face and realized that it was her honesty. Virtue was indeed beautiful, just as he'd read in Plato. But it needed a human face, a human touch. He thought about all the trouble he'd seen in his career, all the shattered human beings, the wrecked lives, and yet here in this place he found someone for whom he felt hope. It moved him deeply. He felt like something fell into place within his soul.

"Michelle?" he asked her. "There's also the issue of Melchizedek."

"Yes," she acknowledged. "I'll tell you all about my research, the virus, everything I know about him."

"Maybe that shouldn't happen," Quarston suggested quietly.

Andover looked at him curiously. She began slowly to understand.

"You're afraid someone else will restart the project, aren't you?" she asked.

Quarston nodded, "Michelle, I think it's pretty clear that Melchizedek is a good man. He doesn't deserve to be hunted for the rest of time."

"You're right," Michelle observed softly. "We should have left him alone."

"We still can," Quarston added.

"How?" she asked him.

"Can you leave Melchizedek out of your story, come up with some other reason why you engineered the virus?" Quarston inquired.

"It's the least I can do," Michelle smiled. "It's time for me to start doing things that help people."

"Thank you," Quarston said simply.

"No, thank you, Agent Quarston," Michelle answered. "Thank you for believing in me."

Quarston looked closely at the woman who sat next to him, pleased to see her smiling, very pleased, he thought to himself. It took a convict, after all, he thought with a smirk.

Quarston squeezed her hand and then lifted her to her feet. Just then they heard the sound of several engines, as four dune buggies flew over the hill behind them and into the temple entrance valley. All three agents grabbed for their weapons, when one of the dune buggies braked hard to stop right next to them. The driver turned toward them with a huge smile, as he removed his goggles.

"Hi there, Quarston! Thought you could use a little help, courtesy of the CIA!" Agent Billings exclaimed.

Quarston smiled hugely at the welcome sight, when Billings added, "I see you found the real Michelle Andover too. Not bad for the FBI."

"He had a little help, Sir," Adams chimed in.

"Yes, he did," added Bartoli with a wink.

* * * *

As Billings and their reinforcements took Michelle Andover into custody, Quarston walked back up to the crest of the hill overlooking the site of the now vanished temple of Thoth. From this vantage point he was able to look across to the hill on the far side of the temple, where he glimpsed two people, a man and a woman who he knew was Anne Horn. The man then stopped at the crest of the hill and turned back toward Quarston. It was the face from his dream. Their eyes locked for a moment and then Quarston bowed his head toward Melchizedek. He raised his eyes again to see Melchizedek and Anne crossing over the crest of the hill hand in hand.

ABOUT THE AUTHOR

Jeffrey Tiel, Ph.D., is an associate professor of philosophy at Ashland University in Ashland, Ohio. He previously taught at the United States Military Academy in West Point, NY, as well as Vanderbilt University in Nashville, TN. He is an award-winning teacher, known for bringing ancient ideas to life. His extensive travels throughout the Mediterranean world—through Italy, Egypt, Israel, and Greece—provide a rich historical context for the characters and plotline of the novel. *The Search for Melchizedek* is the first in a series of novels. Tiel has also authored *Philosophy of Human Nature* and *Faith & Reflection*.

99445309R00249

Made in the USA
Lexington, KY
18 September 2018